BLIND THE EYES

K.A. WIGGINS

SNOWMELT
& STUMPS

FOR THE ONES WHO TRY TOO HARD.

REMNANTS

CADENCE FOUND ME the night I surrendered to the Mara.

I got lucky. They devoured only my disobedience.

Cadence's luck wasn't so good. She's been with me for over a year now, and I'm starting to think she'll be the same impossible child forever.

"So I had this dream last night," she says. "It was about trees. I miss trees. I miss climbing with . . . w-with—I just miss them. We should go find some. Let's go now. Okay? Now. Let's go now. Now-now-now-n—"

"Stop it." I don't have time for her lies. Regulation 3: Distraction is destruction. I must not allow myself to be distracted, nor be a distraction to others. It's why everything here's the same shade of grey: the paint, the carpet, even us. It's the reason for these shapeless, hooded uniforms and masks. It's even why we have to work everyday, instead of letting the computers do it all for us. Distraction leads to dreaming. Dreaming draws the Mara. The Mara would destroy us all—if the Towers of Refuge didn't protect us.

But Cadence hates being shushed. She blows a rude noise in my ear and proceeds to singsong something that mostly consists of her new made-up word, *trees,* looped at different pitches.

She needs to stop telling stories and pestering me. Obviously, she can't have actually dreamt. I'm pretty sure ghosts don't sleep. And no one in Refuge dreams, not if they want to live.

My skin crawls in a not entirely unpleasant way.

"Dreeeams of treeeeees," she warbles into my ear.

"Shut up!"

I swat at her and snag my hood. The ward securing it flies off. I scramble to yank it back in place and keep my mask from sagging. The last thing I need is to expose the uneven dark blotches on my naked face.

Forty grey workers sit behind grey consoles in the grey room, bathed in dingy yellowish artificial light—the windows were painted over back when the waters rose to hide the drowned city. Cadence says it was to stop the drowned looking back. In any case, my decidedly non-regulation colouring would stand out like a vivid stain on the face of such bland perfection. Showing my face wouldn't just be a Regulation 1 offense, either. Regulation 2: Segregation is safety. Minimal contact between workers is essential to our survival.

"Probationary Worker 18-Cole." The voice is nasal, cracking and uneven. "I might've known."

I flush another shade darker.

Division Supervisor Kistrfyv's shoes nudge my shameful black probationary hoodband. His damp, bulbous gaze is neatly framed between the loose mask drawn over his nose and mouth and the crisp, even spread of his hood under the dual bands of a supervisor. They're proper wards, of course, gleaming with protective gold thread. He's dressed perfectly to regulation: baggy, form-obscuring grey tunic and loose pants hiding soft shoes, gloves under drooping sleeves, hood secured with its twin gold wards, and an opaque, veil-like mask covering every inch of admirably grey, medium-dark skin except the narrow opening around his eyes.

His stance isn't quite regulation, though; he leans forward, as though eager. If he weren't the supervisor, he'd be at risk of a violation.

"I don't like him," Cadence says. "He's a bully. And creepy."

I tighten my grip on the sagging hood. Cadence may be a forbidden distraction, but there's no way I know of to get rid of her. She's been around ever since that night in Corrections. The Mara could have killed me, down on Floor 6. It wasn't the first time I'd failed to follow regulation, or I wouldn't have been there in the first place. But instead of ending me, the Mara only ate my dreams—and left a troublemaking ghost in their wake.

I earned my way to a probationary position in the Surveillance Technology Division less than six months later. It's not hard to obey regulation anymore; the Mara took the part of me that could make bad choices. Or any choices. I'm better off without it. If only Cadence would stop getting me into trouble.

"Probationary worker," Supervisor Kistrfyv says again, leaning in too close. "I will not have you destabilizing my division. Submit. Now."

The chair squeaks as I stand. My mask droops. I tuck my chin, partly to keep my face shadowed, mostly because the supervisor twitches and glares whenever my head rises higher than his. Head bowed, I shuffle around the console to pick up the black ward—a mark of shameful failure; I won't qualify for gold unless I can pass probation—and snug it down over my hood. If I could, I'd dream of being invisible. But I don't want things anymore. I just obey.

"Probationary worker," Cadence mimics in a whiny tone so like the supervisor's it makes me flinch, "I demand you extract my head from my butt. Probationary worker, I have nothing better to do with my time than stand here and blink like a fish. Probationary worker, I—"

"Probationary worker." The real Kistrfyv speaks over her in warning tones. "You've held us all up long enough. Submit, and be quick about it."

"He's such a weenie," she huffs.

I twist my hands in the loose fabric at my sides to keep them still and try to look contrite as I mumble through a comprehensive list of my violations: distracting behaviour, immodest dress, lack of focus . . . I wrap it up by mumbling the ritual phrase three times: "I call upon the Mara to eat my dreams."

Rote submission is different than being Mara-taken. It's meant as appeasement, a sort of pre-emptive measure. Void your disobedient impulses, turn over your hopes and desires to the Mara fast enough, regularly enough, and they'll consume the offering and leave the rest of you intact. I've performed submission hundreds, maybe thousands of times. Before Cadence came, often there'd be a rush of emptiness left in their wake. Now, I feel nothing. I don't have enough dreams left to satisfy them; if they came, they'd probably just end me.

Kistrfyv makes me repeat the summons again. Louder. Clearer. Again. I scrunch my eyes shut and tighten my fists. This show of terror seems to please Kistrfyv, or maybe he just gets bored, because he finally lets me stop.

Cadence starts breathing the word *weenie* in a sort of singsong, gasping air in and puffing it out, drowning out Kistrfyv, who has started in on a lecture without giving me leave to sit. My thighs tremble.

I duck my chin another inch to appear more submissive. I need Kistrfyv to be pleased with me. Pleased enough to arrange a probationary trial soon. Pleased enough to grant me a promotion to full worker and hand over the gold band that wards off the Mara to replace my black one. Pleased enough to erase my record of failure once and for all.

Kistrfyv smooths the dual wards around his forehead as if to emphasize his elevated position and keeps lecturing.

"Betcha he's bald under that hood." Cadence warbles an improvised ode to his presumed follicular deficiency at top volume.

I'd kick her right about now, if I could. My legs are starting to ache from standing with my knees locked, but I don't dare shift my weight under the force of the supervisor's damp gaze. To make things worse, the pants on this latest uniform are too loose. They edge past my hipbones, one anxiety-spurring fraction of an inch at a time. Meanwhile, Cadence seems to be experimenting with how long she can sustain each syllable. It's annoying. And distracting. And kind of amazing.

"Aren't you sick of it all?" she says, as if she knows what I'm thinking. "I know I'm bored."

I tense. I prefer it when she's picking on other people.

"Why do you put up with it?"

As if we haven't been over it. As if she doesn't know just as well as I do. Better, even.

"Fight back! Defend yourself. Look at him. He's a shrimp. He's scared of you. You can't be satisfied with this. How can you be so passive? Do something—anything! Do you have a pulse? Hellooo . . ."

I can't respond. She'll get bored with me—or Kistrfyv will, if I can just hold out long enough.

"Don't you want more? You're really going to let that weenie bully you for the rest of your life?"

It's clear she would do things differently, if she could. Her tragedy is that she literally can't. Mine is she'll never let me forget it.

Kistrfyv seems to see past my mask to the exasperated twist beneath. His sneer is so pronounced it escapes the upper edge of his mask. The effect is unpleasant, but not nearly as much as his punishment will be: extra cycles of rec and more Noosh—the dense, flavourless goop that meets all nutritional requirements while ensuring uniformity among the populace. Or it's supposed to, anyway. It drains the color from the other workers' skin, keeps them shapeless and slim and more or less the same. I remain an inexplicably vivid shade of brown, my eyes and hair still too saturated and distinctive. I'm too tall and too bony—which only adds to the misery of the rec cycles. On the bright side, every time they increase my Noosh allotment, it seems to dull Cadence's voice and makes it easier to resist her distractions.

I can see my probationary trial receding further with every blink of the supervisor's bulbous, judging eyes.

He has no intention of letting me live down my failure, letting me blend in with the crowd. He just likes watching me squirm.

I make no further apology, though Kistrfyv eyes me expectantly. He'd probably appreciate a little groveling or a few tears. Maybe I should make more of a show of contrition. Maybe it would motivate him to promote me sooner.

Or maybe it's hopeless. He tops off his lecture with a group chorus of benevolent regulation, watching me the whole time. After, I'm allowed to sit.

I shift, all sharp angles at odds with the smooth, ergonomic curves of my seat, another reminder that I'm never right, even for something as simple as a chair. A wheel squeaks, high and thin. I cringe.

"You're both weenies," Cadence says.

I'd like to tell her to shut up. I'd like to tell her I have no choice, and she knows it. I'd like to tell her it's better than being like her, forever complaining and never able to do a thing about it.

I'd like to, but I won't. As much trouble as she is, she's all I have left. And she'll back off soon, because I'm all she has. All she'll ever have.

STRANGERS

I DON'T HATE my job. Hate is dangerous. Hate is a wish for change. A wish is a dream that can draw down the Mara.

I'm not capable of hating my job. I merely appreciate when I no longer have to be at it. The pressure to focus, to keep from drifting off, to keep from being distracted by Cadence's extravagantly expressed boredom . . . It's exhausting.

Which is the point of work, after all. It's the point of everything. Keep us just occupied and numb enough to stay out of trouble. Even bio breaks are subject to regulation, carefully scheduled to avoid interaction. But I excel at maintaining a modest perimeter, and my posture is flawless. Stooped shoulders to minimize my height, chin tucked to avoid eye contact and hide my face, elbows in, small steps. It's not easy. I have an unfortunate tendency to trip over my own oversized feet, and I seem to be growing. Still.

"I miss colour," Cadence says out of nowhere. Like she does. "When was the last time you saw a proper, rich blue? Or orange? Ooh, I miss oranges too. And fruit. And eating."

My mouth goes dry. A tingle buzzes the base of my skull. "Shh."

"Oh, come on, it's not as if they can hear me."

"But I can." She has to stop doing this to me, reminding me she's a ghost. The dead are strangely distracting. I hurry back to my console and squint at the screen.

"You oughta thank me for breaking the boredom. How you can stare at that thing all day, I'll never know."

Maybe if I pretend she's not there, she'll back off. I start scanning from the submerged lower levels, deserted except for the occasional aquatic patrol, and work my way up floor by deserted floor, past the ebb and flow of the Corrections division on Floor 6 and on to the tangle of codes that marks the higher divisions. Floor 15, Residential, is reliably busy; cleaners come and go all day long. Floor 18 looks empty, though of course it isn't really. The system doesn't track surveillance workers. There'd be no point in sitting here monitoring myself sitting here monitoring . . . yeah, no point at all.

The snarl of worker codes is heaviest between floors 16 and 30, tapering off on the higher levels. As far as I can tell, only a few enforcers and a handful of division leaders ever go that high. Apparently the Mayor lives up there, but if she has a code in the system, I haven't figured it out.

"Oops. You missed one. Hey, if I help you find five more screw-ups, can we leave early? I'm so done with this scene."

A surveillance feed on Floor 19 is patchy, the handful of codes flickering in and out too quickly to represent the actual movements of workers. I flag the anomaly to the field team for investigation.

"Don't ignore me—say thank you. Manners. Honestly, were you raised in a barn?"

I don't understand. Barn? But she's teasing, playful, which is better than nagging. She did save me from an error, after all.

She was also the source of my distraction.

"Thanks," I mutter into my mask. "Now will you let me concentrate?"

She makes a rude sound in my ear. It's only a few minutes before she starts up again, complaining about things I don't understand, distracting, harassing, and occasionally helping, just to change things up.

A good worker doesn't need release from the boredom. A good drone lives for the boredom—or rather, the boredom is what lets us live. So I'm not struggling to focus, counting the minutes through the day. I don't dream of a different life, a better one. Not anymore.

But can I help if I'm forced to listen to Cadence imagine wild and beautiful alien worlds? She doesn't always nag and tease and pester. Sometimes she tells stories, wild fantasies of people and places from the Outside, before the ocean invaded. Colours, not just shades of grey; forms that aren't purposelessly shapeless; food that's something other than flavourless and slurped through a straw twice a day. More often than not, her stories trail off in confusion, usually when she tries to talk about herself instead of just making things up. Because, you know—ghost. She doesn't remember her past. She doesn't know any more about the world than I do.

But she keeps talking while I focus on my screen. Flag the anomalies. Repeat. Build a record of obedience. I've only just sat down after my second bio break of the day when I see it. I have to look twice to be sure. Surveillance is down across a full half of Floor 20.

"Is that . . . ?" Cadence sounds awed. "Full crash? How would that even happen?"

It's a major anomaly. If there were warning signs, someone's going to be in a lot of trouble. I flag it for field service. Whoever gets assigned to investigate is going to be busy for a while. An alert takes over my screen: "Surveillance Technician 18-Cole-: Assigned to task."

That can't be right.

"No way," Cadence says, "you get to do a field investigation? Awesome."

That definitely can't be right. Only senior surveillance technicians are assigned to field duties. I glance at the supervisor's office door and swallow. I should report something's gone wrong and get the task reassigned.

Unless he did this.

The buzzing in my head settles into a deep, pulsing ache. I push back at it, rumpling my hood. He wouldn't, would he? Purposely assign a major field investigation to me, just to see me fail? Or—

I take a closer look at the notation buried in the attached files. Two words jump out at me: "Probationary Trial."

I can't believe it. I'd thought after this morning's incident, I'd be waiting months, years even.

I wring my hands. It's here it's here it's here it's . . . impossible. It's a trap. Kistrfyv is setting me up to fail. I hardly know anything about field missions.

But there's no way to refuse the task, not without admitting failure and giving up my shot at normality. I push back my chair, catch my knee on the side of the console, and almost collide with a passing worker.

"Really?" Cadence sounds delighted. "You're actually going? This is so cool. What do you think Floor 20 is like?"

She keeps up a steady one-sided commentary. I try to breathe and walk at the same time. I clench restless fingers into stillness, fumbling the door to the hallway open. There's a crowd in front of the elevator doors.

A crowd.

Refuge Force. It was all a trap. Kistrfyv set me up, and now they've come for me and they'll drag me back down to Floor 6 to die—

But enforcers wear white, close-fitting uniforms. The figures up ahead are in standard grey, Noosh-bleached features shadowed under their hoods as they huddle distressingly close together.

"You just gonna stand here or what?" Cadence sounds annoyed. It's as if she doesn't even see them, doesn't realize how deeply in violation of regulation it is for them to be congregating out here. Work shifts are carefully staggered to avoid this exact situation. There should never be more than one of us moving between locations at the same time.

One worker in the middle of the group stands out. He's tall, maybe even taller than I am, his shoulders thrown back to show the clear line of his body beneath a carelessly dishevelled uniform. His ID is obscured; I can't tell which division he's with. I've certainly never noticed him before. His hood has slipped, exposing dramatic blue-black strands against golden skin. But even properly covered, he would stand out—his irises are like liquid gold. And he's staring right at me.

"About time," he says.

FREEDOM

I MOVE OUT of the doorway.

"Finally," Cadence says. Then, as I take another step: "Uh, Cole? This way. Cole!"

She's annoyed. It makes sense. It's repulsive, the way those workers are all in each other's space. And that strange man, he's practically malformed: shoulders thrown back, his smooth, angled jawline visible where his mask has shifted to one side. I can even make out the corner of his mouth, upturned. He's smiling?

I feel sick. Or something.

He gestures and the others melt away, apparently taking their cue to leave. He moves closer. Somehow the loose folds of the same shapeless uniform we all wear seem to accentuate his form instead of obscuring it.

"It's been ages, flame." His voice is warm, liquid in a way that tugs my shoulders up around my ears and makes my teeth squeak.

Why does he act like he knows me? Whatever this is, it's very, very wrong. I need to get out of here.

I don't move.

"You don't remember, do you? It's okay, just come with me." He moves closer. "You're in danger here."

What comes out of my mouth bears only a passing resemblance to language. I try again. "Wh—who are you?"

He laughs. "Ravel. I'm the one you've been waiting for."

His hand on my arm. A shock like static electricity prickling across my scalp. A memory: the dead man's face, blue-grey pallor over a bony jaw. That night on Floor 6.

I jerk away. The back of my head thunks against the wall.

"Easy—you need to trust me. I'm here to help you." He slips an arm behind my back and sweeps me toward a door across from the elevator. I've never noticed it before. Never had a reason to.

"I don't like this," Cadence says. "Cole? Do something."

"I'm here to rescue you," Ravel says over her protest. "I know what you want, flame. I know what you need. You don't have to be alone anymore. You don't have to hide among these drones. I can give you back your life."

He sounds so confident. But he's wrong. I don't want anything. The Mara took that part of me. The trouble is, they also took the part that knew how to talk back.

He leans in. The warmth of his breath on my ear makes it hard to focus.

"You're out here on an assignment, right? That was me. I set it up to help you escape. You can't trust Refuge. They're lying to you, lying to everyone. They can't protect you like I can. They just want to use you. You don't remember—you don't know how much they've taken from you already. Come with me. It'll hurt less if you come now. I don't want to see you suffer."

Beyond the door, a stairwell stretches away into the shadows. I turn to look full into his face—far, far too close now. He smiles, all shining eyes and even, too-white teeth.

"Who are you?"

He sighs, and the pressure at my back lessens. "It would be better if you'd just trust me. This is all for you, after all." His teasing tone reminds me a little of Cadence's now. "Haven't you ever dreamed of escaping this place?"

I suck in a breath and twist to look up and down the hallway. How dare he make such accusations?

"Hey." He catches my chin. His gloves are missing. The warmth of his hand scorches right through my mask.

His voice drops, his gaze dazzling in its intensity. "You can trust me. You're meant for more than this. Didn't you ever wonder why you were spared?"

I forget how to breathe.

"Cole, move," Cadence says. "This guy's crazy. Let's get out of here."

Where does she want to go again? What . . . what was I doing? I can't think. I need him to stop talking so I can think, but he just keeps going.

"I made a place to help people like you, flame, a place where you can be what you were always meant to be." He brushes his thumb against my cheek, rumpling my mask. "There's another world at the end of these steps. Freedom has everything you could ever want and more. You just have to reach out and take it."

The concern in his expression seems to hook inside me and yank. I'm on fire. Of course, if it'll make him happy. Of course. Whatever it was that he wanted. Whatever he said—

Wait, what did he just say?

"People like me." I lean away. *People like you.* Other people. Probationary workers? Failures?

"But you're special." He hurries on. "You always have been. You're meant for more, so much more than this. Don't you feel it? Haven't you always known you were different?"

Different.

"This is wrong." It's not a complaint, nor a challenge. It's not even a choice. Just a statement of fact. I take another step back.

I'm nobody special. I'm not tempted by his words—just confused. He sounded so authoritative; I almost obeyed out of habit. But the Mara took the part of me that could be tempted. This has to be a lie, some kind of trick or scheme.

Finally, I get a proper glance at the ID printed on his uniform: 00-Ravel-. There's no division code, no sequence number. He's fake, just playing a part. It's all part of my probationary trial. Obedience in the face of temptation.

And what could be more tempting than someone like him telling me I'm meant for something more than this?

It's so obvious, now I've caught my breath and can think again. It's a final call to dream instead of obey. I need to submit to the Mara.

"You shouldn't be here." My voice comes out cold and even. I'm pleased with how steady it sounds. "You're in violation of regulation."

Dark brows knit together over those molten eyes; so expressive, so pleading. It's wrong to notice; I know it is. I need to end this, now.

"I call upon the Mara to eat my dreams."

"Don't you want to be with me? Why don't you tell me what you want?" He leans in, whispers, "Tell me your secret desires. I'll give it all to you."

Images flicker through my mind in shades of blue and grey as I go cold, colder than their stiff skin. No. The Mara ate my dreams. They took all that away. But if they hadn't . . . What would he say if I told him just what I used to fantasize about? If he knew just how different—how 'special'—I used to be? I shake my head.

"I call upon the Mara to eat my dreams." The tingling starts to recede. The memories fade.

"What's wrong? Please—"

"It's a trick," I whisper, more to myself than to him. "I won't fail. I call upon the Mara to eat my dreams."

For an instant after the final repetition, his face goes blank in a way that clears my head instead of fogging it. But then he relaxes again into an expression of warm invitation. The light returns to his eyes. I'm left off balance, not sure of just what I saw.

"Cole, I'll take care of you. I'll make it all right. Look, just follow me down to Freedom. Just down to the end of these steps, to the life you were meant to live. You know you want this. You won't regret it, I promise. Trust me."

"I won't fail," I say, louder. He looks confused. "I know my duty. I won't be tricked. I will pass probation. You tell Kistrfyv that."

I take another step back and feel behind me for the elevator call button. I flatten myself against the cold steel.

"You only hurt yourself by denying me," Ravel says, one hand outstretched in invitation. "You'll come to me in the end."

There's a whoosh to my right. A door swings open. A worker emerges, head modestly bowed.

"You'll come to me."

It's a breath on the air, followed by a click. When I look back, the stairwell door is closed and Ravel is gone.

4 LEFTOVERS

I NEARLY TOPPLE backwards into the elevator car when it arrives. My heart doesn't slow until the doors close, sealing me safely in.

"Finally," Cadence says. "Talk about messed up. Who does that guy think he is? Creepy, much?"

"He acted in violation of several regulations." The memory drives a wave of heat through me. The things he said— "Unacceptable behaviour, even if it was part of the probationary trial."

"Uh, yeah, unacceptable and weird. You gotta be clear with guys like that. Don't let them think they can push you around."

"I—"

"Let 'em know what's what. You can't humour them. They won't get the picture."

"I didn't—"

"Wait. It's not like you, you know, liked him, is it? Ew. Guys like that are no good, Cole."

The elevator interrupts my sputtering. Floor **20**. I step out into the hallway. My knees lock.

What was I thinking? I don't know how to investigate a broken surveillance system. I have no idea where to even begin figuring out what went wrong. I'm going to fail, and Serovate's going to mock me and ship me back to Corrections, and I'm never going to get out of there and I'll probably die and—

"I have to go back. I don't know how to fix this." I pluck at the hem of my shirt, my fingers fluttering as fast as my racing heart.

"Obviously. Wasn't the whole point to get out and explore? Don't tell me you seriously thought you were coming up here to work?"

Floor 20 is a care ward—declining workers, mostly, waiting out their final years safely ensconced in tiny, separate rooms. Even if I knew how to perform a field investigation, with the space all broken up like this, it would take forever to work my way room by room across the whole floor and figure out what had gone wrong. But I can't go back now. Either Kistrfyv set me up to fail, or Ravel was telling the truth and it's his fault I'm here. Either way, I'll have to figure out what's wrong with the system before I can go back.

I pause at the first door to my right. There are sounds beyond, a sort of gurgling wheeze. Snoring?

"Now what?" Cadence asks.

One more thing I'd forgotten: there are people behind each door. I'll have to invade their space to carry out my investigation. Just the thought of it makes me ill.

"There's someone in there," I say, by way of explanation.

"Well, duh."

"I can't just go in."

"Cool. Don't. This place is boring. Let's go check out a different floor."

"I can't."

"Fine. If you're gonna be a wimp about it, you can just go back to work and stare at your boring stupid screen some more. Or maybe you just wanna go back and see your boyfriend."

I gasp, whirl to face her with my hand raised for a swat—but she's not there. She's not anywhere. It's moments like these she feels . . . I don't know, too close and unfairly far away at the same time.

Before the waters rose and the Mara came, people were made differently. Individually. Gross as it sounds, people apparently got together to make more people. Which is unhealthy and dangerous of course, so Refuge started producing workers in a controlled environment instead. But if I'd been born before, into a family, would it feel like this? Stuck with a bratty little sister to pester me all day and night?

If we weren't both unsequenced—from production series discontinued after only one iteration; not broken enough to destroy, but not valuable enough to bother making more of—I'd even have thought maybe Cadence was one of my series, another Cole who died before she'd finished growing. Being haunted feels like too much connection, like family and more than family, someone you can never get away from, but eventually it's so normal to be together you forget anything else.

I lower my hand. I get why she's annoyed with me. I need to suck it up, push through the awkwardness, get it over with. Instead, I twist my fists tighter in the loose fabric at the sides of my uniform and set off down the hall.

"Now what?" Cadence has been sounding different since we ran into Ravel. Less bratty, more, I don't know. Snarky? As if she's somehow getting closer to my age. Can ghosts age?

I push the distraction away and try to focus. "I should start at the other end, work my way back."

Starting from the far end of the corridor is a great idea. Methodical. Logical. Probably what protocol would dictate, if I actually knew the appropriate steps to take for a field investigation. It's also the perfect excuse not to open any doors for another minute or two.

Cadence laughs at me all the way down the hall, around the corner, and to the end of that stretch as well. I stare at the last door and roll my shoulders, producing a crackling sound from the joints in my neck. I listen for another moment. Silence. That's a good sign. I push it open, hoping for a vacant room, despite the sign beside the door that reads: 20-Bell-. Another only. If she were part of a series, her sequence number would be after the second dash, forming her short ID: Bellwan, Belltu, and so on.

As it turns out, I get my wish for another few moments of solitude. Sort of.

The room is miniscule, maybe twice the width of the overturned cot. The air is thick with the heavy sweetness of the protective airborne sedative used in the upper floors of Refuge to protect us from distraction and disobedient thoughts. Its cloying scent is dense in the small space. Probably a good thing, given the circumstances.

The body is unlike any I've seen. It's partly covered by pieces of the overturned cot. The floor and walls around it are fractured. Gritty white powder mixes with congealing blood. It's as if something ripped through the corpse and right on into the room around it.

The buzzing in my ears mutes Cadence's shriek. Dark stains seep up the soft toes of my shoes.

The corpse is not fresh. Raw gashes scissor across its body. Its uniform hangs in shreds, exposing purpling shadows closer to the floor, grey-white flesh higher up. During the day on Floor 6, the dead were carted off almost immediately. Mara-taken in the night were another matter—I've seen corpses as old as six or even eight hours dead. This one's joints will be stiff by now. It would be impossible to smooth away its anguished contortion even if I wanted to take pity on it, to wipe away the echo of its pain.

What's left of the dead woman's face is twisted in horror. Her bulging eyes are opaque, pearlescent. Mara-taken.

I kneel. There's a smell below the cloying sweetness of the air: bitter, rotten, sharp. Everything about this death is different than it should be, except for the eyes. What happened to her?

The woman—Bell?—must have been very old. Her skin is lined and sagging. Her close-cropped hair is thin; transparent wisps that don't seem to be able to soak up the stain of blood. I've never seen anyone quite like her. One of the side effects of Noosh; it flattens out our differences. All of them, age included. Until it can't, and then I guess we end up here on Floor 20.

I drag two gloved fingers through the powder on the floor: gritty from concrete dust, slightly tacky from the blood that spilled when whatever did this went right through her and into the floor below. The Mara don't leave damage like this. They aren't physical. They eat dreams. They take only what's inside, leaving the shell hollow but untouched, except for those pearl-blank eyes. It's why we're so carefully controlled, why we have the ritual of submission: to keep us as empty inside as possible.

But if the Mara only hunger after the inner life, what slashed Bell here so deeply it tore through the thin carpet and into concrete?

The buzzing in my head prickles across my scalp, spreading.

This isn't happening. This forbidden fascination with the dead—the desire know what they knew and feel what they felt, to become someone else for even a moment—the Mara took it away with all the rest of my disobedience. I don't break regulation any more. I can't lose everything I've worked for. I won't fail again. Any moment now, I'll step away, send for help, submit my longing to the Mara.

Instead, I reach out to touch the corpse's ashen skin.

SUSANNAH

THERE'S A FLARE of piercing light, and everything changes. I'm . . . somewhere else. Sound comes back first: a delicate, distant melody. I've never heard anything like it.

I haven't heard music like that in years, the child thinks.

I peer past an improbably frilly and beribboned skirt. Shiny white shoes swing in time to the gentle tune. I'm sitting at a table set with china and silver amidst a lavish expanse of gently waving greenery, polished wood, and marble pillars.

And here's the strangest, most impossible part of it. I'm not me; I'm her. A small girl in an extravagant, inappropriate dress. I see what she sees, feel what she feels, and, increasingly, think what she thinks.

A shadow hovers over our hands, curdling our stomach: a faded silhouette of withered fingers clawed against white sheets. We gasp at the sudden ache of arthritis. Mama reaches over to press our smooth, childish hand and the vision passes.

The warmth of her touch is alarming and unexpected somehow. We look up into her smiling face, smooth and unblemished—so young, why does that seem odd?—and across at Father, frowning nearsightedly at his menu, although of course he'll order the usual.

My—our— sight blurs at the edges. Everything beyond the glittering expanse of our table is out of focus. I try to pull away from the girl and the air thickens. I look closer. Skeins of translucent, threadlike fibres clog the air, creating a fog-like effect.

Everything about this is wrong. This can't be happening. I can't be here. I can't be imagining this. I'd never.

There has to be some sort of explanation. How did I get here? What's happening?

But I slip deeper into the girl's mind with every one of our shared breaths.

Our heart aches, looking at Mama and Father. We are so happy to be here. But something's wrong, or about to go wrong. We can't remember, and brush away the unease.

Mouthwatering breakfast aromas mingle with the lavish perfume of artfully arranged flowers. We prop a menu against the table edge to scan its decadent offerings. Crisp waffles with cream and fruit. Golden stacks of pancakes, or French toast drizzled with maple syrup. Bacon and eggs.

Eggs. The word tears my consciousness up and out of hers. Cadence has told me about eggs before. Where is she? Where am I? I shouldn't be here.

I can't quite catch hold of why.

There's a distant sense of panic, just on the other side of a heavy curtain. It's pushing toward me, trying to reach me. It thins to only the barest whisper of a passing thought. I drift under again.

The music shifts, the gentle strains now jumbled and jarring, shuddering from distractingly loud and harsh to creeping near-silence. Frowning, we close the menu. A small, ribbon-bound box perches behind it. "To Miss Suzannah Bell" says the cream-coloured tag, in elegant cursive.

Mama speaks, but her voice is lost under a violent crescendo of discordant music. Father, his arm draped casually over her shoulder, twinkles at us above his carefully oiled moustache. He does so enjoy finding the best presents.

We feel surprise. It's Suzannah's birthday?

The question is mine. I surface muzzily from the girl's consciousness.

Suzie, she thinks to me, *but they call me Bell now.*

Suzie seems unfazed at the presence of a second consciousness drifting in and out of her. I squint through the shifting filaments that cloud the air. I'd lost track of them until the girl's name jostled me back into my own head. Suzannah Bell. Bell. It's familiar.

The ID beside the door on Floor **20**. The room with the corpse.

Corpse? She wonders.

I shutter the memory. Impossible as it seems—impossible as this whole experience is—I can't very well be exposing a child to the horrors of . . . the horrors of . . .

What was it again? Somewhere else. I'm supposed to be somewhere else. I'm supposed to be someone else. The memories drift away with my consciousness.

We tug the satin ribbon. The box drops open to reveal the most lovely, delicate little doll. It's flawless, dressed to the finest detail in precisely the outfit we have on, down to the spotless white shoes. Mama and Father had to have planned this all out far in advance. Our eyes prick with tears.

The hair and face are not quite an honest copy, though. The doll's tiny curls are much tidier, shinier, and in all ways more appealing; her face is an absolute delight, with sweet porcelain features and the most gleamingest black eyes, not like our muddy hazel ones at all. A whiff of decay drifts through the air, distracting us. Something's wrong—and if we stop and think a moment, if we just concentrate, we'll remember—

But here's our meal now, sweet and savoury scents drowning out that faint swampiness in a wash of fragrant steam. We sit the doll up against a saltcellar and stroke its curls as we eat.

Click.

Something shifts under our finger. Several faint lines angle across the doll's face. We press. The lines darken.

A grating whisper. The head of the doll splits. It fans open in delicate, sharp slices.

Our fork clangs against our plate. We pull the doll to us, anticipating wonders painted on each slice, or perhaps a hollow compartment hiding another gift. But there's only an empty cavity inside, a flat, unbroken darkness that the chandeliers fail to illuminate.

Our hands shake. There's something here we shouldn't see. We peer down anyway.

A sudden wave of dizziness. The reek of decay is stronger now. The doll slips from our fingers. It drops toward the carpet with slow inevitability. We lunge for it. Then we're falling, everything's falling. The world spins out in a dizzy whirl.

My view shifts as she falls away from me. The threads choking the air tangle around her.

I know what this is now. It has to be a dream, a nightmare, a Mara attack. There's no other explanation that makes sense. This world no longer exists. Maybe it never did. The corpse sprawled beside her cot on Floor 20 and this impossibly young child, Suzie, they share more than an ID. But I don't know how she can be dead in Refuge and alive to be dreaming this now. Unless...

Unless none of this is about her at all. Unless this is my dream. My death.

I stare at Suzie in horror. She sprawls on the floor beside her chair, shrunken and stiff as if she's become the doll that fell. Her mother rises in the distance, elegance itself trailing away toward the ceiling, giant-like. A moment later, her father looms up alongside. Their apparent lack of concern cuts at Suzie's heart. She struggles to understand. She doesn't see through my eyes. She doesn't know what's coming.

The crash of the piano has subsided into ringing silence. The hall feels cavernous and empty. The ghost or memory of Suzannah Bell can still taste decay in the air, and I through her. Her parents hold out their hands as if to take hers, but the angle is too high. She doesn't understand why, not at first. Translucent threads drape from their arms, snarled and heavy. They're unevenly wound ropes by the time they reach Suzie, binding her in place.

The warm, late-morning sun shifts, a flash of stark, blinding light. The long bones beneath Suzie's parents' skin are darkly skeletal silhouettes. Her heart stutters and seizes, her breath caught in her throat. I hold my breath as well, caught in the moment, in her panic and my own horror. The end must be coming soon. Hers, or mine.

A pair of flawless arms reaches past Suzie in stiff, unbending unison. They slip through threads now milky in their thickness as if they're not there at all. A rigid figure with bright curls stalks past Suzie. It takes her parents' outstretched hands. The doll takes Suzie's place without her parents noticing a thing, and that's how I know this nightmare really is almost at an end.

The Mara have come.

The creature holds Suzie's parents' hands as they turn to leave. She calls to them soundlessly from behind a tiny painted rosebud of a mouth, panicked now. What dream, what nightmare is this? Her thoughts snag. *Dream. It's just a dream.* But instead of relief, terror wells in instinctive response.

Her horror makes it harder to keep mine at bay. We both know now there will be no waking, no escape. They're coming for us, have already come, are here now. The only question is, have they already come for Suzie—come and gone and left this echo for me to stumble into? Or has their devouring somehow carried on all this time, past the ending of Suzie's physical form? Or is it not Suzie they're here for at all?

I would run, but like her, I can't move. I'm as formless as a ghost.

She struggles against leaden arms, unable to see the weight of coiled, knotted threads pinning her to the ground. She longs to pinch herself, shock herself awake, close her eyes and open them to her own, real life. She'd even welcome back the endless decades of mindless drudgery, the pains of the years burdening her aged frame. Her longing tugs at me, casting shadows of an aged corpse in my mind.

But her eyes are frozen in place, wide and staring. Her outflung limbs are a dead, cold weight dragging her down. She can't open her lips to form the words of submission, to release her dreams to the Mara and save herself. She's trapped, as immobile and helpless as the doll that has taken her place. Left behind. Abandoned.

The Mara in their cruel mimicry of Suzie let go of her parents' hands. Suzie can't look away from the sight of them again after all this time, so young, so healthy and unaware in their short-lived happiness, even if it is an illusion. The ghost of the years between them creeps back into her mind and memory. They'd never been this happy. This paradise had never truly existed in their lifetime. So much loss. So much pain. She wants to forget. She wants to go back to being a child, protected. She wants them to look again at her, to see her and love her.

I choke on the sensation of her loss, heart racing in time with hers, gaze darting as hers cannot. It's not just the doll that's the Mara, but everything around us. This alien place and these unlikely people are all a part of some elaborate, soul-sucking nightmare. These things Suzie has shown me, they're not real. They were never real. Family. Music. Food. They have to be the product of the Mara, luring her—us? me?—deeper, strengthening our attachment before devouring us whole.

The creature turns and stalks back toward us, glittering eyes malevolent in that expressionless porcelain perfection of a face, a cruel replacement for Suzie's—Bell's—broken, aged weakness. Its doll eyes are clouded with a faint impression of grey and green and blue – the child's hazel eyes, painted over her replacement's bottomless black ones. Suzie's memories roll back over her, the weight of years and so many deaths crashing back into her mind and body all at once.

I'm shocked to realize at least some of what I've seen is from her memories and not entirely a fabrication of the

Mara. Shocked and relieved. Unless this is just another dimension of deception, it's possible this isn't my dream after all. But I'm not sure what's more improbable; that the Mara could have spun all of this out of my imagination in the first place or that Bell could really have been that old. I mean, a family? An actual childhood spent outside of Refuge's walls? Could she really have been produced—born—before the floods?

The porcelain mockery of a face leers, glass eyes full of bottomless, eerie knowing. Black leaches through the hazel paint. The delicately fanned segments of the creature's head, grown so large now, have slipped back together with only the barest hint of their former, grotesque separation. A thin dark line shows just at its hairline; a narrow but seemingly bottomless gap where the skull curves to the perfectly arched spill of its hair.

Something squirms within. It trickles down the porcelain forehead and oozes along the angled line of that painted brow, a gathering oil slick of midnight tears pooling in the socket of one glittering eye. They overflow, streaking over the smooth cheek, spattering with acid heat across Suzie as the Mara loom over her in that flawless replica of her own beribboned dress.

She surges against the burning, struggling to move the dead weight of arms and legs turned to cold, immobile porcelain. I want to cover my eyes, but I can't move, can't escape any more than she can.

The sole of the Mara-doll's pristine white shoe grown to gigantic proportions rises to blot out the light. And falls.

Everything washes away in a wave of shattering pain as the Mara end the nightmare the way I knew they would, in horror and agony and death.

FOR A LONG moment, there's nothing else. Then I'm alone in the dark, whole, my thoughts, my senses entirely my own once more. The ineffable awareness of Suzie's existence that pervaded the dream is gone. There's nothing left but sick, quivering fear. Am I dead too this time? Is it over?

In the darkness, the figure of an old woman coalesces. Her face is bare and exposed, her edges frayed and wispy. It's the broken body of the corpse I reached out to, Bell. The fraying along her edges grows, threads of silver unravelling until she's the girl with the golden curls and hazel eyes.

"Suzie," I say into the darkness.

She stares back at me, her young face etched with sadness. A whispering, rushing sound surrounds us, filling the empty spaces.

"Suzie," I say again, wishing I could reach out to her, reaching for the edges of my own boundaries to try to draw them together and touch the broken child. I feel as shattered as if I'd been crushed alongside her, but the dream was hers, not mine. She was the victim of the Mara, not me. So why do I hurt?

Shadows darken across her face. I recognize the scored lines etched across the corpse of her future-past self. Her eyes cloud over. I need to make it stop, to shelter her, to turn back time to when she was whole and happy and seen. But even as I find my hands and gather my voice, the rushing sound rises and fragments into thousands of shouting, shrieking voices.

She speaks. I can't hear her past the cacophony. The shadows across her darken and split her skin. She throws her head back. Her face contorts in a scream. I can't quite pick it out among the host of howling voices. It breaks nonetheless, as if the gashes across her flesh are mirrored inside me.

I struggle harder to reach her. Countless invisible hands seem to shove against me, hauling me back and away.

Her mouth slackens; her chin tips down. She stares at me with milky eyes and shattered skin. The edges of her are short-cropped threads drifting in an intangible breeze. Darkness wells up in the corners of her eyes and overflows.

It runs down her cheeks in a continuous stream. She smiles, slow and empty.

A wash of light carries it all away.

I'M KNEELING IN a tiny, brightly lit room, reaching out to a corpse once more. I blink. For a moment, it seems as if the tips of my gloves are tangled in silver threads.

SECRETS

WHAT JUST HAPPENED?" Cadence sounds faint.

I clamp my fingers around my elbows and flatten my back against the wall.

"Oh," she says in quite a different tone. "Oh, no, it's okay. You're okay. It's gonna be okay."

I stare at a jagged crack in the paint and try not to see what's left of Bell at my feet. Suzie.

No. It can't have been real; this isn't Suzie, but Bell. A declining worker, old and worn and probably senile. I try not to think about her abbreviated ID. Another discontinued, defective only. Is that why she was killed?

"I don't know what you did just now," Cadence says. "But all this stuff has been coming back to me—flashes of memories from before. It's incredible. You're never gonna believe—"

"I didn't mean to." I tuck my hands out of sight. "I know I shouldn't have, but I just—and then that girl . . ."

"Huh? What girl? You mean touching the body? Yeah, that probably wasn't a great idea. What was that even about? But listen, I've just remembered—"

She starts babbling again, making up some story about her memories coming back, lost friends, some kind of mission, trying to distract me. I'm sure she means well, but it's no use. I have to get out of here. I was just hallucinating, or something. That's as bad as dreaming. The Mara will come for me. With a dead body at my feet, I clearly can't rely on Floor 20's shields to protect me.

But it's like staring at a light for too long; the image of Bell's body has burned into my retinas, and like a phantom behind that, the image of the little girl, Suzie, writhes as it's eaten away by the Mara.

My fingers itch. The buzzing in my head swells against the thought of leaving her. If I touched her again, could I go back? Make it different? Help her? Or at least keep her from being alone in the dark? It's irrational to think I could do anything about her death; incontrovertible proof lies at my feet, staining my shoes. I flatten a hand against the closed door, trembling.

"Are you even listening?" Cadence says, as if whatever it is she has to say matters right now. "Hey, I know that Ravel guy was a real creeper, but he was on to something. Refuge is super messed up. You need to get out of here, like right now. Besides, I really need your help with—"

I thump the door once, twice, then repeatedly, as if the dull *thud* will help me figure out what to do.

"Uh, Cole?" she says, quieter this time. "What's going on? I know it's freaky how messed up the body is, but it's not like you've never seen a corpse before. It's okay, you know? Let's just get a little space between you and this mess."

I ache to go back, to press both my hands on that chill, wrinkled flesh and cry out Suzie's name until I reach her again. Instead, I push on the door and take a deep breath of the clearer hallway air. My gloves leave dark smears against the grey paint. A storm of gritty, bloodstained footprints behind me catches my gaze and won't let go.

"Good," Cadence soothes, "you're doing really good. Just walk away, okay? In fact, listen, Refuge is totally no good—but I think I can get you out. We could both escape—"

"I'm not in the mood for your stories right now."

I can't be here. I can't be feeling this way. The Mara already ate the part of me that could feel and choose and—

"Cole, I'm not playing with you." Her voice is fierce. "This is for real. You have to help me—"

The unmistakeable tone of an elevator car arriving chimes in the distance. We both freeze, listening to the whir of the doors opening. A low grumble of male voices filters around the corner. I strain to make out the words.

". . . just saying, as an inspector . . . more than qualified . . . Her Worship's . . . fail to see what some low-level enforcer . . ."

The speaker's voice is gruff with irritation and nearly drowned out by the heavy thump and scuffle of thick-soled boots. Refuge Force.

They've come for me.

My own thin shoes make a faint squelching as I waver. I want to slip back into the room with Bell and hide, but I've been drawn to her since the moment I saw her. No, I haven't. That's not possible.

"Inspector." The words are soft, deferential, but the tone is slippery. "Don't sell yourself short. Your esteemed intellect surely sees the advantage of a mutually beneficial arrangement. We both live to serve Her Worship's interests, after all, and the, ah, issue in question does seem to be escalating."

They're getting nearer, approaching the corner. I flinch back from the doorway, out of sight.

"None of that, Serovate." The boots stamp to a stop. "I won't stand for your greasy little word games. Precision, man. The corpses are what're escalating. The attacks. Fatalities. Her Worship personally commissioned me to investigate, and I—"

"To be sure, Inspector, to be sure. Admirable precision indeed. I stand ready and willing to support the honourable inspector in, ah, precisely the manner required by Our Lady."

The sound of rustling plastic crackles around the corner. I shrink further into Bell's room. I should have acted sooner, should have reported the death right away. Maybe I could dash out to meet them as if I've only just arrived on the scene?

My knees disagree, weak at the thought of interrupting the bickering enforcers.

"Is that really necessary?" The inspector complains. The rustling gets louder.

"Not at all, Inspector, not at all. I myself see no need for such precautions, but Her Worship did express some distaste at the way the last scene was handled."

"If you'd been doing your duty properly instead of letting that poor worker stumble over—"

"As you say, Inspector, the consequences were less than ideal. Her Worship mandated a more proactive approach to her people's security in future, although I would be more than happy to dispense with erecting a perimeter around the scene, if you would care to authorize . . . ? No? Ah, well. Why don't you proceed with your investigation and I'll just finish up here, then?"

"I don't need an enforcer to tell me my job," the inspector growls, "nor to remind me of my duty to Mayor Ajera."

"Just so. As you say, you've performed your duties admirably. And yet, the wrong workers keep dying despite Her Worship's provisions, and even her specially commissioned officers have done—let's see now, oh yes— absolutely nothing to slow the tide or explain the damage."

"Why, you little, I—"

I shift my weight. I'm going to get caught eavesdropping if I don't hurry up and approach them first. But what does he mean by *consequences*? And *wrong* workers? As if there's a right kind to die?

"So of course," the enforcer continues, apparently unperturbed at his inflammatory effect on a senior officer, "you'll want to have something to show for your efforts today, to remind her of your continued value. After all, the risk to Mayor Ajera's position if these stupid drones realize Refuge can't actually protect them . . . I mean, really. Submitting to the Mara. Little golden halos. The idiots will believe anything if you catch them young enough . . ."

A roaring sound in my ears drowns him out. I press my mask against my lips. Did he really just say that? If that's true . . . If it's true . . .

"Told ya," says Cadence, as if her flippant tone could fool me into thinking she's not just as shocked as I am. "This place is bad news, Cole."

I sink to my knees. *Refuge can't actually protect them.* What does he mean? Refuge is the only thing that protects us from the Mara. The wards. The rite of submission . . .

But behind me is the proof that something is very, very wrong. There's a glint of gold wire in the cracked concrete beneath Bell's shattered body. She was protected and well sedated, if the cloying thickness of the air was any indication. If the presence of gold and sedatives and a lifetime of self-control and obedience weren't enough to save her—

I need to get out of here.

"Enough!" the inspector roars. "That. Is. Enough. How dare you—"

"Easy, inspector. You wouldn't want to go doing anything you might regret. I doubt you'd enjoy spending your overtime supplementing the rank and file—though you have to admit, there is some use for us lowly enforcers, if only as brute force and a clean-up crew."

"Kidnapping children is hardly—"

"—a task for an elevated servant of Refuge such as yourself. Quite so. A messy, regrettable business, to be sure. So perhaps we would better serve Refuge's interests and your own by staying on task and finding a way to slow the rate of casualties?"

A chill ices along my spine, though a part of me recognizes this as an absurd overreaction. Children? What do they mean, kidnapping children? From where? Refuge has solved the massive danger that human interaction poses by growing its workers to near-adulthood since the flood. But if Refuge has lied about what it takes to survive the Mara, what else could they have lied about?

I need to get out of here. Now.

Thud.

"Who's there?" the inspector demands.

The response is a startled murmur. A care worker coming on shift, perhaps, or a declining worker checking on the noise in the hallway. Come to think of it, it's amazing I didn't run into anyone sooner.

Either way, it's a chance to escape. I slip out and ease the door closed with my fingertips in the gap to keep it from slamming.

"What are you doing?" Cadence whispers, even though no one else can hear her.

"Getting out of here. Didn't you hear? The "incident"? Corpses? They're looking for this whole situation back here"—I wave one arm in broad indication of Bell's shattered body, the cracked floor and walls, the surveillance system failure—"and I plan to be gone by the time they turn that corner. Which is any minute now."

The door's propped open by two fingers. I'm arrested by the narrow slice visible through it as I glance back.

Suzie.

All of the sudden, the urge to go back in there, to reach out to her—what's left of her—is overwhelming. I'm not even sure which calls me more strongly: the child, her pain transforming into something hungry and dark, or the pallid corpse. But Cadence is watching.

"Are you kidding?" She interrupts my train of thought with a dramatic reversal of her own. "You have every right to be here. You were sent up on assignment, after all. If anything, running away now is going to cause more trouble. Here's what you're gonna do: report the death like an obedient little drone, wait until they dismiss you and start their investigation of the scene, and then escape."

She's . . . absolutely right. And more importantly, it's the perfect excuse to go back into Bell's room, even sit down again beside her. There's not much space, after all.

Maybe sit so close that when I casually brace my arm against the floor, my fingers might just brush up against . . .

I draw the door open again but hesitate. I didn't like the sound of those two enforcers. Especially the junior one, with his greasily polite little veiled threats. What if they guessed I'd been listening the whole time?

"Now what? Could you maybe try not to look so suspicious?" Cadence says, not bothering to keep her voice down.

I forget to whisper in return. "What if—"

"Did you hear something?" the inspector says.

MORRISTU

THE ENFORCERS' BOOTS thunder closer. Shadows in the distance. They'll turn the corner any moment and see me. I can't be caught like this.

I dive for the nearest door. It's all I can do to hold my breath and jam my hand against frame. With my fingers softening the door's fall, the latch can't click shut and give me away. The boots pound closer, closer . . .

"Wait out here," the enforcer, Serovate, says, his voice clear and sharp just on the other side of the door.

My lungs ache with the urge to gasp for air, but it's not safe. I swallow hard at the dark smears my glove leaves on the doorjamb, and look down in horror at a trail of smudged footprints.

"That's no good," the inspector mutters, rustling away further again. I clamp my lips shut and try not to moan, but he doesn't seem to have noticed me. Yet. He must be talking to the person they encountered by the elevator. "Over here. Now face the wall. Good. What's that ID again? 20-Morris-02? Right, Morristu: You just wait like that and don't look 'round."

Morristu's breath catches. The worker must be terrified to have been detained by Refuge Force. I would be. Will be, any minute now, when they follow the footprints right to me.

"No, no. Now don't get all worked up like that." The inspector seems to be trying to soothe Morristu in the hallway while I panic behind the door. "You're not in trouble—"

"Yet," Serovate says.

The inspector grunts. "I'll have some questions for you after we've finished inspecting the scene. Just something I'm trying out, you understand. Questioning potential witnesses yields astonishing insights, particularly when there are surveillance failures. Technology, you know, doesn't solve everything. It's really quite fascinating, all the tools and systems they made use of in the time before . . ."

I gulp at the word *surveillance*. The inspector clears his throat, cutting his rambling short.

"Well, we'll come back to that. Rest assured, if you follow regulation and offer us your full compliance, I'm sure you'll be back on your rounds in no time."

"Yes, Inspector," Morristu says with a quaver.

I'm surprised by her voice. I've never come across a sequenced female before—only anomalies like Cadence and me. But Morristu is evidence that Refuge sees at least some value in producing females.

Boots scuffle inches away. This is it. They'll notice the footprints and throw open the door and—

"Shall I open the door for you, Inspector?" The enforcer hardly seems to be trying to hide the sneer in his voice.

"Serovate, you're in the way. You know I insist on being first to the scene."

"Of course. Wouldn't dream of obstructing your investigation." Serovate shuffles and scuffs heavily, as if it's too much trouble to pick up his feet.

There's no creak, no whoosh of displaced air, just another moment of breathing: deep and purposeful nearby—the inspector, most likely; noisy and careless, even closer—the other enforcer, Serovate, practically on the other side of the door; and fast and shallow, further off—the panicking unfortunate, Morristu. It's all interspersed with the rustle of uniforms. And the creak of the cot beside me.

I dart a terrified glance over, but its occupant is sleeping, a truly ancient creature, judging by the wrinkles around its closed eyes. Its caved-in chest barely rises with each breath;

only the slightest ripple marks where its mask drapes over an open mouth.

"Well," Cadence says. "That could have gone worse."

I grit my teeth. She's right; I could be out there beside that terrified worker in the hallway, nose to the wall waiting for who knows what to happen. But if I'd listened to her and acted sooner, I might've been able to get control of the situation. Besides, I hadn't counted on this room being occupied.

"Hmm," the inspector grunts from the room next door, his voice muffled through the thin walls. "This one's worse again."

"Oh, I don't know," Enforcer Serovate says. "That kid down on '14 looked pretty bad last week—"

"Look at the floor."

"Ah. Well. Isn't that interesting. Someone's been in here. And how distressing; I've gone and walked through the trail."

I press my hand harder against the door to keep it from shaking. Maybe I should just make a break for it? But if the enforcer clumsily obscured my footprints, they might not realize I'm here. Plus, I'm pretty sure I can't actually outrun them.

"Hmm? Trail?" The inspector sounds distracted. "Trail? No, these gouges. Bit much for the Mara based on the current pattern of escalation, but I can't see any of the drones managing this kind of damage, unless Morristu out there has some serious talents up her sleeve."

Serovate offers an eerie giggle at the inspector's absentminded comment. Morristu moans. The two men shuffle and breathe and say nothing for too long after that. They must be looking at the small room with its untidy bed and gouged, bloodstained floor; the body in the midst of it, horribly exposed, being coldly examined.

I twist my free hand in the folds of my uniform until my fingers stop aching to reach out and the tingling that spreads across my scalp at the thought of her starts to ebb. I'd like to throw open this door and drag both of them out of Bell's room. To slam the door in their faces and keep her to myself. To lay down on the shattered floor beside her corpse and hold her cold wrinkled hand and pull that broken child from the grasp of the Mara.

What's happening to me?

"Someone's been here," the inspector says, finally. "See the footprints there? And there? And this smudge on the door? I don't know how we missed them on the way in. The trail is hopelessly trampled now."

"Indeed," Serovate says. "How remarkably observant you are, Inspector." He raises his voice and demands, "Was it you?"

I cringe back from the door, but it's not me he's asking.

"I d-don't know anything," the woman in the hall stammers. "What's that?"

"Did I say you could turn around?"

"I didn't mean to, it's just— you asked and I . . . And that . . . Is she dead . . . ?"

One of the men heaves a sigh—the inspector, I think—and the woman whimpers.

"You really shouldn't have turned around," Serovate says with noticeable glee. "Inspector?"

"Her Worship won't be pleased to lose another one."

"Not our fault she popped up before we could finish sealing the perimeter. And you did say someone had been in the room before we got here."

"I wasn't . . . I didn't," Morristu sobs.

"She probably didn't," the inspector acknowledges absently.

Serovate barks a laugh. "Likely not. Still, now that she's seen . . ."

"Oh, very well. Go ahead."

"Floor 20 Care Ward Worker Morris 2," Serovate says formally, "you are under arrest for the murder of Floor 20 Former Worker Bell. You will be taken before Her Worship Maryam Ajera, Mayor of the Towers of Refuge, to plead your case."

"But I didn't do anything." Morristu hiccups her plea between panicked gulps of air. "You know I didn't do anything. Please."

I glance at the sleeper beside me, but his shallow breaths continue unbroken despite her wails.

"You know this is kind of your fault, right? That they think she was in there." Cadence says.

I want to snap back and ask what she expects me to do about it.

"Oh, just go along," the inspector says to Morristu. "You're better off with Her Worship anyway. Shields might actually do you some good up there. Wouldn't want to end up like this one, would you?"

"Well, that's done for her," Serovate says, sounding amused at Morristu's renewed sobbing. "Sometimes I wonder about you, Haynfyv. Cold as ice."

"It's Inspector Haynfyv," Haynfyv says irritably, "and I don't know what you're on about now. I complete my duty. Without emotion. In compliance with regulation. As you well know."

The enforcer snorts. "Aren't we beyond that little myth at this point? Surely you don't have to wear your mask with me, *Inspector.*"

"Regulation is regulation. I will continue to uphold it regardless of its current efficacy."

"Or lack thereof, isn't it? Very good, Inspector. You uphold your blessed regulation, and I'll worry about who gets to keep drawing breath. And who doesn't."

Morristu chokes on a sob and falls silent.

I shiver. They can't be saying what I think they're saying.

"Caught that, did you?" Serovate sneers. "Go ahead. Regret your life. Your pointless little existence. All your futile little choices. You'll be over it soon enough. But don't worry. We'll just go out and hunt down a nice fresh little replacement. And I know just where to—"

"Enough," the inspector says sharply. "I've an investigation to get on with. Just because you're enjoying running wild doesn't mean the rest of us don't have a duty to Our Lady. The effects of regulation must be recovered."

"If it ever had any. You were appointed quite recently, weren't you, Inspector?"

I close my eyes. It's not true. They're treasonous liars. Refuge protects us. The shields protect us. Our obedience to regulation and our submission to the Mara protects us. If not . . . If not, nothing stands between any one of us and being crushed like Bell.

"Just get on with it," the inspector growls.

With a final mocking laugh, Serovate hauls the sobbing Morristu away. "Don't forget to keep an eye out for that tech," he yells before getting on the elevator. "Her Worship did say to bring her on up for a chat, preferably unharmed."

I swallow hard. Cadence sucks in a shocked breath. What could the mayor possibly want with me?

"Tech?" Haynfyv mumbles absently from the room next door. I flatten myself against the door. "He knows perfectly well I prefer pre-flood methods to today's unreliable tools . . ."

His absentminded mumbling trails off. There's some shuffling from the other side of the wall. Then quiet. Then rustling fabric. Knocking sounds. Scraping.

I bristle at the thought of the inspector poking around my corpse. Well, not *my* corpse; Bell's corpse. But still. I found it first.

Which is kind of the problem.

"Do something!" Cadence says.

If it weren't too dangerous to even breathe, I'd demand to know what she thinks I could possibly do about any of this. So far today, her endless digs and distractions have done nothing but get me in trouble. But what should I do? Wait here until the inspector goes away again? Will he leave the body? Can I get close to her again?

I roll my shoulders. I need to let that go. Focus.

"You can't just ignore this," Cadence says as if I'm an idiot, as if I don't know I have to get myself out of this somehow. "You can't just turn your back on all of it, pretend it's not real. Listen, I know people who can help you. Just follow me, okay? We can come back and save everyone later. But you'll need help."

"What help?" I hardly dare to breathe the words, but she hears.

"I know people. I remember how to—"

She doesn't remember anything. She can't. It's just another one of her games. One of her made-up stories. Ghosts don't have memories, not real ones at least. But if she did, if there were another way, a place I could escape to, someone who could end Refuge and expose its lies . . . What about that man with the golden eyes, Ravel? What if that wasn't just a test? He offered to help.

I tug at my hood thoughtfully and catch a whiff of blood from my stained glove. Poor old Bell. Poor Suzie. But I have to stop thinking like that. I can't do anything about it now. I was supposed to pass probation, finally, but somehow I ended up bloodstained and hiding out from enforcers in someone else's room—clearly having overheard all their secrets, no less. If I just snuck back to work without having completed my own investigation or reporting the corpse, forget passing probation. I'd probably be shunted right back to Floor 6. And that would be the best-case scenario.

"Tech!" Haynfyv's voice, sudden and loud from the next room, makes me flinch. I bump into the cot beside me. "Ah. That's right. From the Surveillance Division. Why didn't he just say so in the first place?"

There's a rustling sound as the inspector gathers himself next door.

No. Oh, no. I'm out of time.

"Don't move," Cadence says. "He doesn't know you're here. He doesn't know it was you in there, not really."

She's right. If I just stay quiet, he might not even look in here. But beside me, the shrivelled occupant of the cot's eyelids flutter. The mask draws in against withered lips in painful, inevitable slow motion.

A reedy shriek splits the air.

DISOBEDIENCE

THE DOOR CRASHES shut behind me. It dampens the high-pitched shriek only slightly. My pants bind at the knees and threaten to slip past bony hipbones. I clutch them with one hand and race toward the elevator. I'm panting by the time I round the corner. There's a sort of gold tape netting spanning the walls. It looks fragile. I grit my teeth and run harder.

Heavy boots thundering. The inspector shouts. I disobey his order to stop and face the wall. There's no time to feel guilty about it.

Voices murmur and complain from behind too-thin walls. A few doors crack open—a flash of bloodshot eyes under wrinkled brows—and snap shut as I pass. I'd assumed the residents of Floor 20 were mostly deaf or sedated into passivity. The enforcers had shown no particular concern over eavesdroppers.

"He's gaining on you," Cadence says.

My shoes flap on the carpet. One works itself loose. I stumble and kick it away. I charge the security perimeter at full speed, hoping it'll snap or pull away from the walls. It doesn't. I bounce back, wheel my arms for balance, and hurl myself at it again, scrabbling to climb. The inspector's shouts get louder all the time.

"Under, stupid! Go under it!" Cadence yells.

I want to yell back in frustration. The perimeter webbing sags against the floor. I lever it up enough to drag myself underneath. My hipbones scrape carpet. My waistband rolls alarmingly. Then I'm through.

I skid to a stop in front of the elevator, sweating madly, and jam my finger on the call button.

"There's no time," Cadence wails. "He'll catch you first."

She's right. He'll be rounding the corner any second. The perimeter barrier won't hold him for long.

I punch the button a few more times, then whip around, desperate for a way out. I flash back to a memory of gold eyes and white, white teeth, Ravel's arm upraised in a showy flourish toward a shadowy stairwell. Could that stairwell be accessed from every floor? There's an unmarked door directly across from the elevator.

"Go," Cadence says, following the line of my gaze.

I throw the door wide and stumble into the darkness beyond.

"To the right. Right!"

I pull to the side, thundering up the stairs instead of down. My one remaining shoe flaps against the sharp steps, squelching a little and probably leaving prints. I kick hard. It peels free. Maybe the inspector will trip on it.

The door crashes shut behind me. It cuts off the light from the hallway. I stumble in the darkness and bark my shins.

Cadence screams in my ear, "Hurry, faster!" and then, "Stop!"

I reach for the next step and skid to my knees when it's not there. The door slams open below. I stop panting and cringe back into the shadows. Why couldn't I have gone down? Maybe then I could've escaped onto the next floor. But the inspector takes off down the stairs instead of up. I will my heartbeat to slow. His footsteps crash and echo. There's a creak as he reaches another door, a pause, and then a slam.

I let out a sigh.

"Not yet," Cadence warns.

The door slams, and Haynfyv's footsteps sound again, descending to the next floor. He's not gone, but he's not coming back, at least not yet.

I slide one glove up the cold roughness of the wall for balance. My sight's adjusting to the gloom. There's a pale blue light marking the door below me. It illuminates a few steps, the way back. The air is dusty and dank smelling. I taste salt and iron on my tongue, sweat and panic.

I reach out a bare foot to descend.

"What are you doing?"

I risk a whisper: "Going back."

"Are you an idiot? Back where? Go up, stupid. Up, up, up."

There's a dim strip light above the closed door below us. Pale, dim blue like Bell's withered lips, bloodless in death. I need to go back for her. I can't think too hard about what I'll do when I get there. I can't explain it to Cadence, either. I don't know how. It had to have been a hallucination, brought on by the stress of trying to pass probation. It had to be. Not a dream; no one survives dreams. And not a real ghost, either. Cadence is never going to turn and reach out to me with pearlescent eyes oozing darkness like that. Definitely not.

Right?

"It's too late to help her," Cadence says.

I choke.

"Morristu is gone."

Oh. *That* her. Right.

"Besides, you can't risk opening a door and alerting that inspector you're up here. You'll just have to find a different way to make things right. Trust me. Keep climbing."

"Make things right," I repeat. I feel for the wall and edge my toes along until I find the next step. What a strange idea, that I should try to do anything about that poor worker's situation. How could I? It would be a violation of regulation to even remember her name. But better Cadence think I'm worked up about some care worker taking the fall in

47

my place than realize just how much I want to go back to Bell's corpse. Much, much better.

Around the corner, another strip of blue light comes into view: the next floor up. I work my way toward it, careful not to trip and alert the inspector to my presence. His boots still crash on the stairs in the distance, diligently in pursuit, just in the wrong direction.

"Keep going," Cadence says when I reach the next door.

And the one after that. And the next one. My legs tremble. I push my hood back and wipe away sweat.

"Keep going," she urges.

I plant my feet stubbornly and risk a whisper: "he's got to be far enough away. I'll be careful."

I reach for the door.

"Stop!" she screeches, and I jump back. "What are you thinking? It's not safe. Keep climbing."

I reach for the door again, and she yells.

"I'm tired," I reach out once more.

"Wait, wait, wait."

I pause, both hands flat against the door.

"Just wait. Let's talk it out. You're not thinking clearly."

"He's so far away now. It should be safe to get off."

I pause, listening pointedly. There are distant echoes every time a door crashes shut again. I can barely make out the sound of the inspector's boots on the stairs.

"Get off?" Cadence says, incredulous. "Get off what?"

"The upper floors—"

"And go where?"

"Home."

"Cole."

"What?"

"Really?"

"What?"

"You can't go home."

"Of course I can. Listen, it's safe enough, and I'll be careful, and—"

"*Cole.* You. Can't. Go. Home."

The hairs prickle up on the back of my neck in a this-is-bad-but-you-haven't-realized-it-yet sort of full-body shudder that starts tiny and grows. "Oh."

"Yes, oh. What did you think? That you'd just sleep it off and head in to work tomorrow morning as if nothing happened? Refuge Force were looking for you anyways, remember? That inspector even saw you."

"Just my back. That could be anyone." I know full well I'll be on record as the surveillance tech on site.

"Don't act stupid. Even if Refuge Force were that useless, you really think you could just go back? Pretend you didn't see any of it? Didn't hear any of it? Go along merrily passing probation and working away in that dreary little death trap of an office?"

It's not until she says it that I realize that's exactly what I'd hoped for. No, not hoped. I don't hope. Planned. I'd been planning to go back and pretend nothing had happened. Keep my head down and follow the rules.

I turn and lean against the door, then slide down to the cold floor with a thump.

The rules. Regulation. It was all a lie. Or at least, it is now. Maybe obedience had done some good in the past. Maybe not. But by the enforcer's own admission, neither physical shields nor obedience and surrender are any guarantee of safety from the Mara. There's no reason behind any of it—Cadence's death, or Bell's, or my survival. They didn't eat my dreams to spare me, to make me the perfect drone—they ate because they wanted to. And Refuge, sending me to Corrections, putting me on probation—all my hard work, all that self-control, self-denial, the clenched fists and the bitten tongue—and for what? It doesn't matter what I do, or think, or say. There's no point to any of it.

Despite myself, a little shiver of anticipation works its way up my spine. I've been living surrounded by corpses waiting to happen all along. It just turns out I'm one of them.

DISCOVERY

IT CHANGES EVERYTHING, knowing Refuge has been lying to us. Obedience to regulation doesn't keep the Mara away. Surrendering my dreams and desires to them never saved me. But it's crippling to even think about what's left. There's just no point. Noosh—pointless. Work—pointless. Passing probation . . . Staying away from corpses—pointless.

I lurch up the stairs, pulse pounding in my throat. I'm overreacting. It's too simplistic to dismiss everything. After all, how will I live without Refuge? There is nothing else. Nowhere else. I don't have any dreams left to help me find a way forward.

The image of Ravel, confident, mesmerizing, floats up from the roiling chaos of my thoughts. Ravel and his impossible offer. What did he call that place? Freedom? But even if I were willing to go to him, he said "down at the bottom of the stairs," right? And I'm going up.

"Cadence," I whisper. It's really more of a wheeze. And an excuse to stop climbing. I slump on a sharp-edged step, panting, for a few moments.

"What?"

"Why am I climbing? Like, besides that the inspector went down. Thanks for that, by the way."

"Haven't you been listening?" she says incredulously. "I'm saving you."

Saving seems a little dramatic, but okay. She's a dramatic person. And she's not wrong.

"But what's the point?"

"Keep climbing."

I groan.

"You do get that you can't go back, right?"

"Pretty much."

"And you're clear turning yourself in to save that worker wouldn't help anything, yeah?"

I hadn't considered trading myself for Morristu, but she doesn't need to know that. "Yeah."

"So you need help. A way out."

"Out?"

"Out."

"Oh. I thought . . ."

"Don't you ever listen?"

"You said that already."

"You need to get out of Refuge." She enunciates as if she thinks I really am an idiot, when she's obviously the one without a clue.

"There's nothing out there." The city has been an uninhabitable, flooded wasteland for generations, overrun by the icy ocean and drowned in toxic fog, only the Mara left to prowl its corroded towers and submerged streets.

"Oh, really? Fine, since you know so much: what do you want to do?"

"You know I don't—"

"If you say 'want things' right now, I'm going to scream."

"—want things."

"Stop it."

"It's not my fault—"

"Stop it."

"I can't—"

"Enough. There's nothing wrong with you."

"How can you say that? Just because I got lucky and survived doesn't mean—"

"Why did you touch the corpse, Cole?"

I stub my toes on the edge of a step and bark my knee. I have to sit down and clutch it for a moment until the pain fades. It's good timing. I don't have any idea what to say to her.

"It's not a trick question. Too hard? Here's an easier one: Why didn't you report the field assignment when it first came in? You knew you weren't ready for it. No? What about that creeper in the hallway you couldn't take your eyes off of? Why did you procrastinate when you first got off the elevator? Why did you hide from Refuge Force? Why did you run?"

"I-I don't—"

"What does a good drone do, Cole?"

"I—"

"A good drone obeys. A good worker follows regulation. If the Mara took your dreams and you can't want anything, and you just live to obey, why are you listening to me right now?"

I want to be anywhere but here, in the dark, cold concrete scratching my back. I want to curl up on the floor next to Bell's body. Not really an option. Doesn't stop me from wanting it.

I want to go back to work. Slide into my desk and pretend I never moved from my console. Definitely not an option. I'll never pass probation now, and I can't stomach the idea of sitting there with my black band for all eternity, shoulders hunched against Supervisor Kistrfyv's sneers.

I *want.*

My nails dig right through my gloves into the concrete step. When did it happen? When did I become this needy, this selfish, this demanding? When did my dreams return? Did I grow new ones?

I should call the Mara right now, surrender voluntarily, before I'm too full of wishing and wanting and dreaming to be drained without being killed. If ritual submission even works. But I can't stop. I don't want to. What I do want is the last year of my life back. I mean, all that work trying to fit in and earn their acceptance, wasted. I'd love to shout the truth about Refuge for the entire division to hear, to see the look on Kistrfyv's face as I rip his authority to shreds . . .

I mean, wouldn't it feel great? At least, for all five minutes before the enforcers came and dragged me away. Besides, no one would listen. No one would believe me. It's not as if exposing Refuge's lies would make a difference . . .

"Anything?" Cadence asks, apparently done waiting.

I don't want to say no, so I start talking without a plan.

"I can't go back." It's as if I can hear her eyes rolling, but I plod on, ticking off the things I know so far. "And I can't help anybody, and—"

"I didn't say that."

"What?"

"I didn't say you couldn't help anybody. You should. Help people."

"They won't listen to me." The appeal of destroying Refuge's authority is not lost on me. If Refuge no longer existed, I wouldn't be a probationary worker. I wouldn't even be a failed trainee. It might not even be a problem that Noosh had never worked properly on me. If everyone else's life were turned upside down, mine wouldn't stand out so much. But . . . "They have no reason to trust some probationary worker. They'll think I'm crazy. There's no way I can convince anyone by myself."

"Which is why you need to do what I tell you. You can't survive on your own, right?"

I nod.

"So you need allies to help you bring down Refuge," she says, as if it's so simple and obvious a next step it really goes without saying.

A memory of Ravel's outstretched hand and the shadowy, descending stairs beyond flickers to the surface. She continues before I can point out she's been leading me in the wrong direction.

"It solves everything. Think about it: Refuge's after you now, so by exposing its lies, you not only secure your own safety, you earn a place with strong allies who'll help you get the job done."

It makes sense, kind of, although it's weird how serious Cadence seems as she explains. Still, I warm to the idea of any plan that involves attacking Refuge. All that wasted effort to behave and obey, to make myself small and silent and invisible and empty. Why not tear Refuge down? Why not make them all suffer for my misery? Mine and the others', living and dead.

Okay, new plan. Take down Refuge. Find allies to convince the workers they're being lied to (and take care of me). Which means I'm going to Ravel after all, just as he said I would.

It's been too long since it was okay to feel. I think I should feel, I don't know, indignant? Embarrassed? Maybe it's embarrassed; my face is warm and my pulse is speeding up. But it's almost like excitement. Despite my entire life falling apart in the space of an hour or so, maybe this day is going to turn out after all.

But this is Cadence—silly, flighty, troublemaking Cadence—telling me to use what I know to buy my way into a new life. She doesn't have the greatest track record when it comes to having a solid grasp on reality.

"This isn't just one of your made-up stories again, is it?" I don't know what I'll do if it is, but better to know it now than later.

"Would I do that to you?" she says.

10

ETERNITY

CADENCE AND I are alone in a world of near darkness. Dying.

At least, I'm sure *I'm* dying.

My heart races, about to burst. My muscles quiver on the verge of collapse. My uniform is soaked through with sweat. I even pulled my mask away from my face, not that there's anyone here to see. The breath rasps in my throat, tasting of blood and pain. I think I'm going to pass out.

This must be why Refuge never bothered expressly prohibiting use of the stairs. Assigned health cycles never prepared me for anything like this. I've lost count of how many times I've scraped and bruised my shins and elbows. Kicking off my shoe to avoid leaving a trail of blood seems pretty pointless now; between the sweat and the scrapes, I'm leaving quite the mark on these stairs. But it's hard to be too worried about pursuit when the burning in my legs competes with the fire in my throat for attention.

"You're doing great," Cadence says. "Almost there. Can you believe how clear the air is in here?"

I'd strangle her if I had the energy. And if she were corporeal. As it is, I can barely summon the will to raise a hand to the next step. Pause. Now my knee.

I've been crawling up this stairway for an eternity and will continue on for all time. I can't remember why I started, and I don't have the will to stop. I am a machine, set to continue until the parts wear out.

Scratch that. If I'm a machine, I'm definitely in need of maintenance. My throat is hot and tight, my tongue thick in my mouth. My lips are cracked as if all the moisture has leached away already. My stomach stopped grumbling a while ago. I've missed my Noosh for the evening. I've never missed a meal before. I'm not sure what will happen to me.

"How much further?" I say.

Cadence snorts. "You're being ridiculous. Get over yourself. A little exercise is good for you. Weakling."

She singsongs the last word as if she's reverting to her usual childishness, faking echoes since the stairwell can't bounce them back.

I pretend not to hear her. Nice that she's back to her chipper, pesky self. "So, how exactly is climbing stairs going to help me get allies? Who are these allies, anyway?"

"Wait and see."

"I think I'd rather just go to Ravel, thanks."

She changes the subject instead of responding; we've already argued about it, repeatedly. It's not safe to go down; Haynfyv headed that way. Besides, Cadence apparently knows people who'll help me if I go up. I didn't like this plan much from the start, mostly because it involves more climbing. Also, because I'm still afraid she's making this all up . . . and maybe a little because it doesn't involve Ravel. Cadence did have a point about the risk of running into Haynfyv. Of course, heading for the rooftop sounded a lot more reasonable several floors ago. Right about now, being dragged off by Haynfyv doesn't sound so bad. I bet he'd give me a drink of water, at least.

"You want to tell everyone the truth about Refuge, right?" Cadence reminds me, as if I've forgotten the plan already.

Not right at this moment, I don't, not if it means climbing until my heart gives out. I'm more and more ready to quit on this plan, or at least her part of it, if she doesn't start delivering soon. Of course, the thought of backtracking after how far I've come is horrible in its own right.

"Right," I say, reluctantly, "so why am I killing myself alone in the dark?"

Maybe not the best choice of words.

Cadence doesn't seem to notice. "Just trust me, okay? It'll make more sense later. I just need to . . . If we can get to the roof, I'll remember more and—"

"Wait, what do you mean 'remember'? I thought you said there were people up there."

"It's—he's . . . It'll help, okay? I'll remember more, and we can find—find—allies. I'll help you find allies on the roof. They'll take care of you. I promise."

I start crawling up the stairs again. It's not that I believe her. I'm growing more and more convinced this stairway will never end and there's no destination and no help for me at the end of it.

But there's an edge to Cadence's voice I don't like. I wonder again about the girl, Suzie. If what I'd encountered had been her ghost—just if—then could the same thing happen to Cadence? Could I stop it from happening to Cadence?

I crawl onward, distraction helping to dull the pain. When I run out of stairs, it's not so much a surprise as a revelation.

I press forward dumbly against the door at the end of the stairs. Pause. Press again. Shuffle in a circle until I'm back facing the door.

Stairs stretching down into shadows. Door ahead. Walls. That's it.

I made it.

I draw a deep, rasping breath and start coughing. My tongue is buried under a blanket of bitter dust. My lips are cracked. My throat burns. I curl on my side against the door and listen to the sound of my heartbeat slowing.

There's a noise beyond the door. Sharp, high calls, piercing and far off, behind a faint rushing sound that rises and falls like one of Cadence's less inspired songs, like breathing.

Sweat stands out on my skin, already growing chilly. My clothes are soaked. I'm shaking from terror, or something like it.

Cadence is entranced. She breathes something that sounds like "seegles."

The word means nothing to me. I have no interest in meeting the source of that horrifying, alien sound.

A groaning, rattling roar starts somewhere far below. Suddenly, I'd much rather meet these "seegles" of Cadence's than whatever monstrosity is surging behind me.

I strain upwards and slide along the door until I feel a handle. The door flies open, snapping at its limits and bouncing back before the onrushing air shoves it away again.

The thought of roaring and shrieking horrors is wiped from my mind in an instant.

I have discovered light.

BEAUTY

IN THE INSTANT before I curl in on myself in anguished pain, brilliance unmatched by any I have ever encountered overwhelms my senses.

I must have more.

But for the moment, all I can do is rock with my head in my arms.

"Cole." Cadence's voice is hushed, awestruck. "Look."

I peer between my fingers. They're lit from without, a tangle of radiance and shadows, colour and texture, with a depth and a range I'd never imagined existed. Each finger rimmed in light, translucently red.

It's so warm. A rough, gravel-covered expanse stretches out before me. Past that, a raised edge and—

Colour. All colour. And somehow, light and colour at the same time.

White light, so bright I can't look at it, wreathed in warm tones of gold and red and purple shading to blues and greys. Ripples and movement above and below, the light shifting and sliding. Ocean and sky, Cadence says. A channel of brightness falling on me, curtained by a shivering rush of water from the sky. Sun shower, she whispers. Air stirs, casting a fistful of drops against my face. Wind. Rain.

It is impossible. It's more than I have ever known and yet somehow terribly, painfully familiar. It's overwhelming and intense and *there*.

"Sunset. That's the sun. It looks like at the end of the day," Cadence says, but her words are distant, dry information compared to a scintillating reality. There are dark, still things out there beyond the edge, framed against the riot of light and colour.

"Towers." She says absently. "Hush, I think something's coming back to me."

I creep closer to the edge, staying low in a crouching shuffle, exhaustion and pain forgotten.

Past the jagged edges of the crumbling towers, the rain rolls back to leave a cool stillness, sky above and below divided by heaped blue forms in the far distance. The movement above is a slow swirl; the movement below, a steady rocking shimmer, darker, fading into a formless, muddy mass that swathes the towers in murk. The fog covering the drowned feet of the city is ugly, but the ocean . . . I'd never imagined water could look like that.

Creatures wheel and dive in the sky above, emitting the high-pitched cries I'd heard earlier. Seegles, then. One swoops and lands nearby. It too is a marvel of shape and texture, colour, and motion. I hardly notice my feet have brought me near, until it launches itself in a sudden flurry.

It leaves something behind in its wake.

"Feathers," Cadence says.

They're floating. Drifting on the air, so slowly, so lightly. Swirling, dropping, and rising again.

I lean against the edge of the tower, transfixed. What would it be like to be carried by the air like that, cushioned, suspended in the warmth of that brilliance, aloft in the ordered riot of colour and motion, swaying, dancing, spiralling on invisible currents?

"Is this why you wanted me to come up here?" I ask.

She doesn't reply. A chill crawls up my spine. In such a wide-open space, I can't sense her.

"Was it to show me this?" I say again, to fill the—not silence; gravel shifts and clicks beneath my feet, the seegles call, and the wind shushes and rustles and roars—but to fill the space between us, to fill the absence of her voice.

"I don't . . ." she whispers.

Relief makes my head spin. "So, what's the plan? How do we show people all this?" I wave my arms at the sea, the sky, the mountains, the other towers, and the murky fog covering the ocean lapping at their feet. "And more importantly, where's all that help you promised?"

"I don't know. I thought once I got up here . . . But it's not coming back. Just give me a little more time, okay? I know I can remember, just—just hang on."

The sky darkens. I shiver. It's getting colder. The view looks less thrilling and more intimidating by the moment.

"Seriously? What was the point of making me climb all those stairs if there's nothing up here? You promised this wasn't all just another one of your stories—"

"I'm not making this up! I'm not lying to you. Just wait, okay? I just need a little longer."

I should've known better than to trust her on something this big. She doesn't know anything. She's just some dead kid playing for attention; it's not like she has to suffer the consequences. I'm the one stranded on a rooftop waiting for a ghost to tell me my next move.

This is stupid. I'm stupid. I should've changed course when I remembered Ravel's offer and saved myself some pain. Maybe I will anyway. Cadence's plan is good, even if her help isn't.

I can earn Ravel's trust and aid with what I've learned about Refuge, use it to buy myself a new life and dismantle my old one. He was offering an awful lot before I even knew anything, and he already knows there's something wrong with Refuge. He seemed persuasive; all those people around him. He'll be able to get the word out about Refuge's betrayal, to help people, to convince them . . . if any of what he said was real in the first place. I have to find out.

I'll just rest another minute here, before breaking the news to Cadence. Her little game is over. The gravel pricks my skin through the thin, damp fabric of my uniform. It's chilly, but that's not why I'm shivering. It's the thought—the memory—of a pair of gold eyes that somehow worked their way into my head and made me want to break the rules and whisper my secrets all in the space of a few minutes.

And then, finally, I give in to the temptation I've worked so hard to suppress for over a year now and let the buzzing sensation at the base of my skull diffuse into a thousand tingling pinpricks across my scalp. I'm uncomfortably aware of Cadence's presence. I still don't know if Refuge's prohibition on fantasizing has any bearing on the Mara's attacks or not. I do know the idea of Cadence realizing just how much I obsess about the dead is more than a little awkward. I uncurl, examine one scuffed, bare hand against the gravelly rooftop. Then I let it drape limply, trying to picture his in its place. His hands were bigger than mine. What would he look like dead? Would he go quietly or in anguish? That impossibly warm skin gone cold . . . How could someone like him ever look grey and still? Would I like him as a corpse?

Would he like me?

I stare, heavy-lidded, at my fingertips. The coppery tone of my skin's too vivid to easily take on the perfect, toneless grey of the dead, but as the light fades and I relax into the cold, I can almost see it. Can almost feel it, the flush of my cheeks fading to pallor. The stains around my eyes stand out starkly as gravity drains the blood.

I am not lovely. My face is too broad across and too hollow at the sides, never mind the ragged-edged birthmarks splashed across my cheeks and forehead. My hair is too bushy, overlong and ragged and curling around my ears. But, in the pallor and stillness of death, I look almost acceptable. Almost worthy. I am an appealing corpse. I would stay with me if I could.

I slip deeper into the fantasy. Time passes. My limbs stiffen in the late stages of death, purpling at the edge of the ground with drained blood. The eyelids draw back.

Milky clouding covers the deep brown of my irises. At this late stage of death, my pupils have contracted again, and I seem to stare back at myself dully under half-raised lids.

Um. Except that's not me. I'm apart from my corpse, lying beside it on the rooftop as it bloats and the flesh starts to slip. The fantasy takes on a horrifyingly real weight and clarity. The tingling shifts to terror as the corpse contorts and raises itself. I scramble away. Its mouth opens. Dark sludge bubbles at the edge of its lips as it laughs without the use of lungs.

"Cadence!" I back away until the edge of the roof scrapes my legs. "Cadence!"

The corpse shifts closer, not walking so much as falling and catching itself again with a jolt; again; again.

I want to hold my breath against its stench, but I can't stop the screams now, can't stop calling for Cadence, calling for anyone to come and make this stop. I know she can't help me, not really, and anyway this is all a nightmare and it's my own fault and no one can help me because no one survives the Mara. It doesn't stop me screaming and pleading and begging for help as the corpse sheds its flesh and presses skeletal hands against my shoulders.

And pushes me off the edge.

12

FALLING

IR RUSHES AGAINST me. It stings my eyes and steals my breath, stripping away what little warmth I have left.

I can't see anything, can't feel anything except the wind of my fall. The cloying stink of decay surrounds me. I know the ground is rising to meet me. Once it does, I will not be. I sense hunger and greed and dark pleasure. The Mara wait for me.

This is not what I wanted. This is not how I'd imagined death. This is not beautiful and still. It's not thrilling and forbidden and delicious. I don't know what I'd hoped to feel, but this isn't it.

Is this what they experienced, those frozen, final forms with their fixed expressions? Every corpse I've ever fantasized over, longing to understand what they felt and knew in those final moments. Is this what I've come back to over and again? It's terrifying.

I am horror, and even that will soon be gone.

I am despair.

Dream and you will die—the fear, the reality that keeps us all in line. Refuge regulation was my salvation, and I faithlessly abandoned it at the first opportunity. This terror is nothing more than I deserve. This is my due, what I earned by listening to Cadence and reaching for something more. It's too late for anything, even regret.

One traitorous thought lingers, so close to the end. At least I got that one moment of wonder. That storm. That glorious sunset. That light. That freedom.

That moment was mine, and mine alone.

IMPACT. THE FORCE of my fall wrenches my limbs.

And yet.

I'm a mass of bruises and scrapes, a collection of pain, but I *am*. Something shifts beneath me. My head rolls to one side, supported on a warm and resistant surface. Heat radiates along my side. Someone caught me? How? I should be dead. No one survives the Mara. There's no way they'd spare me twice.

A distant rumble fades in and out; buzzing static. A voice. Finding I do indeed continue to have a body, I make an effort to open my eyes.

A failed effort.

There's a jolt, then roughness, a hard surface. The warmth withdraws. Indistinct sound, far away. Why can't I hear?

A figure wavers into focus through my lashes, outlined in a blurred corona of brilliant light. It fades. The world is silent.

MY EYES OPEN to a world I have never seen.

The air is sharp, icy, clear. Like my mind. Everything feels more real, more present. A fog has lifted I never knew was there. The light—what light there is—is collected in an enormous shining disc and scattered against a deep and welcoming dark.

Grit scratches my stinging palms. Every muscle aches. My stomach cramps and my mouth is dry. Black silhouettes against the glittering sky mark towers. The irregular outlines of mountains in the distance are reflected under a net of stars shimmering on the surface of the inlet.

It is mine alone, my own perfect paradise of hidden night. It's glorious. I'm perfectly, completely alone, as I have never been. No minders, no trainers, no workers, no supervisors. No Cadence.

No one to give me words. No one to supply the knowing behind simple experience. Mountains. Inlet. Moon. Stars. Paradise. Glory.

But no, these words, these ideas, they're made up things. They belong to Cadence, not me. I turn, clutching at the empty night for her, my companion, my sister, my ghost. The night is still beautiful, but now the head-spinning beauty seems cruel. Mocking. Where has she gone, my trickster, my storyteller?

The Mara. That had been a dream, hadn't it? Falling. Dying.

But I'm still here. Did Cadence sacrifice herself for me? Was that who I felt, there at the end? That voice on the edges of my consciousness, that presence?

Stillness echoes inside me. She left the words but took the stories, the trouble and the noise and all the too-muchness of her presence.

I push to my feet, stand swaying, shuffle further from the railing. I glance at the doorway back into Refuge. I don't know what I'll do there, but I can't stay here. Despite all the beauty, it's dangerous. I don't know how I survived, but I'm not willing to give the Mara another shot at me. That was not how I imagined death. Not beautiful. Not shivery-good. It was horrible.

"That was amazing!" Cadence crows.

I trip, a gut-churning moment of free fall. Gravel scores my hands, ripping the skin.

"What's wrong, clumsy?"

"Where were you?"

"Huh?"

"Where did you go? You've never gone before."

Ever.

"What are you talking about?" Her excitement shifts to exasperation. "I just found the meaning of life, and you wanna chat about where you go when you sleep?"

"I wasn't asleep." I don't bother to keep the frost out of my voice.

She abandoned me. I was calling for her. And yeah, fine, she couldn't have saved me, but it's her fault I'm up here in the first place. And now she's not even listening, chirping along as if nothing's happened.

"Forget it," she says. "It's not important."

"Not important? Not important? I nearly died, and it was all your fault."

"Whoa, what? Died? What are you talking about? Listen, it worked. Just like I told you. More of my memories came back, and it's insane, see, I think I was actually sent here, and there's this guy, Ash, and—"

"Shut up!" My voice is still raw, but I scream once more for good measure. Shocked silence rings in my ears. "I've had enough of your stories. Stop pretending. This isn't a game. My whole world got destroyed today, or hadn't you noticed? I trusted you to help, or at least not to lie to me too. And what did I get? A pointless, painful, endless climb to some rooftop so I could get killed by the Mara while you play your stupid little game. You don't care about anyone but yourself. And you know what the worst of it is? There's no point. None. It's not like your stupid fantasies are ever going to mean anything. You're d—"

She makes a sound, painful and high-pitched and raw, a hurt whine I can feel in the back of my own throat. I breathe raggedly for a moment.

I won't go there. I don't have to.

"We're done," I say instead. "This is it. I've had it. You cause nothing but trouble. I don't care if you're full on insane or just a vicious liar. Or maybe this is all some sort of elaborate prank by the Mara. Is that it, Cadence? Are you even you anymore? Hello? You know what? I'm done. I'm going back down those stairs, and I'm going to get my own allies.

I'm going to find that Ravel guy. He'll be able to convince everyone of the truth. At least he seems to think I'm worth something. And you can just stay up here and . . ."

I'm not too sure how to threaten a ghost, so I illustrate my resolve by slamming the door behind me instead. She can wait out there on the roof and freeze or dissipate or whatever nasty thing happens to ghosts, for all I care.

I've got a mission to carry out.

13

DETERMINATION

I SCOOT FORWARD and feel for the next step. Crisp, crystalline alertness is leaching away into the cold concrete. My skin stings where I've scraped it raw. More parts of my body ache than I knew I had. I'd be starving if I weren't already too parched to care about filling myself with anything but water. I think about the submerged floors at the base of Refuge longingly. All that water, just sitting there. And somewhere between me and that endless dark water, Ravel and his "Freedom." Maybe. But the shadows seem to heighten every sensation, including anger, and Cadence just won't shut up.

"Listen. I really don't think this is a good idea.

"I don't understand what your problem is.

"Seriously, you can't just keep ignoring me like this. Cole. Cole. Colecolecole. Come on. Let's talk about it.

"I don't trust that guy. I thought you didn't, either. You're smarter than this. Please. Just stop, okay?"

I've decided to ignore Cadence's existence. She's decided not to let me. We're at an impasse, but I'm not going to be the first to cave.

"Fine. You don't want to talk? Then I'll talk."

I want to point out she's been talking this whole time, but then she'd win.

Refuge Force are probably still after me, lurking around the stairwell. I stumble down the stairs as quietly as I can, wincing with each step and straining to hear danger lurking around the sharp corners.

"Cole, I'm telling the truth. You have to believe me; it's not just a story. I really was sent here for a reason. And if you'd just go back up there, I'm sure I'd remember enough of it to find the way out. I think Ash's coming for me. There's something I have to do. Please, Cole. Please."

Her pitch rises, but she can't stop me. She's always had a habit of making up improbable stories, but this is ridiculous and manipulative, and I won't let her get to me.

Or—I try to shove the thought away, but it lurks in the back of my mind—what if she's really broken now? What if she's like Suzie and the Mara are eating her from the inside, turning her against me? I'd wanted to believe it was Cadence who'd saved me, but she clearly has no idea what happened or how close I was to ending up like her. Or maybe that's the point. Maybe she wants me dead. Stuck playing her games forever.

I press on down the endless stairs; a raw-edged eternity of dimly lit doorways, shadowy steps, and Cadence's unrelenting pestering. I'm desperate for a drink, some Noosh to ease the aching hunger, desperate enough to sidle up to one of the doors and lay my head against it. Maybe I could just sneak out onto the floor and grab a quick drink. If I move fast, I'd probably get away with it.

I can't hear anything past Cadence, demanding to know what idiocy I'm up to now. I crack the door open, squint into the light, and freeze. There's a distant clomping, boots approaching. I want to turn and run. Instead, I ease the door shut. The footsteps near and stop. Whoever it is must be waiting for the elevator. It sounds its arrival. I sag with relief.

"You really should go back up," Cadence says.

I wish I could trust her. I wish I could get out of this dark stairwell. I wish I could go back to this morning, when all I had to do was stave off boredom, stay out of trouble, and focus on my simple, routine work. I wish I could go back to the rooftop and take joy in the fleeting beauty of the Outside, of that impossible world I've only just discovered.

But I ruined that for myself the way I ruin everything, retreating into blind obsession. Now even that's destroyed. The transcendent, unreachable beauty of death has proven ugly and horrible. I have nothing.

"Cole, come on," Cadence says. "You're always like this. Stop making things worse. Just listen to me, okay? We just need to go back to the roof and—"

"Enough! I don't care. You want to go? Then go. Just leave me alone."

I thud down the stairs, almost glad of the pain, the exhaustion, the thirst. It's real.

Here's the truth: What Cadence wants doesn't matter. What Cadence thinks I should want doesn't matter. Refuge has been lying to us all this time. I'm not sure anymore if wishing and wanting actually leads to death or not, but it definitely doesn't accomplish anything by itself. I can't go back. I can't escape into fantasy. The cold touch of a corpse can't make anything better. There's no beauty or goodness to be had there. I know I can't help anyone by myself, least of all me.

So what does that leave?

I stomp down the next step, and the one after that. Each groan I swallow sounds in my head: *Ravel, Ravel, Ravel.*

The name echoes and becomes meaningless over the long, dark, painful descent. Or maybe it's not meaningless; maybe it's full of too many meanings. Ravel: help me. Ravel: make things right. Ravel: save us all.

I'VE LOST COUNT of how many doors I've passed, how many floors. I hardly bother opening my eyes any more, trusting my body to know the aching pattern of step-step-step-flat stretch before another door, turn-scuff-step-step.

Even Cadence has fallen silent. Sometimes there are sounds, footsteps, the rustle of fabric behind the doors as I pass. It helps break up the monotony. Sometimes I get a whiff of something, the familiar heavy sweetness of the ventilation or a musty sharpness. But mostly there's unending, dreary sameness and pain.

I want to stop. I want to keep going. I want to get to Freedom and hand off all my problems to Ravel. It's easier to keep going than to make the decision to quit, easier to plod forward than think about what other options I have or don't have.

And then, it's easier not to think at all. I continue, continue, continue. Impact. I hit a solid surface with knees and nose and rebound, grinding my raw hands in the dust as I catch myself.

I edge back from the door. Blink at it stupidly. I've reached the end. This is it.

I don't know exactly what I'd hoped to find at the end of this journey, but it wasn't a door like any other, flat and blank and dark below a pale blue light.

I lean my forehead against the cool surface. The door vibrates a little in time to my pulse.

No, it's the other way around. A distant, deep, repetitive *thud* works its way through the bones of the building and into me through the surface of the door. There's something on the other side. Ravel. Freedom. It's really there.

I made it.

14

SIXERS

S UDDEN, STARK LIGHT sends me reeling. I'd more than half expected to run into the submerged floors before finding Ravel, but the corridor on the other side of the door is bare concrete block, and perfectly dry. A tangle of pipes and cables clutter the ceiling. The distant thumping is a little louder now, echoing around a sharp corner up ahead. I'm reluctant to leave the shadowy, familiar quiet of the stairwell, but Ravel's somewhere out there. I need his help. And more importantly, I need a drink. I stagger down the corridor, weaving, clutching the nearest wall to stay upright.

"Just for the record, this is a terrible idea," Cadence says. "You don't know what's down here. You have no reason to trust Ravel. I really think you should turn around and go back up to the roof. Seriously, I just know if I had a little longer, I'd remember everything, Cole. Everything. And then I could help you—"

Voices swell from a second corridor crossing the first, as if they've just come out of another room.

"No please," one sobs, high-pitched and breathy and sloppy with terror. "Don't, don't. Please. I didn't do anything, I didn't—"

It's Morristu, or someone who sounds an awful lot like her.

The second voice confirms it.

"You didn't?" it exclaims with mock surprise. "You didn't do *anything*? Well then. What a shame you heard so much."

The enforcer from earlier, Serovate. Why is he down here? And more importantly, can I make it back to the stairwell without getting caught?

"But I didn't, I didn't, I didn't," Morristu wails. "Why did you bring me back here? I can't be here. I can't."

Serovate barks a laugh. "Even Her Worship agreed you're mine now, but by all means, keep trying. You know how much I enjoy it. It's almost worth the wait. How many years has it been now, Amy? Since you left it, I mean. Wouldn't you like to be reunited?"

There's a thump, a choked gasp. I step back, and wince at the scuffing noise. Worse, I've left splotches of blood all the way back to the stairwell. If Serovate turns the corner, he'll see me. And even if I can creep back to the stairwell, if he notices the trail I've left . . .

"Please," Morristu whimpers. "Please, at least not her, anyone but her—"

"Don't tell me you want to play the mother now—after all I've done for you? What exactly do you think you have left to bargain with?"

I eye the other side of the juncture. What if I could slip past while Serovate's distracted? There's no help behind me, but if I could just reach Ravel . . .

"Must you?" a third voice complains in muffled tones. He sounds bored, but the texture of his voice is strangely familiar. Where have I heard it before? "I hardly think—"

"And you're not expected to, are you?" Serovate chuckles, panting a little. "Let's make a little addendum to our arrangement, shall we, princeling? Call it a bonus for making sure the little lady wanders your way instead of into Mama Dearest's clutches. Do you have any idea how hard it is to arrange a fake probation trial at the last minute like that? And keep Haynfyv off the scent of some clueless little drone? She left a bloody trail. Literally. Took some work to scuff it out, I can tell you. So, how's about you enjoy your pleasures where and when you can, and leave me to enjoy mine?"

I can't remember how to breathe. He can't be saying—

"It was all planned," Cadence whispers. "All of it, right from the alert this morning. But why? Why do they want you?"

I should be offended. Instead I wish everyone shared her opinion. I mean, what possible use could the mayor have for me? I've never even met her. Now, Kistrfyv ruining my life, I'd believe, but the other voice isn't his.

I edge closer to where the corridors intersect and peek around the corner. The stranger has his back to me. He's in a standard-issue grey Refuge uniform with an astonishing triple-banded ward haloing his hood. I've never seen a Refuge official that highly ranked before.

It's also the first time I've actually seen Serovate. He's short and slender, even delicate-looking—not at all what I'd expected. Mirrored goggles shield his eyes. His mask hangs askew, exposing a sliver of pallid skin and just the edge of his mouth. His white Refuge Force uniform is wrinkled and stained. He's fixated on the cringing figure at his feet, Morristu. If I ran now, he'd see me. But if he'd just turn a little further, the edge of his hood might screen me from view . . .

"I won't have you bringing your filthy business down here," the stranger tells Serovate. Distaste adds the slightest edge to his bored tones. "Move along."

"Careful, boy, or I might have to let slip something of our special arrangements to your—"

"Oh, don't start with me, sixer. Especially not after failing to bring back—"

I'm not surprised when Serovate spits back something even coarser. Calling someone a "sixer"—as in Floor 6—is wishing for their death, a wish that could just as easily get you killed instead. The stranger must be very stupid, or very careless, or very, very much not a fan of Serovate.

"I wasn't the one who failed to capture my prey." Serovate's voice is so low I can barely hear it.

The other man is silent at that, or maybe I just can't make out his response past Morristu's shuddering sobs. Morristu, who's suffering in my place. If it weren't for her bad timing, I'd be the one cringing at Serovate's feet right now.

It's a violation of regulation to think that way. It's not allowed, imagining what others think or feel or experience. It's even worse than feeling or hoping or dreaming yourself. It's unsafe.

But there is no safe because regulation is a lie.

I dart another glance around the corner. Morristu chokes and stares back. Her tearful eyes widen and flick to the stranger. She's going to turn me over to them. She's going to sacrifice me to buy her freedom. She throws her arms around Serovate's feet. He looks down.

"Please," she moans. "Please. Let me go."

Her voice rises to a shriek on the last word.

"Run!" says Cadence.

I dive across the exposed intersection to the corridor on the other side. Shouts ring out. I race for another crossroads down the hall and veer left, then right at the one after. The voices fade in the distance. I whip around the next corner and collide with a dark figure. There's a flash of gold and a faint jingling as we go down in a painful tangle of limbs. The stranger knees me in the stomach. I curl over and catch an elbow to the head. I roll toward the wall, throwing my arms up as a shield.

But instead of another blow, there's only the patter of footsteps retreating. The small, dark-cloaked shape pauses at the corner.

"Who are you? What are you doing here?" she demands, shoving back her hood just enough to reveal a soft mouth and delicate chin with oddly warm-toned skin—not the pallor of Refuge, but neither as dark as mine, nor as radiant as Ravel's.

I lean against the wall and gasp for air, eyeing the stranger. She doesn't seem to want to hurt me after all. Maybe I just surprised her. And she's not wearing a Refuge uniform. Could she be one of Ravel's people?

"What do you want?" She tugs her hood forward again, her hands concealed in the loose fabric of the cloak.

"Lie," says Cadence. "You don't know if you can trust her."

"I'm looking for Ravel," I say. "Do you know how to get to, uh, Freedom?"

The woman stiffens. "What's your business with him?"

"Don't," says Cadence.

"He invited me. I want to join him. Is Freedom nearby? Can you help me find it?"

The woman's soft lips flatten, but all she says is, "It's near. Ravel—he's expecting you?"

"Yes," I say without hesitation, as if he's waiting this very moment to welcome me in. The woman appears to believe me.

"Go back."

Or possibly not.

"Changed my mind," Cadence says. "I like this one."

I glare at the cloaked woman. Still, she hasn't actually come out and threatened me, so that's a plus. I take a step toward her and sway on my feet. I slump against the nearest wall, shake my head. "I can't."

She purses her lips. "I don't know what you've been told, kid, but it's not what you think. You won't find what you need in Freedom. Go home."

"I have no home," I tip my head against the wall, too tired to raise it. I want to take the words back as soon as they leave my lips. Speaking them makes it too real. "Please. I have no other choice. I need Ravel."

She snorts at that, her mouth twisting. "Little girl, no one needs that kind of trouble. Whatever your situation is, I promise you you're better off dealing with it than running away to that spoiled little—"

"Please." I duck my head. My scraped hands catch my eye. When did I lose my gloves? I don't remember. I fold my hands together, the shamefully exposed skin blackened with ground-in blood and dirt, and shake the loose sleeves of my uniform down over them. Then I think better of it and raise my hands to the cloaked woman, showing her the stains.

"Please. I need help."

The words feel sick and wrong in my mouth, but she takes my dirty, scratched hands in her own. Her nails are painted orange and purple. Sunset colours. Their brightness distracts me only a little from the gentle, forbidden warmth of her touch.

"There's another way," she whispers. "If it's truly as bad as all that, there's another way. I can help you. But right now, there's someone else who needs me more."

There's a burst of sound—a door thrown open somewhere nearby, voices and something beyond the voices, that deep, bone rattling thump grown louder again.

She backs away. "I have to go. I'm out of time. I'll come back for you. Just hang on."

I want to chase after her. Instead, I knot my fingers in the loose fabric of my uniform and rest my chin on my knees, waiting for the voices to draw near. I'm too tired to run anymore, even if Serovate is right around the corner.

Cold seeps up from the floor. I want to go home. I want to take a shower and go to bed and wake up to a world where this day never happened. So tired . . .

But I can never go back. And even if I could, impossibly, pass my probation and be welcomed into the ranks of Refuge workers, would I? Knowing what I know now?

I still can't grasp the magnitude of the lies. Everything I know, everything I've ever known, hinges on Refuge's ability to protect us from death. And what about Cadence? How many of her impossible stories are true? No. Cadence is a liar. Or insane. Or possessed by the Mara. And there's no point sitting here slowly freezing as I sift through unanswerable questions. Ironically, just like she's always pushing me to, I have to act. Go back or go forward; those are my only options—just as soon as I gather enough energy to get back on my feet. And with both Inspector Haynfyv and the creepy Serovate somewhere behind me, that really leaves only the one choice. I stand.

And then the voices swell as their owners round the corner, and the choice is made for me.

"Cole! Welcome! I see you decided to join us after all."

Ravel.

WELCOME

"R AVEL," CADENCE GROANS.

My heart stops. Stutters. Starts up again in double time.

A high-pitched voice titters in the darkness: "Look at that. You scared the kid. Better keep those hands to yourself, Ravel."

I feel his laugh in my knees. Voices murmur amused agreement. Several others stand in the stretch of corridor beyond Ravel. They stare shamelessly.

Something's wrong with them. Their mouths, the whole lower halves of their faces, are scandalously exposed. Their eyes are framed by colourful structures, each one different, and their hoods are thrown back to bare the tops of their heads.

One man's head is smooth and shining under the lights, with dark, complicated designs swirling across his skin. Another has a ridge of bright green down the centre of his scalp and a series of orange and blue dots trailing away on either side. Feathers swoop across a woman's forehead and down the ridge of her nose.

Ravel looks almost normal by comparison, his hair only a little longer than regulation, shiny and black. It almost covers the winking lights at his ears, gold a bare shade brighter than his skin woven through and around the curve of his ear, piercing the flesh. Iridescent oil-slick feathers start somewhere behind his ear and curl down around his neck to tremble along his collarbone, just above the line of his uniform tunic. His eyes are brilliant behind a black wire lattice that spans from ear to ear and nose to brow, setting off the warm tone of his skin. The rest of his face is distressingly bare.

He raises a hand in casual dismissal. The others melt away. He reaches for me. I flinch, the shock of touch meeting the exhaustion of my spent body. My knees feel like rubber. He catches my scraped elbow. Shooting pain shocks me upright, keeps me from fully collapsing. Cadence is hyperventilating. Or maybe that's me. He's ignoring it, either way, which is awfully nice of him.

"Welcome. I can't tell you how pleased I am you're here," he says. "I've missed you, flame. What took you so long?"

I'd forgotten the shocking heat of his touch. His hand on my shoulder, his breath in my ear, that radiating warmth at my back. I would jump away—I really should—but every muscle feels disconnected and numb. It's so hard to focus. I finally shrug his arm off and lean against the wall. Its cold seeps into my burning skin and drains the heat from my head.

This is it. I need to explain, to tell him what I heard. He has to act against Refuge, to save everyone.

"They're after me." I keep my face turned to the wall, afraid to look up and see his face go cold and distant, offended at the trouble I'm bringing to his doorstep. "I don't know why, but—"

"Who's after you, flame?"

His thumb traces the arc of stains along my cheek. I flush. My mask's been down this whole time. I hardly dare to dart a glance up at him, but he looks merely concerned, when he should be terrified or furious.

"Refuge Force," I whisper. "They knew I'd be there. They chased me. When I tried to come here, they were waiting for me, and—"

"Shh." Ravel leans in to press his bare forehead against my hooded one. The wire around his eyes scrapes my nose.

"You don't have to be afraid anymore. They can't reach you here. I won't let them."

"But what about—"

"This is my place. You're safe, flame. No one can hurt you or take you away now. You have no idea how long I've waited for this." He strokes my head, shoulders, arms, numbing my responses, clouding my mind. "There's so much more than that strangled existence. You were made for more. I can't wait to show you how much more."

I let him coax me from the supporting wall. His voice, his nearness, his touch, it's all wrong—dangerously, fascinatingly wrong. It violates everything I've ever been taught was right. Safe. But he's real, and he's here.

"Escape," Cadence orders, but I'm not listening to her anymore. "Think, Cole! Why's he treating you like this? He doesn't even know you. This guy has no reason to help you. You need to get out while you still can."

I'm not going to believe the lies of Refuge. I'm not going to let it, or her, control me. I came here for a reason: I need an ally, and Ravel seems so eager to help.

I turn to him. Those golden eyes, mesmerizing, a wild creature entirely focused on me. He's reaching out again, a hand on my shoulder, another stroking lightly down my arm. It's horrible and it's amazing, and I can't remember why exactly it should stop. He's been speaking for some time, drowned out by the torrent of Cadence's outrage and the roaring in my ears.

Turns out, it's one thing to decide on a course of action; it's another to suppress a lifetime of training. I can't help feeling shocked by the way he casually violates regulation at every turn. Ravel guides me down the now-empty corridor, around a corner, and toward another door. I break out of my daze enough to start catching his words.

"—going to love it, like nothing you've ever imagined. So much more than Refuge could ever give you. I can't wait for you to be free of all the lies."

Cadence moans. "Seriously, this is weird. I really think we'd be better off without this guy."

She's always so dramatic. It's going to be fine. I'm going to be fine. I want to know whatever it is Ravel has to show me. I need to earn his trust, to learn what he wants and meet his expectations. How else am I going to convince him to be my ally?

My steps falter. What was it, again, I wanted his help with? Wasn't there something I needed to do?

He lifts my chin with one hand and stoops to catch my gaze. My breath stops, caught in the liquid wonder of his eyes.

"You want this," he says.

I want this.

"You were made for this," he tells me.

I was made for this.

"Don't look, don't—" Cadence's voice is cut off as he leans in, hands gentle on either side of my face, fingers edging past my hood, threaded through my cropped hair. My vision fills with gold and black, light glittering out of darkness.

"You're going to love this," he says.

I believe.

He's right. I've wanted nothing as much as I want to please him, to discover whatever mysteries he has for me. I'm not surprised when he pushes open a door to reveal another bleak hallway, and then another. He supports and guides me. I can go on forever like this, wrapped in calm surety and golden liquid heat. I'm here for a reason. I can trust Ravel. I choose this. Whatever this is.

An eternity later, our journey ends in another door. The distant throbbing is a strong beat now. I can feel it through the soles of my feet, low and steady under a wash of sound from beyond the door. It makes my blood race and my head spin.

He lifts my hand, places it against the door, his own covering it so I'm caught between ice and fire.

"Welcome to Freedom," he whispers.

16

DUST

FREEDOM IS ANOTHER world, utterly alien. Overwhelming. I'm caught between the imperative to surrender to its mad intensity and the fierce need to fight it off, to draw stillness around myself in a shield and retreat from the chaos.

Ravel's arm behind me is an anchor and a weapon, security and danger wrapped up in treacherous warmth. He steers me onward as Freedom's inhuman inhabitants draw back to make way.

I take it in flashes, unable to cope with the whole. Heavy-lidded eyes droop under lashes that flare, teal-feathered, over orange mesh. Winking hemispheres form an armoured, angular pattern across the scalp. Black lips gleam, reflective with a wet, mirrored sheen. Shining metal glints from incisors.

There's no safe direction to look. Above, the light scatters in all directions, lurching and spinning and washing the surging landscape in an erratic ebb and flow of shifting shades of blue. Below, my scraped toes shrink away from the twisting, stamping, twirling creatures. The air is thick with spice and sweat.

I fear being absorbed into the frenzy, but the press of thrashing bodies parts around Ravel, breaking away with teeth bared in welcome, or rage, or hunger as he sweeps me along. I want to take it all in and shut it off at the same time.

Ravel steers me through a curtained barrier. The stillness of the room beyond is like breaching the surface of water. The suddenly distant, low thumping of muted music seems to resonate through the floor and pool in the base of my skull.

Ravel laughs. "Spectacular, isn't it?"

He pulls me down onto a low structure. It's strewn with brightly patterned throws and piled with cushions, though the shape is more like a bed than a chair. The light in this room is soft and steady.

Cadence mutters about getting out while I can, but my ears are still ringing and the arc and dance of blue light spots my vision.

At a gesture from Ravel, two figures move into the foreground. Their costumes expose almost as much as they cover. Sleeves dip to cover the hands or trail away to expose arms ringed in elaborate bands and intricate markings. Paints slip across the faces with little regard for the underlying topography. Glittering eyes peek out from beneath heavy, dark lids, encased in lacy nets that scandalously expose the lower part of the face.

I smooth my mask, tucking both sides securely under my hood.

The attendants' hushed voices belie their exotic decoration, incongruously modest against the visual excess. The man offers an armful of something to Ravel, while the woman advances toward me carrying a tray. Ravel drapes an arm across my shoulders and reaches for the tray with the other.

"It's called 'dust,'" he says, "See all the gold catch the light? This will help."

The cup is a marvel of delicate glass etched and sculpted with flowing lines. Glittering flecks dance in pale golden fluid as thin as water. I raise the cup cautiously, fold back the lower edge of my mask, and inhale delicate blossoms and spice. I take a sip. Though the liquid is cool to the touch, it burns on my tongue and lips. I cough and nearly spill the rest.

Ravel grabs the cup and tips the remaining contents into my mouth. Squirming, I swallow another mouthful. Heat scorches out to every tingling extremity. A sense of calm pleasure spreads with it. The room feels very large.

"Better, right?" He flashes that easy grin of his again. "I can't tell you how pleased I am to have you here, Victoire. You don't mind if I call you that, right?"

I blink. He takes it as permission. "It's all part of the magic here, flame. We throw off our old drone names along with Refuge's repression. Freedom's all about individuality. Personal expression. You understand."

I don't, but there's too much going on and I can't seem to focus enough to tell him. The female attendant exchanges her tray for another her counterpart supplies. His hand lingers, steadying the weight as she takes it. It's inappropriate. Offensive. Or that's what I should be thinking, anyways. But if anything, it just seems . . . I don't know. Nice.

Ravel's staring. I forgot; he's waiting for a response. I need to say something.

"Refuge. Lies." My tongue feels thick and clumsy.

"It does that." He laughs. The transparency of feeling in his expression astonishes me; I can't look away. "I knew you were special, Victoire, from the first moment I laid eyes on you. You see more, don't you? You see the truth without ever having to be told. I knew you would."

I'm warm and content. He's quiet—the attendant removed the thing around his eyes and is busy painting his face with gold and black, drawing dark rims around his lashes to make his wild eyes burn amidst a wash of shimmering gold.

"Not safe," I say, wondering if only using very short, clumsy sentences is what he means by being special.

"No, that's just it, isn't it?" he says eagerly, smearing the fresh paint on his lips. "All those rules suffocating the life out of you, damn regulation breathing down everyone's neck. Ritual submission to monsters. It's all a big hoax.

For all its control, Refuge can't save anyone. So what's the point of it all?"

The attendant wipes the smudges clean and starts over. She dusts his dark hair with gold so it glitters among the inky strands.

"Control?" I think not of Refuge but of Cadence, who seems to have settled down to watch warily. She's always trying to tell me what to do. Come to think of it, I'm surprised she doesn't have anything to say about all this.

"Yes, that's the heart of it, isn't it?" He waves one hand in emphasis. "That's what it's all about. They tell you what to be, how to be, who to be. Dictate every movement, every thought. They control an army of drones. But, you and me, we're too smart to stay put and do as we're told. I can't tell you how long I've waited for someone like you, flame, someone who really gets it. And, while they brainwash the masses, the deaths stack up. It's all wrong."

"All. Wrong." I nod ponderously. My head feels too big.

"That's why I created Freedom." He settles his arm back around my shoulders. I don't pull away. "To save people from all that misery and repression, from the fear of death. Refuge preaches control—self-control, complete and total control of mind and body—and submission to the Mara, but they can't stop the dying. It doesn't work. So, what's the answer?"

"Lies," I say again, sticking doggedly to what I know. I came here with a purpose, I'm pretty sure. It had to do with lies. And truth. Is this the truth? I feel like I'm forgetting something important.

"The answer"—his fingers press emphasis into my skin—"is obvious. It's the opposite of everything Refuge stands for and tries to enforce. It's indulgence. Pleasure. Sensation. Experience. Connection"—he squeezes tighter—"and, in a word, Freedom. Freedom of action, of thought, of behaviour. Living, Victoire. That's what we need to do, just live, and seize what we want, and stop worrying about all the ways things can go wrong."

The attendant threads new rings and chains around the curve of his ears, at his brow, and around his lips.

When he turns to smile down at me, even his tongue has been pierced with shining ore. She finishes her work by dipping a brush in the same black that outlines his eyes and painting glossy fresh ink over the sharp-edged patterns at his temples and down the sides of his face. I narrow my eyes and try to look alert while thinking far too slowly.

Living. What does he mean by that? *Freedom, not control.* Touching, and too much noise, and way too much skin—not wearing the uniform, masking the eyes but not the lips, that's what it looks like to me. What was it he said about the fear of death? That the Mara don't care what we do? Submitting our dreams and desires doesn't save us.

I nod and the room dips with me. It makes a fuzzy kind of sense. If Refuge has been lying to us, and workers are dying despite following regulation, the obvious solution is to do the opposite of what we've been taught. Is that the truth I was trying to share? Isn't he helping me do what I wanted? He's saving people, right? And I'm safe now. So everything's the way it should be.

There might have been more to it, something different, but the memory is distant. I nod some more, as if the gentle movement will help me remember.

"What are you here for?" Cadence says, almost as distant and indistinct as my memories, but I know her voice. I recognize that tone.

She's displeased. I don't feel good about that.

I don't feel bad about it, either.

17
VICTOIRE

RAVEL PULLS AWAY, careful not to jostle my refilled glass of dust. He strips off his tunic, and I barely remember to be horrified. It helps that Refuge and its regulations seem so far away right now. I'm very warm and sort of heavy-feeling, somehow.

His skin is covered in bold black designs like those on his face, the marks sharply curving and twining across his chest and around his arms from shoulder to elbow. He shines under the diffuse, warm light as attendants rub oil and even more gold into his skin. They sweep fresh paint across him, linking the designs so ink flows seamlessly from the existing marks, a single interwoven pattern from hairline to wrists. It's mesmerizing.

"Victoire?" Ravel flicks my rumpled mask free, tipping my hood back in a fluid motion that doesn't leave space to startle away.

It unsettles something in me that had nearly gone to sleep. I frown.

"Cole! What are you here for?" Cadence snaps, still distant, still displeased, still trying to get me to do whatever it is she thinks I need to.

I snag the half-remembered thread of my mission and present it to Ravel.

"The truth." I shift on the cushions. Ravel smiles at me, his eyebrows tipped together above his mask in that twist that makes my head spin and my stomach flip. "People need to know the truth. About Refuge. They lied. The Mara—"

"See, that's why I can't get you out of my mind, Victoire. You're not like anyone else. Even after all their programming, you're able to think of others. Despite all they've done to you, you've held on to something essential."

I'm warming up to the way he thinks I'm special. He seems to see it as a good thing to be different. But, the way he talks about me, the things he seems to see in me—is that true? Do I think of others? Do I recognize problems and see through lies?

The Victoire he sees is appealing. I'm just not sure she's me. I'm also increasingly less sure it matters.

I sip carefully from my glass of liquid fire, heat welling through my skin.

Ravel stands very still, a glimmering statue of brightness wound about with shadows, and regards me through his glittering mask. He seems more himself now, a wild thing of burning eyes and fierceness, than he had in the sterile halls of Refuge. It's strange to think of that first meeting—was it really only a few hours ago? It feels as if I've known him forever.

He holds out one black-and-gold-threaded arm to me, his hand open in command, invitation. His nails are sharp, fading from bright to dark, and pointed. I don't remember when they did that. There's a whisper of silk and the glide of hard gold at my back as he draws me out and past, the heat of him like a furnace as we trade places.

I clutch his hand. "You'll tell them the truth? You'll bring it all down—Refuge? End the dying?"

It's what I'm here for, after all. I remember—though I can't quite recall why it's important. But I want to be the Victoire he wants, the Victoire he sees—and it seems like the thing he'd want her to say.

He's gone rigid, his expression blank and unreadable. Something catches in the back of my throat. I got it wrong. That's not what his Victoire would say. It's not what he wanted at all.

My fingers flutter as if I can craft a better answer, a better version of me out of their dance. Finally, Ravel's lips curve in a smile.

"If you'll help me, flame, everyone can learn the truth. Refuge's days are numbered." He leans forward, suddenly intense. "It's a rebellion, Victoire, that's what it's all about. Freedom. That's what I need you for, what I've waited so long for. My goddess of victory. Together, we'll draw everyone to the truth. With you beside me, who would dream of resisting? Who would choose Refuge over this?"

He gestures grandly. I'm not quite sure if he means himself, this room, the wild party raging outside?

"Death itself bows before the master of Freedom." He grins up at me. "And that's the truth, flame. When you're ready, my Victoire, I'll show you just how well you've chosen."

I avoid his gaze as the attendants approach. Such boasting is cause enough for the Mara to take a man, or so I'd been trained to believe. But there he sits, fearless. I try to match his confidence, to hold myself steady and not flinch away from the fluttering brush of hands. The attendants keep glancing back at Ravel too. For approval, or maybe just to see him, to drink him in.

The hum and thud of the frenzy just outside this haven is distant but penetrating. The rhythm seeps through the floor and forces my heart into new and unsteady patterns.

"Don't trust him," Cadence whispers from a great distance, so great a distance I could have mistaken her voice for my own, if I didn't know her ways so well.

"I will not be controlled," I breathe, barely moving my lips so the attendants and Ravel won't notice and take offence; it's for Cadence, and she knows it.

She gasps. "I am not Refuge. You know that. This place is no good. Ravel can't be nearly as powerful as he claims. You're not safe here. Who's going to stop the Mara?"

Not Refuge, the Mara. She's lost sight of the mission in all this. Caught up in her own fantasies, she's spun it into something grand and impossible.

"Enough." It's hardly more than a thought, the slightest parting of my lips, heavy now with paint.

It hits Cadence as if I've spat in her face. "Fine. You know, I thought you'd be smarter than this. I thought you'd want to make a real difference, but you're just another drone. I should've never even bothered with you. I'm done."

She goes, leaving a dark, empty space behind. It gnaws at me, but I will not call out for her. I'm better off without her. I'm not going to worry about where she's gone, what will happen to her without me, what she might turn into. Or be eaten by. That's her problem now.

I don't need her manipulations and deceit. I don't need anyone to tell me what to do. I've found my ally. Ravel will take care of me now. He'll take care of everything.

The attendants' hands still, withdraw. I feel cast adrift in a sea of sensation. The light filtering past my eyelids is rose-dark velvet shot through with flames. I float alone and exposed in the inferno.

In the distance, a spark of silver flickers to life. It stretches and grows, sending out delicate tendrils. Cadence?

"My goddess of victory," Ravel whispers.

I open my eyes, slowly, fighting the weight of heavy eyelids. His molten gaze is dark, reverent; his lips curve possessively.

"Show her," he says.

The attendants draw back a fold of fabric along the wall to reveal a tall mirror. I have become like them and not like them. Become more. The girl in the glass is bright where he is dark and dark where he is bright. Impossibly sharp and fine. Her skin glows a deep copper. There's too much of it showing—far, far too much. The bruised, aching lengths of gawky limbs have taken on an elegant, ethereal slenderness through whatever magic the shadow and sway of gauzy fabric and paint and endless chains and bangles have conspired to cast.

I don't recognize myself. The craft of Ravel's attendants takes my breath away.

Painted gilt swirls and coils across the girl in the mirror, delicate and fluid, paired to reflect and enhance Ravel's sharp, bold inked patterns. It forms a glittering filigree that stretches from her shoulders and collarbone, up her neck and across her face, seamlessly melting into the edges of a lace mask.

The dark stains of my marked skin are buried somewhere under the paint and glitter and lace as if they had never existed. My own rough, dark hair has been magically transformed, the short-cropped strands bound to a wash of feathers that shimmer from chestnut roots to pale tips. They're covered in the same gold shimmer that glints in Ravel's inky curls.

They are reverse mirror images, he and she. His presence is solid and dark, intense and commanding, brilliance contained and channelled; hers is deep yet delicate, narrow and bright. His hands trace sharp lines across her shoulders and down her arms as his breath makes the feathers dance in her hair. They whisper secrets, fluttering and rustling a refrain: *you were made for this.* I dance with them, weightless and tumbled in the force of his presence, and the world dances with me, spinning and blurring in the distance.

When he presses me through the curtain back into the chaos, I am a new creature. His creature. Victoire. I have left Cole behind along with Cadence and abandoned the icy, still, awkward self who fears the noise and the press of bodies, the overwhelming of the senses, the loss of control.

Control is a lie, I remind the part of me who stands at a distance, chronicling this event.

The new, exotic creature I've become embraces the dizzying spin. The blue lights follow Victoire now, deepening to purple, sickening to green, and then fiery orange as she spins through one throbbing room after another. The gaze of the crowd is her right; their adulation, her due tribute.

"Ravel!" they call, ecstatic. "Victoire!"

Victoire twists toward Ravel, surrendered to the wildness of the dance. She moves in steps I never learned, drawn by his hand and his gaze, buoyed on a wave of certainty.

Cadence had no power to do anything. And Cole would never take action. No one would listen to her, follow her. Cole couldn't help anyone. But Victoire can say anything. Do anything. Victoire can get Ravel to break down Refuge's lies and save the workers. She throws her head back and laughs, wild in the midst of the madness, loud and careless with it. It's so simple. All she has to do is let go and be.

And yet there's a part of me that resists being left behind, being thrown off and swept away by the yearning, hungry, exhilarating magic of being Victoire. A part that watches her from a cold, still distance, naming her as other. This part allows her to be only because she pleases Ravel, because she meets his expectations and fills a purpose.

This is my choice. Victoire is my choice; a creature made for him. I am alone in the invisible dark, looking on. He is the dark heart of the flame and Victoire his own white-hot core within it, surging away but inextricably joined, consumed. Together, they take flight.

18
REBELS

THE POUNDING BEAT still rings in my ears. Gold sparkles and tiny feathers cover the pillow. A blanket drapes over the crimped remains of last night's costume and smeared paints. It's the first time I've woken alone—in days? weeks?—without Ravel bouncing into the room to call me back to the floor, or his attendants nudging me awake to paint fresh designs across my skin.

Bangles clink. They've left pale imprints in my skin, quickly flushing red as the blood flows back. I ought to stay awake long enough to strip them off next time. I sigh in relief as the weight of all that heavy gold lifts and my head clears.

My feet hit the ground, bringing a host of new complaints. Fresh blisters from ridiculous shoes. Sore muscles. Skin raw from being painted and stripped and painted again one too many times in a row. At least the scrapes and scratches from when I ran away from Refuge have mostly healed.

My stomach flips at the memory of that terrible night. Cadence had promised so much, and it had gone so wrong. The beauty of those first moments on top of the roof still haunts me, though. The shocking coolness of the storm's final gasp. The mind-bendingly glorious sky as the clouds moved off and the night came on. The light, the openness, the movement. It would almost be worth that climb to breathe the open air again . . .

No.

It had been a dream, and dreams lie. Dreams cannot be trusted. Dreams lure you in with promises of your heart's desire, of everything you hope for, of fantasy and fiction made flesh. And then as soon as you reach for paradise, they turn and crush you.

How much of that insane night was even real? Maybe there had been no end to the stairs. Maybe that whole revelation had been a lie. That light, that space. That broken, decaying version of me spun into being by the Mara to seek my end in terror and pain. That silvery, indistinct presence that brought me back out of the darkness, only to leave me alone and afraid in the night.

It couldn't have been real.

"It was all real. You know it was real. You remember."

I'm surprised to hear Cadence's voice, and pleased, and then angry. Where has she been? Why has she come back? How did she guess what I was thinking? Or had I spoken aloud?

"It wasn't real. There's no way it could have been."

"Cole, I really think—"

"Don't."

"This isn't—"

"Enough. You said I needed an ally. Well, I found one. On my own. A real one, not one of your made-up stories."

I have a new life now. A safe place. A strong ally. I completed my mission in less than a day. Ravel is all about taking down Refuge, helping people realize the truth and get free. Now all I have to do is keep him happy.

Although, now I think about it, I'm not sure I ever did manage to tell him about those enforcers covering up the Mara-taken deaths. He hasn't mentioned any actual plans to start moving against Refuge, either. I should really track him down and make sure he knows just how bad things have got up there.

"You can't just go around trusting everything you're told, Cole. Something's not right here. Something's been keeping me away."

"You're just jealous Ravel wants Victoire in the first place."

It's a nasty and irrational sort of thing to say, but it's too late to take it back.

"Come on, seriously? You're letting him change your name? Your identity? Do you have any idea how creepy that is? Listen, I know things were crazy before and some of that's my fault, but I've been doing a lot of thinking, and my memories—"

"Ravel isn't the one manipulating me."

She falls silent, probably fuming at the implication. I ignore her.

I'm barely dressed in Victoire's vague, filmy, crumpled costume from last night. I drag the blanket off the bed and clutch it around myself with one hand. Modesty is a Refuge value, not a Freedom one, but I'm not quite up to living that particular truth in this moment. Regulation is a lie, but it's also—I don't know, comfortable. Familiar.

I stumble through the thick drapes that hide the doorway. The fabric tangles around my free arm, which is good, because I need its support when I see what's beyond.

The exotic world of Freedom, chaotic and busy and alive, is no more. I don't know this place. It's an empty, silent shell. The floor is cracked and gouged, the ceiling gaptoothed, missing tiles exposing a skeletal framework of narrow trusses and exposed piping. Dangling light bulbs flicker, leaving the corners drenched in shadow. There's no trace of the brilliant blue hall that should be beyond this door.

Everyone's left me. Everyone.

A shimmer of pallid flesh taunts from the corner of my vision. I whip around to look, but there's nothing there. No corpse. No dead thing, recent or long gone. That's for the best. It has to be. There is no death in Freedom, and I choose Freedom. I choose Ravel. I choose truth. I choose . . . I wish I'd chosen to stay in bed.

I shiver. Debris shifts and crunches underfoot. I can't find the blue room, nor the purple one, nor the green or the orange, nor even even the shockingly white one Ravel showed me only last night. There's nothing here. Maybe it just goes on and on like this, unending mazes of broken corridors and abandoned halls. What if Freedom and Ravel were a dream, too, and I'm alone and there's nothing down here. Maybe this isn't even a real place and I'm already dead and—

"What's that?" Cadence says.

I slump in relief. Not that I need her or anything.

A gust sweeps down the corridor, heavy and damp with a sharp edge of salt. This whole area under Refuge was supposed to have been underwater—what if whatever drained the flooding fails? Another gust. I pull the blanket tighter around my shoulders. A curtain on the sidewall flares and settles, revealing an opening I hadn't noticed before. Warm light and distant murmuring spill around the edges of the fabric.

I hold my breath and step with excruciating precision. I'm at once relieved and embarrassed at the view. I probably shouldn't be here.

The room is much like the one I woke up in, with the same elaborately draped walls and low, cushioned furniture around the edges. Familiar, delicate cups of dust are held carelessly in the hands of a freshly painted and jewelled Ravel and several other men dressed up like poor imitations of him, each with swirling dark ink running waist to scalp.

He's speaking, the lines of his lean body tight and focused. Something inside me turns over in awe of how casually he flaunts his rejection of regulation, of how easily he does the forbidden, of how much further I have to go to match him.

The others are seated, canted toward him, intent. I lean in despite myself to catch his words. He is a bright and beautiful thing.

"It's men like you," he says, burning eyes fixed on each in turn. His voice is honeyed and warm but strong, a sweet liquor. "Visionaries. Freethinkers. You see the evils of Refuge. You throw off their poisonous promises and see through false comfort and security. You courageous few seek out true freedom. Freedom to experience. To feel, to taste, to see. To possess."

The men nod and murmur approvingly. This must be the rebellion getting their marching orders. Good. Ravel's taking action.

"This is your chance." Cadence says. "Go now, while they're distracted."

I don't want to look away. The presence of these lesser men only serves to reinforce his supremacy. I made the right choice, coming to him for help. He'll set things right. I probably don't even need to take the time to tell him what I learned. He seems driven enough as it is. My mission is really and truly over. All I need to worry about are learning the ways of Freedom and getting over my regulation-fuelled hang-ups.

I roll my shoulders under the woven blanket, shrugging it back a little, not quite ready to let it drop away but moving in that direction. Victoire. Be Victoire. Be free.

But something's not right. I'm sure I'm not needed here; Ravel has things well in hand. But there's something about the leaders of his rebellion. The men are soft and pale, blurred and streaked in a sad mimicry of his fierce beauty. Where his eyes are intense, compelling, commanding, theirs are dull and self-satisfied. Where his face is strong and sharp, theirs are merely hungry. They drink him in and pant for more.

Are these the ones who are going to stand up to Refuge, who are going to break through to the indoctrinated workers and set them free? Are these my allies? I'd never have a chance at making it through to anyone on my own, but what exactly are these sad excuses for rebels supposed to contribute?

"We've shaken the evil at the heart of Refuge," Ravel says, and the men murmur in approval. "We've won over the key to the enemy's schemes and struck a devastating blow against the power of Mayor Ajera and her minions."

There are scattered cheers at this, a clink of glasses. The men seem pleased but less excited about the development than I am. What key? How close is Refuge to falling? I lean in further, eager to hear more.

"We've snatched what Her Worship most desired from her grasp and crippled her control," Ravel coaxes a louder cheer from the intoxicated crowd, "and just in time for tonight's exchange, when we mark the rise of the master of Freedom and the decline of the mistress of Refuge."

The cheer is more enthusiastic this time. I'm still trying to work out who's doing what as Ravel continues.

"You are the first of many, the brave pioneers." He prowls back and forth in front of their watery gazes. "You have taken on the burden of leadership and are honoured for it. Lead the revolution in abandon, in excess, in every pleasure and delight. Live your freedom in defiance, and bring Refuge to its knees."

My breath catches in my throat. It's an inspiring speech, but it doesn't quite ring true. I mean, it sounds impressive, but what are they actually doing about Refuge?

The men rise, abandoning their cups and moving toward the exit all at once. I spin to run away before they see me and collide with something soft. I'm surrounded. I don't know how they moved so quietly, but a cluster of exotically dressed women clogs the corridor, watching me. Behind them, attendants unfurl fiery orange-hued drapes along the walls and lower lighting rigs from the shadowy recesses of the ceiling.

Freedom is coming back to life.

SCHEMES

I TRIP ON the thick curtain to Ravel's chamber, my feet tangling. The dark, perfumed fabric binds around me as I fall, keeping me blessedly hidden.

There's a murmur of voices; high titters and low, pleased rumbles from beyond the muffling drapes. Squirming only wraps the folds tighter around me.

"Should have listened, should have gotten away while you had a chance, stupid stupid stupid st—" Cadence mutters fast and low, like a prayer.

I hate her. It's her fault we're in this mess. If she hadn't distracted me—

"So." Ravel's voice is a spear of ice.

Ice that melts immediately in a flush of embarrassment. Suddenly the heavy drapes are stifling. I can't breathe.

"What have we here? A fine mess you've gotten yourself into, Refuge spy."

The drapes unwind in a dizzy whirl, dumping me unceremoniously in a dirty, sweaty heap. I have no intention of looking up.

His delighted laugh breaks my resolve. "What a wonderful surprise, Victoire." He extends an elegant hand. The dark devices inked on his skin ripple hypnotically with the motion. "So glad you've joined us. I'm sorry you had to wake up alone; I had thought you might sleep longer."

I blink at him stupidly. Not that he seems to notice. My stupidity, that is.

"What's the matter?"

I don't know what to say. I just got caught eavesdropping, but he doesn't seem angry, just concerned. Maybe I can risk a question.

"What's the exchange?"

"How much did you hear, flame?" The edges of his smile are too tight.

"Oh, not much." I talk fast to cover my mistake. "Just that you've got the rebellion well underway, and something about a key and an exchange and, well, I just wanted to know how things were going, and if maybe you might want some help or anything? I never did get a chance to tell you what I learned back in Refuge."

He relaxes. "Sure, sure. In fact, I was just about to go get you."

Trust Cadence to get me worked up for nothing. Ravel has it all under control. It's no one's fault but my own if I'm failing to learn and adapt fast enough.

Attendants transform the shell of the club in the background, unfurling rolls of fabric hidden in the ceiling: orange nearby, white just past that, green back the way I'd come. Long, complicated-looking racks of lighting are carefully lowered into place. Musty air stirs with spiced, sweet perfumes and billowing dust. I can taste it on my tongue, dry and gritty, but the way it dances in the beams of coloured light is strangely beautiful.

Ravel's followers are mingling with the women in the shadows. I look away, horrified despite myself and uncomfortably aware once again of the press of Ravel's body against mine.

He traces my gaze, and I feel his laughter. I need Victoire to take over and help me perform the role I've chosen for myself, but instead of sweeping in to save me, she's strangely distant. No one but Ravel is looking; she prefers an audience.

I turn and try to channel Victoire, to pull on elegance and confidence and be what he wants, but I can tell my eyes are too wide. I stumble, and my arm knocks against him in a way that's clumsy and sharp, not pleasing at all. He steadies me.

"Let's get a little space, okay? Just you and me."

He steers me back through the green and purple and blue halls to the chamber I woke up in. Ravel waves the attendants away and pulls me down beside him. He lounges, one arm flung around my shoulders. I tuck my knees up against my chest and pull some cushions closer. It's strange to have so much of my face exposed, never mind the rest of me, especially when he strokes my cheek and feels the tightening of my mouth.

"It's okay, it's okay," he says soothingly, not unlike Cadence.

I relax a little. He appears content to sit with me for the moment. I know I should get it together and try harder to be what he expects.

I watch the attendants standing at the far wall instead. Underneath the paints and other enhancements, their skin is very pale. Not the greyish, Noosh-induced paleness of Refuge or the blue-tinted pallor of a corpse. My head tingles, but the usual wave of fascination with the dead dulls in the face of so much else to contend with. No, their flesh is something else entirely, a blank white canvas. Its uniformity is another layer of paint. The man shows dark, rich skin at the inner crease of his elbow where the paint has been smudged away. The woman's skin at the hairline, where sweat has washed it clean, is a warm, soft tan.

She shares a glance with the dark-skinned attendant, drifts closer. His ring-wound fingers trail across a bobbing spray of pink tendrils on her shoulder and settle on a painted patch of skin at her hip. Her soft orange lips quirk up ever so slightly.

"Huh," Cadence says, apparently watching too. I'm not displeased by her presence.

There's a sort of tremble in me as I watch them, the sort of shiver that is stillness instead of motion, but Ravel seems to feel it anyway.

"What's wrong, flame?" He traces the lower edge of my mask with his thumb. "It's a lot of change at first, isn't it? What can I do to make it easier?"

"Flame?" I say, instead of answering his impossible, absurd question.

His grin widens. The gold paint melts to red inside his mouth, and there's the flash of more gold thrust through his tongue further in.

"Cole, right? In the time before, coal was a black stone that burned, the source of fire. You're my flame, Victoire, fuel for the rebellion, spark and fire and victory once the ashes settle."

My mouth is open, but there's nothing to say to that, really. Cadence snorts, unimpressed.

"Rebellion?" I wince at how many of our conversations seem to take place in monosyllables, at least on my part. "Is the exchange part of the rebellion?"

Ravel's lips tighten, but when he answers, his voice is warm and light. "Of course. Everything I do is rebellion."

"And what should I do?"

He laughs. "It's not so much about what you do as who you are."

Maybe he didn't understand the question.

"I mean, how does the rebellion work? What do you need from me?"

"Oh, nothing, really," he says. "Just follow your desire. I've always known you were meant to be here."

What does that mean? I wish he'd just tell me what he wants. I never realized how simple, how useful, it had been to have regulation written and memorized and clear.

He leans in and strokes circles on my knee with one sharp nail. "Freedom is all about what goes on inside, you know? What does Refuge teach? No, don't recite it. Just think about it. It's all control, right? All about keeping people down, locked away from each other, from themselves. No dreams, no hope, no ambition, no feeling, no desire. But it doesn't work. You've seen people die?"

He doesn't wait for me to answer, but I nod anyway. Oh, have I seen people die.

"So, there's no point to it. None. Control—meaningless. Obedience—meaningless. Refuge's existence, structure, hierarchy, shields—meaningless. If you can die anyway, why bother with any of it?"

He pauses, as if I might have something to contribute. I wrack my brain. My lips part a couple of times without anything behind them, but he's patient, poised on the drawn-out moment with characteristic elegance.

In the absence of any response that will clearly please him, I reach for something plain and honest. "It helps," I say, testing each word, "to feel like you can do something."

"But that's just it." He nods and rubs my knee raw in enthusiastic circles. "You have to get away from worrying about what you have to do and focus on just being. If regulation leads not to life, but to death, doesn't it stand to reason that the opposite of regulation leads not to death but to life?"

He waits for me to catch up, but all I can think is: what does this have to do with an exchange?

"So, what's the opposite of regulation? What's the opposite of control? Indulgence. Abandon. Rebellion. We're safest when we're most alive, most ourselves, most caught up in dreams, and wants, and wishes, and ambitions. Selfishness, flame, is the greatest protection there is. So"— he pats my knee in emphasis—"all I need from my Victoire here is for her to indulge in anything and everything her little heart desires. Yes?"

I gulp.

"What about everyone else?" I breathe, afraid to give the thought voice.

Ravel's nail stops tracing circles for a moment, starts again, stroking my knee this time. I can't tell if he's doing it to distract me or if it's an unconscious expression of his own commitment to selfish indulgence.

"Ah, that's what makes you so unique, flame, that ability to look outside yourself. You see so much, don't you? Just be careful it doesn't get in the way of your own needs. Can't have anything happening to my Victoire, after all."

He runs his knuckles across my knee, a disturbing, overwhelming sensation. Maybe it's a test, a reminder to accept sensation instead of defaulting to my regulation indoctrination and pushing it away. He talks as if he knows me better than I know myself. It would feel reassuring if I weren't so afraid that he's confused me for someone else.

"Rebellion," he says thoughtfully, as his knuckles go *bump bump bump* over the knobby bones of my knee, "starts inside, right? Disobedience. Indulgence. It's practised; it's choices. I just make a safe place to practise. I find the ones who are waking up, and let them know there's somewhere they can indulge their hunger. The more who wake up to their needs, the more the rebellion grows, until we can drag our brothers out from their slumber and overthrow the seat of control entirely."

His gaze is distant, his movements slow and methodical, bumping back and forth across my knee.

"What if they don't wake up? When do you take the truth to them? What if they die first?"

And what about me? Am I as "awake" as he seems to believe? Have I always been awake in a sea of sleepers who dare not dream? What if I'm just not as hungry as the people Ravel talks about? What if I don't know how to indulge? And what about all the damage in the meantime? Children kidnapped? People dying?

Then I think about the dead and the shameful, thrumming, tingling sensation of wanting. I feel a little better. That was waking up, wasn't it? Even if it wasn't the right thing to want. Even if it turned out what I thought I wanted was horrible and painful and scary and wrong.

And then he says, "If they die, they die."

EXCHANGE

T'S NOT THAT I don't realize something's wrong. Cadence's shocked gasp would have clued me in, if nothing else. It's just . . . his attitude makes sense, even if it is kind of horrible.

People die. Refuge can't protect them, and they should know that. But, if they're not ready to know, not ready to learn to live another way, isn't it better to leave them be? Doesn't each one of us have to choose to learn, choose to obey or to rebel for ourselves?

Isn't that why I ran away from Refuge when I first learned the truth? Because there's no way someone like me could convince anyone of it anyway? Well, that and it wasn't safe for me there, and I was being chased by enforcers, and Cadence had lied and said she knew what she was doing. But mostly because I knew it was impossible for a valueless probationary worker to get people to realize they were being lied to and controlled in the first place.

It all makes sense. I still don't like it.

"Can't we make it stop—the dying?"

"That's my girl." Ravel squeezes me close. "So kind-hearted. But think, flame. How would we do that? What is there to stop the Mara from taking a life?"

"What about submitting the—"

"Ritual submission? No." He laughs. "More lies. That's one of my favourites, actually. It's from a bedtime story, a legend from another place in the time before the floods. A chimaera, a sort of imaginary mashed together beast spirit called a "baku" was said to eat dreams—or more specifically, nightmares. If a child had a bad dream, he would call to the baku to come and eat his nightmare three times. But the baku, while useful, had a dark side. It shouldn't be called carelessly, for it might be hungry and eat all the good dreams, all the desires of the dreamer, and leave him a hollowed-out shell.

"When my—when Refuge first encountered the dream-eating Mara, they simply transplanted this legend as a sort of charm or remedy. It has no practical effect. If the Mara come for you, they're not going to be satisfied with just part of your dreams. They don't care for half-measures and repressed desire."

He's wrong. The Mara took my dreams, the night Cadence found me. They ate my disobedience—I know they did. But to explain to Ravel, I'd have to admit just what I'd lost. Somehow, I don't think the Victoire he expects is the sort of person to have an unhealthy obsession with the dead.

"But think," he continues, "nearly all of us will die eventually. It's inevitable. What cannot be accepted is never living—and that's where we can do something for the masses. What's the real threat to living? Is it Mara attacks?"

I nod.

"Or, is it really the fear of death and the control that gives others over us? Doesn't Refuge use our fear of being killed by the Mara to prevent us from living in the first place? So, what's the worse threat?"

"Even without Refuge, we still have to fear the Mara."

"That's just it." He jumps to his feet and paces. "That's the heart of Freedom. If the threat of the Mara could be controlled, channelled—if we could know where, and when, and who would die—we wouldn't have to fear death. And that, flame, is the Exchange."

I stare blankly.

"It's going to blow your mind. Get dressed. You're helping me defeat the fear of death tonight, and I want you looking your best."

Ravel snaps his fingers at the waiting attendants, gives me one last delighted grin and is gone in a surge of music before the heavy curtain drops shut.

I mull it over as the attendants work around me to prepare for the night ahead. Ravel's theories are astonishing, but I still don't see how the rebellion works. I'd like to talk it over with Cadence, but she's gone silent again and the attendants would think I've gone crazy.

I watch them, the way they speak in a language of glances and touch: the lift of an exposed shoulder, the press of an elbow, the quirk of a lip. The woman's almond eyes, narrowed in subtle amusement; the brush of the man's hand on her hip, so light for someone so large; untold ways to communicate when a body isn't covered over and hidden away by a uniform. No wonder Refuge didn't want us to see this. They'd never have controlled us if we could speak without words.

Later, in the midst of a wide hall, under strobing lights and buoyed by a throbbing beat, I find this language of touch and glance, brush and smile, all throughout the many-headed mass of revellers. Victoire experiments in it, trying it out on Ravel, who stays close, dancing with her in the island of space left for them as they move through the tinted rooms. Beyond the white hall is a violet one that I've never seen before, and beyond that, one hung only in flat black velvet. Deep crimson light glances off sparkles and studs as if the dancers have been caught out in a bloody rain.

I let Victoire take over, while the still part of me that observes from a distance watches the way the others look at us, coming back again and again to Ravel and Victoire. I watch the way their riotous dress and movement makes them indistinct instead of individual. It makes them less than while they try so hard to be more. The rebellion, it seems, is really a series of small, individual mutinies against regulation.

It's a diffuse movement. And I've apparently joined it just by showing up.

But here's the thing. I had—have—a mission. A purpose. A reason to keep going. Doing. Being.

Tell people the truth about Refuge. Bring it down. Stop the dying.

Though really, it was more like: find someone to tell people the truth about Refuge. Find someone else to end their control, their abuses, their lies. Find an ally to make us all safe. It had been a silly mission, anyway, just something to hold on to, something to keep on keeping on with. I'm no hero. Had I ever really intended anything beyond finding a safe place to escape Refuge's pursuit, its judgment? To escape that black mark of failure around my head?

Ravel's given me what I wanted, a place to exist. To survive. But can I really practice self-indulgence and wait for the rebellion to take hold one worker at a time while I hide out from death down here?

Victoire leans into Ravel and smiles at the thought. She raises one slender arm gracefully, delicate traceries of gold catching the bloody light. He takes her outstretched hand and spins her in a shimmering, dizzy swirl. He bows, laughing, his gaze dark with admiration and something more. Victoire's pleased with his attentiveness, powerful with it; shoulders back, chin level, drawn up to her full height proudly, letting the ornaments drape back and away.

It's embarrassing. Frightening. But I choose this, choose her, choose the selfishness and hunger that comes with being her. I let her take control.

"How you have grown into yourself." He strokes a hand down her arm. The fine hairs on the back of my neck raise, but Victoire makes no sign besides a small quirk to her lips. "I can't tell you how much it pleases me to have you here with me, inspiring our rebellion, my golden goddess."

"Goddess?"

"But of course," he insists. "You, my Victoire, are our icon, the perfect fantasy we worship, absolute freedom and abandon, the promise of eternal pleasure. I knew it the moment I first laid eyes on you."

"Ravel," Victoire murmurs, laying her cheek against his shoulder.

She is pleased with the flattery, but I feel a twinge of discomfort. That's not quite what he told me before. What happened to being different because I notice things, because I was trying to help other people? Not that that's really who I am, necessarily, but it's just . . . different.

I need to trust Ravel.

I'm not sure I can.

VICTOIRE LOSES HERSELF in the flash and swirl of the dance, caught in Ravel's overwhelming presence. They're undeniably beautiful together, gold and shadow guiding a slender flame.

I can't get caught up in it, though—I'm watching for the promised "exchange." And though Ravel has insisted nothing can harm me here, all his talk of Refuge has me worried about pursuit. If those enforcers ever figure out where I went, could he really stop them from taking me?

Black velvet swallows the sanguine light. It's the darkest of the halls. Shadows flow along the walls—some sort of attendants in dark cloaks that blend into the background. They're the ones who transformed the space from bare underground warren to this gorgeous madness. Their purposeful movement sets them apart from the general roil of pulsing dancers.

A sweep of light picks out one man, arm thrown up to brush aside the wall covering as he enters the hall from some concealed entrance. His skin is so lined; it reminds me of the age-worn skin of the corpse, Bell.

Ravel notices the direction of my gaze. "Well chosen, flame."

He points at the cloaked man. The music falls silent. The whirling figures stumble to a halt and scramble back from the startled attendant.

"The Exchange," Ravel says into the sudden hush.

"The Exchange." The crowd roars back.

The sound is low and scattered at first. It gains intensity and speed, every dancer within view striking his or her right heel on the floor, generating a pounding beat. Spotlights gather around the man in the cloak. He turns and flings himself against a sudden wall of bodies. Arms shove back at him, denying escape.

"My lady chooses you," Ravel says over the stomping. "Dream for us."

The attendant falls to his knees. Ravel tugs me forward, and the crowd makes a path as we approach. Up close, the whites of the stranger's eyes are starkly framed in a simple fabric mask. His mouth moves, but no words make it past his lips.

Please. He's shaping the word please. Over and over again. I can't breathe. All I can hear is the desperate strangled sound he makes, as though he's choking on the word.

"Don't look," Cadence whispers from a great distance.

"Your sacrifice for our freedom." Ravel seizes my hand and presses it on the stranger's sweat-dampened scalp. His hair is rough beneath my palm. I feel something brush against my free hand. I look down, but nothing's there.

"Your sacrifice for our freedom," the crowd roars.

I struggle, but Ravel won't let go. The stranger shudders under my touch.

"It's the Exchange, Victoire. You chose him; I was watching. It's a beautiful thing. Don't shame him by pulling away. He knew the risk he was taking coming here."

One or both of us shakes harder at that. Tears run down the man's face. My eyes sting in response.

Ravel reaches out and wrenches away the man's mask. I look away. I don't understand what's going on. I don't want to understand. The stomping beat has worked its way deep inside me, quaking and threatening to send me to my knees.

Again, something brushes my free hand. The air seems thick, cloudy. I blink. Nothing's there. A loose thread, maybe. I scrub my hand against my hip, a damp stain marring the silk.

"Leave it alone," Cadence whispers, a little louder. "Get out of there. Now."

Ravel tightens his grip. The cloaked man's breath hitches. Ravel says, "Your death for our life."

"Cole, don't!" Cadence screams.

Her voice is washed away as the crowd roars Ravel's words. The stomping races faster, a speeding pulse. The invisible thread pulls taut.

I won't look. I don't want to see. But I feel it against my palm, the sudden stillness.

The silence is ringing.

I look. His panic-widened eyes fog over with a pearlescent sheen. Mara taken. Eaten alive.

His shell slumps to the ground. The crowd cheers.

Ravel releases my hand. I hold it away from me. Cadence sobs in the background. The music starts. Dancers whirl.

The corpse's head is tilted awkwardly against the ground. I can't look away from those blank eyes.

He's dead.

My scalp tingles. I reach up and yank at the feathers in my hair, ripping them out in handfuls, trying to make the traitorous sensation stop. Glitter falls like rain. I didn't mean to . . . I didn't know . . . I never meant to . . .

But the truth sings through my blood: It's my fault he died.

21 LIWAN

RAVEL GRABS MY wrists. Feathers spill everywhere. I shake my head, yank against his grip. It's Cadence who's crying, not me. Not me. I don't deserve to cry.

It's my fault. I want to tell him. Ravel. I want to tell him it's my fault, but I can't. I can't get the words out, I can't breathe, I—

Ravel lets go of one hand and tucks me into his side. I bury my free hand in my hair again and yank.

"Oh, flame, no. No, it's okay. It's okay. I thought you understood. I didn't expect—it's my fault. I should have prepared you better."

He curls over me, shielding me from view, and sweeps me away from the dancers, back into the stillness of the private room. He settles me onto the bed and kneels, reaching up to work my hands free of the snarled mess of hair and feathers.

He doesn't let go as he looks over his shoulder. "Dust."

The female attendant scurries out of some hidden alcove with a tray and offers it to him.

"Do I look like I have a free hand right now?"

I cringe. His expression gentles in an instant. "No, don't be afraid. You're safe here. You're always safe with me. You have to believe that."

The attendant's face is rigid beneath her mask. She offers me the cup. I clamp my lips and lean away. At a glare from Ravel, she presses the cup to my mouth and tilts.

I gulp some down despite myself. Her gaze is hard. Does she know? Did she hear the stillness and the pounding and the crowd's cheer after he fell? Does she blame me?

My breathing speeds again, despite the dust scorching the back of my tongue.

"Another," he says.

The attendant pours another glass. I shake my head.

"It will help."

When I still refuse, he covers my nose and tips it into my mouth. I choke. Most of it goes down anyway. After, I'm calmer. I can't hear Cadence's sobbing.

"He . . . he died. He just died." I swipe spilled dust and smeared paint from my face. Then I keep scrubbing, tearing off mask, bangles, chains—along with the paint on my arms.

Ravel just looks at me, his face set as if he's the one hurt.

"You've seen death before," he says, finally.

I shake my head. "It's never been my fault. Why did you make me do that? Why?"

"It's not like that. I truly thought you'd understand, Victoire." He gets up, sits beside me, not touching, just there.

His disappointment—his distance—slows me down inside. I'm so cold.

"The Exchange," he says, "it's a trade. A bargain. The Mara let us live in peace, but there's a price. I designate a sacrifice, a victim for them. They leave the rest of us alone. It's better this way."

I focus on breathing, on not hearing him.

"The Mara take lives, indiscriminately. This way, the rest of us get to live without the fear of death, free to enjoy everything life has to offer until our time comes. I lead them. It's my right, my—our—responsibility to choose the sacrifice."

I don't look at him.

"I need you, flame. You're special like me, even if you haven't remembered yet. Together, we'll rule Freedom, bring down Refuge itself. You're meant to be by my side. I had to show them all that. Show them your power. They know you now, respect and fear you. And the Mara won't touch you."

I don't want this. But Victoire stirs within me, traitorously eager at the idea of all that power and hungry for the immunity he promises. I shove her back down. This isn't right. I can't be a part of this. There has to be another way, a better way.

"It's the only way," Ravel whispers, as if he can hear my thoughts. Then he looks away, speaking to the attendants. "Get her cleaned up. The night's not over."

I rise to protest, but he pushes me back against the cushions. "Where would you go, flame?" There's a spark to his gaze now that I don't like. "There's nowhere for you to be but right here."

I shove to my feet as soon as he gives me room to. He's right. I have no other option than to keep him happy, nowhere else to be. But I can't just sit still and do nothing, either.

He whirls as if angry I won't stay put. I back away. My feet tangle. I trip, arms flailing, grabbing at threads too fragile to hold my weight.

And then I keep tumbling. It's dark, unremittingly, endlessly.
Light comes.

And then I'm with him. 12-Lee-01, Liwan in his—our—thoughts, one of the older trainees in Refuge, nearly ready to graduate to a work division.

He's angry, barely even trying to seem compliant. It's not fair. I tried so hard to be good in Training and still got dragged off to Corrections. His frustration seeps into me, merging with memories of my own discontent. I slip deeper into his mind, his thoughts, without really meaning to, deep enough that *I* and *he* becomes *we*, *us*.

We're suspicious of everything. The bland food, a liquid diet of flavourless, thick goop is supposed to dull the warm tint of our skin and fade the near black of our hair and irises, smooth it out to blend with the herds of grown workers. But the Noosh isn't working on us as fast as on some of the others, or we'd have been transferred to a workplace by now. A future as a Refuge worker holds no promise for us, anyway.

We've learned to force down the Noosh as they watch and then purge most out later. It seems to make a difference.

I claw back up to my own singular consciousness, astonished. It never occurred to me to do such a thing, though I felt just like he does, angry and ashamed. His looks are actually a bit like Ravel's. Did Ravel ever hate himself; ever feel like a failure for his differences too? Or has he always been so confident? Ravel . . . I was just with him. What am I doing here? How did I get here? I'm in Liwan's head like I was with Bell, but I didn't touch a corpse, and it's not like when I'm Victoire, either. We share a body and a mind, but I let her drive our actions and thoughts. Here I don't seem to have any ability to step in and influence Liwan. He feels separate, like Suzie did. But I didn't mess up this time, didn't indulge in temptation, didn't feel the warning, beckoning tingle.

Liwan seems to realize I'm with him at some level, thinking with self-conscious clarity: *My head feels so much clearer. Purging the Noosh makes a difference, for sure. I learn faster than the others. But I've learned to slow down, play dumb and let my mind wander. In the world I escape to, I live with others. Their eyes focus; they see me. They smile. Laugh.*

He recreates the scene for me, layering a sort of phantom image over the bland walls of the training room, wispy and half-formed. It feels different from what Suzie shared with me. There's longing, yes, but less of a desire to be seen, more loneliness.

He misses his family, says Cadence. If I had a body in this—whatever this is—I'd have jumped at the sound of her voice. *And who's Suzie?*

What are you doing here? I ask, without the benefit of a mouth or lungs or ears, which seem to have very little to do with communication just now.

You really shouldn't be here, she says. *You shouldn't be able to see this.*

I want to ask what she means, but Liwan's projected image sweeps in, growing more solid as it surrounds us on all sides. It's disturbingly reminiscent of Suzie's dreamscape in the way it blurs in the distance.

I look for the Mara, but I don't sense their hungry darkness. At least not yet. Just the small, dim room, doors and windows covered to keep out a thick yellowish fog. Two adults and a small boy that could be Liwan, and a tiny, squirming thing with the same dark hair and eyes. In Refuge, a trainer is leading a recitation of regulation. Liwan's grasp on the made-up world wavers and slips away as he mechanically recites along. I mouth the words to help him, but—

"Liwan."

"Trainee Worker 12-Lee-01," the trainer repeats himself, "remember Injunctions One and Three. Dreams lead to death. An idle mind draws down destruction."

Liwan mumbles an apology and focuses for a few minutes until the trainer's attention moves off and he feels like he's gotten back into the flow of things. We slip away again.

Bàba wants us to climb a building with him. He says you can see past the fog if you go high enough, to where the water isn't haunted. We try, but we're still too little. He gives up and takes us home, paddling between monstrous skeletons of corroded steel and shattered glass.

Cole, you need to leave. Cadence's voice jolts me out again. *It's not safe for you here.*

I feel as though I've followed Liwan through minutes, hours, days, though it can't have taken more than seconds for him to show me. It feels dangerously close to dream territory. Is that what she's afraid of? But I don't sense the presence of the Mara at all. I pull back from Liwan, squinting. Translucent threads fill the air.

Are they coming?

She doesn't answer for a long moment. *What do you see?*

Where to start? Do I tell her about Liwan listlessly trailing through his training? Or about the adventures he's spinning into images one or both of us is probably hallucinating? Or do I try to describe the even more improbable threads that clog the air in both worlds, neither of which I should be in right now? Why is she even asking me? Can't she see for herself? Or is she somehow in my head, doing all this in the first place? Manipulative little liar.

What should I see? Nothing. Everything. Fantasies of a stupid boy who'd rather lose himself in stories and risk his neck than behave. Like someone else I know.

I'm not your enemy. You need to leave. It's not safe for you here.

Right, as if I have any say in the matter. It's not like I can do anything. Besides, she's probably trying to force me to make up with her. If she's somehow in my head, making me see things, trying to make me listen to her, the only thing I can do is ignore her until she gets bored and it all ends. I focus back on Liwan.

Mama says there's another way to see past the fog. It's dangerous, but she says we should see. Just in case, we should get to see. She seems sad. Bàba says it's best to go just before dark. Easier to get away. Prettier. They're afraid of something. We're not sure what.

We dress in layer upon layer of dark clothes, covered over with a loose cloak. The fog is even heavier than usual outside. Bàba says hurry, hurry so we can still see it.

In Refuge the trainers divide the trainees into groups, jolting us out of the story to comply. There was a moment in the fog where it had seemed as if it could have been getting to be a dream, as if the Mara were circling. But now it's just normal, everyday life—except I'm still stuck with Liwan.

What if this isn't Cadence's fault? What if it never ends? Can I influence Liwan somehow? Get him to escape to Freedom too? It's not as if he's really safe here anyway. But when I try to tell him about the doors across from the elevators, he doesn't seem to hear.

He's bored. It's tediously slow work. You can't go too fast, make too many mistakes, or stop working. You have to go at exactly the right pace. Apparently, this is calculated to keep your mind and body occupied without being too exhausting.

Liwan is faster and smarter than he should be, though, probably because of the way he's learned to purge Noosh from his system. Once his body settles into the rhythm, he slips away again to his projected world, pulling me in deep this time, so deep I almost forget it's all just Cadence's doing in the first place.

Bàba paddles quickly. The fog is thinner here. We can see higher, past the crumbling buildings to where there's nothing but light. We run aground. A building on the edge of the city, only partially submerged. The top is covered with dark sand. Bàba boosts us on to the shifting surface of this beach and keeps his hand on our shoulder as we walk to the other side. We gaze out over glittering waves at a far shore and distant mountains painted in the crimson glow of the sunset. We've never seen so far or so clearly. The dipping sun is warm on our skin, the wash of waves on the shore soothing as bàba tries to tell us something, something important. But a shadow falls.

I feel the Mara approach. I have no voice to warn him. I don't know what called me to him, or why I should witness this at all, but whether it started as a vision or a memory or the manipulations of a ghost, Liwan's imagination has conjured a dream. And the Mara are hungry.

Monsters march along the sand, clothed in stiff uniforms and heavy boots. Our father is ripped away. Salt and a foul sweetness mingle in the air. Hot blood pours down our face. Sand sucks at our feet, dragging us down.

I try to pull away from Liwan as I did from Suzie at the end. I even call for Cadence. She calls back helplessly as the Mara sweep in to claim their prey.

22 VISIONS

HIS IS WHAT I see: Liwan, trapped in the smallness and weakness of his child's body in the dream, flailing as he's drawn deeper into the heavy sand. The sand has arms, grasping fingers clothed in an enforcer's heavy white gloves. The glorious riot of light on the waves has been eaten away by the darkness, but I can still make him out beneath the ropy threads wound about him. I witness the stretched, churning horror of his face as blood not his own drips down his hair.

What light there is exists to illuminate the ruin of his bàba. He's sinking faster than Liwan, sand crawling up his face, choking the slack mouth, clogging the blank eyes, until there's nothing left of him but a damp stain. Liwan howls and sobs and begs for him to return, pleading for what's done to be undone, crying for forgiveness as the sand creeps past his waist and the snarled cords draw tighter. I cry with him, horrified, broken for what he's lost.

But, at the same time, I see this: the trainee 12-Lee-01 pauses under the sickly golden glow of shielded lights and leans on his scrub brush a moment too long, weighed down by heavy tangles of translucent threads. A trainer's eyes narrow in the grey expanse above his mask, ready to correct, then widen as the boy tumbles forward, rigid. Trainees scream and scramble away as he falls, writhing on the floor. Liwan's mask is pushed sideways as he squirms and chokes. Tears run freely from his eyes, blood from his nose.

It's a dizzying sort of double vision and more: doubled hearing, doubled smell, as if all my senses exist simultaneously in both unlikely locations, with seaside rot and rank fear alongside the too-sweet artificial fug of shielded air seeping through Refuge's ventilation.

Liwan shakes and strains on the floor, his body awash in spilled cleaning fluid and snarled in barely visible coils. At the same time, he's drawn deeper into the sand, dragged by tangled threads and phantom arms, his voice weakening as the heavy grains weigh him down, refusing him air.

Don't look, Cadence says. *You shouldn't be here. You can't help him.*

Make it stop. I say. And then shriek, begging, as the Mara come.

The sand bubbles and shifts. Something presses up from beneath: dark hair, rough skin, a loose grin under hollow eyes. Grains run from every crease and cavity in a continuous stream as the Mara in bàba's form rear above. The creature wears an enforcer's uniform, but its mask hangs loose, showing sharp teeth under an empty stare.

In Refuge, Liwan's body jolts. The floor cracks beneath him. His leg bends at an impossible angle and his ribs creak. He's beyond responding now, barely alive, but the small version of him in the dream reaches a trembling hand to the face of the sand monster, not pushing it away but pleading, seeking comfort. The Mara bat the boy's hand aside, reach for his throat, and squeeze.

Make it stop.

I can't, Cadence says.

It's not right. Both the almost-grown trainee, crumpled and alone on the floor in Refuge, and the child being crushed in a dream—they don't deserve this. Liwan might not have been the most obedient trainee ever, but there's no way he could have done anything to deserve this anguish. Nothing could be bad enough to justify this.

But that's just it, isn't it? Obedience and disobedience have nothing to do with it. It's random. The Mara are hungry, and they take what they want, and all that's left—

If Liwan isn't dead yet, he will be any moment now. A tingling sensation across my scalp distracts me, that shameful fascination with the dead trying to take over . . . But this is different, knowing him before all that's left is the empty shell. I can't accept this, his being alive and wanting and living and struggling, and then not.

If I knew where my body was, I would rush the Mara and scoop sand away from the boy's face with both hands. I'd rip into that tangled web and tear it off of him. I'd plunge into that empty ring of cracked and crumbling floor, dive past the staring trainers and gutless trainees, and hold Liwan's head up, help him breathe even if he has only moments left to do so.

But I can't move. All I can do is scream for Cadence to make it stop. The Mara-beast swells.

And shatters, pierced through in an explosionof silver-white light.

I curl against the stinging burn of its brilliance. When I manage to look back, Liwan lays on his back in both Refuge and the dream, trembling and teary but sucking in huge, grateful breaths. There is no trace of threads, neither tangled around either vision of the boy nor filling the space around him.

The brightness around the child in the dream fades, drawing down into a tight beam held by a gently glowing figure that drops to its knees and gathers up the small boy. In Refuge, Liwan relaxes, breathing evenly. The trainers hesitate, looking furtively at one another, but make no move to step forward.

The glow around the stranger dims further, until I can make out features. He's big, maybe even taller than me and certainly broader. His face is unmasked, bare under the coating of light that shimmers over it. He cradles the small boy, brushes grains of sand from his face. Something inside me turns over at the sight of it. Then we're no longer on a beach. The dream is fading. Though my strange, twinned vision still holds both in view, Refuge now seems the more real of the two.

The man cloaked in silver light looks up, his face drawn and sad. Then he goes rigid, the light flaring around him again. Did he just see me?

That shouldn't be possible. I can't even see me. Though, actually, I can feel the edges of myself again.

" . . . " the stranger says, words on the edge of hearing.

His lips move. He stands, child-Liwan in his arms. The silver light surrounds and covers him, brightest in his eyes and the lines around them, starkly outlining an expression I struggle to name. He takes a step toward me, and then looks down as Liwan's figure starts to fade. When he looks up, there are tears in his eyes.

In Refuge, Liwan sits up, gasping with pain as he shifts his broken leg. Then that fades out too. I'm left in a featureless space with the stranger. He draws closer, speaking words I can't quite hear, his face knotted with pain. There's something more there, too, a sort of pleading, and longing, and . . . I don't have words for it.

He's so close. His eyes are dark. Not a darkness of dying and ending but the darkness of a night sky lit with starlight like that one perfect crisp moment on the rooftop so many days ago. Even as his trembling hand reaches out, he and I and the whole space around us fade away.

" . . . Cady . . . " It's barely a whisper, a voiceless echo.

I'M BACK IN Freedom, sprawled on the dizzying patchwork of rugs. Ravel helps me to my feet. "You all right, flame? Too much dust?"

I cringe, disoriented and raw inside. The memory of Liwan sinking into the dark weight of sand, writhing as the floor of Refuge crumbles beneath him, haunts me. And the light-swathed stranger, reaching for me with an expression I can't name.

"Victoire?" Ravel's voice is uncertain, reminding me of the way the stranger's hand trembled as he reached for me.

I shake my head. It wasn't real. It was a dream, or a hallucination, or . . . Cadence.

Ravel tilts my chin up and sucks in a breath. "Flame, what's going on? What is that?" I make a noise of complaint, but he doesn't let go. "What happened to you?"

He hauls me in front of the mirror. Faint silver light rings my pupils, as if the glowing stranger is still reflected there. Even as I look, it dims and goes out.

"I knew there had to be some reason she wanted you back after all this time," he mutters. He sits me down on the edge of the bed and kneels, holding my hands. "It'll be okay, I promise," he says, making a visible effort to speak softly. He runs his thumb along the side of my hand and smiles. "Just tell me what happened."

"Don't tell him anything," Cadence says.

I open my mouth to snap at her, or maybe to scream. It's her fault. It must be. But I can't say a word, not with Ravel so close. He tightens his grip, sharp nails cutting into my skin. "Flame, I really need you to trust me if this is going to work. I can't keep you safe if you don't. We can't stop Refuge if you won't let me in."

"Seriously, don't say anything," Cadence says. "I'll explain it all later, okay? Just don't tell him what you saw."

I press my lips together, trying to think. If I anger Cadence, what will she do? Storm off in a huff again and refuse to talk to me for a while. Not so bad. Inflict more twisted hallucinatory visions of death? Not so good, but if they're not real—and they can't be, not since I'm still alive—then it's not like they're really a threat. But if I disappoint Ravel, what would he do? Would he send me away? If he stopped taking care of me, I'd have nowhere to go, no one to help me. And out of the two, he's the only one who might have a chance of keeping me safe from the real dreams, from the Mara. He's also the one I know for a fact could turn me over to them.

But as horrible as it is, the Exchange is power, right? Power to stop the dying. I don't want to be afraid any more. I don't want to see any more children get hurt.

"It was a dream," I say, all in a rush.

"Cole!"

"A dream . . . Victoire, flame, I know it's been a bit of a night for you, but I need you to focus, okay? Can you tell me what happened to make your eyes like that?"

"He doesn't believe you," Cadence says, relieved. "Just don't say anything else. He'll give up soon and leave you alone, and then we can escape."

"It was like a dream. You have to believe me. One moment I was here, and then the next I was with this boy, up in Refuge, and it was like he was the one dreaming and the Mara came and—"

"You're still here," he points out. "You're not dead. It can't have been a dream. So, flame, I really think you must be hiding something from me. I need you to trust me with the truth, okay? Remember how important it is we all know the truth?"

I push past him and jump to my feet to pace. "I'm not lying. I'm not making it up. Cadence is the one who tells stories—it was probably her fault in the first place. I'm telling the truth. There was this boy and it was just like Suzie's dream except Cadence was there, and then this other guy, and that's where the light came from, and he made it so no one died, and—"

"Cadence?" Ravel says.

I wind my fingers together, twisting until it hurts, then make my way back to the edge of the bed and sit. "She's my ghost."

"Your ghost. Cadence is your—" He stares as if I've gone insane.

"Well, not my ghost, exactly, but she's dead and she haunts me. So . . . a ghost. Anyway, when the first dream happened, I don't think she was there, but this time she was, and—"

"Cadence takes you to dreams? Your ghost does? Flame, I don't think you—that's . . ."

"She doesn't take me, exactly." I clench my fingers in my lap until the joints ache. "With Suzie, I kinda . . . I, um, touched what . . . what was left, and then . . . it just sort of happened. But this time I didn't do anything, I promise, I was just here, and then I was with the boy, Liwan and then the Mara showed up, and then this guy came along and sent it away again and then I was back here—"

"There was a man who fought the Mara? In your dream? Who is he? Is he here? What can you tell me about him?"

I relax. Ravel's getting drawn into the mystery, too. Then I remember: the important thing isn't the stranger who killed the Mara, it's whether the Mara were real in the first place, or if it was all somehow one of Cadence's made-up stories. I don't know which is worse. If Cadence can get in my head like that, make me see things that aren't there, she could make me see or believe anything. But if the dreams are real, even if I've somehow survived this long, it's only a matter of time before the Mara kill me too.

"I don't know anything. He just showed up at the end. He seemed to know me—or, no, Cadence. He was looking for Cadence. And then I was back here. What if it happens again? Is it because of the Exchange? Am I being punished?"

Ravel takes my hands again, but he jitters a bit, as if he's having trouble sitting still.

"Listen to me. These are not dreams, okay? Dreams kill. And I have an arrangement with the Mara. They know you're mine. They won't touch you. This is just a—a side effect. Of the haunting. That ghost of yours, she's messing with your head, making you see things."

"I never—" Cadence begins, but I speak over her.

"It's not real?"

"What other explanation could there be? Dreams kill. But you've survived."

Ravel gazes at me with those molten eyes of his and his brows all tented up and confirms everything I want to hear. Cadence has been acting weird ever since the dream—or vision, I guess—of Suzie. She's always been bossy, trying to make me think like she does and do what she wants to do. And those drills Liwan was doing in Refuge, they're just like I remember. Is Cadence taking my memories and weaving them into visions? How could she think I wouldn't notice?

"Cole, don't listen to him. He's lying to you. He's been lying this whole time."

"I'm going to help you, okay, flame? I'm going to take care of you. It's all going to be all right. You just have to listen to me. You just—you just tell me any time that ghost starts trying to show you something or tell you lies, and I'll help you sort out what's true. I'll keep you safe."

"Cole, come on, why would I mess with you? You know me, you know I wouldn't do that. We just have to escape, and then you'll understand everything. Or, or not even escape, just get away from him, okay? I'll explain everything if you just give me a chance."

I close my eyes. Ravel is going to help me. He's going to take care of me.

"Victoire? Flame? You trust me, don't you?"

I nod. He's the master of Freedom. He has the power to keep me safe. I tell him everything: what I saw with Suzie, and on the rooftop, and with Liwan. And he promises none of that was real, all of it was something Cadence came up with, a new way to manipulate me and control my emotions and make me do what she wants. He suggests perhaps the Mara are getting to her.

The way she shrieks over him when he says this makes me afraid. Maybe I've really known all along that she was being eaten away by darkness. Maybe she even tried to tell me, in that first dream—or vision, I guess. But he promises I'm safe now, that he can keep the Mara away from me, and he'll do what he can to keep the Mara away from her, too. He tells me to rest, he has to go out now and take care of some things.

I'm relieved to be left alone. I relax. It's the closest I've been to peaceful in days. I'm out of sight of any authority that needs pleasing; no one needs anything from me just now. I drift in and out of sleep, hungry but too worn out and full of dust to wake up enough to get something to eat.

So maybe Cadence is able to get inside my head again because my guard is down. But that's not what it feels like. It feels as if something snags around my hand. It feels as if there's a sharp tug, and then I'm flying away from myself.

It feels as if the darkness rises up and swallows me whole.

23

FUCHSIA

THIS VISION IS different, again. I'm alone in my body. At least I think I am.

"Leave me alone," I yell at Cadence. "I don't want this. I don't want to see any more."

"I'm not the one doing this, Cole. If you hadn't gone and told Ravel everything, if you'd just trusted me and helped, I could have explained. You're ruining everything."

She's angry? Fine. Two can play at that game. I don't have to listen or even talk to her. I can just wait for it to be over.

At least this vision is in a pretty setting. I recognize the rooftop of Refuge. I'm sitting cross-legged on the sharp gravel under a magical vista. Shades of blue fade to midnight, all pierced with stars.

I go to the edge to get a better look. The skeletons of crumbling towers are framed against the radiance of a full moon, their submerged feet hidden by sickly fog. At the edge of the city, it thins over the ocean. There's something else—I step toward it, and it vanishes; back, and it reappears. A slender silver thread, like a strand of starlight or a moonbeam stretched across the city.

I reach out, expecting my hand to pass right through it, but it's cool and solid in my grasp. I tighten my fist and feel a sudden pull. My sight sharpens and zooms in along the length of the thread toward the top of a building at the edge of the city.

A woman is there, Outside. Her skin is rough and reddened, her hair long and tangled, clothes patched and faded. She crouches on a patch of dirt in a raised box, working around stringy, pale plants.

The vision shifts into more familiar territory, bringing me her thoughts, her feelings. Perhaps it's because of the distance, or her age, but her thoughts seem simple, dull. Smaller, somehow. I'm not as immersed in them as I was with Liwan, or with Susie.

So tired, she thinks. *I'm so tired. It's cold. I'm hungry. It's too hard.*

I want out.

Never enough food. Work all day long, grubbing, clearing, hauling more dirt. Light's too weak for growing. Wind's too strong. All that salt—

It's a rooftop garden. Cadence names off the plants for me, and even I can tell they don't look good: pallid carrots, shrivelled potatoes, wilted greens.

I don't like this. The woman—Fuchsia, the name comes to me—feels different than Suzie or Liwan. She wants different things. She's as angry and bitter and small as the produce of her pathetic plot. But I do feel something for her pitiful life, if only gratitude I don't have to live it.

Can't stand it—dirt under nails, ground into skin, on my clothes. Dirt everywhere. When it rains, mud.

I don't like her, with her bitter, small thoughts and exhaustion, but her isolation hurts. Suzie had Mama and Father until the end. Liwan had mama and bàba and the unnamed little one. But Fuchsia has nothing beautiful or warm or good to hold on to or dream of. The Mara will come for her in the end. It's heartbreaking to think she doesn't even have something to wish for until then. I want to rail at Cadence, but then I remember I'm ignoring her.

If only Granddad hadn't been so stupid. Fuchsia slumps against the raised edge of a bed of carrots. *If only he'd taken Refuge's invitation back when it still took in folks. If he'd let my parents go, even—*

The pale, insubstantial end of another moonbeam thread noses its way out of the fringe of her grubby dress and wavers, reaching out into the air.

I'd've been born one of them, Citizen not Street, grubbing in the dirt. I hear rumours; there's light, heat, running water. Clean clothes every day, 'n no one starves. Oh, to be clean, really clean, even for a moment. To sleep in a safe, clean room with a full belly . . .

Her longing resonates. All she wants is what I had, and I went and risked it all for what? To tell people there's just a chance they might not be safe? That they've been abducted and lied to and betrayed—and also cared for and fed and clothed and given a life to live? I don't want the life she has, her worn, painful-looking skin and hard, hungry eyes.

But I have Ravel now, a place to be, warmth and food and safety. I have to do better, thank Ravel for all he's done for me, maybe find a way to bring—what did she call them? Streets?—as well as workers into Freedom after Refuge falls. If they joined us, even with the Exchange, wouldn't it mean more life for all of us and a reduced risk of death?

Somehow, Fuchsia seems to pick up on this thought. Threads nose their way out from her in all directions as she proudly thinks at me: *I've a plan. See, there's this one enforcer. They say he's different, he'll bend the rules. Take you in from the cold. I'd a friend, she told me about him. Went with him. Never came back, 'course she wouldn't, why would she? No one leaves Refuge, 'except enforcers. I'd give him whatever he asked, anything, if I could only find him, if he'd take me away from here.* Her hollow gaze turns inward. Threads waver off in all directions. *He looks so fine in his uniform.*

She scrambles to her feet, swaying, one arm clutched around her middle, the other outstretched. Threads trail from her fingertips. A man in Refuge Force uniform moves toward her, drawn along a chain of silver threads. The way he minces along as if the ground under his feet is greased and slick seems familiar.

He sees me, knows I'm better 'n this. The scene strobes in and out, surroundings changing with each flash, time slipping by in an instant. The snarl of threads radiating from her seems to grow thicker, stronger with each flash.

I don't recognize the opulent rooms of Fuchsia's imagining—or Cadence's, really. They're like nothing I've ever seen before. The way Fuchsia pictures herself, clean and dressed in bright, flowing clothes with shimmering hair, is neither like the wild excess of Freedom nor the severe modesty of Refuge. She's somehow picturing all this without the benefit or disappointment of reality intruding. I can't help smiling at the blissful way she sinks into her vision, the hopeful way she imagines Refuge, but such idealistic perfection is too good to last.

Fuchsia raises food to her mouth, trailing a milky clot of threads. It rots before our eyes. The enforcer is there in the blink of an eye, as if summoned by the tangled cords, forcing the slop into her, pressing her down over the table, hand at her throat.

I know it's nothing more than a cruel fantasy inflicted by Cadence, but it feels as if the Mara are really here. I sense their hunger. And despite all my training, all that practice at ignoring others, despite knowing it's not real and Fuchsia's just a figment of Cadence's imagination, I can't take it. I can't accept her suffering and death, even if it's imaginary, even if she's not an innocent, not a child, not anything. I don't want to see this. I want it to stop. I want to make it stop.

I call out, but there's no sound, just crackling static. I claw the air, push drifting tendrils of translucent thread aside.

The enforcer shifts and changes. Fuchsia's flailing hands weaken under the weight of the snarled cords. I watch from some distance above and at the same time from within Fuchsia.

We cough, the ripe stench of decay filling our mouth, threads drawn tight around our throat. The enforcer shoves a mass of mouldy slop in our face. His other hand chokes at our neck, cutting off our air. We kick, flail, trying for an elbow to his gut. Our nails scrabble at his face, grasping for an eye to gouge, skin to shred, but they scrape against the porous grit of exposed bone. Empty, weeping pits in a bare skull leer down at us. We'd scream, but his hand's clamped over our mouth. Our lungs burn—

Distantly, someone cries out, *Cole, Cole!* The part of us that is not Fuchsia responds, trying to pull back. We're both too weak now. Darkness sweeps in.

A silver figure steps out of nowhere and tackles the thing the enforcer has become. Its roar batters me back and away from Fuchsia. The stranger—*Ash,* Cadence cries, and I tuck the name away for Ravel—pursues the monster with whirling blades, each blow slicing through hanks of thread as if they offer no resistance at all. Quick, but not quick enough.

The beast's bone-white head cracks the ceiling, its eyes empty pits that smoke and boil over with sludge. It bats him back, knocking him away in a tumble of limbs. Fuschia scrambles along a wall that stretches and warps, no doors. The floor cracks under the monster's weight, cratering with each step.

I flail against an invisible barrier. Fuchsia scrabbles against the wall for a way out as the Mara closes in. If I could just reach her, I could—I don't know, it's as if I could reach her, I could stop it, stop all of this, but I can't find a way through the tangle of threads. It's too late—the beast's claws reach her. She screams—

24 ASH

USCHIA SCREAMS AS the creature rips into her. It sprouts a single silver horn between the smoking, drooling craters where its eyes should be.

It bellows. The light draws swiftly downward, splitting it in two. The pieces ignite, a flash inferno that devours the world.

And then everything's quiet. I'm at the edge of the rooftop again, gazing toward the moonlit sea, one hand upraised as if plucking an invisible string from the sky.

A slight scraping sound. I turn.

Light glimmers, as though he reflects starlight like the distant ocean. He's younger than I'd realized. He looks up from tucking away a blade, eyes wide and wary. His face transforms, grim determination melting to something softer.

"Cady!"

"Ash," Cadence says in return, joyful and clear.

But it's my lips that move as she says it. I try to speak. The words catch in my throat.

He rushes to me. "What happened? Where have you been?"

Up close, glimpses of colour show under the swirling mist that covers his skin: warm brown, pale tan, shadows under his eyes.

"Um, things got complicated," Cadence says through me. What I want to say—*Who are you? What do you think you're doing? What's going on?*—is lost under her words. "But what took you so long? Where are the others?"

"Plan's changed—just me. It was harder to get past the barrier than I'd expected. Even after I found a way into the city, I couldn't reach you for days. And then when I did . . . You just about died, Cady. I was nearly too late. Why weren't you fighting back? Where are your parents? When did it get like this?"

Parents? So she really is—was—from outside?

Or at least, that's what she wants me to think. I take step back, putting some distance between myself and the boy. He shifts his weight as if he wants to reach out and stop me. I don't understand why she's forcing me to be silent, using me to speak to him, as if he can't tell the difference between us.

"Cady? There's not much time. Where's your anchor? I'll come find you."

Almost died? Cadence asks, but the usual way, not through me. Ash just keeps watching with those starlight eyes.

"I don't—I don't remember," she uses me to say.

Ash stares. "You don't know where your anchor is? What's wrong with you? You look so . . . Are you alone?"

"I'm—" She pauses, and I take another step back as Ash reaches for me—or her, I guess. "No. It's fine. Refuge. We're in Refuge, or below it, really. They call it Freedom, a lawless space at the foot of the tower. It shouldn't be that hard to find."

"Figures. It's nearly impossible to reach. I run into patrols every time I get near that area. It's like they know I've been looking for ages."

"You'll find a way. It's . . . it's good to see you again, Ash. You've, um, grown."

He smiles at that, reaches out again. This time, I don't move away, but it feels like everything else does. His touch is insubstantial, dissolving like mist along with the landscape— dreamscape?—around us.

Then he's gone. I'm in Freedom once more. Ash's silver-lit silhouette still wavers behind my eyelids when I blink.

"He's coming back for me," Cadence says.

He saw her, not me. *Cady*, he said. But it feels like I know him. I know that shadowed face, those wide eyes, that rigid determination. The midnight sky gathered for a moment in the shape of man to save us, more alien than the anonymous revellers in Freedom dancing their mad dance at Refuge's feet, yet more familiar, as if I've always known him.

No. It's Cadence who knows him, and he, her. I've just picked up on and gotten mixed up in their sense of familiarity through some mistake, some strange side effect of her haunting. Or is it calculated? Is that what Cadence wishes? That I didn't exist? That she could . . . what? Take my body? My life? Be me—or just live instead of me?

"I tried to tell you about him," she says, but her frustration is subdued. Stronger is the excitement in her voice, so strong it jumps to me like a spark and fizzes through my veins. "Ash. All grown up and come back for me. We have to go to him."

I shake my head at her, distracted from rising horror, as she must intend me to be. "That's impossible. He was never really even here."

"Oh. Right," she says with an air of great revelation.

"Just give it up. I'm not going to get sucked into your crazy delusions." But I'm distracted by the memory of dark eyes under a sheen of silver.

"You have to help. We're supposed to be on a mission to stop the Mara. You saw him fight. Just think of how many people we could help."

It's a tempting thought: pick up where Cadence left off. Take her place, her partner. Join this Ash in the fight to save everyone. There's just one problem: none of it's true.

ANGE

EVERYTHING ALL RIGHT? Is it another vision?" Ravel's female attendant leans over the edge of the bed. She produces a delicate cup of dust and presses it to my lips. "Ravel's orders."

Her eyes are hooded, inscrutable as she tips the drink into my mouth. It burns down my throat. I slump against the cushions as warmth seeps through me. With it comes a heavy, dizzy feeling that erases my frustration with Cadence. I taste sweet spice on my tongue and lick my lips for stray drops.

"Feel better?" The attendant asks.

I can't place her tone, her expression, not with the bright distraction of her mask and the weight of the drink's heat pressing me down and away from myself.

" ...? ...!" says Cadence.

I can no longer make out her lies. Nothing to fear. Nothing at all. If I were less numb and content, I might feel a pang that Ash isn't real, isn't coming for me, but reality and unreality alike seem so distant now. And anyway, I have Ravel.

"It was another vision, wasn't it?" The attendant whispers. "I can see it in your eyes."

Her features are outlined in arcs and accents of bright colour behind a purple and orange mask. Her clothes flutter as she moves, her skin painted in the same sunset palette right down to the nails. It's hard to tell where fabric ends and flesh begins.

She glances all around the chamber before stepping close.

"Ravel will want to know. Why don't you tell me? I'll write it down for him so you don't have to remember."

She flickers away to the other side of the chamber and reaches behind the drapery, one eye on me all the while, as if she doesn't trust me to be left alone. Maybe she fears Ravel—I can entertain the thought that he might be a fearful thing without fearing him myself, in this empty-full nothing-everything space.

She looks around the chamber again before stepping close. "Tell me."

Her dark eyes seem tired and lined behind all the paint and the glitter, her cheeks hollow over incongruously soft lips and a delicate chin. There's something familiar about her.

"Ravel will want to take you out again later," she says, more sharply. "It's easier this way. Why don't you just tell me, kid?"

I'm confused. What does she want, again?

"What's wrong with you?" Cadence says, her voice so distant I can barely make it out, so indistinct the words barely even register.

I raise one finger to admire the painted, shaped nail. Nothing's wrong. I feel amazing. Or rather, I feel nothing and everything all at once, which seems amazing.

Something snags under my touch. Darkness crowds the corners of my vision.

"Hey! Focus, you've got to focus." The attendant snaps in front of my face. "You can't do that. It's not safe, drifting off like that."

"Like . . . ?" I can't quite string the words together.

"Too much dust, huh?" The woman cuts her eyes at the empty glass. "You've got to focus, though. Don't let the dreams take you."

"Dreams?"

I work at making the appropriate expression, dragging my brows together in confused denial. I hadn't been dreaming. Wasn't she listening when Ravel explained about the visions?

"Listen, just try to focus for a minute, okay? He'll be back soon. I know he says you'll be safe here, indulging in all Freedom has to offer, blah blah blah. It's not that simple. Look, there really isn't time to explain it all right now. Just, how can I put this?"

She flutters a hand in the air and bites her lip, which transfers orange paint to her teeth. It's not a good look. She looks toward the back of the room. "Give me a hand here."

The other attendant brushes aside a wall hanging and approaches, ducking his head to eye the main door. His lips are aubergine to match the rest of his midnight-hued costume, though startlingly pink on the inner edge when he smiles.

"Haynfor, nice to meet you." He bobs his head in a friendly way.

The ID is familiar, as is his voice, though I can't quite place it. Maybe I'd met one of his series in the past.

The woman smacks him.

He rolls his eyes. "Cass, at your service. This delightful lady, by the way, is Ange."

"See? Was that so hard?" Ange says with an approving nod.

She darts in to press her lips to his. Orange and aubergine don't mix well, but he smiles as she pulls away and slips an arm around her waist.

"Right, love." Ange darts another glance over her shoulder at the door.

It makes Cass look again, which causes the feathers in her hair to tickle his nose. He sneezes.

"Cass. Focus. Ravel's little princess here needs a little guidance. Help me convince her to stay alive long enough for us to—"

Cass clears his throat, and Ange presses her lips together. "Right. Well, anyway, handle it."

"Sure you want to risk it?"

He's remarkably neutral as he asks the question. Ange's glare is sharp as glass. She hisses through her teeth and turns to me.

"Look, kid. I know you're from up there. I know something had to have happened to make you come here. You don't have to tell me anything. Keep your secrets; you don't have to buy trust from me. Not for this. Not yet. This one's on us. Chalk it up to my soft heart"—Cass snorts, and she digs an elbow into his ribs—"or maybe I just don't like to watch kids die. Or whatever. For now, you've got your own personal guardian angel looking out for you, no charge."

"Right over her head," Cass says.

Ange snorts. "Anyway, just listen to the big guy."

He raises his eyebrows at her, and then me, and says, "Don't dream."

Ange swats him. "Yeah, I tried that already. If you don't help properly, I'll send you back to wait alone."

"You know I love it when you're fierce." He pats her head.

She wrestles his hand off, losing feathers in the process, but her lips quirk up at the corner. Their obvious comfort with one another reminds me a little of Cadence and Ash.

I shove the thought away and get angry instead. "I. Don't. Dream." I've had enough of people doing and saying whatever they want to me.

"See?" Ange says to Cass, ignoring me. "She doesn't get it. I've seen her drifting off; seems pretty high risk to me. She won't be easy to get away from Ravel, either. Any ideas?"

Cass looks at me. I stare back, feeling tired and irritable. What's wrong with them? How did they both miss Ravel explaining about Cadence and the visions?

"Can you feel the music?" he asks.

I blink.

"The beat? Can you feel it?"

Cass reaches out to my knee and taps it once, again, again, each touch spaced out evenly, in time with the distant throbbing of Freedom. Then he moves his hand, patting the cushions beside me, a little stronger, so I can still feel the impact.

"You can want if you act on it, if you fill that want immediately," he says. "It's the wanting without having that calls the Mara. Refuge tries to teach you not to want, to empty yourself and stay hollow, but that's not possible—or not human, anyway. And surrendering to the Mara only gets you killed. Ravel has a different answer. He believes he can fill your wants with Freedom, keep you so full that you have no room for longings that go unfilled. That's his real angle, not all that nonsense about the Exchange."

Cass lets me sit with that for a moment. "You're not someone whose desires are so small and simple, though, are you? You really can't help dreaming. You call out to the nightmares without meaning to. You're too alive, too hungry, not empty but not full and satisfied, either."

I'm insulted. Of course I can empty myself. Of course I don't dream.

I try to rally enough outrage to give voice to my protest, but Cass is still thumping the cushions beside me. He moves his other arm to tap out a complex pattern on my bare knee at the same time.

Ange drapes her arms around his shoulders and leans in. "The masks don't help," she whispers, raising one hand to her own, but not removing it, not going that far. "They only keep us from seeing the wanting in each other. Dust doesn't really help either, at least not for long, not for the strong ones. It just dims things."

"There's a way to fill yourself without being full," Cass says, still tapping, "a way to keep yourself distracted and focused at once, so the Mara don't feel the hunger in you. Listen to the beat. Feel it. Let it fill you. Carry it with you even when it's not there. It's simple"—he stops tapping, but continues rhythmically thumping the cushions beside me—"and complex"—he starts up the racing taps on my knee once more—"and if you learn to hold on to it, it can keep you safe."

"Well, safer, anyway," Ange adds. "It'll help you hold out long enough."

Cass searches my face. I'm about to say I don't get it, don't know what they're talking about, but something in his low voice makes me stop. Maybe it's just the foggy, distant feeling of too much dust, but it makes a sort of illogical sense. The first thing I noticed about Freedom was the beat, the way it underpins everything here, working its way through the floors and walls and up into my bones, the way the high melodies and countermelodies play and fill you and draw you into the dance. I haven't been dreaming—but it couldn't hurt to take his advice and focus a little more on the beat. Maybe it could keep Cadence's visions away too.

He steps back, resting his hand for a moment on Ange's bare shoulder in passing.

"Well done, love," she murmurs. She touches his hand before he pulls away, smiling back at him, darts another glance to the door, and turns to me. "We're just trying to help you. You're not safe like this. Not with him. You understand, right?"

She presses my hand. I don't respond, though her words sounded a little like a threat. I look past her to watch Cass's retreat. He reminds me of Ash. Not that Ash is real.

But if he were, would he look at me the way Cass looked at Ange?

"Hey! What did we just say?" She grabs my jaw. Her touch isn't gentle. "Don't go drifting off like that."

There's a rustle of fabric, noise. Ravel sweeps into the room. Ange's grip shifts.

"Refreshed, flame?" Ravel flings himself on the cushions beside me as Ange fusses over my face. He bats her hands away. "It's fine, just put her in a wider mask or something. We'll be out late. I trust she's been dosed appropriately? Good. You're all dismissed until morning, then. Take your pleasure as you will."

He looks pointedly at Ange's smudged lips. Her gaze is shuttered as she backs away. It's as if she stopped being a person the moment Ravel arrived.

Ravel slips an arm around me and sweeps us off into the fray, not giving me a chance to mention my latest vision, or Ange's warnings, come to that. The effects of the dust have mellowed just enough to allow me to keep up but not so much I don't let the music in and let the dance take over.

I reach for Victoire, for the glittering spectacle Ravel seems to expect when he says her name. She's confident and coordinated, brilliant and bold and unfazed by the mad excess of Freedom. She's the key to fitting in, becoming who Ravel expects me to be, earning his approval, supporting his rebellion, and releasing the workers from Refuge's lies.

But I reach for the beat at the same time, not to guide my steps but to ground me. To keep me safe. To keep me full.

26 MANNFOR

WAKING UP IS not fun.

I'm all twisted and knotted up in a blanket, the fabric sweat-damp and gritty. It's like I've been slurping sour fog, my mouth sharp and fuzzy at the same time, my tongue swollen and heavy.

I should probably roll over and see if I can press down the queasiness, but even the slightest twitch makes my head pound and the room spin. I swallow hard, eyeing the distance to the facilities—a distance that rolls and stretches as I peer along its warping length. Will the misery be worth it? Do I have a choice?

As it turns out, no. No, I don't.

My body makes the tumbling rush to the cool safety of the bathroom without me getting too much in the way, drastically reducing the amount of cleanup someone will have to deal with—Ange or Cass, probably. Ugh. The chilly condensation of the facilities soothes the sticky heat of my face. I'll just stay here forever.

I last all of a minute before chattering teeth drive me under the shower head to let the steaming water soak through what remains of last night's outfit. The spray rinses tiny, reflective specks of glitter, swirls of white and gold paint, and spiky, wet feathers down the drain.

The memories are heavy and oily. Although steam is filling the air, I can't stop shaking. I can't. It's just . . .

Darkness, heat, abandon. An endless, exotic crowd of hungry revellers. Transformation. Glitter and shine and sweat. Liquid fire that scorches my tongue and settles deep inside. Feeling that heat rise on my skin and dance, every nerve alive. I don't have words for it.

That's a lie. Ravel taught me the word for her, the elegantly careless creature who owned Freedom last night, who dominated it alongside him, careless of death. *Victoire.*

Victoire, not me.

Not me.

Cadence whimpers. "Cole," she says, just that.

No! It wasn't me.

My stomach heaves. I barely make it out from under the stream of water in time. After, I curl on the floor. If I hold on hard enough, I won't shake. I can stay like this, safe, whole, alone. Forever.

"Not you, Cole?" Cadence whispers.

I curl tighter. Steam softens all the hard edges, diffusing the light. Everything feels so far away. Even her. I trail my fingers against the tile, watching the way condensation beads and bursts.

There's something else, too, as transparent as a drop of water but resistant when I poke at it. It clouds over like steam, a single, shimmering thread. It pulls away from the wall, trailing down at an angle. It's hard to tell where it's attached.

I give it a tug, remembering too late where I've felt this gossamer touch: every time Cadence inflicts another vision on me. I'm annoyed, and frustrated, and scared. Then I push away all the wanting for things to be different and pull on the empty-fullness of the beat like Cass showed me.

It's fine. I don't mind, not really. I refuse to. There will be longing, and then fear and pain, and then an end to it, and none of it will be my fault. I can't do anything about it.

And maybe, after the end, there will be Ash. Though I really shouldn't let myself look forward to meeting him. I know better. He's just a fabrication of Cadence's.

But I can't see anything. What if I'm trapped? Lost in some kind of in-between state? Or is this something else entirely—a dream, a real one?

Something crunches underfoot. My weight shifts forward. A dull, reddish glow grows somewhere off in the distance. I'm okay; it's just a place without much light. And I wish it'd stayed that way. Things are squirming, masses and masses of them all across the long, low, darkened room. Ugh. The floor is covered with heaps of some type of insect. If this were my body, I'd be throwing up again. But since it's not, I just feel his bored discontent as he shuffles along, shaking a wide container to scatter a fine rain of particles.

There's no double vision, no twinned realities—not so far, anyway, just this miserable, dim place. It's somewhere in Refuge, judging from his uniform hood and mask, but I can't think where.

The worker turns and heads back in the opposite direction. A pale strip of blue light above a door on the far wall marks an exit. He stares at it as he shuffles along. The light shifts and darkens until it's a pair of eyes gazing back at him through the narrow window of a uniform. Her uniform, standard issue except for a pair of heavy, high boots like his, bears division ID code 22. Nutrition Supply.

Noosh. Oh, no.

"That's messed up," Cadence says.

I silently agree. Then I feel better. None of this is real. It's all straight out of her imagination, so I definitely haven't been slurping down mashed bugs every day of my life. Probably. I can't dwell on my disgust anyway, because the Noosh worker, 22-Mann-04, is too fixated on the woman with the blue eyes. Threads nose out from him and radiate gently into the darkness. The woman has the next shift after his—the grubs that will become Noosh need constant feeding—so he gets to see her for a handful of seconds in passing each day.

We watch the exit, anticipating the moment we get to pass her in the corridor. If we hurry, we could finish a couple of minutes early, reach the elevator as it brings her to us. She'll be looking at the floor, waiting quietly. We'll get a precious extra second or two to watch her, see her lashes raise, her eyes crinkle in welcome, and glance away shyly. Wouldn't she recognize what it meant for us to go to the effort? Doesn't she feel the same way as us, trudging through every other minute of her day to get to the one that we're in?

As his wish takes form, the squiggling mass of grubs vanishes. They're replaced by a length of corridor choked with reaching threads, familiar elevator doors spreading to show a slight figure who looks up in welcome. Mannfor reaches out to her, hesitantly at first, then with growing confidence. She slips a warm hand under his mask to brush her thumb along his lips and run her fingers through his close-cropped hair.

Which is awkward for me. And astonishing. His dream is in clear violation of regulation. It lacks Liwan's open rebellion, but unlike the trainee, Mannfor doesn't seem to question or reject Refuge's teachings. He just yearns, quietly and persistently, for something he knows he can never have—and when that yearning produces something real, he sinks into it without a qualm.

He feels such satisfaction, such awe, as the blue-eyed woman steps closer. He accepts happiness, welcomes it, her, with open arms. She stretches up, slips aside his mask and presses her lips to his.

I can't quite put a word to what he feels, then, what I feel through him. There is excitement, of course, satisfaction, pleasure of a sort, but alongside his wanting, there is a lack of want. He seems to experience a kind of completeness, as though her touch has fulfilled all desire.

Is that why Cass and Ange touched lips yesterday? Does it feel like this every time? Would I feel like this myself, in my own skin and no one else's, if someone did this to me?

I consider Ravel, but find it hard to associate the sort of peace Mannfor is experiencing with Ravel's force of presence. Kissing Ravel seems like a burning thing.

I think of Ash. Though clearly capable of violence, the way he reached out had held the same sort of uncomplicated welcome Mannfor feels with the blue-eyed woman.

There's just one problem: Ash thinks I'm Cadence. Or rather, two problems: that, and the fact that Ash isn't real.

I'm angry, and then I'm not. I can't be, not while Mannfor's thoughts and emotions and sensations overwhelm me. His contentment is shifting, disturbed by more wanting. He holds his blue-eyed woman. The skein of threads between them tangle and strengthen.

When she pulls back, she grins, flashing serrated rows of teeth. Her tongue licks out, long and thin and pale as the squirming grubs they both tend.

We stare. He doesn't understand. I'd close his eyes, to spare us these final moments, but then we'd miss Ash's grand entrance, and despite everything, that's all I really have to look forward to in this. Plus, I don't have any control of Mannfor's movements anyway.

The woman's mouth widens, a slash from ear to ear.

Mannfor tries to pull away. His breath speeds as he panics, but not his, ours, because I'm closer to him in these final moments than to myself.

It holds us tight, arms snaking around us, constricting. We fix horrified eyes on its teeth, but it's the thing's arms that squeeze the breath from us. We cry out. It cracks our ribs and snaps the long bones of our arms.

Our mouth gapes, unable to draw breath. Our face twists, tears running freely, but it never moves to bite us. Our heart stutters and stops. Our head rolls back with blank eyes.

I separate from him then, released from his pain, and look down at his corpse. The threads clogging the air vanished with his consciousness. He's simultaneously covered over with squirming grubs in the Noosh cultivation room, and spattered across the elevator.

His is the sort of corpse that used to make my scalp tingle with fascination. The lines of what he's witnessed are carved into his face as its livid hue fades to a waxen pallor. But I lived his death, every overwhelming moment of it. There's no mystery. I'm more interested in why Ash hasn't shown up yet.

Then the twinned vision rolls away and Mannfor's form coalesces in the void that's left. He hangs in nothingness, limp, chest caved in. But he stares at me, aware.

"Don't, Cadence." My voice is almost steady. "Enough. Don't do this."

She's mimicking what I saw with Suzie, whatever that was. She lied to me, acted like she never saw it.

"Cadence. Seriously, don't. Make it stop."

Mannfor's edges are frayed and wispy. The rippling threads radiate into the darkness. Or nothingness. It's hard to tell the difference. His head flops forward. He has to roll his eyes up to keep staring at me, pleading with me. They're clear. For now.

I would cover my face if I could. Even though I know this is all just Cadence messing with me, I feel like a monster for taking his suffering so casually, dismissing it as uninteresting.

His gaze hardens. He's no longer begging, or maybe it's just the way he glares up from under dark brows, unable to raise his head. I hate Cadence for doing this to me, but I can't hold out against his display of disembodied torment.

"I'm sorry. I couldn't stop you. Couldn't save you. I'm sorry."

A whispering, rushing sound surrounds us and fills the empty spaces. Mannfor's chin sinks a little further. His eyes strain to keep pinning me down. The fraying at his edges works its way in, as though he's unravelling. Blood wells and tips out over his lashes to carve fresh lines down his cheeks.

"Mannfor." I wish I could reach out to him, wipe away the blood, smooth his face, raise his chin so he can at least look at me like a man and not a broken thing. "I'm sorry."

It's all I can say, so I make it mean more; sorry I can't make this stop. Sorry I cared so little about your suffering that I only wanted to get it over with. Sorry I still know more about what's going to happen next than you do.

I'm screaming into a cacophony of rushing noise now, as it rises and fragments into hundreds of shouting, shrieking voices. Mannfor opens his mouth. I strain to hear, hoping for something that will make this better. I know it would only be Cadence speaking through him, but I still want to hear *it's okay*. Or *I don't blame you*. Or *it's not your fault*.

He speaks, but I can't hear. Blood trickles from his mouth as he shows his teeth. His face contorts in a scream. I can't pick it out among the host of howling voices.

His narrow eyes tilt up at the outer corner. That's where the cloudiness spreads from. Or maybe that's where the colour drains to, the life in them seeping away.

I struggle to reach him. It's as if countless invisible hands are pushing against me, pulling me back and away. His mouth slackens, his chin rising as if his spine hasn't been pulverized, as if the threads are weaving him together instead of fraying him apart. He stares at me with empty, pearl-white orbs and smiles, slow and sharp. His teeth are serrated. His smile widens. There are rows upon rows, marching away into the void inside him. Then the darkness surges, overflowing his lips and pouring from his eyes.

I scream against the unfairness of it, against Cadence for forcing me to relive my helplessness, for introducing me to guilt and then steeping me in it.

Darkness drowns Mannfor's corpse. When it washes away, I'm alone on the bathroom floor, shivering, listening to Cadence gag in the background.

I hate her for pretending to be horrified by what she has created.

27

COMPROMISE

I DRESS ON my own, rustling around behind the wall hangings to find the stash of clothes and decorations and paints and even a pitcher of dust, all prepared and waiting. There's no sign of Ange or Cass.

It's time to take control of the situation. Even if Cadence's visions aren't real, from what the enforcers said, I know the Mara are still taking people in Refuge. If we could reach them and get Refuge out of the way, even with the horror of the Exchange, wouldn't that be better? One life for so many more?

I'll convince Ravel to save the workers right now. Maybe that's been Cadence's plan all along, to shock and motivate me, but that's almost certainly giving her way too much credit. She's sick, more twisted than I could ever have imagined. I see through her now. She takes joy in tormenting me.

I might not be able to stop her, but I can do something about the torment of others.

In my head, I sound much more determined than I feel. My stomach tells a different story, tangling into knots like the threads that drag me into the visions. I'm going to need all the confidence I can muster, which is why I choose a veiled mask from the shelf. It feels comfortingly familiar, brushing Refuge-style down the bridge of my nose and deflecting my breath back at me. It's the best of both worlds, the elaborate costume of Freedom with the comforting familiarity of Refuge modesty. I want to send a message: I don't care what name Ravel wants to call me, and I do want to please him, but I'm not just his doll. I need him to listen to me, properly listen, tonight.

That's the plan, anyway.

Ravel gathers me to him with an enthusiastic: "Victoire!"

He examines my costume. "That's a good effort, flame." He brushes back the veil on my mask, touches my lips with his thumb, and sighs. "But I'd like to make a few suggestions?"

He says it like a question, a warm lilt at the end, but though his lips smile, his eyes are sharp amidst the glittering frame of his mask. He lounges on the cushions, which I've rearranged carefully to hide leftover paint smears and glitter.

"Ange," he says, jogging his heel.

He doesn't yell, but there's immediately a rustling behind the far wall. Still, it's a few moments before she appears. She hurries across the room, eyes on the floor.

"My dear Angelique," Ravel says, with a beckoning flourish. Her shoulders are very tight and straight as she steps closer. "I trust you spent an enjoyable evening?"

"Uh-oh," Cadence whispers.

Ravel's voice is at its most liquid, golden and warm and smooth. The pink feathers in Ange's hair tremble, but the rest of her is rigid. Ravel swats a cushion off the edge of the bed and pats the clear space it makes beside him.

It's one of the places where I'd smeared paint in my sleep. Bedraggled feathers and glitter smear his palm. He cocks his head.

"Please, sit and tell me about your time off. Victoire doesn't mind waiting, do you, flame?"

Something's wrong. Was it my fault for getting dressed alone? I'd been hoping to make time to talk to Ravel in the quiet before the club really got going. But complaining about being kept waiting doesn't seem like a good move.

"Cole, do something."

Cadence sounds worried, which is absurd after all the twisted crap she's put me through over the last couple days.

"There, see?" Ravel croons, beckoning to Ange with both hands now. "My Victoire doesn't realize her own value at all, does she, Angelique? She has no idea how precious she is to me. How essential."

Ange perches beside him. Ravel grips her arm, pulling her off balance to land half on his lap. Her arm is pale where his fingers press in, but her face is smooth, her eyes hooded as she stares at the floor.

"You see, dear Angelique, some things, some precious few things are essential," Ravel slides his hand up her shoulder, smearing paint and glitter. He pauses, tendons ridging his skin as Ange's face pales, then slides his hand down again, slipping under her arm and around her waist, where his fingers stroke, slowly, slowly as he continues. "And others are, well, not."

His nails circle hypnotically on her skin, leaving white trails that flush red after a moment, spirals and tangles of red. His other hand strokes the side of her face, and then grips her jaw, tightening as he says, "So what I need from you, darling, is to help lovely Victoire here remember just how precious and absolutely essential she is to me."

His nails bite in as he jerks her head in an exaggerated nod.

"And while I know you understand this perfectly, I'm just not seeing the evidence I'd like to see that you're committed to what I value. So please, why don't you tell me"—he runs his thumb up to part her smudged lips, scraping his nail along her teeth *tck-tck-tck*—"just what's so important to you that you fail in your service to me and mine?"

"Pig." Cadence's voice trembles. "Do something, Cole! Are you really just going to watch this?"

But I'm not Cole, am I? I'm Victoire; he just said so. Precious and essential—and not, just now, trapped in his lap while he asks dangerous questions. I need Ravel's power, his way with people. I need him to keep thinking I'm something special, to keep wanting me. Besides, I'm done letting Cadence try to manipulate and control me.

But I squirm, thinking of Ange and Cass last night trying to help me, bantering and cuddling. Kissing. I feel bad about it, I do, but there's nothing I can do or say that could stop Ravel from scolding her for breaking the rules and not doing her job. He's only disciplining one of his staff. I shouldn't judge Freedom by Refuge standards. Touch isn't a crime here.

But I do need to get him to focus on me, if I want to talk him into taking action against Refuge.

"Don't you like how I look?" I say, and though it's my voice, it's Victoire's attitude infusing it. "Doesn't this please you?"

The words come out pouty and teasing, artfully pleading on the surface and confident below. I do a little pirouette. Ravel's attention shifts from Ange. His foot stops bouncing in the air. I step closer, a Victoirish swing to my hips making me a little unsteady, my own ungainly awkwardness making it worse.

"Oh, flame," Ravel breathes, tilting his head, "you're incandescent, of course. But I can't have my Victoire tired out by menial chores when there's a whole night ahead of us."

"Oh, but—" I pause on purpose, as if suddenly shy. I'm terrified, queasy, light-headed, and not entirely sure where I'm going with this. Shy doesn't even begin to cover it.

Ravel's hands still. Then he shunts Ange off to the side and stands to take my hands instead.

"Sorry, flame. It's been a rough day—one too many incompetents to deal with. Too many failures getting in my way."

I struggle not to cringe as he spits out the word "failure."

He strokes my hand, searching my face. "What is it? Tell me, go on."

"It's just," I say, a little high, a touch too breathless, but he's glowing at me, intent, and there's nothing for it but to push onward, "I-I sent her away, so we could, you know. Talk. Alone."

"Alone." He tilts his head, looking at me from under his lashes. "You sent her away?"

I nod, a little teary, but I think it just seals it for him.

"Um," Cadence says, "good job getting Ange off the hook. But seriously?"

I burn to tell her to shut up, but with Ravel so close . . .

"Ange," he says, sliding one hand around to the small of my back, "my Victoire wants some alone time with me. Out."

I bite my tongue to keep from shuddering and glance past him to Ange, standing wide-eyed by the bed. She shakes her head in sharp, tiny movements. A bead of blood wells up and slips down the side of her chin.

"Stall," says Cadence.

As much as I don't trust her, that might be a good idea. "B-but I realized after I sent her away it's a lot of work dressing the way you like. So maybe Ange could wait until we've had a chance to talk and then fix my mistakes?"

Ange nods and wipes away the trickle of blood on her face.

He tips my chin up. I avoid his gaze, examining the winking gold threaded through his ears. "Well, if you're sure that's what you want, flame."

Heat radiates off him. It makes little glittery lights dance at the edge of my vision until he steps back so I have room to inhale.

"Go clean yourself up," he says to Ange, who's carefully gazing at the floor. "Then wait for me to call. We will be requiring your services tonight after all."

He flings himself on the bed once more, scattering cushions as he takes over the space, half reclining.

"Join me," he says.

It's not a question.

28

MARYAM

R AVEL REALLY LIKES touching. This is increasingly clear the longer I spend with him. It's a problem for a few reasons. First, he never seems to get enough of it. Second, it's uncomfortable and terribly distracting. I know it's not considered disobedience in Freedom—quite the opposite, in fact—but it's one of the harder rules to adjust to here. Third, it gets in the way of me communicating effectively with him, and that, after all, is the point right now.

"I, um, I wanted to . . ." I shrink back. He tightens his grip, so I'm worse off than when I started. "I wanted to talk. Um, can you, can you not . . . ? Just, can we just talk, you know?"

I've lost all my Victoirishness in a bundle of signature Cole awkwardness, and I'm too busy squirming to get enough of the right words out. I don't see any way out of this. I need Ravel's help, and he seems to need me half in his lap. He's never pushed it before like this. Cadence is nattering away indignantly, which isn't helping, either.

"Just, I need . . ." I wedge my elbow down between us and lever myself away a little.

Ravel tents his eyebrows at me in a melting sort of way. I try again.

"So I had—Cadence sent more visions." I scoot toward the edge of the couch-bed while I have the chance.

"And I know you wanted to know if that happened again, and actually it gave me some ideas about the rebellion, and—"

He pulls me back, unfazed. "Oh, flame, there's all the time in the world for talk. It's not important."

"I—I really think it is." I push away, though he seems to take my hand on his chest as an invitation. I try to repeat the elbow trick, end up overbalancing, and land in a heap on the floor. He laughs.

I talk fast, outlining the visions of Fuchsia and Mannfor. I don't like telling him about Ash, but he prods when I get vague about how the visions end. I end up spilling all of it, even how Cadence won't let me speak to Ash.

Ravel's quiet for several long minutes.

"I don't see how it could be any clearer, flame," he says at last. "That ghost of yours is bad news, and it's only getting worse. I've got to take care of something later, but I'll stay with you as much as I can, okay? I'm sure I can keep you distracted enough she won't be able to get in."

I bite my lip, not sure whether to be relieved or worried about this development. If he really can keep the visions away . . . But I'm afraid to ask just how he thinks he can do that, and it wasn't why I wanted to talk to him in the first place.

"Actually, I was thinking not so much about what I'm experiencing, but, you know, like, with the Exchange, if we could bring more people in, then it wouldn't be so bad after all?"

He slips to the floor in a tumble of cushions. "The only people I care about right now are"—he points at me, making a little circle in the air with his index finger— "and"—he thumbs back at himself, grinning.

I scuttle backward. "And I'm grateful to have a place here, really, I am, but those enforcers made it sound like the Mara were taking more and more people, and I thought if we could just get them out of Refuge and down here—"

"Enforcers?"

"When the surveillance system was down, you know? On Floor 20? They didn't know I was there. It sounded like there had been other deaths, but the body was really messed up, and they said things were getting worse and—and the shields didn't work anymore, and neither did following regulation, and the mayor had commissioned them to, I don't know, do something about it or figure it out or—"

"They talked about M—" Ravel swallows the rest of the word, sighs. "Victoire. Flame. I appreciate you taking the time to share your story with me. This is fascinating, although of course I knew it all already. You say they were on special commission to the mayor?" He pauses, ever so slightly, before the word *mayor*. "Think carefully. It might be important."

"Yes, I think they both were, or maybe not the inspector . . ." I frown. It had been ages ago, and I'd been so freaked out at the time. "At least, at first it sounded like both, but then later I thought it might have just been the junior enforcer, even though he looked like a mess."

"You met him again?" Ravel's voice is gentle, but his fingers drum the floor.

"Well, I never really met him, I just overheard them, and then at the bottom of the stairs the enforcer was there again, talking to someone, but I ran away, and I don't know if he even knew it was me—and anyways, they seem to have stopped looking for me, and I'm so grateful for all you've done, but I think it's really important that the other workers know about Refuge's lies and that they're not safe, you know, even if they're not ready, and—"

He scoots closer. "Poor flame. You're overwhelmed, aren't you? It's been hard on you, I know. But you're here now. Safe. You know I'll take care of it, don't you? You know I won't let them get you?"

"It's not about me."

He's slipping away from the point again.

"Flame, really. I'm a little disappointed. I thought you trusted me. If I didn't know better, I'd be hurt."

"I—I didn't mean—"

"Oh, but you did. You always do. You never trust me, never believe I can handle it on my own. You all wish I'd never been born. None of you ever—"

He jolts to his feet. I scramble backwards. My hand catches on the edge of one of the heaped carpets blanketing the floor. I lose my balance. My head smacks against the floor, a gap in the rugs.

Ravel looms, his shadow falling over me. His eyes have gone glassy. My ears are ringing. I don't understand. What's wrong with him?

"Send me away, don't send me away." He sways on his feet, unfocused. It's as if he doesn't see me at all. "It's too late, Your Worship, too late for me, too late for you, too late too late. Your fault, all your fault. Why won't you look at me?"

I push up on my elbows. The room swims. His blank gaze shifts slowly, so slowly. I half expect to see his golden irises gone pearl-white.

"Don't you trust me, Ma-ry-am?" He hisses, staring past me as he leans in. He plants a foot on my chest and presses.

"I don't know what—"

Then I feel the thread snag around my fingertips. I seize it, perversely grateful to Cadence for the reprieve.

SHE LOOKS OUT on glimmering brilliance. Mirrors line the walls to multiply the opulence. She herself positively shines, the silken gold of her hair matched by her glowing gaze, startlingly like Ravel's but round eyed and framed by flawless skin no line or mark has ever dared mar.

Her name is Maryam, but nobody has called her that— just Maryam—not to her face, not in a very long time. She's addressed as *My Lady* and *Your Worship* and *Mayor Ajera*. I know her, or of her: Mayor of the Towers of Refuge, Chief of the Council of Guardians, First Mother to the Citizens, Breath of Tower Regulation.

Of course, I've never seen her. I have no way of knowing if she actually looks like this, or if it's just the way Cadence imagines her, weaving a fantasy out of Ravel's ravings. I don't understand his obsession with the head of Refuge, and caught in the midst of Cadence's vision, it's hard to remember none of this is true. The mayor doesn't share Ravel's astonishing eyes. It's just Cadence weaving scraps of memory into a trap for my mind. Or an escape.

I melt into the golden woman.

A rabbit trembles on our lap as if aware it stands out like a target, shockingly white amidst the richly gleaming hues of our audience chamber.

We soothe it. It brings us no pleasure to see lives taken, but what can we do? No more than we have done: protect those who would entrust their lives to us, sacrifice the few so we might protect the many, preserve the faithful and regretfully expose the rebellious in this unending devils' bargain. It really is better this way; controlled, balanced.

In the time before, there was no meaning, no pattern. People just died, good people and bad people, obedient people and troublemaking people, and there was no reason and no way to protect them. So much hurting. Such fear and anger. Once, the rage and the loss had even threatened to take us. The memory has become distant, faded—the feeling of that small, warm body, scarcely the length of our forearm, with such fragile, tiny fingers and toes. How cold, how stiff he had been, lying there at the end.

We will never forget, not after all these years, nor for all the years to come. It was our source, our reason, our meaning for continuing, for playing these terrible games, for making these cruel bargains month after month. The masters cursed us with this terrible beauty, this never-fading youth. We will never be free. That final ember of distant memory smolders, buried deep in our wrinkled, aged heart beneath ever-renewed skin that has hardened around us like a shell: smooth, and beautiful, and strong.

I surface, gasping into consciousness. The similarities are eerie, the way Cadence gathers the threads of Ravel's rule in Freedom and feeds them into the story. How dare she fabricate such lies?

But . . . maybe there's a deeper purpose. It's manipulative, but it feels like she's been showing me all of it for a reason. To make me care, to remind me of myself and my—our—mission. To push me to see, and to question, and to act.

The vision pulls me in again.

They come. Shadows bubbling fog-like around the edges of draperies and walls, twisting, churning columns of nothingness that hide the true masters of our once-beautiful city. The air sours, the rich scent of flowers and spice turning, decaying, sticky and bitter on the tongue. Small breezes snatch at the edges of the wall hangings and make our gown and hair dance, tickling our face and caressing our skin.

The rabbit cowers in terror.

We remain serene. It is their game to hint at horrors in the twist and warp of indistinct form, to threaten and torment with insubstantial images, but it has gone on too long. We will not be moved by the Mara's games. Not like this.

The formless masses spin together, coalescing into two shapes, one man-height and one tragically smaller, their silhouettes achingly reminiscent of those we lost so long ago. Too long ago. They have tried this tactic on us too many times for it to truly sting any longer.

"My lords," we say.

"Our lady." The breeze sighs in our ear. "We await your report."

It is part of their game, we're sure, to demand reports on our efforts to control Refuge, to maintain the masses in obedience and order, to arrange and preserve the protections around them. The Mara surely know of everything done within their borders better than we do, for who can stop them going where they will? And yet we make our reports, dutifully, passionlessly, while they poison the air around us.

The rabbit's panicked heartbeat slows.

We speak in unhurried, rehearsed tones. Our throat grows clogged and swollen. We report accelerated Noosh production, increasing need for chemical suppressants, adjustment of working hours to quell an increase in energy and creativity until the additional suppressants can be generated. We are concerned the ranks of workers are being thinned out. It's getting increasingly difficult to replenish them. Also, the corrosive fog is damaging our infrastructure and necessitates repairs. We try not to sound accusatory.

The Mara make concerned noises that ricochet on the choking drafts. They seem amused at the irony of our situation. They fall silent when we report that the latest corpses exhibit unusual marks and environmental damage, though we are sure we suppressed every hint of accusation that could have crept into the account.

All that remains of the rabbit is a sunken pile of bones under desiccated leather. We run one bony finger over it lightly. It collapses to the floor between our sagging thighs. Our breath rattles, bruising our weakened lungs. Our chin droops, neck grown unable to bear the weight of our balding head. It's painful almost beyond bearing to maintain our steady, calm gaze.

We fall silent, our reports completed as they had begun, without inflection or complaint.

"You've been hiding something from us." *The Mara wait until we're finished, until we are at our weakest to bring the accusation. If they'd allowed it, our heart would have stopped.*

"My lords," *we rasp, searching for an excuse.*

"You conceal our enemies. You wish to be freed?"

"I conceal nothing. There is no threat."

"The girl survives."

We pause, considering. Would they end us if we admitted to concealing the child? Would we at last be free? But there is no true freedom left in this city. Perhaps no true freedom left in any place beyond it. We'd hoped the strangers would be able to tell us, but only the girl survived. Neither her parents nor her mind reached us intact all those years ago. We'd hoped, one day, she might remember, but . . .

"It's me," Cadence whispers. "She means me. I remember. My family. We were like Ash. We were sent here to fight. Against the Mara."

Her voice drags me out of the horrifying, fascinating play. The woman decaying before my eyes. The warped columns of poison fog speaking from everywhere and nowhere at once.

Her imagination is unparalleled. I can't envision what she would have been like alive. What she would have been able to do, if she'd lived in a place where such a powerful imagination wasn't a death sentence.

What if Cadence's visions were never about me at all? Just fantasies to give her own weird, ghostly existence meaning and importance? Has she been leading up to this supposed revelation all along? But . . .

"Then why am I here?"

"I don't know. Somehow, the way I am with you, something has crossed over. Some of my—our power—has transferred to you, brought you into all this. I'm sorry, Cole, I really am, but you're a part of this now. You can't just ignore it. You have to believe me."

I'm drawn under again as Maryam speaks.

"There is no threat," we repeat. "Outsiders came, years ago, it's true. The adults were dispatched quickly. There was a child, but she was simply used as any other, wiped clean and added to the workforce. She's gone now. I don't have her. I harbour no enemies of my lords."

"She's no child now," the Mara say with many voices. "We know what was done. The cost of disobedience is high, Ajera. Do you still desire to continue in your service?"

We swallow thickly and cough. This is our chance to give in, to accept death. If we didn't suspect it no longer held true escape, if we didn't still perhaps have one left worth sacrificing for, we would have given into our longing for it long, long ago. But how very interesting they should bring up the girl now, so soon after we lost her. So soon after he took her. What threat does she hold to nightmares as powerful as they? There may yet be hope, if his rebellious selfishness doesn't doom us all.

We sigh over the memory of a proud face and a pair of defiant golden eyes. He's not our son. Our son is dead. But Ravel is something to us. Our responsibility. Our last bond.

"*I will continue,*" *we gasp and sigh with relief as our ageless, perfect form is renewed.*

"*What is the price of your service?*" *The voices continue, chorusing through the ritual.*

"*I entreat the obedient ones be spared through the disciplining of their thoughts and the rite of surrender and the brilliance of the sacred gold. Let the wards of the many be renewed in the blood of the few.*"

"*Your price is granted.*"

And the masters are gone, leaving us alone in our golden chamber with a tiny, desiccated corpse at our feet and a burning hatred in our heart.

29

HAUNTING

RAVEL IS ROCKING, arms wrapped tight around himself. He's scored lines over his biceps, a criss-crossing tangle of tracks weeping red over black ink. He babbles, begging forgiveness, his voice pitchy and uneven, uncharacteristically high and boyish.

I hurt. The memory of Maryam Ajera's suffering clings to me, and behind it lurks Ravel's unfocused glare and the pressure of his foot bearing down on my sternum. When I take a breath, it rasps. I cough.

His head jerks up at the sound.

"Victoire! Oh, flame, you shouldn't have made me—I really didn't want to hurt you like that. You understand, I know you do. You know I'm so sorry, don't you?"

I concentrate on breathing and avoid eye contact.

He runs a fingernail along my cheekbone where it meets my mask. "It was another vision, wasn't it?"

I shake my head. His nail digs in, just a little.

"I can see it in your eyes, flame, remember? Tell me."

"Don't talk to him." Cadence sounds tired. "Don't trust him. He's been lying to you this whole time."

And that's what it comes down to. Who's been lying to me? A dead girl, delighting in inflicting torment—or just caught up in her own fantasies and dragging me along for the ride? Is that really Cadence? But the alternative is even harder to accept, that she has, I don't know, magical powers to survive dreams.

Powers that somehow absorbed into me as she haunted me, inadvertently ruining my life—and then all this time, Ravel's been using me to what? What's the point for him? To learn things he shouldn't know, like a magical surveillance system? Or does he just get a rush out of messing with me?

I can't sort it out. The threads are too tangled. There's too much I don't know. But there might be a way I can find out who's telling the truth.

I tell Ravel about dreaming Maryam—all of it. I tell him about the mirrored room and the golden woman and the forms the Mara took, a man and an infant. A muscle at the side of his jaw ticks. I tell him about the rabbit and how Maryam crumbled, and he blinks fast and looks away. I tell him how she made a deal to offer sacrifices to the Mara in exchange for control of Refuge, the chance to save some. I point out how very similar that sounds to the way he runs Freedom. His teeth grind. I tell him how, at the end, she thought of a small boy with eyes like his, a boy she wouldn't call son, a boy she kept living for.

He turns away. "Remember, flame, they're not really dreams. We've got to do something about that ghost haunting you. She's crazy. Dangerous. Don't listen to anything she says. Trust me."

"He's lying to you. Why can't you see that?" Cadence sounds close to tears.

"I know," I tell him, resting a hand on his shoulder. "I know now she's been lying to me all along."

"Cole! I promise I haven't. Don't do this."

"I trust you. I know you're doing the best you can for us"—his face lights up— "and I think it's amazing what you've built here, I really do. But Refuge needs to fall. The dying has to—if it can't stop, at least be less. We have to make them understand, bring everyone together. Please, Ravel—"

"You're too naïve, flame." He takes my hand, eyes smouldering, but I'm not drawn in this time. Not even a little bit. "If it weren't for me, you wouldn't have survived this long. You don't understand how things really work. Just listen to me, and everything will be fine."

I lift my chin and smile, slow and sharp, as if I'm Victoire.

He nods approvingly. "It's time for another Exchange. You'll choose the sacrifice."

"Cole, no!"

I nod. He bows with a flourish, kisses my hand, and bounds off, pausing at the door. "Ange, make her ready for tonight."

"Cole—"

"Not now."

Ange appears beside me, Cass at her elbow.

"You're her," I say.

She freezes. "I don't know what you mean."

Cass shifts his weight.

"I met you, that first night when I ran from the enforcers." I say. "You tried to warn me. Why did you leave me there?"

"Ange." Cass's tone is warning and pleading at the same time.

She sighs and runs a hand over her hair. "What do you want, kid?"

"Can you help me?"

She looks at me for a long moment. Cass peers over her shoulder. She reaches back for his hand and they do that thing of theirs, a silent conversation.

"If you really want to go, we'll get you out," he says finally.

She nods.

It's a start, but it's not good enough.

"Where?" I ask. "I can't go back to Refuge."

Ange shakes her head. "We can't tell you. But it's away from here. You'll be safe there."

"Ravel won't be able to reach me? Or Refuge's enforcers?"

"No one from up here knows about it, not unless they're one of us."

"Good." I take a deep breath. "That's a start. Now, how about the rest?"

"The rest of what?" Ange says blankly.

"The people. The dancers. The workers. The ones outside. What about them dying?"

"One thing at a time, kid." Cass looks like he's trying not to laugh. "Let's focus on you for now and worry about the rest later, okay?"

I frown.

"I'm not going anywhere unless you tell me why you're willing to let me in, and how you're going to help stop the dying."

If Cadence's visions—or dreams, apparently—have shown me anything, it's that just surviving isn't good enough anymore.

"What are we going to do with you?" Not waiting for an answer, she demands of Cass, "What are we going to do with her?"

"You could start by calming down, love." He slips an arm around her shoulder, softening the words. "She doesn't understand. How could she? If anything, at least she's learning to ask the right questions."

"I said—"

Cass's look brings me up short. "Hold your horses, kid. We'll help you—and you're not wrong to want to know why and what you're in for with it—but there's no time, and frankly, there's not much reason for us to trust you."

"I'm not staying here another night."

Tense lines bracket Ange's mouth. "It's too soon. She's not ready. We're not ready. Ravel's not done with her. He'll know something's up."

"So, we leave her here. Clean her up and send her out."

Ange gives Cass a look, then stalks away. She vanishes behind one of the wall hangings at the back of the room. Her sarcasm is muffled as she says, "Of course we do. What's one more kill?"

Her arms are full as she walks back. She dumps it all next to me and perches on the side of the bed to press a wet cloth to the side of my face. She's really going to send me out to Ravel.

"Please, I—I can't sacrifice someone like that again. But if you're not—"

"We're on the level, and that's about all I can tell you until we know you won't fall back into Ravel's hands or Refuge's. We happen to be in a position to help.

You're just going to have to take our word for it for now. We're already risking our place here just to help you."

"You're spies?"

Cass chuckles. "Ange's the one on crusade. You should've seen her face when she figured out being the man's stylist was the best way to stay on the inside. I'm just here to keep her out of trouble 'til I can convince her to settle down. Word of advice: don't fall for a crusader." He winks. Ange rolls her eyes.

"We mostly keep our heads down," she says. "But you say you need to get out now. So, here we are. How's your memory?"

"Um . . ."

"Cass? Can we give her a map? Do you know how to read a map, kid?"

"Better not risk it," Cass says. "She can just follow the lights."

"Listen close, okay? It's not that hard." Ange twists fresh feathers into my hair. They're not tiny white down this time, but longer, mottled brown and dull red with a broad curl to them. "When you get out, head for the green room. There's a spot on the far wall, just before you hit the orange room. Look for blue lights, low on the wall, like this high"—she taps a gold armband clamped a couple inches above my elbow—"flashing repeatedly, but faint, right? Because the light should be green. Follow them if you get lost. Push where they stop; the door's just beyond. Cass will get someone to guide you from there."

"What about you?" I turn. She shoves my chin back so she can keep working on my hair.

"I'm staying here to buy time. Ravel will come back looking for you. I'll pretend I misunderstood and sent you out after him already. He'll think he's lost you in the crowd, maybe captured by enforcers—"

"Refuge Force is out there?" I dig my fingers into my palms.

"Probably not," Cass says. "And anyway, they'd have a tough time recognizing you like this."

He has a dull red garment for me that matches the feathers. He fits it over my shoulders and adds a matching belt, broad but not too tight. When he turns me to a mirror,

I'm a new kind of alien. The feathers form a sort of cap over my head, closer to the colour of natural hair. A wide mask flattens my face, and the costume pins all the diaphanous layers down, darkening and broadening my shape. There is still a touch of glitter, but not nearly as much as I've grown accustomed to.

"You won't attract so much attention like this," Ange explains, tugging some of the layers smooth and tucking others back from my legs. "And you'll be able to move faster without all that gold weighing you down. If Ravel does catch you, it'll still look like we've done our jobs. Not well, but . . ."

"It took a lot to get this close to Ravel." Cass pulls Ange back and fits her under his arm. She hangs onto his hand over her shoulder, turning to press a kiss onto his cheek before fixing sharp eyes on me. "We can't risk losing this kind of access. But it's going to be okay; you'll see. With a little luck, we'll be able to spirit you away and get back to business as usual in no time. Unless the boss here says we can cut the charade and take you ourselves . . . ?"

He raises his eyebrows at Ange. She swats him. He shrugs, grimacing comically. I grin at their antics; it helps keep my stomach from turning over at the thought of actually walking out the door.

"Cole, we don't have time for this," Cadence says. "We need to go find Ash."

I ignore her. Even if she's been telling the truth this whole time, there's something she doesn't seem to have worked out yet. We have no idea how to get out of Refuge. Even if Ash were real, he wouldn't be the ally I need, not right now, anyway. Cadence can wait a little longer. She owes me that much.

I stare at my feet, just breathing, feeling the ache in my chest that Ravel left. I don't have the best track record with allies. It turns out I couldn't trust him to save anyone. I never had a chance of convincing him to do anything he didn't already plan to do. Or not do. Will this group Ange and Cass are in be any better?

It'll have to be. I'm out of options.

30 RECONCILIATION

I STRAIGHTEN MY shoulders and watch Cass and Ange. The way they can communicate comfort and assurance and acceptance and determination just through touch is astonishing. Ravel's body only speaks a language of control, always broadcasting, but never receiving.

I'm finally ready to go.

"Hurry." Ange smiles, but the edges of her mouth are tight. "We'll see you when we can."

"We'll see you soon," Cass corrects. "You're gonna be fine. Trust me."

I'd like to. I like the rough, warm way they talk to me and to each other. I like their casual touch, so unlike Refuge reserve and Freedom heat alike.

I slip out into the maelstrom of Freedom carefully, keeping my gaze low to avoid eye contact. I watch out of the corners of my eyes for Ravel, enforcers, or anyone else shoving against the rhythm.

"Cole," Cadence says over the noise, nothing now to interrupt her but the endless beat, the twisting melodies. "We need to talk."

I hunch my shoulders. "Not now. Wait a little longer." I cross from the blue room to the purple.

"Look, I'm sorry about what happened on the rooftop, I really am, but I'd have thought by now you'd have realized how important that was, making contact with Ash—"

"Enough!" The nearest dancers' steps stutter at my shout. I duck my head and scurry past into the green hall before they can take a closer look. "I don't have time for this. I know you're all messed up from being dead and having no life of your own to live and all, but I'm way too busy trying to salvage mine right now."

"Really? I'm not the one who's always looking for someone else to make things better. Yeah, I'm dead. I know, okay? I don't have a voice—"

"You don't have a voice? Is that some kind of joke? When you won't let me even talk to Ash, and steal all his attention, and—you know what? This is all your fault in the first place."

"Look, I can't do anything. We both know that. But you can. So why don't you stop running away and shoving your problems on someone else all the time?"

"If it weren't for you making trouble in the first place, I wouldn't have had anything to run away from. You don't get to tell me I haven't been trying. I've done the best I could. It's not my fault if you could've done better. I'm here. You're not."

Cadence doesn't say anything.

I've gone too far. I'm at the border of the white room already. I need to backtrack. I head for the nearest wall, slipping and bumping and diving between bodies until I reach it.

"Whatever made you think you needed Ravel to speak for you?" she says finally, so softly I barely hear her over the wash of sound.

Stupid question. Finding allies was her idea in the first place. Besides, I don't want to talk to people. And they don't want to listen to me. What would've been the point of trying to expose Refuge's lies on my own? I'd have been captured immediately. And even if enforcers hadn't dragged me off before I could get a word out, the first worker I tried to convince would've turned me in for violating regulation.

"Tell me," she says. "Tell me why you trusted him to help you instead of me."

"You just don't get it." I kick the wall, forgetting it's really a huge, stiff curtain. It absorbs the force, rendering my action meaningless. I put my back to it and slump, letting the fabric cradle me. "You're too close. You don't see how I can't—"

"I would have helped you."

"You couldn't. I'm just too—people just don't like me. They can tell there's something wrong with me. They wouldn't have wanted to listen."

"There's nothing wrong with you, Cole."

"Oh, really? I'm obsessed with death. You don't think that's a problem? You don't think that makes me wrong?"

"Are you?"

I flush. What does she know? I shove away from the suffocating wall and throw myself into the mass of dancers, fighting through them toward the green hall, elbows hammering my ribs, feet tripping me up.

"You know I am. You've always known, haven't you? Right from the start. I bet it's because of you, I—"

"Tell me what it's like. When did it start?"

"You know when it started. That man, that night. On Floor 6. You know. The Mara-taken. I got in trouble the morning after."

"Why did you do that?"

"I—Oh, I don't know. Because I wanted to, okay?"

"Why did you want to?"

"Really?"

She waits.

"I just . . . He was just so still, and the way he looked . . . He'd been through something, felt something terrible. Incredible. Something. You could see it on his face. Even with those eyes, you could see it in him."

"So, you went up to him. Touched him. And then what?"

"Nothing. Then nothing. Just, cold, empty, still. And I liked that, too, in its own way."

Someone's elbow jabs the worst of my bruises. I curl over; catch another that sends me stumbling to my knees.

"What else?" Cadence is focused, relentless, ignoring the way I'm about to get trampled. "It's not like you went around seeking out Mara-taken all the time. Why do you think you're obsessed?"

"I don't even have to touch them, really." I gather my feet, get tangled in trailing fabric, and trip again, bruising my knees.

I'm not sure why I'm saying all this to her except it's easier than fighting about it. And it doesn't feel bad, exactly. It's almost a relief to finally have it all out there. "Mostly, I can't touch them. I'd get in trouble. But so many died on Floor 6. Just looking at them, I'd—There's a feeling to it, like a buzzing, aching sort of pressure at the back of my head, and then it would sort of tingle all under my hair. After a while, I didn't have to see someone die. Just remembering or thinking about it was enough to start obsessing all over again. What they looked like. What they must've felt."

I give up on trying to untangle my legs and crawl. When I run into another fabric wall, I look up. There's a blue light flashing along it about three feet up.

"Then there was Suzie. Bell. You remember, the Mara-taken on Floor 20. That's when it started, the dreams. That's because of you, right? You said when we were with Maryam it's connected to you somehow."

She's silent long enough that I think she's gone away again. The music starts to work itself into my bones and my head and my chest, smoothing out my movements, teasing out Victoire from the small place she retreats to when there's no audience to impress.

And then Cadence speaks, hesitantly, as if I might run away, even though she's the only one I can never run from.

"I think it's all because of me, everything that's happened to you. I didn't mean for any of it to happen, but . . . You've seen Ash fight, right? He's special; he can enter the dreams of others, fight for them, save them. I was like him, before.

"I'm sorry, Cole. I never meant for you to be involved, but it seems like you've been picking up on what I can—could—do at some level all along. Somehow, something was blocking the dreams until Suzie, and blocking my memories too. And even before that . . .

"You're not obsessed with death; you're drawn to it. There's a difference. What you describe—it's a summons. You're being called to people in trouble, the way I would have been. For Ash and me, it's how we reach the victims. How we save them. I don't know why it's happening to you. I didn't think it could."

I brace my hands on the stiff green fabric of the wall. Blue light winks over them. I can't breathe. "Why didn't you tell me sooner?"

"At first, I didn't know what was happening any more than you did. When the memories started coming back . . . I didn't handle it well. I didn't know enough at first. By the time I'd remembered more something was blocking me. There were hours, days when you didn't seem to hear me. Or maybe it's that you wouldn't listen. You'd already chosen Ravel."

I'd realized the dreams had to be real when I saw Ravel's reaction to Cadence's supposed vision about Maryam, but I hadn't had a chance to think about what that truly meant. All of them, everything I saw . . . All of it was real?

My head spins. Just who was Cadence, before? And—oh. *Oh.* Ash.

31

CASS

I FEEL SICK in a different way now, a fluttery, light-headed sort of way.

Since Cadence is telling the truth, since I've somehow been infected with some ability she had in life, if the visions are of real people, of their final moments caught in deadly dreams, since she and Ash were alike in their power to enter those dreams . . .

Ash is real.

Ash is real.

Absurdly, I swing around and scan the crowd, as if now that I've realized he's alive somewhere, of course he'll be within sight, coming for me. Or rather, for Cadence—which gives me a sinking, shadowy feeling, with a beam of light at the heart of it. After all, the one thing I know about Cadence for sure is she's a ghost. She's dead, if not quite gone.

Ash may be coming for her, but it's me he'll find.

The blue lights wink out to a blank patch of the fabric-concealed wall. I've found the way to Ange and Cass's promised safety. But what if Ash comes looking for me and I'm not here?

I scan the crowd more carefully, half expecting him to step out from around a dancer and hold out his hand.

"What's the matter?" Cadence asks.

"What about Ash?"

"We have to help him find a way in—or maybe find you a way out, if he isn't already here. Don't tell him I said it, but he's got serious skills." She falls silent, as if she's looking around for him, too.

It fills me with hope. He's here, he'll show up any minute, he'll come for us. I take a few steps away from the wall and stand on my toes, trying to see further into the crowd.

When I feel a hand on my shoulder, I spin, arms outstretched, grinning. A stranger wearing crisp, form-fitting white stares back through an enforcer's goggles.

"You're her, aren't you?" he says. "Just what did you get up to, worker, that Her Worship is so set on getting you back?"

His voice is familiar, gruff and measured: Refuge Force Inspector Haynfyv.

"I—I don't know what you mean. You've got the wrong person."

"Figures her boy would be the one hiding you. That Ravel's been getting right out of hand lately. I knew all that nonsense about intruders sniffing around outside had to be a smokescreen."

I drop, hoping to duck out of his reach. He's too fast for me.

"Division 18 Surveillance Technologist Cole,"—he pins my arms and cinches my wrists together—"you are hereby detained pending investigation of your involvement in the murder of Former Worker 20-Bell—"

"I didn't kill anyone." I cringe as soon as the words pass my lips, remembering the cloaked man who dropped under the combined pressure of my hand and Ravel's.

"Probably not," he agrees, surprising me into stillness. "But Our Lady wants to see you either way, so you're coming with me."

He drags me into the crowd, seemingly unaware of my best attempts at resistance. The mayor wants to see me. Why? Is it about Cadence somehow? Do they think they can get to her through me? Figures. Just when I've finally sorted everything out with her, she makes new trouble for me.

"It has to have been Ravel," Cadence moans. "He's gone and told them about Ash. That's why Ash hasn't been able to reach us. They're looking for him. You have to escape. You have to warn him."

I squirm and twist. I kick at his feet and even slump, using my full weight against him, but Haynfyv keeps his grip.

Then Ravel's there, flanked by Cass; all fists and scoring nails and snarling teeth. Haynfyv flails and goes down. I lunge for the exit.

"Get her out of here," Ravel yells, pinning Haynfyv as dancers scramble away.

Cass pulls me away, muttering low: "We can't risk it now. Just come quietly, and I'll get you out later, okay?"

"How did he find me?"

"The enforcer?" he says, tucking me under his arm like I'm Ange. I don't fit as neatly as she does. I feel all elbows and shoulders and too-pointy chin. "Just bad luck, I guess. Sorry. Maybe something about the way we did your costume caught his eye."

"But Haynfyv never even saw my face." Of course, he would have checked Refuge records for my profile by now.

Cass stops. "What did you call him?"

"The lead enforcer—Inspector Haynfyv—I escaped from him right before I came here." I tug at Cass's arm. "Shouldn't we hurry?"

"Hayne . . . five . . ." He turns and stares.

Ravel has the inspector on the ground, but he's stopped beating him.

"It can't be." Cass moves back toward the inspector and Ravel in a daze, as if he's forgotten all about me.

"Didn't Cass originally introduce himself as part of the Hayn- series?" Cadence says. "You have to stop him."

I clutch at his arm. My fingers snag on a thread. The crowd around us blurs, wavering. My vision splits. I'm both Cole being dragged along as Cass stumbles forward and Cass himself, caught in a vision—a dream.

This can't be happening. Ravel controls the sacrifices through the Exchange. The Mara don't just take people in Freedom, not the way they do in Refuge. But even that seems to have been a lie. I can't deny what I'm seeing right now.

Cass is just a boy in his dream. He holds his arms out to an even smaller child who runs to him, drawn along a shining skein of silver threads, to be swept up and spun in a dizzying circle, giggling.

The dream turns; the child slips. Lands wrong. A sickening crunch. Boy-Cass races to his side. His eyes open. I feel Cass's relief as if it's my own, but the part of me that watches from a distance can see the thick weave of threads binding Cass to the deadly monster in his arms.

Ash, I beg, *Ash, you have to come, you have to stop this.*

But he's not here. He isn't coming. The child grins over boy-Cass's shoulder, too wide, too dark behind too-sharp teeth. Darkness pools in the corners of its eyes. All Cass wants is his brother back, his baby, safe in his arms. Somehow, seeing Haynfyv and hearing his name triggered this in him, this wanting. This longing. And it's going to kill him.

I can't let him die. Cass helped me. He has to go back to Ange. This time, it'll be different. This time, I'm here with him, truly here in body, not just some formless, watching spirit.

"Use the threads," Cadence says. "You can see them. Feel them. It might work. Untangle the threads and he'll be free."

But my hands are still bound. I can't move the way I need to. I have to bob and stretch to gather up the threads. One catches my eye. Bright and strong, it arrows away into the crowd. A sharp-eyed, sunset-painted face flashes through my mind when I tug it. Ange.

"Remember," I plead.

Cass jerks. He lifts his head.

"Remember Ange, Cass. This isn't real. Don't you want to go back to Ange?"

I haul on the thread, and it loosens, elastic. Then it thickens and glows, a dense cord stretched from Cass out into the press of bodies.

"Ange." He twists to look back over his shoulder. The thing in his arms snarls at me. "Who's Ange?"

I tug at the cord again and claw with the other hand against the mass of near-invisible threads that bind him to the monster wearing the form of his brother.

"Cass, you have to remember. You have to go back to her."

The creature sinks its fangs into his neck.

He cries out and shoves it away. "Ange! Where's Ange? Where's my brother? What is this?"

The child-shaped creature swells. Small, chubby hands warping with sickening, gristly pops. Claws rip Cass's shoulder. It darts in for another bite.

"Cass, don't you want to go back to Ange?" I drag at that thread, while in the other part of my twinned vision, his body bucks and bleeds over the gashed floor.

I'm too close to the attack, part of it, not separate. I can't worry about that now, can't let myself feel the pain. I can't look away, can't stop trying to pull him back from the edge. "Cass, remember!"

And somehow, he does. As he releases the longing for his long-lost brother, the binding threads fade around him and the single cord I know leads to Ange strengthens in my grasp. The monster too fades around the edges. Its claws swipe without drawing blood. It glares past Cass with hollow eyes and curls its lip in a snarl. There's a rising tide of whispers, sobs, screams, shrieks; a thousand voices one over the other until they drown out my pleading.

"Cass!"

But he's looking down at the child in his arms again, the child with soft hands and mussed up curls and an innocent smile. My hands are slick with blood, too slippery to hold on. The nest of threads around the brothers snaps taut and darkens. Cass hugs the monster close as if he's forgotten what made him bleed.

"Don't give up. Try again." Cadence urges.

I can't work my fingers back into the weave. I don't want to see, don't want to feel. At the end, I look away and wish for Ash. But the waking-world versions of us jerk and convulse in my doubled vision, the ground beneath us crumbling as the Mara take Cass apart and ravage his surroundings.

Dancers slip and scramble at the edge of a growing crater, scrabbling on hands and knees to get away from the attack. Ravel and Haynfyv stare, frozen.

Then everything fades away.

32

PLANS

STARLIGHT. THE ROOFTOP. Everything hurts. Ash kneels over me. Is it a dream? It can't be reality.

My lips shape the words, "What happened?" and then, "Why didn't you come sooner?" but nothing comes out.

"We can't last much longer. You have to hurry." Cadence says through me instead.

He looks away, swiping a hand across his face. The silver mist over his skin roils. The shadows under his eyes are darker than before.

"Why didn't you fight back? Why didn't anyone help you? What's going on in there, Cady?"

"Hurry, Ash."

He's still refusing to look at me—at her—when he responds. "I didn't realize how bad it had gotten. I didn't know. I'm so sorry, Cady. I'm trying, I am, but I just can't find a way in. Every time I get close, it seems like there're more patrols in the way. And something about that place— as soon as I get near it, everything just goes numb. It's like I can't see, can't hear, can hardly think and—"

I want to tell him it's not his fault, to stop the hurt in his voice. I reach for him, but can barely lift my hand. I gasp at the pain. He turns and catches it as it falls.

"They know you're out there. They're looking for you. There has to be something you can do, some way in," Cadence says. "You just have to try harder. We can't afford for you not to. There are things you need to know, things you all need to—oh. Of course. It's the gold."

"Gold?"

Cadence ignores me. "They line the walls with gold, wear it, even drink it. That must be what's keeping you out. That's what kept her from—"

"No. I'll try harder. I can handle it," he says.

"You can't." Her voice chokes out of me. "You know you can't. It's so obvious now. I'm not even sure how I've held on this long. No, you'll never be able to reach us. It's not safe. Go back."

"You can't be serious. If you think I'd just leave you to—"

"You have to go back. Tell them—tell them we've failed. I've failed. It's not your fault. Refuge, it's too far gone. The mission's over. Go back, tell them to come up with something else."

"Cady—"

"You know it's the only choice. Don't make me order you."

He laughs at that, a humourless bark of a laugh. "You know that's not how it works. You might have been stronger than me when we were kids, but the Travellers—"

"Just go," she whispers.

His face hardens, stone, but it's as if cracks are forming, lined in silver. "I don't want to leave you here. I can't."

"You can. Go. Before the dreamscape fades, let me see you go. Let me know you made it out. At least give me that."

He swallows a sound in the back of his throat. Stands. Turns away.

I can't stand it. I can't let it all end like this, not when I've finally gotten free of Ravel's lies. "Wait. Please."

He can't hear you, Cole. Don't make this harder than it needs to be. I'll explain later, she says to me alone.

We watch him walk away, the silver on his skin diffusing into a mist that clouds his form.

"Later will be too late," I say. "I have an idea. Trust me." I don't, actually, but I'd say anything to keep him from leaving. "Just don't let him go."

I'm afraid she won't listen, won't stop him, but finally she calls out, "Wait."

He stiffens, the mist thinning around him, drawing back down to the surface of his skin, but he doesn't turn.

Talk fast.

"He can't get in because Refuge Force is looking for him." I think out loud, desperate for a plan. "And we don't know a way out. But what if he could know where the Refuge Force patrols are stationed? Avoid them?"

Wouldn't that be convenient? Unfortunately, that's not part of his power, or mine.

I grin then, through the pain and the fear and the guilt. The only reason Refuge Force's out there looking for him is because I trusted Ravel instead of Cadence. But I can fix this.

"I can get him in."

Explain.

"I was trained as a surveillance tech, right? What do I do all day but stare at maps and track Refuge Force movements? I can guide Ash around the patrols."

"We have an idea," she says through me.

He turns, ducking his head as if to hide his hope from us.

What about the gold? she asks. *I'd forgotten after all this time, but it's like an allergy for us, or a poison. It explains why it took so long for you to start entering dreams, why you couldn't hear me when you were on the dust, and why Ash couldn't reach us before. But you seem to have built up some resistance. Why not just find the exits and leave on our own? We can meet Ash outside.*

It's not a bad idea—but I can't just give up like that. I have to end Refuge. I have to. I can't just walk away, even if she and Ash can. I have to stop the dying. No more kids. No more . . . friends. Ash could help me do that, if he could reach me. I know he could. I just have to find some way of getting him in here.

"We'll find paths with less gold. Unshielded zones like the stairwell or Floor 6. He'll be okay once he's in. But as soon as I leave Refuge, there'll be no one to keep track of the patrols, and they'll have moved around by the time we get down to ground level again. I'd get us caught trying to escape on my own, but maybe with Ash's help . . ."

Cadence mulls this over, sighs, and relays the plan to Ash. It's strange to hear the same words passing through my lips, in her voice this time.

Ash nods. "How long before you can move?"

The ground beneath me turns to liquid. Everything wavers and starts to fade. His hand tightens on mine, as if he can hold me here, but I've learned to recognize the way these dreams end, irresistibly and all at once.

"I can wait," he says, fast and low, bending over me as if his closeness can hold off the ending of the dreamtime. "Don't push too hard, Cady. Stay safe."

The fading of the dream brings fresh pain surging up. I gasp and squeeze his hand, but he can't hold off the darkness.

"Be careful," he says as reality rushes in and crushes me.

"SHE'S GONE, YOU drone." Ravel's voice slices through the darkness.

"And whose fault is that?" Haynfyv says. "Your mother's been throwing everything she's got into bringing this one back. Don't expect she'll be too pleased to hear—"

"Spawning a clone is not motherhood, sixer. I owe that woman nothing. There's nothing left here worth taking with you. Move along and tell Maryam how you got her precious key killed."

I can't lift the unbearable weight of my eyelids. Ravel's words swim in the murky fog of half-consciousness. A key? Ravel's mother. Or creator. Maryam. The mayor is Ravel's . . . Am I dead? I hurt enough that I doubt it.

"Flame?" Ravel whispers.

I moan. Not dead, but back under his control. I'd been so close to getting away, and now . . .

"Don't move," he says. "The inspector thinks you're dead. I—I thought . . . Just keep your eyes closed. I'll keep you safe."

There's scuffling, too many seconds of hurting, and very little else to concentrate on. Ravel's voice in the distance is nearly drowned out by the endless beat that shakes the floor beneath me.

"Take her away," he says. Something jostles me. Pain. Then nothing.

ANGE BLURS INTO view. She's painting something acrid and slick over my skin. I don't hurt anymore.

She looks faded, pale and grim and still. At first, I don't remember why. Then I can't stop the moan that rises to my lips. Her rigid shoulders pull another fraction straighter. Her bright mask is trimmed in feathers and ribbons that trail back over her head and down her cheeks like a flood of fiery quivering tears.

"I—" My throat is dry. I cough. The spasms wake a deep ache in me, though my skin doesn't hurt, and if what I remember is true, it should. "I tried to stop it. I tried to bring him back. I didn't mean for—"

"You couldn't have done anything," she says, brittle and ungentle but not accusing.

She's rigid to the point of breaking. I picture her casting sly glances up at Cass, nestling into his side, her lips gentle and quirked up at one side as she presses them to his. His face, hope cloaked in humour as he teases her about settling down. A future they'll never reach.

"She's right," says Cadence, tears in her voice. "You couldn't have done anything. It's not your fault."

That only makes it worse. I couldn't stop it, couldn't save him. Couldn't save anyone. But Ash could have. If he'd been there, he'd have saved Cass and Ange wouldn't be hiding under a mask. She'd be with him; strong, happy, gentle Cass.

If Ash were here, everything would be better. I wouldn't have to worry about Ravel and his expectations, his recipe for the perfect Victoire. Or enforcers tracking me down. Or finding a way to make the workers realize the danger they're in. Or any of it.

If Ash were here, maybe Cadence could stop haunting me, stop dragging me into the dreams of others. At the very least, no one would be dying.

If Ash were here, everything would be right.

The problem is, getting Ash here is going to take another dream. To be immersed in someone else's longings so deeply I can't separate myself from what they want or the pain when their dreams turn on them. More suffering. More hurt. What if it's Ange next time?

She looks away, as if she can't stand to hold my gaze.

"I'm sorry," I say, because it needs to be said.

It was my fault; Cass was there for me. And I say it because I am sorry. I don't want him to be gone. I don't want her to be hurt. I don't want that to have been my last memory of him, those horrible, wracked, wet-sounding gasps and the vicious crunching.

"We'll get you out soon." Ange's gaze settles somewhere over my head. "It'll just take some time. Try to hang in there."

I want to tell her it's okay, she can stop trying to help now. She can stop trying to hold herself together. I want to tell her, but I don't. Better to leave her out of it.

She pauses a moment longer, as if she expects some sort of response. Then she nods, the edges of her mask fluttering, and takes her healing paste away to the back room.

I should go now. I shift my weight to one side and groan at the sharp bite of pain.

"Cole?" Cadence sounds worried.

"We've got to get Ash." I grit my teeth and heave another couple of inches.

"Oh. Um, Cole?"

"Mmph?"

"Clothes."

I look down. Right. Better get that sorted before I head up to Refuge. Which raises a different issue: where am I going to find a uniform? It's not like I can just wander back wearing feathers and paint and ask to use a console. Which means not only do I need to track down a uniform, find a way back up into Refuge, climb hundreds of stairs, avoid being noticed, chased, or caught by Ravel or enforcers, walk back in and sit down at my old desk without anyone noticing, I'll also have to navigate being pulled into one or more dreams, connecting with Ash in dreamtime unreality to send him instructions, and then finding a nearby and safe location to wait for his arrival.

So that won't be hard at all.

33
STAIRS

I YANK A blanket up, wince, and squirm a little deeper into the cushions. I need to move, to hurry up and get Ash here to save the day, but the mountain of barriers feels overwhelming.

"What about Ange?" Cadence asks.

I consider it.

"I don't want to ask for her help. She's done enough." Sacrificed enough.

"But what happens to her if you just vanish?"

Oh. At the very least, she'd get in trouble with Ravel for letting me escape. At the worst, it might blow her cover.

" . . . right," I say, as if I were totally planning for that as well. "Which is why I'll—"

"—pretend to be injured until Ravel gets back, and then sneak out when neither of them are around? Good, I thought so."

I gulp back the bitter taste that rises at the thought of Ravel showing up, expecting to see Ange taking care of me and instead finding me gone. I don't want to picture his reaction, the kind of damage he could do. But if I wait a little longer and rest, I might be able to find a way to sneak out without getting Ange blamed for it.

I tuck the blanket closer, nestle into the cushions, and let my head tip back. I focus on making each limb as bonelessly limp as possible and hope I look convincingly unconscious.

It reminds me a little of pretending to be dead, pursuing that cold stillness out of fascination and a desire to understand. The memory makes me sick to my stomach. It also triggers a traitorous little thrill that prickles across my scalp. Then I have to start again, consciously relaxing each muscle.

There's a burst of noise as the door to Freedom flies open. I struggle not to tense up and undo all my painstaking work.

"Victoire." Ravel flings himself down beside me. The bed bounces and shakes.

I let my head loll away from him, hoping it looks natural, and peek under my lashes to watch Ange approach.

"How is she?" He runs a finger down my shoulder, slipping the blanket to one side.

I quash the shiver that wants to surface and bite my lip so hard I draw blood. Ange sees. She glances away.

"She'll live," she says, fierce eyes blank and fixed on the floor.

"She'd better."

His nails are sharp points against my skin. I clench my fists under the cover of the blanket.

"She's cost me an awful lot. Do you have any idea how much damage that little unplanned death caused? The ripples—there are idiots who think they can do my job. Take my place. As if their inferior little minds could ever comprehend what I go through to keep this place alive. If it weren't for her gifts, I might almost wish I'd never been there when she was taken."

I unclench my fists just in time. He pulls my hand out and strokes it, rotating my arm and fluttering the points of his nails near the paste-smeared lacerations.

"She was in worse shape then, though not as bad as those parents of hers. Worm food."

My parents? He's gotten me confused with Cadence. Which . . . actually makes so much more sense. All this time, he's thought I was her. Did she look that much like me? Or has it all just been a mix-up in Refuge's records?

"Of course, her value would double if I could get my hands on that little friend of hers outside. You have no idea how busy that's kept me these past few days. How hard I've had to work."

It really is all my fault. I was the one who let him know about Ash in the first place.

"When's she going to wake up? I could use her support out there. Another Exchange would go a long way toward appeasing the masses, regaining their confidence."

I trap my tongue between my teeth and bite down until all I taste is the sharp sweetness of blood.

"She's not strong," Ange says. "She'll take some time to recover. She needs rest."

He drops my arm. I open my mouth to gasp at the pain and catch myself just in time.

"Fine. She rests. You're finished tending her?"

"For the moment."

"You're sure she won't wake up?"

"It seems unlikely, but I can make no guarantees."

"Fine." He stands up and steps away. "I'm understaffed now. I'll need you with me tonight. Hurry up."

I bite harder at that. How careless his tone is, how casually unconcerned about Cass's death. How can he not care about what happened?

Two sets of footsteps leave.

"Coast's clear," Cadence says. "Well done. You'd better hurry, though. No telling when he'll send someone to check on you."

I roll off the bed, groaning and smearing blue paste all over. Whatever Ange gave me keeps the hurting remote and numb as long as I stay still. I pad gingerly across the floor and start poking through cupboards and shelves behind cleverly draped openings at the back of the room. There's a pitcher of dust standing out and ready. It might dull the pain. Better not. I'll need a clear head.

My uniform is buried under rolls of fabric, cleaned and neatly folded. As much as I've craved the comfort of familiar Refuge modesty, I can barely bring myself to touch the thing again. But to bring Ash here, to have him make it all? It's worth the way my skin crawls as I pull it on.

Then I take it off again and roll it up tightly.

"What's wrong?" Cadence asks. "Hurry."

"It'll stand out," I seize a handful of fabric from another shelf and try to figure out how it's meant to drape. "I can't move through Freedom wearing that."

"Oh." She's silent for a couple of moments. "I saw a good mask two shelves up."

It's a great mask, a heavier, darker twin to Ange's. I'm afraid it was Cass's, but it fits me well enough. I need it too much to hesitate for long. I roll a deep violet garment around the bundle of my uniform and tuck the whole thing under my arm. I'll have to change in the stairwell. If I can even find my way back to it.

That's when I feel the draft. I turn to the blank space between two shelves and poke the heavily-draped wall. It gives. I shove through to a bleak, starkly lit concrete corridor.

"So that's how they got around so quietly," Cadence says.

Ange and Cass had a back entrance the whole time.

"Should I . . . ?" The cool, musty air raises goosebumps on my arms.

"Can't be any worse than wandering through hordes of dancers, hoping to stumble across an exit. I say go for it."

I let the curtain fall on Ravel's exotic cocoon of a chamber and step into the echoing grey corridor.

I STAGGER DOWN the hallway, one hand on a wall, stiff and hurting and worried.

"What happens when Ash gets here?" It's not so much a question as a reminder, a kindness. She needs to realize. I can't let her be surprised by it.

"He'll get you to safety," she says, missing my point, or ignoring it. "I'll make sure of it. That's the first thing. Then . . . then we'll come up with a plan. He's got a mission, and I—" Her voice quivers. I think she's going to say it, but then she doesn't. "The mission must be completed. He'll find a way. Somehow, he'll find a way."

I walk in silence, listening to her breathe. It's weird there's anything to hear, since she has no lungs, no mouth, no heart to feel with. No mind to think with. What is a ghost, anyway? What is she, that I should feel sorry for her, and also jealous of her, and also guilty?

And, because I'm guilty, and jealous, and sorry, I don't say it, don't force her to acknowledge what she is, what she's lost, all she'll never have again. I don't ask if it's wrong to call Ash to me when he thinks he's coming for her. I don't think she wants me to ask.

It's all for the mission. I can pretend if she can that bringing Refuge down and saving everyone is what matters most, that it's all any of us care about. That's mostly true, anyway. Stopping the dying, the threat of the Mara masked by the lies of Refuge—and come to that, Ravel has been lying too—matters more than what any of us want or feel. This is the best thing I can do. I have to get Ash to Refuge. I can wait until after to break the news to him that Cadence has repeatedly refused to share: his childhood friend, his mission partner, and the girl he loves—if his tone and the gentleness of his touch have anything to say about it—is gone, and she's never coming back.

So when I round a corner and there's an all too familiar-looking door, I think I can be forgiven for pausing a moment too long before pulling it open. It's not really a failing to drag my feet and wallow in pain and hesitate. It's not unreasonable to sink down and lay my head on the steps when I reach them and refuse to look at the endless climb ahead. It's totally understandable to spend a moment alone in the shadows, clinging to the way he begged me to take care of myself and pretending he really meant it for me.

Then I start to climb.

HERE'S THE STORY I want to tell: I push through my pain and race bravely up hundreds of steps, sneak fearlessly into my old office, masterfully communicate an ingenious route to the heart of Refuge, and boldly sweep off to await the arrival of my hero.

Here's reality: I fight for each step. I'd like to stop counting, but I can't. I have to get to Floor 18. I've made it four floors. Already I feel as if I can't move another inch.

It was cold when I started out. I'm dripping with sweat now. I haven't changed into uniform yet. Just the thought makes me ill. My breath rasps, and speeds at the thought of enforcers sneaking up behind me unheard. Yanking me back down all those hard-earned, sharp-edged stairs. Every muscle burns. My knees and palms are raw. I'd been reduced to crawling before I'd even reached the first floor.

I can't do this.

"Don't give up. You're doing great. Keep at it."

If Cadence weren't a ghost, I'd shove her down the stairs. Instead, I wheeze menacingly. It's all I have energy for.

Floor 5. Then Floor 6, where the failures are sent to die. I hold my palm to the door as if I'll be able to feel the misery of those trapped on the other side, the failures and the broken, the sacrifices . . . But we're all sacrifices, aren't we? All the way up to the very top. Wasn't that Maryam's nightmare?

I keep going. Cadence starts talking. Maybe it's to distract me, or maybe it's because I'm finally free of Ravel's influence and she's not afraid I'll spill everything. She explains how the threads are things people want and how they call to the void of the Mara. How the hungry monsters follow the threads of desire and then hollow out what they find at the other end. How she was trained to untangle those threads and use them to make victims strong against the Mara, to keep them safe, alive. She thinks some of that must have been passed to me, that I might be able to learn to use her skills, at least as long as she's with me.

I ask about the threads, about how I feel them now before the dreams even start. She says using them as a conduit to reach the dreams before they turn is an advanced skill, far beyond what I should be capable of. But many things have gone beyond what she expected—the severity of the attacks, the way they damage the surrounding landscape, the frequency. The Mara shouldn't be able to do that, she says, and it's getting worse.

And while she explains, I drag myself up the stairs. After a while, the pain is so complete and so constant I kind of forget about it. There's an empty space in my mind neither Cadence, nor pain, nor fear, nor defeat can really touch. I stop questioning if I can keep going and just continue on.

"Stop."

I keep climbing for several steps before I register her voice and huddle there, halfway to Floor 19, to spend a few moments coming to terms with the fact that I made it. Then I strip off my sweat-damp costume and pull on the familiar uniform. I draw the hood up to hide the feathers woven into my hair and fasten the veiled lower mask over my mouth. I hope Ange cleaned enough of the paint from around my eyes that I don't draw attention.

The hood-fastening band folded into the parcel of clothes is an official gold ward, not my familiar, detested black one. I never passed probation. I never completed my trial, was never awarded full status as a worker. I have no right to wear the gold ward.

I pull it on anyway.

34

DRONES

T HE STEADY, DULL familiarity of the workplace is soothing. At least, that's what I tell myself. Repeatedly.

After all, the whole thing is engineered to be as soothing as possible: the bland space, the shrouded forms, the soft tap of fingers, the muted rustle of cloth. Warm air carrying a sweet scent that slows my breath and coats my tongue.

No one looks up when I ease the door open. A fine film of dust covers my console, but no one so much as glances over when I settle in the chair. Why would they? It's against regulation to show interest in others. They probably haven't even noticed I've been gone.

It seems laughable now, how worried I was about what they thought of me, imagining them staring constantly at the black probationary band I no longer wear. I almost miss it. The gold ward must be tighter. My head throbs.

I do have to hurry, though. I can't risk attracting the attention of the supervisor. Kistrfyv might notice my return. Unlike the rest, he always paid a creepy amount of attention to me. I tap to wake up the console, and there it is: Refuge, zone by zone, level by level, streaming code showing the choreographed movements of workers.

Refuge Force are tracked by the system, unlike sedentary divisions like my own. I hunt for their division ID, the prefix 09-, on the lower reaches, looking for the points where they vanish off the grid. I'd been told that whole area was submerged in the flood, but now . . . I'd seen no signs of water in Freedom. The level must have receded since then.

It takes a while, but I find four points where enforcers seem to breach the outer reaches of the tower complex, one for each of the original towers. Of them, two are heavily used, one less so, and the last shows only the occasional trace of a pair of enforcers pacing to the boundary and back.

I point it out to Cadence, murmuring under my breath so as not to draw the attention of my neighbours. She doesn't respond. I lean back and reach for the threads of dreams, eager to tell Ash.

I nearly fall out of my chair. I can't feel any threads at all—and now I think about it, haven't since leaving Freedom.

I trail my fingers through the air slowly, pretending to stretch. The air is as empty as it should be—if I were normal and dreams didn't call me through my fingertips.

What do I do?

"What's the matter?" Cadence's voice is a distant echo. "Hurry up and tell him."

"There's no . . . I—I can't feel any threads."

"That's not—oh."

"What if they don't dream at all up here? What if they don't want anything? I'm never going to be able to reach him."

"Even this lot can't be that dull. You already know there are deaths in Refuge. It has to be something else. Maybe it's just because you're injured. You're too worn down. Just give it a moment, it'll come to you."

She's right. That has to be it. I've seen people die in Refuge. They're not as perfect as they make out to be. I never was.

I stare at the display and track the movements of enforcers combing the borders of our enclosed world and wait, hope, for a dream to come. This setback could be a good thing. There has to be a pattern to the enforcers' movements, if I can only figure it out. Once I know that,

I'll be able to get Ash in and then, eventually maybe, get all of us out without getting caught.

But the bland familiarity of the work is too reassuring, too simple. My mind keeps slipping back to the spin and slide and sensation of Freedom, holding it up and contrasting its vibrancy with the dullness of my former life. I remember the way the thick air caught the motion of the lights, the painted beams, dancing phantom bars of colour that spun and swirled. The sound—oh, the music. It throbbed in the base of my skull, danced on the edge of my tongue, sweet and sharp and heavy like the scent on the air. In Freedom, the sound is just there, inside you and all around you, an extension of the air.

I sway a little in my seat to scraps of melody, to a pulsing beat that lives only in my head. It hovers over my tongue, buzzing to be heard. It's a new type of pain to be still and pinch my lips closed over my teeth and hold the sound inside. I have to forget what Cass taught me; I have to stop clinging to the beat to ground myself.

I need a dream to come to me. I need to want, to be distracted and drawn in.

So I let go, let my mind wander in all the forbidden ways. I ask all the questions I've spent a lifetime avoiding. And I realize, after so long spent trying not to long for anything, I don't even know what I want. Not to return to Freedom—not really, despite its pleasures, not after Cass's death, not after running away from Ravel and his dreams and desires for me. If anything, I wish I could go back to my own familiar room with my own bed and rest, take time to recover before trying again to change the world and stop the dying—the dying I've feared and hated but see no evidence of here at all.

That terrifies me more than anything, the lack of horror here. It's all so safe and familiar and dull, the way it welcomes me in and makes it hard to truly believe it's possible to leave.

I have to destroy Refuge. Have to end its threat, the banality of its insidious lies, the half-truths so deeply programmed I still have trouble seeing past them after all that's happened. And to do that, I need Ash.

I prod at the throbbing headache building behind my eyes. The ward around my hood shifts under my fingers, and I shove it higher, loosening it. There's a quick glitter and flash—my neighbours' glances, furtive, over and away back to their own business. Instead of hiding, I glare back, daring them to comment.

A silver thread drifts across my vision.

I snatch it before it can vanish.

LOOK AT THEM, row upon row of drones. Empty-eyed tappers. Machines. Our machines, each one of their lives in our hands.

We roll our neck, luxuriating in the spine-tingling thought. It's our choice, who to single out and who to ignore. It's not complete freedom, of course. We have a quota to fill: one in fifty to recommend for sacrifice. But to our drones, our dominion is absolute. They never realize how much power we have. They're not meant to know. They're not strong enough to know the true workings of Refuge.

Not like us. We're special. Smarter, stronger-minded.

There's a particular pleasure in store for us today. We smirk in anticipation. We selected this next sacrifice some time ago. Indeed, we thought she'd been taken already, but now she's shown up again, diligently tapping away as if she'd never left.

I pull away from his twisted mind, gasping. It's the supervisor, Kistrfyv. He's the next victim, and the worker he looks out at with such hate is me. He's been singling me out for special torture all along. It wasn't my imagination. He intended for me to die right from the start. He never planned for me to graduate from probation at all.

My stomach turns over at the thought of spending any more time in his head, but I have no choice and no capacity to resist. I'm drawn back in. This time, my awareness is split between Kistrfyv's perspective and my own, though I have no control in either reality.

The way she bends and shrinks when we reprimand her is satisfying. We've missed it. We may regret it once she's been removed. When we were newer to our position, we diligently selected the weakest drones for reassignment or sacrifice, but for the last several cycles, it has amused us to select for homogeneity. Our current crew is nearly all of a uniform height, which is unexpectedly gratifying. We do so enjoy patterns like that, our little systems. It's probably why we were placed in charge of the division. That and our obvious superiority.

Irritatingly, when they sent us that gawky probationary worker, she unbalanced our careful cultivation, poking up out of the uniform mass of drones. Even worse, we were told explicitly she was not to be sacrificed, merely observed. It took months before we found a turncoat enforcer willing to make the necessary arrangements. Now she's back as if she'd never left, flaunting a gold ward we never granted her as if she'd passed probation with flying colours.

We smooth our hood. It's important, when dealing with lesser creatures, to display marks of authority.

The door to Kistrfyv's private office swings open. He set me up to fail. He hired someone—Serovate?—to make sure I wouldn't come back. It's his fault. Everything comes back to this greedy little man. The air is choking.

It really is so very pleasurable, this part of our duties. And we're so terribly well suited for it. We ought to be rewarded after this sacrifice. Isn't it a milestone? The tenth from our division? Twentieth? Something like that. Of course, there must be a commensurate reward, a special bonus for excellence. We'll be promoted to division head, surely. Larger quarters, more benefits, better food. In fact, isn't that an enforcer now, sent to summon us for our advancement? We wait with dignity, repressing the urge to squirm with pleasure.

We're glad for our mask. The air seems unusually thick today. Unhealthy brownish-gold. We blink several times, squinting through the fog. The enforcer must be quite tall. We crane our neck. So very tall . . .

The room seems to shrink around and away from him, our deliciously docile drones blotted out behind the dark silhouette framed in sickly golden light. We taste salt and swallow once, then again, gagging on the thick, strong flavour. There must be something wrong with our mask. The enforcer looms closer still.

We lean back a little to see his face. His mask has gone missing. His exposed nose and mouth are grotesque. It's not just the impropriety of a bare face. The nose is barely there, two high slits over a gaping void of a mouth with grasping, writhing edges. Above, pearl white orbs weep viscous black tears. We recoil. Our tongue convulses behind our teeth, but no sound makes it past the thickness in our throat.

The creature's sleeves fall back. Boneless ropes of flesh flail out and wrap us in damp heat.

35

TRIUMPH

THE DESTRUCTION SEEMS veiled in a filmy mass. The nearly transparent threads that bind Kistrfyv to his dream are layered so thickly I can barely see through the web. His uniform is shredded, the double-ringed hood ripped away. Long scratches along his bald scalp weep dark lines like combed-over strands. The heavy folds of ashen flesh at the base of his skull and around his jaw are mottled with terror.

It's horribly, shockingly intimate—in a way, even more intimate than watching through his eyes and hearing his thoughts—to see him exposed like this. The tang of terror clots the air, a high note to the heavy, musky rot that chokes out from the spreading mass.

The floor shakes under the violence of the attack. Cracks splinter outward. Consoles judder across the floor. A fine rain of plaster sifts from the ceiling.

It's happening too fast; I'm not prepared. I hadn't thought about what might happen if the next dream was near my waking body—what did Ash call it, my anchor?—like the one that took Cass. I might not survive long enough to meet Ash.

We scream as it tears at us. The floor cracks beneath us. The wide-eyed faces of our passive drones go spinning by. It slams us against the ceiling. Shards rain down.

The seething mass around Kistrfyv spreads higher, wider. It cracks the frame of the door to his office and blows out the observation window. Indistinct forms writhe and dart in the jaundiced fog. There are eyes, too. Cold. Hungry. Intelligent. Pearl-white but not blank, not empty. A long, dark tongue slicks out and caresses a torn length of flesh on Kistrfyv's face. He's on the ground, curled around the ruin of his belly, his legs bent in places a human leg does not bend. His back bows. He screams.

The cold eyes roll with pleasure. Then the Mara look directly at me and sweep a barb against Kistrfyv's throat, choking his screams.

Then we are elsewhere. I face the shattered remains of Kistrfyv in the void. He looks at me but doesn't try to speak, doesn't try to plead. There's no rush of voices to drown mine out. I don't try to talk to him, not to apologize nor to offer help I cannot give. His pale eyes are full of distaste for only a moment. The void swallows him.

I come back to myself in a rush, but the nightmare doesn't end. A column of thick yellow fog churns. Tiles splinter. Lights shatter overhead. The nearest workers scramble to get away. Others sit, staring at the blood blossoming through their uniforms, too docile to understand.

I'm so cold. My hands shake, balled into fists at my side. But there's a knot of heat deep inside me. It sweeps out in a dizzy rush. The world is stark, lit in sharp-edged silver light. Knifelike shadows fall away in every direction.

This is unacceptable. Absolutely unacceptable that the Mara should invade my world, harm my people. Revoltingly unacceptable they should savour a meal, play with it in front of my eyes, and still be unsatisfied, still reach out to devour more.

I shake, but it is not out of fear now.

"Try it," Cadence breathes. "Reach for the threads."

I barely hear her encouragement. I don't think she could stop me if she tried. I tear away my hood and mask. I need to breathe, to see, to stop the ache and the cloudiness in my head.

The huddled form on the ground that was once Kistrfyv is very still in the midst of a spreading, dark pool. The threads binding him in place have melted away. I stalk through the outer edge of the fog toward the beast shrouded within. It gathers shreds of the miasma around itself, growing darker, larger.

Some distant part of my mind wonders what I'll do when I reach it. Die, probably.

"Don't lose focus," says Cadence. "Hold on to that feeling."

Fury washes heat and ice through my skin in turns, pulsing. I raise a hand as if to strike the creature and seize a knot of nearly invisible threads. I wrap my hand around them and yank.

The creature hiding in the fog is rocked back as if by a blow. Tendrils puff off into nothingness.

"Yes!" Cadence shouts.

The dark bulk of the Mara in the fog tenses and coils as if to spring.

I dig my fingers into the threads of desire. The light around me bends. Stabbing beams of silver-white arrow toward the beast. It wavers, roars, rears back. A single, bright flash tears from ceiling to floor.

I sway in the force of the Mara's howl, battered by waves of damp heat. The beast explodes into nothing, cracking an invisible shell and leaving me raw and trembling. An overpowering stench rushes in.

He's there. Ash. His bright blades fade from white heat to a polished gleam. The light around him soaks into his clothes, silvers his skin, and glimmers in his eyes. His fierce, focused face creases in regret, gazing on the ruin of the man lying broken at his feet.

Then he catches sight of me.

"Cady."

I sway. "Refuge Force . . . There's a way."

Cadence doesn't repeat my words to him. "It's no good," she says instead. "We thought—we looked for a way—but with this much damage . . . The system's down. We won't be able to trace their movements. I'm sorry, it's not safe. You need to go."

Ash's jaw hardens. "It doesn't matter. I'm not leaving you alone in there. I'll do whatever it takes to finish this mission. You just find a safe place, okay? Wait for me. I'll find a way."

"No. It's over, Ash."

But we're so close. I just beat back the Mara. I just snuck into Refuge, infiltrated the security system, and took on a nightmare—and survived, mostly intact. I'm not giving up now.

"Cadence, tell him to wait. I'll find him a way in."

I'm sorry. We need to be realistic about this. It's better if he survives, if he takes a message back to the Travellers. The mission isn't worth—

"You think I care about your mission? The one you've never really even bothered explaining to me? I have my own plan: stop the dying. End Refuge. Ash's the only one I know who can help. So no, I'm not going to just sit back and let him go. I'm going to do whatever it takes to get him in here in one piece, and then we're going to take this place apart from the inside. Tell him to wait, Cadence."

You're not being reasonable.

"Tell him."

Fine. It's on your head if he gets caught.

She acts tough, but she caved too easily. She wants Ash here just as much as I do.

I stare at him as she explains through me, willing him to listen, to wait for me.

He starts to respond and blinks out of existence, the dreamscape wiped away between one word and the next.

I drop to my knees, caught between hope that he won't abandon us, fear he'll rush in and be captured or killed, and behind it all, as the hot blood soaks through to my skin, elation at victory wrapped up in a defeat. My teeth are gritted in a fierce grin, some part of me savagely delighted at the way the Mara shredded under my attack.

That was no failure.

REFUGE FORCE IS on its way and soon everything will go back to normal. We're safe now. That's what the announcement said.

I'm out of time. They'll be here any minute. I need to get away, or I'll get caught.

Dampness spreads across my knees, ground dark into the creases of my gloves. I scrub my hands against my thighs, unable to wipe away the clinging stains soaked into the fabric. I can't have it on me. Can't have him on me.

I never liked Kistrfyv.

That shouldn't be true, but it is. There is no like or dislike. There is simply the role Refuge guides each one of us to play. But whether it is—was—his role or the man himself, I'd hated it. Him. And he'd hated me. I'd seen it in his eyes, though I shouldn't have been looking. I hadn't even dared to name the feeling back then, but I'd seen his fixation, a burning hunger always to be higher, always to be stronger, always to be more.

And for me to be less, even though I was less than nothing to him. Just some failure.

I inhale the reek of hot blood, of human flesh turned inside out and sinking into the floor, spattered on the walls, ground into my skin. The light is suddenly too bright, too far away, my skin stretched tight and itchy.

Failure. But I hadn't felt like a failure when those gossamer threads brushed the ends of my fingers. It hadn't felt like failure when I sent silver light cutting down them and into the Mara. Some part of me wants to cheer. More than that, it wants to see if I can catch hold of those threads again, bring down another beast.

Enforcers pour into the room. In the midst of my successful resistance against the Mara, I've ruined my own plan. There's no way to access the surveillance feeds now, no way to guide Ash in.

"Head down, push forward," Cadence says. "You'll have to escape and try somewhere else."

I duck my chin and shuffle as if I'm just another shell-shocked worker. The first enforcer to reach me grabs my elbow and shoves me further along, minimum personal perimeters apparently cancelled by the crisis.

"Keep moving." He stoops to yank at some fool huddled under a desk.

I allow myself a sigh of relief. He didn't notice anything out of the ordinary.

Then Inspector Haynfyv steps into the room.

"Head down," Cadence says again. "He hasn't seen you yet. Head. Down."

I want to break and run, but there's nowhere to go. So I do as she says, slouching as I shuffle toward the door. I can't help glancing up as I pass the inspector, but he's focused on the heart of the damage.

His goggles sit askew, the skin around his left eye raised and puffy with bruises. How did Ravel get away with attacking an inspector? Is it because he's connected to the mayor? Is that why Refuge has left him and Freedom alone all this time?

An enforcer hauls me clear of the doorway and shoves me toward a huddled mass of workers in the hallway.

They stand with shoulders rounded, heads down, hands clasped in front. Obedient, with perfect form, as if their supervisor hasn't just been shredded right before their eyes. As if their uniforms aren't spattered with blood and their flesh torn. A few of the more alert ones clutch their elbows and rock. One is actually crumpled in a corner, whimpering.

I back into the crowd, trying to look convincingly shell-shocked, and keep backing until I bump into the wall. Refuge Force load the elevator, five workers herded by two enforcers at a time. If I time it right, I might be able to slip into the stairwell as the elevator door closes. The trouble is, enforcers are hauling the nearest workers in for each trip. I have to find a way to edge closer without getting shoved in for my plan to work.

There's a brief interval between filling one elevator car and the next. The silence is broken by uneven breaths, the rustle of cloth, distant clatter as enforcers sift through the wreckage. None of us are going to be going back to work any time soon.

I keep edging along until I feel the ridge of the stairwell door under my fingertips. The elevator door opens across the hall. A pair of enforcers starts hauling in workers. They look at me, reaching.

I exhale, long and shuddering, and let my knees go limp as if I'm losing consciousness from shock—a tempting thought. It's a risky move, drawing attention to myself, but the enforcers grab the next worker within reach without bothering to haul me up.

The elevator slides shut. I feel for the stairwell door and slip through the narrowest possible crack. I'll go one floor down and wait for the threat to clear.

The cool, dark concrete feels good. I just need a moment. I strip off my soaked gloves. The light uniform clings, cold and clammy, where blood has soaked it through. I pluck it away from my skin, wishing I'd thought to bring a change of clothes.

The door beside me bursts open. I shove away from the wall. Someone grabs my arm. There's a sharp jab.

Everything slows down.

My head is heavy. I swivel it toward the enforcer, eyes suddenly hot and bruised. The syringe is smaller than I expect in his gloved hand. It's hard to focus on, with two—make that three needles. He yanks. I stumble and knock my head against the doorframe. He pulls me into the bright corridor.

I don't feel pain. It must have been at least partly anaesthetic. Odd details stand out. Light glinting off the polished edge of the elevator door, pain-bright. An uneven smear of dark crimson where blood has spattered the enforcer's heavy boots.

The enforcer hauls me to the elevator. I slump in a daze, staring at my own splotchy footprints.

"This will help, princess."

His voice is familiar, oily and ingratiating with the barest undertone of a sneer. Everything feels heightened to the point of overload. Too close to focus on. Unbearably distant at the same time. The enforcer's voice bubbles and echoes. My mouth tastes of steel and candy. My tongue is thick. Light flexes and batters at me from unexpected angles.

There's another sharp jab to my upper arm—not pain, just a sudden pressure. The light fades. The elevator dings its arrival in the far distance.

SUPERIOR

T HE CEILING LOOKS familiar. Home. My bed in Refuge?

"Shake it off," Cadence says sharply, but from some distance.

I brush her aside and stretch. My muscles are loose and relaxed, with no soreness or bruising. Everything feels excellent. The cool brush of the sheet, the sweet-scented air, and even Cadence's bad mood serve to accentuate my pleasure.

I raise my hand against the gold-netted light and regard the red-edged splendour of each finger with ponderous fascination. I twirl it over and back, feeling the air, examining the tiny, clear-ridged swirls on the pad of each finger, the darker lines where my fingers bend. They've been scrubbed clean. There's no trace of blood or grime.

"You can't give in," Cadence says. "You can't just let them do this to you."

It's not that I don't know why she's upset. I should fear those lost hours, the missing pain. Someone erased the marks of death as if it had never occurred. I should resent them, fear what I've lost to unconsciousness.

I don't. If anything, I'm grateful for Refuge taking it on, taking away the burden of responding.

"Don't let them make you into a drone again. Think. What happens next? What about the mission? What about Ash?"

I close my eyes. Golden light shines through my eyelids in wavering patterns of red and yellow. Figures dance and sway in the light, dark eyes flashing. I feel Victoire's eagerness rise as if it were my own. It ebbs almost in the same instant. What do I care for the pulse of a beat, for the eyes of many, for the touch of heat and sweat? That is Victoire's passion, not mine. I will not succumb. I am not Ravel's dream of me.

In my mind, I gesture, and the dancers stumble apart in a wash of pale, clean light, the throbbing beat faltering and fading as they go. I paint the walls in green and grey; muted, soft tones interlaced with a deep, rich blue.

The salt-laced breeze carries a high-pitched cry. The gentle air fades into velvet night. Sharp stones prick underfoot. Crystal pinpoints overhead—scattered diamonds around the luminous face of the moon. Every shadow is sharp-edged and crisp except his.

His light-dark eyes gaze into mine, startled and wide. "Cady."

Then he's gone. My heart pounds as if I've just dashed up the stairs to the roof all at once. I must move or it will burst out of me and leave my body limp on the bed. The floor is chill on my bare feet. I crumple and rest my arms and forehead against its solid coolness. My heart tries to hammer its way out of my chest.

Ash.

I reach for Cadence. She's not there. I choke on the cloying sweetness pouring from the vents along the perimeter of the room. There are echoes, as if Cadence is calling from a long way off. I can't make out her voice.

Cady. He'd called to her, his face bare, exposed, so full of feeling it embarrassed me even as it drew me in.

Ash can save us all. He has the power to stop death. He can put an end to the hurting, to the lies, to the control. Refuge, crushing us one by one under the weight of regulation, even as the Mara cull the docile herd of helpless drones. I just have to call him to me, and he'll put an end to it all. Somehow.

Cadence hasn't ever really explained about the silver light. It seems almost an extension of him. I want to know more about him, to understand. I want to know why he calls out "Cady" but looks at me.

I cough suddenly, and gag. The vents; they're pumping too much sedative through the air. I scramble on hands and knees for the door. It's not where it should be. This room is much bigger than my own. Where am I?

When I reach the door, it won't open.

"Settle down, princess," an all too familiar voice snickers behind me. "What's your rush?"

Serovate's sitting on the bed, his fingers rubbing over and under one another with restless energy. How long has it been since I had to consciously suppress my own hands from playing out tension and wanting for all to see? I set my back against the door and tuck my knees close. I'm wearing a shapeless, plain shift. It doesn't cover nearly enough.

"What do you want?" I cough, ruining the effect.

"The real question"—Serovate tips his head—"is what do you want?"

Even with the barrier of his mirrored goggles, I can't help squirming under his gaze.

"I don't know what you mean. I . . . Why am I here?"

He tips his head a little further, looking at me from an angle that would have hurt my neck. Then he tilts his head over to lean it on the other shoulder.

"Perhaps a demonstration is in order." He pulls my pillow into his lap and wraps himself around it. Then he unhooks his mask and shoves his hood back, leaving his face bare except for the goggles.

"What do you see?" he asks.

"Cole, he's not safe," Cadence says, as if I can't tell.

He cups a hand over his mouth—thin-lipped, too wide—and breathes loudly. He drops his hand and flaps both arms in wide arcs timed to the wheezing breaths. The dramatic gesture reminds me uncomfortably of Ravel.

"Get it now?" he says, tipping his head. "No? Pity. Normally the ones that make it this far are a bit sharper than the rest of the herd. Unless you're just that good at hiding it, hmm?"

I push to my feet slowly and feel behind me for the latch. It still doesn't open.

"You're not a prisoner, if that's what you're thinking," he says pleasantly. His mirrored goggles wash out my reflection until it's as pallid as a dead thing's. "Quite the opposite, in fact. Why don't you have a seat while I explain?" He pats the bed beside him. "No? Well, suit yourself, princess. I hope you don't mind if I make myself comfortable."

He pulls his dingy gloves off one finger at a time to show incongruously pudgy hands, stained dark around the nails and knuckles but otherwise as pale as the rest of him. He kicks off his boots and proceeds to sprawl on the bed, propping himself on an elbow, feet drawn up, pillow still snuggled against him. He pets it as he speaks.

"Ahhh. Much better. All those formalities—so stuffy. It's really not my style. Such a pleasure to snatch these moments away from it all, as I'm sure you'll find. Which brings me to my next point. You, Series Cole, formerly of Division 18, Digital Surveillance Technology, are a superior."

I take a deep breath, only now realizing what the enforcer had been alluding to with his theatrics: the air is clear.

"Now, I know what you're thinking." He kneads the pillow, his head tilted at a painful-looking angle. "You're just not up for a promotion, it's such an honour, so on and so forth and such. But it's not a job title so much as a description. Yes, it comes with its own responsibilities, but really, it's more about being recognized for what you are, not about being expected to do anything. At least not until you're ready."

It's eerily like Ravel's speech.

"I don't know what you mean."

He smiles that thin-lipped smile and flops his head in the other direction.

"Such modesty," he says, not altogether approvingly. "You're special. Unique. Capable of seeing, of understanding, of doing so much more than the drones. I understand you are already aware of more than"—he coughs slightly—"regulation details of our situation here.

As you well know, there's a dangerous element the Refuge superiors work to moderate. Most of our drones simply don't have the capacity to confront that reality. You, Cole, have demonstrated awareness and resilience in the face of core realities that lesser beings cannot be challenged with."

He blinks slowly, his lips stretched wide in a grimace that he seems to intend as a smile.

"In doing so, you have come to the attention of Her Worship and the superiors as a candidate for elevation. I do apologize for our methods in extracting you from that distressing situation earlier today, but we felt it was in your best interests to manage the transition to superior in a controlled manner."

I bristle at the word *controlled.*

"But as you've had the chance to observe," he says, "the situation has been managed in your best interest. You will find there are numerous benefits to being a superior. Your rooms enjoy advanced shielding. Yes, rooms—a suite has been allocated to your use. You'll have full access once we finish our chat here."

He gestures again, as expansive and dramatic as Ravel posturing for the masses.

"You'll notice we didn't bother masking you as you slept. Unnecessary within your suite. I'm sure you'll enjoy the expanded slate of recreation options you'll find in the adjoining room, and when you're ready, you'll have full clearance and a meaningful position in critical decision-making. In short, regulation no longer applies to you; you apply regulation."

He finishes his speech with a flourish as if he's said something grand and noteworthy, and maybe he has. If he's telling the truth, there's more to Refuge's lies than I ever could have imagined. And the invitation to be on the inside, to see behind the scenes to the inner workings of Refuge control, to have the opportunity to influence those workings . . . If this is real, how many lives could I help save?

But it's ridiculous to believe him. I'm not special, just unlucky. And haunted, which is what all this comes back to. They don't know about Cadence; she's the one who's special. She's the one they really want. Just like Ash.

That's what this is about, isn't it? They think I'm her.

I want to laugh in the enforcer's face. But the kind of access they're offering . . . clearance at the higher levels of Refuge authority might be useful. Is there a way I can appear to accept while sending for Ash behind their back?

I raise my chin, and look down at the pale, grubby little enforcer lounging on my bed.

"I find your methods lacking." I channel Victoire with everything I have, putting on her confidence, her selfishness, the way she drinks in the admiring gazes of all who surround her and grows stronger from them. "But it's about time someone noticed what I have to offer."

Serovate laughs. "As you say, princess, as you say. In fact, Her Worship has had her eye on you for some time. If it hadn't been for several regrettable missteps by less elevated entities, you would of course have been welcomed as a superior much sooner."

"Of course."

Missteps like him taking a bribe to get me out of the way?

"But you'll be wanting a rest." He pats the pillow in his lap, sighs, and reaches for his boots. "I'll leave you to explore your suite and freshen up. Enjoy yourself. I'll check in tomorrow to see if you need anything."

He regards his mask with another heavy sigh before drawing up his hood and pulling the protective face guard over his nose and mouth. Framed in the dingy, stained white of his uniform, my reflection seems even paler. He walks toward me—toward the door—as he pulls on his gloves.

I step to one side elegantly, as if my skin doesn't crawl under his gaze.

He leans in. "Welcome, princess. Do enjoy yourself." He opens the door and oozes out.

"Freaky," Cadence says. "Let's get out of here."

I wilt, alone in this room that's so familiar yet different. "What if he's waiting out there? Also, clothes."

"Ah."

"Also . . ." I'm not sure where to start. "Do you know what floor we're on?"

"Does it matter?"

"I've got to find another console with access to the surveillance feed, whenever it comes back online. That kind of access probably isn't available to any division lower than 16 or so."

"You're assuming we can even make it to the stairwell," she points out.

I scrub a hand through my hair. One step at a time. First, find something decent to wear.

That part's easy. There are cabinets set into the wall. Inside hang plain uniforms with my series ID—Cole—but no division ID. It makes me stop and stare. No longer just an only, I'm also placeless and jobless, adrift in the rigid Refuge structure. To see it laid out like that, stark letters against the fabric . . .

I open another cabinet and forget all about it. There's a stack of patterned garments cut like uniform tunics, and pants but without hoods, footwear, gloves, or masks to match. It's as if the wild style of Freedom ran into Refuge conservatism and got diluted but not slaughtered outright.

It's unexpectedly appealing. I pull on a set with a faint blue and green pattern and start trying doors. There's more than one, as it turns out. I save the one Serovate used for last, afraid of finding him leering back at me.

The first door opens on a large bathroom. I stare at my reflection. Traces of Freedom remain: lips unevenly smeared with gold, smudges around my eyes, bits of glitter. The pale paint Ange used on my face has mostly worn off from where it hid the spray of stains on my skin shaped, now that I think of it, a little like a Freedom-style mask. The whole mess of it looks stark and wild. The light against the mirror reflects in my eyes, the shimmer highlighting wide pupils.

I don't look like myself; or rather, I look like everything I have been and done smashed together. Dull, indecisive, dark Cole, spattered with Victoire's fading glamour and a touch of fierceness left over from recently facing down death.

I rub at the blotches around my eyes as if they'll flake off like the paint.

Then I try another door. The room beyond is covered in fabric hangings, paler than those of Freedom but, like the strangely patterned uniforms, reminiscent of both worlds. There are several consoles set into the wall. My pulse quickens. I wake one. There's a whole range of choices I'm not familiar with. None of them offer what I need to help Ash.

I move to the next console and select a setting at random. Music fills the room. Like the uniforms and the wall hangings, it's a subdued reflection of what Freedom offers. Instead of ground-shaking, bone-rattling beats and skirling melodies, it's regular, even, moderate. Still, it's music. Music. In Refuge. Maybe there's something to what that creepy enforcer was saying after all. What else don't I know?

"Try another door." Cadence seems uninterested in my discoveries.

She wants to see Ash. I don't blame her. Or at least, I try not to. It's not her fault she's the one he can't wait to meet. But it's not mine, either. The thought of meeting him for real—and having him realize I'm not her—sends my pulse racing and my stomach churning at the same time.

The next door opens to a room the same shape and size but filled with different hangings and consoles, none of which provide the access to the surveillance feeds I need.

That leaves the final door, the one Serovate left through. I half expect it to be locked, for this to be a prison, albeit a large one filled with surprising conveniences.

"Hurry up," she says.

I push. The door opens into another identical room. There's food; not Noosh, real food. The sight of it makes my stomach twist and groan. I pull my hand back almost immediately. Serovate has drugged me at least twice already.

There's another set of doors off this room, one to a second bathroom, though I can't imagine what I'd need two for, and the other . . .

I hold my breath, lean against it, and listen. Then I ease it open until I can peek out.

"Finally," Cadence says.

37

REUNION

HERE'S NOTHING I can use in the first suite I
search, or the next, or the one after that, all of
them unlocked and for good reason. There's
nobody inside. I search down the corridor in one
direction, then the other, terrified I'll walk in on another
superior or an enforcer or Serovate himself.

But by the sixth suite, I'm just frustrated. It's obviously a
residential floor, nothing more. Cadence and I have a
whispered debate over whether I'd be better off creeping
through the stairwell or brazenly calling up an elevator car.

As it turns out, it doesn't matter. The next door changes
everything. The far end of the room seems to vanish
beneath a thick film of translucent threads, but when I get
closer the clouded mass resolves into a sheet of dingy plastic,
and beyond it, what looks like open sky. The outer wall is
missing, the edges of the room shattered, with a translucent
tarp tacked across the opening. Past it, bits of gold wire and
steel rebar poke out of crumbling concrete and tattered
drywall. I clutch the doorframe and eye the long cracks
snaking across the floor and walls. Someone had to have put
up the barrier, but I wouldn't want to trust my weight to the
floor that close to the edge.

"You see them?" Cadence says.

My first instinct was right after all. Countless wafting threads trail right through the plastic sheet. I reach for one, and the world blurs around me.

I'm standing once again under the midnight sky on the rooftop. It was daylight moments ago, in the waking world.

Ash rises from a crouch to greet me.

"No dream? Where are the Mara?" I say before he can open his mouth. No point trying to hold a conversation if we're going to have to turn and fight any minute now. Not that he can hear me.

It's just a dreamscape, Cadence says as if I'm an idiot, even though she's never properly explained how this works. *It's not like someone has to be dying for you to get here. Looks like the broken wall is enough of a breach in the shields to let us dreamwalk.*

"Sorry for the wait," she says through me.

"You're here now." Ash shrugs, but his gaze is fixed on me as if he's worried I'll vanish any second. "So, what's the plan?"

"About that—we're still trying to sort out some, uh, complications. We lost access to the surveillance system. We'll have to find another console before we can guide you in. But the good news is we found a breach in the outer wall, so we'll be able to contact you whenever we need to."

"How high?"

"What?"

"How high's the breach? Can you get out that way?"

"Out? It's got to be at least a dozen stories up, probably twice that. I didn't stop to count. A bit high to jump, don't you think?"

"Not jump, climb. I'll rig something from another building. You up to it?"

I gulp, feeling the blood drain from my head. Climb out the side of Refuge? But at the same time, a twinge of excitement stirs. If I don't have to find a working console to guide him in, I could be much closer to meeting Ash in person than I'd realized.

I shove back the excitement. The point of all this isn't to finally meet Ash, much as the idea fascinates me. If I take Cadence to him and the two of them get back on track with their mission against the Mara, who'll make sure Refuge falls? But if I can get him here, I'm sure he'll realize that's what needs to happen first. What if Cadence could convince him to climb into Refuge instead of sending me out?

"Tell him no," I say. "I can't make it."

Are you sure? What if you just—

"Not a chance."

It's not as hard as you'd think. Ash'll make sure the line's secure, even rig up a bit of a harness for you if I ask him to. I really don't think we should risk him coming over here.

"No. Tell him."

"We're not up to it," she says. "You don't know how much I wish we were. But listen, the connection's clear enough like this. I can pass along all the intelligence the Travellers need. Maybe it's better this way. You take word back, and we'll find a way to stay hidden, keep collecting data, see if we can slow the rate of attacks or something. We're getting stronger."

Oops. Luckily, Ash seems to agree with me. "I'm not leaving without you, Cady. You're coming back with me, or I'm not going at all. If you're not strong enough to climb out on your own, I'm coming in."

"Ash, don't be like that. You know I want to—it's been so long—but this is bigger than either of us. We can't be selfish. The mission is too important."

That's a lie. It's absolutely selfishness keeping her from giving in to the desire to meet up with Ash in the waking world. She doesn't want him to find out about her. Too bad I'm just as selfish. Cadence wants to reunite with Ash, but fears it even more. Ash wants to save Cadence. I need Ash here. It's so easy to reach out and lay a hand on his arm, to use the face he thinks is hers to plead silently for him to come and rescue us.

He takes the bait.

"Enough, Cady. It's decided. Wait there. I'm nearby. It won't take that long to find a way in, now I know what to look for."

He turns. The dreamscape goes with him. I can barely stop myself from cheering.

We did it. We called Ash—and no one even had to die. He knows where we are now; he's on his way. For real. Like, real body, real time, not-going-to-vanish-any-second real. And we're safe and alive—well, I'm alive, and Cadence is still Cadence.

It was a lot easier than I'd expected, actually. Maybe this hero thing has more going for it than I'd feared. But now I've got more to worry about, like what I'm going to do when Ash actually gets here. More specifically, what I'm going to do when he realizes I'm not her.

"How long do you think it'll take?" Cadence says, as if I have any idea.

"You tell me."

"Don't be like that. I'm on your side, Cole. We're good now, right?"

It has been hard to switch gears from thinking she's been torturing me to seeing her as an ally. Not that I have to admit it to her, necessarily. Besides, she's still annoying. And the one Ash's coming to see. And save. And fight alongside. Which brings up all sorts of new issues.

"What happens when he gets here?" I reach out and yank the plastic. It's nailed to the wall, but after tugging for a few minutes, most of it pulls free. It falls in a crackling heap at my feet.

Cadence is quiet too long. "Ash will know what to do," she says finally. "He'll want to make sure we're safe first, and get whatever intelligence we—I—can offer. Then—"

"But what about—" *What about you?*

I can't say it. How can I ask her? But we're all going to have to deal with the reality of her death, of the lie Ash has believed all this time. She's talked to him in the dreams, kept me from telling him. Because of course, that's what I would have done. I never would have let him believe I was her, at least not for this long.

So many things left unsaid; so much more I can't say to Cadence.

You're dead.

You can't help Ash.

You can't have him.

Anyway, it's not about me. Or her. I've done what I've done for the good of everyone. Ash has the power to stop death and maybe the power to stop Refuge's lies, to help everyone see and choose for themselves what to do and how to live. We all need him. And if he happens to dismantle the system that taught me I was a failure and made me work every minute of my life to live up to impossible standards and earn its approval for no reason . . . Well, all the better.

It happens fast. I'm not prepared at all. There's a dull sound. The end of a heavy cord embedded in the floor. Not my translucent barely-there threads, but a real, solid, dark cord. A few breathless minutes later, there's a sort of zipping noise and he's there.

"Cady." Her name sighs out of him as if he's held it so close so long it's a part of every breath.

I shake my head. She makes a soft, half-swallowed sound.

"Cady." He comes to me all in a rush, falling to his knees, gathering me in. He smells of salt and starlight, the scent of the open air under the night sky. He crushes me so close I can't breathe, then pushes me back, running his hands over my face, my shoulders. His fingers are rough, calloused, and dark under a sheen of silver that, even in the waking world, seems to swirl over and through the skin.

This close, it's as if I can peer past the mist right through to who he is below. His skin is a sort of uneven tan, pale along the ridges of his face, shadowed under round brown eyes. His hair is as black as his gear, and long by Refuge's standards. I blink. He's covered over with silver once again, his eyes glowing with light, the angles of his face broadened and filled out with it.

"Cady, you're all right. You did it."

My lips quirk up in acknowledgement, which is wrong. I have to tell him. I have to push him away, make him understand. I thought once he saw me in person, he'd realize. I'd hoped the dreams were what confused him, that Cadence had somehow shown him herself in the dreamscape and not me, just as she'd taken my voice.

That's a lie. I'd hoped for exactly this, for Ash to look me full in the face and pull me close, to want me and not her. But the longer I relax into this, the longer I accept his longing and joy, the more I'll hurt him when he realizes the truth.

"Ash, I—"

"Someone's coming." Cadence says.

I hear the boots too late. Ash whirls to his feet and pulls a pair of long knives from somewhere under his dark, complicated-looking jacket. Plastic sheeting rustles.

"Stay back," he says, as if I'd throw myself at the door or set myself shoulder to shoulder with him to fight whatever comes. As if I'm her.

I can't take it anymore. I can't allow him to keep thinking I'm her, when all along she's been—

"I'm not Cadence." I struggle to my feet. "I'm not her, I—"

Ash looks over his shoulder at me, the silver on his skin swirling thicker, ranging further from its surface. "What do you mean you're not—"

"Cole, not now," Cadence shrieks over him.

The door flies open, dragging his attention away. Serovate grins through the opening, his mask dangling from one side of his hood.

"Well done, princess," he says, throwing up his hand.

There's a sharp sound. Ash jerks and crashes to the floor. Cadence screams.

He lies crumpled, his head turned to one side, his arm caught under his body, his face gone empty. Blood seeps from his shoulder where one of his own blades has sliced through fabric and into flesh. Silver mist boils around him for a moment, then draws back to the surface of his skin. His eyes are half-open and blank but for the movement of silver over their dull gleam. Not pearl-white Mara-taken blank. Just flat, unseeing brown and black.

He's gone, just like that. It's my fault. I never should have made him come in the first place, never should have distracted him with my stupid, selfish demands.

Serovate steps toward Ash, plastic creaking underfoot. I howl and rush him.

"Cole, watch out," Cadence shouts.

Serovate laughs. He catches my arm and twists it back and in. I'm forced to my knees. There's a now-familiar stab of pain. I stare at the sharp gleam of steel as the syringe pulls away.

"Very well done indeed, superior," he sneers down at me.

Darkness gathers in the corners. Plastic creaks under my knees, spilling a bright trail of red toward me. Cadence yells something in the far distance.

I hit the floor in what feels like slow motion and bounce once, my gaze reeling from Serovate to the crumbling walls and landing finally on Ash's blank gaze.

FAILURE

I'M IN DARKNESS, or more correctly, in nothingness. Featurelessness, and a slow becoming. Shapes emerge like a landscape obscured by mist, fuzzy and indistinct.

Sounds filter in, distant and unclear. The growing light is unsettling, but it also brings a strange peace. That form hidden behind the mist, that voice I can't quite hear, that silver gaze. It's painful. But it is good.

I drift between sleep and waking. Everything hurts, but the hurt is more distant when I sleep, when I go away into that other world. While I sleep, I am safe. For now.

When I wake, a painted face hovers over me. My skin aches and stings. Something's poured down my throat. I choke and cough, setting off fresh waves of pain. Voices. They make no sense. I drift back to a place where nothing connects, but the nothing is fine. Nothing is good. It's better. Better than what, I can't quite remember.

The next time I wake, there's a different face. Black and gold curve around warm, high cheeks and brilliant, molten eyes. Strikingly beautiful. Familiar. He looks angry. He speaks. I can't make sense of the words. I close my eyes.

There are others. Still, shadowed faces. Impassive, bright faces that come and go, scanning across me carelessly. And still more faces, rough, reddened, fearful faces in my memory, faces with bright, terrified eyes and then still, dull, dead eyes.

And the one face I cannot see, the one that waits and hides in the drifting, is the only one I want to see.

The mists are thinning. The light is no longer painful. I can almost see him. I'm about to break through. I have so many questions. There's so much I want to know. He reaches toward me through the mist. It ripples and ebbs. His distant voice fades, filtering in and out of range, calling out to me, calling my name.

I OPEN MY eyes to a maze of colour and screw them shut fast. I pull my arms and legs in convulsively. It launches me into a dizzy spin that knocks me into space for a panicked heartbeat. Painful impact. My eyes fly open again.

Then a familiar, calming fuzziness takes comforting hold.

No more aches and bruises, no deep throbbing pain in my chest, no more stinging cuts. I sprawl in a boneless heap on the floor, concrete and cracked tile covered by piles of vibrant rugs. The texture of the floor—I've never noticed it before. It's engrossing. I could stare at it forever. Subtle pitting, grey on grey with hints of shadows and deeper shade at the edge of each layer of carpeting. The drape of twisted fabric over my knees; shadowed valleys and peaked folds. They flex with the slow rise and fall of my breath. The curious wrinkles of a lacy glove over my hand, highlighting each joint. I tighten it into a fist.

I feel nothing, though bright red seeps through the fabric. I watch it grow, touch a finger to it, paint the vivid colour across the bumpy texture of the floor and up the tangled fringe of a purple and orange rug. It soaks in too quickly. It doesn't run like it did on the—

"How dare you," Ravel says.

His tone is bland. Everything is bland. His hand on my shoulder is a slight pressure, not painful, not even warm. It just is.

The room starts to move in fast, sharp jerks. I let my head loll back to look up at him shaking me. The ceiling lights reel in the far distance.

His molten eyes blaze out of that surprising expanse of golden skin, unshielded by any mask. His head is bare and unadorned but beautiful all the same. I understand his appeal in a detached sort of way, but I feel nothing. I don't feel.

I must not feel.

"Stupid girl." Ravel shakes me again, his voice low and controlled. "What were you thinking? Do you have any idea what you've cost me, how much your selfishness has undermined my power? Why couldn't you have just listened to me?"

Selfishness. A thread of memory prods me to remember why he's unhappy with me, why I deserve his anger. I ran away. I went to help Ash.

Ash. I shove that thread away before it gets too close, before it weaves itself into something larger, something hurtful.

"You never look at me." He cups a hand around the back of my head. "Why don't you see me? Why aren't I enough for you?"

His face twists with emotion, but even with him forcing eye contact, it's hard to focus, impossible to care. He's upset about something. Not about something, about me. I should calm him down, reassure him. He doesn't need to worry. I'm here now.

I frown. Why am I here with Ravel? In Freedom? Wasn't I—

There's a voice yelling from far away. It wants me to remember, but I can't. I won't. This is better, this numbness, this emptiness. I blink, slowly, and curve the edges of my lips at Ravel in reassurance.

He wants Victoire. I can be her—or rather, she can be me. Glittering, hungry, heartless. Just like him.

I pull back, letting her rise to the surface. A smile stretches my face, self-satisfied and smug.

Ravel raises his eyebrows at me. "All that effort to get you healed up, and now look at you. Useless. Just another mindless Refuge drone."

He releases my shoulder. My head thunks against the floor. The room swims.

He stares down at me. Sighs.

"Fine. We'll just have to work with it; you've been gone too long as it is. You cost me an awful lot of credibility. You're going to help me get it back. Starting now."

He extends a hand to me, as if I'll just pick myself up off the floor and go dancing after him.

I stay.

Victoire goes.

She comes back late in the morning, drunk on liquor and music, tingling with adoration and new bruises. I refuse to hear the screams of the Exchanged still echoing in her ears, refuse to see them begging, falling. It's not my fault. None of it's my fault. I can't do anything.

Victoire doesn't sleep. Neither can I. We roam the room, chasing Ravel's staff out of the alcoves and tearing through the cupboards, tossing fabric and paints in rainbow masses across the floor. We watch attendants creep out of the corners and tidy the mess away.

The first day and then next, they force the soporific glasses of dust into our hands and down our throats. After that, we reach for the pitcher of golddust. At first, we screw up our face against the burn. Later, we can't even feel it. It doesn't make us sleep, quite, but it slows everything down. It makes the colours brighter, the patterns more entrancing, the throbbing beat wider and deeper. It keeps the screaming far, far away. Along with everything else.

Ravel comes and looks at us and speaks. His voice is as wide and deep as the beat, too slow to be words. We grin up at him, chuckling. How silly he sounds.

Then the laughter melts. His face softens. He holds us while our eyes burn and we choke on memories we can't quite grasp. After, he goes again, dimming the lights in his absence.

We drift. When he comes back, the whole cycle repeats. There are days and nights and more days, and with every new night, there is the Exchange, until the panicked faces and crumpled bodies blur into one in our minds. An avalanche of pearls raining down on us. It takes more and more dust to keep from remembering.

So we dance and laugh and rage and devour and forget. And then, finally, the darkness sweeps us away, and I am torn from Victoire and forced into someone else.

It pursues us, the dream that devours. We moan, seeking the light, the silver that saved us.

"She needs help," Cadence says, jolting me out and away from the broken creature's mind. "Look! She's not going to make it on her own."

I look. At first, I mostly follow the sound, the gasping, tortured cries of the woman. I peer into the shadows. They seem to brighten around the flailing figure. But it's not her ragged, mud-crusted finery, tangled nest of hair, or dirt-crusted fingernails that hold my attention.

Shapes coalesce out of the sickly yellow fog, spinning and darting around her. Her eyes are black in her grimy face, the skin scored with dark lines, rough and reddened. Tears carve mud tracks down her cheeks as she rolls and scuttles, hitting out with both hands at the swarming things in the fog, blurry and indistinct as if caught inside a moving cloud.

I've seen something like it before. I don't want to let the memory in. It's easier to be Victoire, careless Victoire who savours the thrill of the ragged woman's fear.

"You can't just let this happen." Cadence sounds horrified.

The woman strikes out. The things squirming through the fog hit back. Red trails rake her arms, blood spattering crimson. Her voice rings out, shrill and high: "Silver. No. Silver. Silver! Please." She wards off blows that send her skidding across the floor. "Silver, please . . ."

She's nearer now, the light brighter around her. She catches sight of me. Her eyes round with hope.

"Silver," she breathes, crawling on all fours toward me.

"Fight back. Save her, like Ash did." Cadence yells, as if she can force me to remember.

I just watch.

The floor buckles and cracks behind the ragged woman. The things in the fog bunch together and seize her ankle. They yank. There's a horrible, thick pop. She howls and scrapes the ends of her fingers bloody on the floor. She's dragged backwards, her eyes fixed on mine, desperate, anguished, hopeful, accusing. It's as if she recognizes me somehow and can't understand why I won't act to save her.

And something in that look brings it all flooding back to me, and under the dirt, or maybe because of it, I know who she is. Fuchsia. The woman from Outside. The one Ash saved.

The Mara are there with her, dressed in fog like a swirling cloak, huge and hulking. The floor buckles under their force, tile and concrete cracking. I expect them to throw her against the wall, but they don't let go as they haul her backwards and swing her in an arc that reaches full extension with another snap. A final howl of anguish ends in a whimper as the Mara bring her back around to crack against the floor.

Fuchsia is silent as she lies crumpled on—no, in—the floor. Blood flows freely from the corners of her mouth and nose. Her eyes fix on mine. The light in them clouds over with pearlescent film.

The fog-shrouded Mara stomp across and through the floor and the remains of the woman broken on it, trampling with a weight and fervour that reeks of evil delight. The floor shakes long after the light has gone from the eyes of the crumpled mass under the beast's feet. I don't want to see what becomes of her, but I can't turn my gaze away from the sick yellow glow that fills the hall, pulsing and swarming and beating against the floor.

Shadows grow until the only thing left is a fading reflection of silver against the pearl sheen of Fuchsia's still eyes, fixed on mine until the end. Then I too slip into the darkness.

39

SHAME

I T GOES ON this way for days. The cuts heal. The bruises fade. The endless glasses of dust become a little less numbing. The Exchanged die and the dreams come, and with them, more deaths. But not Ash. Never again Ash.

The fuzzy distance is wearing away, bit by bit. It's harder to be satisfied with the hungry adoration of the crowd, with Ravel's calculated attentiveness, harder to surrender to the beat and bounce back after each death.

But I have to be Victoire. There's nothing else left. Even if I could break away from Ravel, what would be the point?

There comes an hour, a minute, a quiet breath alone in my chamber when I can't keep it away any longer. My eyes burn and my heart clenches, and a high keening works its way up my throat as the threads of memory weave back together.

It's all my fault.

I lured Ash in with the promise of saving Cadence and completing his mission. I was stupid enough to think Refuge wouldn't be watching. I bought into the lie of all those empty suites, as if I really believed I was special, some kind of superior deserving of trust and access and power. I ran away from Ravel in the first place, grasping for more after he'd given me a place to be, a place to belong.

I got Cass killed. And Ash.

And for what? So I could feel special? Important? So I could believe there was meaning to my existence, that I had a mission, a goal worthy of sacrifice, worth living for? Perhaps it was something less: so I could play the hero to the people who'd shunned me, dismantling the world that taught me I was worthless.

I've been such an idiot.

Here's the truth: no one in Refuge cares they're being lied to. Not only would they never have listened to me, they'd never have listened to Ravel, or Ash, or anyone who came in and threatened their familiar, safe world.

So much suffering for nothing.

"Snap out of it," Cadence says. "You have to get it together. You're all that's left."

Her voice breaks. How does she keep trying after everything is gone? Why does she bother? Why is she still here?

"Go away." I close my eyes and press the heels of my hands against their heat. "Just leave me alone. No more."

"Cole."

"Just go." I sit up fast. "Just—"

It's not Cadence.

Ange stands beside my bed. "It's time to get you out of here."

I slump back and pull a cushion over my face. "Go away."

"Show a little gratitude." She yanks the cushion away and tosses it across the room. "Do you know what I had to do to make this happen? Do you have any idea how hard it was?"

Her lips are deep purple, just like Cass's. She wears one of his masks. The paint around her eyes is red. She hasn't forgotten.

I roll over and pull my knees up to my chest. "Go away," I say into another cushion.

Ange yanks this one away too. She grabs my shoulders and drags me up off the bed. She's terribly strong, much stronger than her size would suggest. I remember how she fit under Cass's arm, how fierce she was and how calmly he handled her, letting her lead but always just behind her. My eyes burn.

Ange opens her mouth, those aubergine lips snarling as if she's ready to let loose. She drops me and turns her back.

"It's not your fault," she says between slow, harsh breaths that almost hide the quiver in her voice. "That he's—that he's gone. It's not anyone's fault. It's just what happens. That's why we have to keep fighting."

She only knows about the one death, the one that matters most to her, but for me, there've been so many now. Cass's wasn't even the worst. A high, raw sound scorches its way up from my chest and gets caught at the top of my throat. I bite down before it can work its way out.

"I'll get you out of here," Ange says. "I promise. You'll see, when you're away from all this. It's not—it's not that bad."

I turn away. "I don't need anything from you." The words come out haughty. Victoire's words.

"Nevertheless," she says.

Then she goes.

I walk too fast to the back of the room, seize the pitcher of dust, and tip my head back, gulping messily until I can no longer stand. The pitcher falls in wet shards at my feet. I join it.

Ravel finds me there. He raises the lone glass cup on the table in one hand and looks down at me.

I gaze back disinterestedly.

He flings the delicate cup. It shatters musically on a patch of tile exposed when the rugs rumpled beneath me. He grabs a handful of my cropped hair, hauls me across the room. He hurls me against the cushions and roars for the attendants.

There should be pain, and fear. I'm too full of Victoire and dust to feel it.

Ravel stands over me, enraged. He seizes my shoulders and shakes. Bangles and chains clatter and chime on my limp arms. One hand goes to my collar and pulls me forward while the other draws back.

My head snaps to the side with the impact, skin raging hot immediately after. I let my head fall to one side, as if unconscious.

Ravel cries out as if he's the one hurt. "No! No, no, flame, no, I didn't mean to, I . . ." He crushes me to him, huddling on the platform.

I can't summon enough interest to care about the pain, neither his nor mine. But Victoire in me is not displeased with his reaction.

He glares over his shoulder. "You've given her too much."

The attendants scurry to clean away the glass and spilled dust behind him.

"Yes, Ravel." Ange is impassive.

"She's no good to me like this."

"Yes, Ravel."

"Clean her up and bring her out to me when she's able to perform properly."

"Yes, Ravel."

His words are cold, but his hands are warm, gentle, and insistent. My lips curve in a faint smile as he leaves the room.

Ange brings out her paints again and works over me.

"It's a dangerous game," she whispers. "You can't survive like this much longer. There's only so much dust your body can take. And Ravel won't tolerate it forever. His authority is being questioned after so many unscheduled deaths. He needs a way to regain their confidence. More than that, he needs something to make him feel confident. Someone. Don't push him too far."

I refuse to respond. She paints over my bruises and wraps a delicate gold filigree half-mask over the damage. I loll against the cushions and trace a line of embroidery over and over.

"Listen, you stupid kid." Ange grips my arm, pressing the cuffs and chains savagely into my bruises. "I'm telling you, he's going to turn on you if he doesn't get what he wants. Your only chance is to get out. I'll make sure no more dust is put out tonight. He wants you clearer than this, anyway. The effects will wear off slowly, but he'll try to keep you distracted, overwhelmed. He'll use power and pleasure, the beat and the light and the flesh to control you, to make you into what he needs."

She leans in close, trying to force eye contact. "Don't let it take you. He'll try to use it on you, but the truth is, he gets just as high off his own drug. It works on him more than he'd like to admit."

Ange holds my head so I can't turn away. "Slip away before tonight's Exchange. There's a door, a way out. You remember. Follow the blue lights. I'll make sure someone's waiting. They'll help you, take you to safety."

I look past her to the entrance to the chamber. Watching and waiting, feeling the muffled beat shake the floor and tremble up the platform. It slides into my bones, pulsing.

This is what I choose, to be lost to the spell of Freedom, my mind empty, my body full of sensations and longings, of light and sound and touch that come from nowhere and go nowhere, but simply are, and are everything.

40

EXPOSED

VICTOIRE GLORIES IN the energy of the dancers. It shivers across her skin in a thousand-thousand tiny, delicious sparkles, glancing off flecks of paint and glitter and rolling with the drops of sweat. I make myself small within her, pushing away the touch of those hands, the frenzied worshippers dancing their death around us.

The Exchange takes place in ritual silence, broken only by the stomping beat. But whatever arrangement Ravel had with the Mara is broken now. We perform the Exchange hourly, desperately, in every room from blue to black, but between sacrifices, more screams pierce the frenzied melody in a weird counterpoint harmony. I don't know what magic Ravel has to make everyone stay, if it's the dust and the music, or the hunger inside them, or simply that they have nowhere else to go, nothing left to live for. Like me.

Victoire leans into the numbness of dust to keep going, drawing it down and through herself until it changes into something else. It sparkles in her eyes and laughs from her mouth. She'll stay here forever, her hurt and fear painted over in mesmerizing patterns and wound through with beautiful chains until it is become something she flaunts, just another source of power.

Her ears don't hear the screams choked off, the dying gurgles and desperate gasps as the Mara devour one victim after the other. She refuses to see the attendants struggling to clean up the carnage, the dancers with their carefully shuttered gazes fixed on the light above and not the terror below. Ravel works ever harder to hold their focus.

Yet another shriek rises, drawing something out from inside of me, surging past Victoire's studied carelessness.

Anger?

Fury. Horror. Determination.

Rebellion.

Cadence breathes the words into my ear without sound. I can't truly hear her here, with the dust buzzing through Victoire's veins and the music ringing in my ears.

Her words are dangerous, but I'm locked up around myself as tightly as I can be. There is no more space to turn away.

With each shriek that sounds from the shadows around us, my world flashes silver, as if in mockery of what I've lost.

In. Out. Darkness shot with coloured beams one moment, a stunning wash of light the next. It's as if there's a hook set in my insides, and with each cry, with each pulse of brilliance, it yanks, pulling me up and out of the safe, compact core that I have wound myself around.

"Choose to be better than this. Fight back." Cadence's voice is clear and strong in the moment the world pulses out, washed away on a silver tide.

But there is no choice, no point even in dreaming about anything anymore. There is only death, painful, horrible, but inevitable. It's the natural consequence of this place, this rebellion, any rebellion.

Immune for the moment, Victoire leads the charge, drawing the pitiful, mad dancers in her wake even as Ravel draws her along, a glittering thing to catch the eye and lead it away from the nightmares descending.

All of my life has been a smooth, featureless shell; encircling, safe, untouched.

Broken.

Cadence has been poking holes in that shell for as long as I can remember, flaunting her mask-less, vulnerable existence, tempting and teasing and telling stories, luring me into stepping out of bounds. Now Victoire has shattered the shell and started flinging the pieces like weapons, spreading the damage to everyone within range while hiding behind her jewelled mask. She's a weapon in the hands of a master manipulator, and I have lost all my safety.

No, there is no choice. All my choices have been taken from me.

Ravel spins Victoire. She laughs, fabric floating in her wake. Chains fling out and slap sharply when she ends her spin in his arms, her back pressed against him. He seems to revel in his dominance, displaying his mastery to the crowd as he runs a hand along the side of her face. Victoire leans into him.

"Enjoying the dance, flame?" he whispers, the sharpness of his nails tracing white lines on her skin. "Enjoying all I give you? All I've made you? Don't you wish you'd never left me for that pathetic Outsider?"

His fingers tighten around the edge of her mask, digging painfully into the soft skin above her ear.

"I see the way you search the crowd," he says. "I see the way your eyes rove, dreaming of your little boyfriend. Don't worry, flame. I'll erase every last mark of your betrayal. I'll forgive you and end his suffering soon."

He can't mean Ash. Ash is dead. But then who?

I uncurl and shoulder Victoire aside to ask, to press him for answers. If Ash survived . . . if he's been alive this whole time . . .

But the music has stopped. Every eye in the hall is on us. The black hall.

"The Exchange," Ravel says.

No. Not again. I can't. I wrench my shoulders, but Ravel just tightens his grip.

The crowd stares, wavering. The spotlights shine on us alone. Where is the victim?

"The Exchange," Ravel repeats. He stamps behind me, slow at first, then faster, as the dancers join in.

"Will you dream for us, flame?" he says over the racing beat. "What will you sacrifice for our freedom?"

He can't mean . . . He wouldn't. He just said he'd forgive me. He needs me, doesn't he?

At the same time; a looping refrain in the background: Ash. Where's Ash? Is he alive?

Ravel tears my mask from me. I try to curl away. He holds me there, exposed under the crimson lights. The crowd leans in to watch the spectacle. The Exchange, the ritual of controlled death that lets them pretend they're safe from the Mara.

I glare back. I won't clamp my eyes shut. I won't wait in the dark for the Mara to take me. I'll watch the nightmares come until the moment they steal my sight.

"Trust me." Ravel whispers. "You never trust me enough. Would I let my Victoire be taken from me?"

I growl, wriggling against his grip. The room is eerily quiet. The dancers' gazes flicker, confused. Where are the Mara?

"The Exchange answers to me," Ravel roars out over the crowd. "The Mara answer to me. Don't look to them for life or death. You look to me."

The music starts up again at his signal. Ravel spins me away and back in a stumbling simulation of renewed dance.

The Mara did not descend to claim his flame as a victim. It's a triumph, an incontrovertible display of power, a sign that it is not ritual and mask, not devouring monsters, but Ravel himself who decides who lives and dies. His mastery, on display for all to see.

The crowd lets out a collective sigh and resumes its frenzy.

"He's alive!" Cadence's voice is near once again, strong and present. "Cole, Ash's alive!"

The screams start up again in the distance, despite Ravel's display. His mouth tightens. It seems less likely the Mara obey his whims, and more likely they've abandoned the pretence of the Exchange altogether. Freedom dances on regardless. The world washes silver and then red.

Threads brush against my fingertips once more. I know this feeling. I name it.

Fury.

No more lies. No more death. If Ash is alive, there's still a chance to make things right. I have to find him.

Ravel tugs me close. His eyes narrow. He searches my face—exposed—and I struggle not to let him see me behind Victoire's paint and glitter. I have to do something quick, or he'll dose me up again and let the dust keep me compliant, keep me *her*.

"Dust," I whisper. There's something there that can help, if only I can push past fear and make it happen.

"Yes," Cadence says, before I've even had a chance to consider the plan. "That'll work."

I look up at Ravel and lick my lips, thinking furiously.

"I need—" My gaze flicks to him and away.

He pulls me closer and settles his grip. I flinch.

"No," Cadence groans, "use it. C'mon. Just channel Victoire."

The advice is good, even if I can't manage to make eye contact. I lean in gingerly. My skin crawls and my stomach churns at the sweat-slick heat and the smell of him, so close, too close, I can't do this . . .

Another scream rings in my ears. There's the rumble-snap-crash of ceiling tiles falling. The world washes silver for less than a heartbeat, pure and clean, and then I'm back. Threads brush at my fingertips, and it's a sort of pain not to reach out to them.

It is enough.

I pretend my brush with death was exhilarating instead of panic inducing. I look up into his eyes, those lovely, persuasive, devious, mirror-like golden eyes, and try to believe for a moment that he is good and kind.

Or at least persuadable.

"I need . . ." I put a bit of a moan into it, licking my lips delicately.

Ravel watches the line of my throat, the edge of my lip where I catch it between my teeth. I start to panic. He's not going to buy it. He'll see right through me.

Then he chuckles, smirking. It's a bit pathetic, really, how easily he accepts it. How willing he is to believe I've forgiven him for offering me to the Mara, even if it was all staged. He takes my arm and steers me past the reaching, grasping crowd.

But it's too soon to revel in my small triumph. For this plan to work, I have to get well out of his reach.

"Make him believe," says Cadence.

I tug against Ravel's grip, rolling my hips. He pauses.

"I don't want to go back there," I whine, leaning into the crowd, gyrating with the beat. "Don't want to stop. Can't I stay here?"

Ravel grins and lifts a hand. He's looking for an attendant. That won't do. I need to get out of his sight—or at the very least, his reach.

I squirm a little closer again, trying to channel the shuddering into a sort of shimmying dance. It's awkward. He doesn't seem to notice.

"I like it when *you* bring it to me," I whisper, my lips almost brushing his cheek, astonished at my own daring.

Ravel doesn't seem to mind. I don't like the look of his smile. He wraps an arm around me.

"Demanding, aren't we?" He squeezes until a chain pops a link and goes skittering down my back.

I jump. Ravel laughs. He pinches the edge of the chain and yanks. It slithers away and wraps a couple of times around his hand with a snap. He raises the fist to his mouth and presses the chain to his lips.

"Be right back." He tightens his grip until it cuts a white line into his flesh. "Don't enjoy yourself too much while I'm gone. I'll expect my reward when I return."

Cadence swallows. It's hard not to follow suit. I lower my lashes and hope it looks coy instead of nauseated. Ravel tears himself away and moves off through the crowd.

The bodies close in behind him. My knees sag. I've only won a small victory. It'll take more than a little flirting to save Ash.

I really don't want to be around when Ravel gets back with that drink.

I RACE THROUGH half the colour halls before I realize don't have any idea where to start looking for Ash. I scan the crowd, hoping for inspiration. There's a thud. An overenthusiastic dancer catches me with an elbow to the back. The force spins me away to face down the length of the hall. A soft voice whispers: "That way. Follow the blue light."

A slowing swirl of lights traces a blue arc along the wall to the corner and melts into shadow beyond. Ange's escape route. Or maybe not. The walls change from violet to orange, not green and orange. It's a different route than last time. Where Cass died.

I lurch and nearly fall, then shove the memory away before it overwhelms me. Instead, I look around for the dancer who pointed me in this direction. No one seems to pay me any attention.

There's a gust of cold air. A dark-cloaked figure shoves a flap in the wall hanging aside. Pale light flashes against the gloomy violet background.

"Hurry," His voice seems deliberately obscured, presumably for the same reason he keeps his face shadowed. "This way. Hurry."

The hanging drops back in place. It could be a trap. I open my mouth to ask Cadence what she thinks I should do. I close it before the words can escape. Not this time. My selfishness got Ash into this mess. It's my responsibility to save him.

I push through the opening. Someone grabs my arm.

"What took you so long?" Ange yanks me through. She holds on until I catch my balance. "Hurry up. There's no time. When Ravel realizes—"

"I can't go with you." When she grabbed me like that, for a second I'd thought I'd made the wrong choice and been captured once more. I'd forgotten she was planning a rescue. But I'm not the one who needs rescuing. "They have Ash. Ravel, he said—I think my . . . my friend Ash, he's alive. I can't go with you. I have to save him first. It's all my fault, and I have to—"

Ange shakes her head. I take another step out of range. She's smaller than I am but stronger. I have to find some way to convince her to let me go.

"Hurry up," she repeats. "It'll be better for your friend if you're safe first. I'll go back for him as soon as you're clear."

"You know about Ash? You know where he is?"

He's alive. He's really alive. Cadence whoops in the background. Maybe just this once I didn't ruin everything.

"Take me to him. I'm not leaving without him."

Ange turns on her heel. "Fine. As soon as Ravel realizes you went after your friend, it'll be impossible to get him out anyway. I'll explain on the way."

She slows at the next corner and cocks her head, listening. The dark hood she wears slips. She's still wearing Cass's mask under her cloak.

I feel the brush of threads at my fingertips. Light flashes silver-white around me. There's a moment of darkness and a rising shriek of anguish. Then I'm in the stark, bare corridor again.

Ange looks back at me. "Keep it together, kid. There's more going on here than you know. If you want me to get your friend clear, I can't be worrying about you, too."

"How do you know about Ash?"

"Not so loud. We're not the only ones who use these halls." Her voice barely rises above the sound of rustling fabric and pattering feet. "Even I can't fix it if we run into some of them. Ash, is it? We knew that sixer had brought in someone new right around the time he handed you over to Ravel. Took a while to figure out who."

"Sixer—Serovate? The enforcer?"

Ange snorts. "Among other things. He's all tangled up in the worst of the mess." She slows near another corner and signals me to stay back. "There's no time to say this gently. He's warped beyond understanding. He takes delight in breaking things—people, in particular. Your friend—Ash? You need to be prepared. There may not be much, if anything, left."

Cadence chokes.

I freeze. "What?"

"Shh. Keep moving." She motions me around the corner. "Serovate. He—well, you'll get the idea soon. But whatever happens, whatever you see, you've got to keep going. Be quiet. Be fast. We do what we can, we keep moving, and we save our reactions until later. I've seen you shut it all off when Ravel pushes you too far. I've seen you fake it. You can do this. You have to, if you want to live. And if you're lucky and we're fast enough, maybe your friend gets to live, too."

"If." I feel the possibility of Victoire within me, asking if I need her to come out and take over. I push her back. "If you knew Serovate would hurt someone, why didn't you save him sooner?"

Cadence makes that choking noise again, a swallowed sob. It breaks the barrier in my mind and sets free a flood of images: Ash's broad, tanned, star-dusted face, pallid and blood-speckled and empty.

And then we're at the final door, and through it, and the reality is worse.

FORGET

I LOOK AWAY, shutting out Cadence's cries and Ange's low, vicious cursing.

The room's large, stripped down to concrete, and starkly lit at the far end. It highlights each glinting implement and dark stain.

Ange rushes in without hesitation. I stumble forward, finally letting myself see. He hangs from his wrists, clamped in steel. His ankles are bound too, but with chains, not cuffs. He's been left with just enough slack to squirm, but not enough to brace himself against. That would have been important, to keep him from kicking, to keep him from a moment's rest. He'd have experienced enough pain without the added misery of constant strain against every joint, every muscle.

My stomach churns. I fall to the stained floor and vomit. There's so much blood. It's not a dream, or from the inhuman attack of the Mara. There are gleaming tools laid out on the counters: tiny, fine blades and great, tearing ones that rip and rend and—

I heave again, bringing up nothing but thin bile.

"He needs your help. Hurry," Ange says.

I run my arm across my mouth and reach for the clasp around his left wrist. It looks simple enough to unhook from the outside.

"Wait." Her shoulder is under Ash's limp arm. She's already unclasped the other side. "Get that ankle free first, and brace yourself. His weight will drop the moment his arm's free."

She's too short to support him on her own. Already, his weight is too much strain on his left arm. I lean down to unchain his ankle, and there's a meaty *pop* followed by a raw cry. He flails, brought to consciousness by the dislocating of his shoulder. His knee clips the side of my head and knocks me back.

"Get over here." Ange struggles to brace him while he convulses.

I call to Cadence: "Calm him. Convince him to let me help. He'll know your voice."

"I can't," she whimpers, not through me but to me and me alone. "He can't hear me."

"Cady," he chokes out anyway.

I cringe. "We're here to help you. We're going to get you out of here. But you have to hold still, okay?"

He seems to hear me. I get one arm around his front— fever hot, slick with blood and sweat—and angle to catch him as soon as the final cuff lets go.

"Cady, it's all gone wrong. Sorry—I was supposed to be the one . . ." He gasps. "I wanted to be the one to save you. Go. You have to get out of here."

Ash screams when we catch him, jostling his injured shoulder. He convulses and goes limp, his head rolling back. Even with my added height, the sudden drop of his weight is too much for us. We're forced to our knees.

Cadence wails his name, sobbing so loudly I can barely hear Ange muttering "hurry, hurry" as she stumbles to her feet. I stagger up beside her. His blood squishes underfoot. I try to avoid his shoulder, but there's nowhere to hold him that's not carved or burned or broken.

We drag him into the shadows, through the door, down the corridor, and the next. Ange curses. Cadence wails. I refuse to look down. He's alive. That's enough for now. It's everything.

"Put him down here," Ange says as we round another corner. "Is there somewhere he can go? Someone to take care of him?"

She produces a pair of matching dark cloaks identical to hers plus a few extra lengths of black fabric from some hidden pocket.

I shake my head. "I don't know."

She sighs. "I figured. Okay, here's the deal: my people will take you both in for now. But to get to the nearest escape route, we'll have to cross Freedom."

I look at the blood pooling beneath him, then back at the mess we've left in our wake. How much can he afford to lose and still live? How far behind is pursuit?

"Put this on." She shoves one of the cloaks at me. "We'll bind him up enough to slow the bleeding. Set his shoulder. And then we're going to get to safety. If anything happens to me . . ."

There's a tug on my hand. Translucent threads snag between my fingers. Her voice spirals away in a wash of silver light. Roaring darkness. Anguish and terror. I try to fight my way back to Ash, but it's too late.

It's another dream. Enforcers are everywhere, grappling with figures in mismatched rags. Blood flows. All the while the dreamer wails. An enforcer swoops down and seizes her. She's so young. He carries her off over his shoulder. She howls and reaches back for the fallen, her parents, begging wordlessly for them to stand. I struggle not to be drawn in any deeper, not to feel her anguish, not to feel her calling the Mara down.

It's a raid, Refuge Force kidnapping children from the streets to bolster our flagging population. Streets that were supposed to have been submerged by the floods. Seeing parents cut down as they try to protect their children, as horrific as it is, feels inevitable, familiar, a foregone conclusion. It's the reality behind the trainee Liwan's vision of his father's corpse swallowed by the black sand. It's like—

I scream from within the protective circle of mom's arms. She tries to shield me from the sight of dad crumpling to his knees. There's a flickering against shattered concrete as his light fades and goes out.

I gasp. It was there and gone in a flash. That wasn't this child's dream. It felt different. What was that?

"Oh," Cadence says. "No, th—that . . ."

Does she know what just happened? What it means? I'm drawn into the street girl's dream again before I can ask. Her grief and longing call the Mara. The enforcer fades. The crumpled, bloodstained figures rise. They hold her close. She closes her eyes and nestles in. Safe. Home.

There's another flash. The perspective shifts again.

I struggle, bound and bleeding, in a golden room in front of a beautiful woman. A black-haired boy with eyes shining with the same inhuman golden glow as the woman's peeks out at me from behind a floor-length mirror. Someone's holding me back. I can't throw myself on mom's body at our feet, can't try to stop the bleeding, can't wipe away her tears. All I can do is obey. With her last breath the light leaves her eyes and flows into me, along with the command: "Forget."

"Don't," Cadence cries. "You're not allowed. You can't. Leave it alone, Cole."

"What was that? What's happening?"

Before she can respond, my focus is tugged back to the dream. The Mara move to finish their child victim. The part of me that remains separate tears at the threads filling the air, searching for the ones that will stop the dying. Too many children have suffered. Too many families have been broken. Too many girls have grown up alone. Or not at all. I won't let them ruin anyone else.

I dig both hands into the snarl of threads and pull. The Mara suffer with every thread I make straight. I braid the threads into cords and ropes of undiluted power. They cringe from the onslaught of brilliant light. It burns them away.

I grin into the darkness, a vicious thrill sweeping through me. The dream dissolves, leaving the new orphan in the hands of Refuge but in no immediate danger.

Then Ange is shaking me. "Don't you dare."

Her grip is too tight. I need to ask Cadence—was it multiple attacks at the same time? Why did she warn me off? That room—those people—

But Ange doesn't give me another minute to catch up. "You want your friend to live, you want to survive this, you hang on, you hear me?"

I can't let myself think about what this must feel like to her, what it must take for her to keep going. I just nod and pull the cloak tighter around my shoulders.

Ange leans back. "Good. Brace him. I'll do the rest."

I hold Ash up and pass the roll of black fabric to her until it's wound thickly enough to soak up the blood.

He drifts in and out of consciousness, moaning. "Worthless. Leave me. Cady, just go. I can't—don't want you hurt."

Ange jams wadded fabric between his teeth. I brace him, feel the jolt of pain as his shoulder pops back into its socket. He screams around the gag. The hurt ratchets through his body and into mine—

"YOU'RE ASLEEP." CADENCE sounds younger than she has in a long time. "Or not really—passed out, more like— but I've always thought it sounded embarrassing to say 'fainted,' so let's go with 'asleep.'"

She's nervous, babbling. I mean to tell her so, but it's like the dreamscape with Ash, and I find I can't speak.

"You don't have to," she says. "Not to me. We have one voice for a reason. It's the last piece. I can't protect you for much longer."

She's scaring me. I want to ask what she's talking about, but I don't have the will to force the words out.

"I'm telling you that's not how it works. Well, never mind. It's better this way. Forget for just a little longer."

Forget what?

"All of it. It won't help us to remember yet. Forget."

ANGE IS PINCHING my arm, her other hand clamped over my mouth. She sits back on her heels and glares at me through Cass's mask.

"Don't you dare do that again. I can't get you both out safe. Next time you drop like that, we're leaving him behind."

"I can do this." I hope it's not a lie.

We stagger under his weight. I'm on the right this time, his arm around my shoulders and mine around his waist. Ange guides us through the maze of corridors back toward the crush and noise of Freedom. We pause every few feet for her to dart back and swipe up smears of blood in our wake, or forward to check for enemies around the next corner.

I hear them moments before she stiffens and eases back. The tromp of heavy boots had almost been drowned out by the muffled beat of Freedom. She flattens herself against the wall and waves me back. I stumble and almost go down under Ash's weight. She catches up just in time to help.

"Hurry." Her voice is oddly thick.

She urges me faster, faster, until we drag Ash around another corner. Panting, I let him slide to the floor, back against the wall. Ange darts out to swipe up the last telltale drops of blood. She dives around the corner in the nick of time.

I raise a questioning eyebrow.

"Don't," she says.

I lean past her and peek around the corner.

42 RESCUE

REFUGE FORCE. I knew it had to be, from the steady sound of their boots, so unlike the soft padding of a worker's slippers or the bright, tapping ring of Freedom's impossible footwear. And I could tell it was more than one.

But what sends the blood draining from my head in a cold, dizzy wave are the children in their midst. The bigger ones stumble along barefoot and grubby between ranks of goggle-wearing enforcers. The smaller ones are carried, limp in the arms of their captors. All are dressed in faded, dirty scraps of fabric completely unlike the revealing costumes of Freedom or the bland uniforms of Refuge. Children from Outside.

"Stay back," Ange says. "Don't let them see you."

I don't listen. The enforcers aren't wary; they trudge along, impatient at the slow pace. The children themselves are eerily silent, heads down, steps stumbling and awkward from shock, or maybe sedatives, or some combination of the two.

I search their white-suited ranks, hopelessly. I don't know what would be worse, to think of the child I saved from the Mara left to the elements, or to see her here, bound and defeated. Finally, I spot her tied between two larger children, limping along with her arms tucked to her chest.

Ange hauls me back from the corner. "Are you insane?"

I twist away. "Did you know? Those children—they're from Outside, aren't they? I recognize one of them."

She looks me up and down. "You'll explain that later. Yes, I knew. Even those fools in Freedom know, at least through rumour. You didn't actually believe Refuge's stories about growing people, did you?"

"I—I'd heard, but I thought even if it was true, they must just take a few from outside, maybe supplement the workforce when they couldn't grow enough or something. To take this many all at once—"

"You really don't get it, do you? Why would they bother with all the different series? What's the point when they hate differences so much? Why wouldn't they just produce endless copies of the same person? Unless they can't 'grow' people at all."

"But . . . why lie about it at all?"

"They tell you just enough to keep you from asking questions. They train Growers but don't mention where the children come from before they're hooked up to the machines. They call it a series ID, but it's taken from family names; it helps to keep track, numbering them off. They have to keep siblings apart so they don't trigger flashbacks in each other. Anyone who figures it out, who asks the wrong questions, well, there's always Floor 6 if they don't make it to Freedom first."

I don't know where to start. Has it always been this way? Aren't any Refuge workers grown? And if they're not, where did I come from?

"Focus." Ange points at Ash, slumped against the wall. "You want your friend to survive? We have to move. Now."

"What about—" I gesture at the captive children, still shuffling along the bare corridor.

"We have to go. If we can get your friend here to safety, then maybe."

I seize on this. "We can help them? You know where they'll be?"

"We can't do anything for them now. One day . . ."

"She's right," Cadence says. "Ash has to be your first priority. Get him to safety, help him recover.

249

Once he's better, we can work on ending the threat of the Mara and bringing down Refuge. Then those children will be safe right along with everyone else."

I shake my head, though of course she's right. Of course that's the only thing to do. I have to put Ash first.

"For me? How lovely." The familiar voice is gleeful, slippery as ever.

Serovate. The hair stands up on the back of my neck. He's so near. Too near. Ange and Cadence are right; we need to get Ash out of here now.

I shove to my feet. Ash's eyelids flicker. He groans and rolls his head. It hits the concrete wall behind us with a solid *thwack*.

"What was that?" Another enforcer's voice rings out, echoing against the concrete.

Ange clamps a hand over Ash's mouth. He's already gone limp again. She slips under his arm and waves a frantic hand at me in a *hurry up* gesture.

"Oh, do focus," Serovate drawls, amusement heavy in his voice. "Now, which one of these darlings do you suggest? One of the older ones? Any put up a decent fight on the way in?"

There's a whimper, followed by the sound of impact and more rustling.

"Mmm." Serovate hums, a musing, pleased sound. "Or perhaps one of the little, tender ones. They go fast, but they're good fun while they last."

There's a muffled squawk and a thump. I'm frozen in place, straining my ears to hear. Ange waves again, impatiently.

"Cole," Cadence says, harsh. "You can't help them. Go now."

"I've got it," Serovate says. I twist away from Ash to hear better. "These are all awfully small. I think I'll just take a handful of new toys."

"Her Worship ordered—"

"Oh, she did, did she? Well, I'm sure they've not been logged yet. You'll just have to get more before your next report now, won't you? Or are you volunteering to take their place in the playroom?"

"Cole," Cadence says. "Stay on mission."

I shake my head. I know. I know the only thing to do is to get Ash to safety, but something in me can't walk away.

They shimmer behind my eyes: Suzie, crushed and swallowed by darkness; Liwan, fighting for his life on the training room floor as Refuge supervisors looked on and did nothing. Cadence, a shadowy silhouette trapped forever at the edge of childhood, never to step beyond.

Ange reaches across Ash and tugs my sleeve. "You can't help them," she whispers. "It's hard, I know. Make the right choice. Help your friend. Do what you can."

I shake my head, eyes prickling with heat. Ange presses her hand against Ash's side, where blood has soaked through his makeshift bandages. She drags her fingertips down my cheek.

I gasp. The heat overflows my eyes and streaks down to mix with the blood—salt and iron on the air.

"It's your only choice." She's compassionate but unrelenting. "Save him."

Choking against the unbearable tightness in my throat, I turn my back on the captives and strengthen my grip on Ash.

"It's the right thing to do," Cadence says.

"Keep going," Ange says. "Hurry."

I keep going. One foot, then the other. It's the right thing to do. The only thing I can do. Ash has to be safe. The Mara have to be stopped. Refuge has to fall. This isn't just about me anymore, about my vengeance, my victory over the ones who've kept me down. When Refuge falls, no more children will be torn away from their families and subjected to the twisted whims of bad men or the oppressive control of Refuge regulation.

But Ash's hurt, bad. He's not going to be staging uprisings any time soon. Which means those kids Serovate seized . . .

I can't accept it. I can't do anything about it, but I can't accept it either. If only Ash were strong enough to take down Serovate, at least, to save them that trauma.

What if someone else could stop him? Ravel?

No, even putting aside how he must feel about me at the moment and what it might take to earn his help, he seems to have some sort of arrangement with Serovate. And there's no love lost there for Ash. No, Ravel's not an option. What about Ange?

I study Ange's profile, strained under more than just Ash's unconscious weight. She's lost so much already because of me. Cass never would've died if I'd kept my mouth shut. Distracting him like that was unforgivable, even if I hadn't realized people could be attacked in Freedom. Ange is already doing everything she can to help us. There's no way I can ask any more from her.

"You're doing great, kid," she says, glancing over at me. "Just keep it up. We'll be out of here in no time."

It takes another few steps before I can get the words out. "I'm sorry about him, you know. Cass. I tried to stop it."

"It's not your fault." Her tone is flat but not unkind. "No one can stop an attack. It's fate. When your time's up, it's up."

"But if I hadn't distracted him with his brother . . ."

It's stupid to argue about it. I put my head down, remembering the gentle way Cass had teased Ange. Remembering his desperation, those final moments in the dream, caught between wanting her and longing for a past that—I now understand—Refuge had ripped away from him.

"I knew," she says. I can barely hear her over the scrape of Ash's feet dragging on the concrete. "It was my fault, not yours. I knew his brother was still alive in Refuge, knew he was an inspector, knew there was a chance they'd meet one day, but—"

"He wanted to go to you. I could feel it. He wanted you, too. He just couldn't fight them."

"You can't know that." Ange's knuckles pale where they grip Ash's arm.

I don't know how to explain to her that I can, and I do. I don't know how to explain what it is to be sucked into the darkness of other people's desires, into their dreams,

252

to feel what they feel and want what they want. To feel them be destroyed by it and then be left alone in the darkness. Even now, the insubstantial press of countless threads, the longing of hopeless souls calling out tangle around my fingers, pulling at me, drawing me to them.

I look down at my hands, wrapped around Ash, and they're there: tiny gossamer threads, the nearly invisible fragments of wishes; strong, thick silver cords, longings and desires shining with a moonglow; heavy, murky threads, nearly chains, of desperate, unrelenting, grasping want. I shift Ash's weight to free a hand and stroke the threads. Some are delicate, and others so strong I want to pull away.

Cadence was wrong. There is something I can do. Something I have to do.

CARNAGE

I 'M GOING BACK."

Ange whips around to stare.

"I know how to stop him. Serovate. I can keep those kids safe and buy you time to get Ash away."

I hope.

"I don't believe you," she says. "And I'm not letting you kill yourself out of some misplaced sense of guilt. Give it up. I know it's horrible, but there are some things you just can't fix."

I nod at her assessment. "I can't do much. But I can do this."

Ange studies my face. "Tell me."

"I can't explain—"

"I'm not letting you go without a plan. Just spit it out."

I keep my gaze fixed on the threads, tangling my fingers in them, terrified they'll vanish. "Ravel's Exchange gave me the idea. I can tell when and where the Mara will attack. Don't ask me how. I just can. I'll get Serovate to chase me, then substitute his life for the victim's. With him gone, we're all better off. It's the right choice."

She stiffens at her own words thrown back at her, opens her mouth to protest, and closes it again, studying me. "You're sure it'll work?"

"Yes." No.

"Cole," Cadence says, "this is wrong. Don't do this."

"You'd have to be quick to stay ahead of him," Ange says.

"I think he likes the chase. He won't want to catch me too quickly."

She nods, affirming my guess. My stomach churns at the thought of going back and drawing that monster's attention, of hearing his boots echoing in the corridors behind me. I raise my chin, trying to look determined and fearless.

Ange snorts.

"This is wrong," Cadence says. "You can't use our power this way. This is different than what Ravel made you do. Those deaths are on his head, but to choose to sacrifice someone . . . You're not a killer. I know you can't stand the idea of those kids getting hurt, but think long term. You just have to wait, okay? Ash's safety is what matters most."

I nod, conceding her point, but as we push through to Freedom's violet hall, I pull away.

"You'll manage from here, right?"

Her lips twist in a half-smile, though she looks at me as if she's saying goodbye. "Fine. Be careful. Find us after. Don't risk the green room entrance. There's an access point at the far corner of the black. Just walk into the space where the walls meet. I'll send someone to lead you the rest of the way."

I smile back through the queasiness and Cadence's yelling. She can't see the best solution. She's too clouded by fears and attachments, by her connection to Ash. That must be why her power passed to me.

I see clearly now. My selfishness and fear of taking action has caused so much pain, so much damage. I know what I have to do to atone. It's time to start to making things right.

I turn and push back into the cool, echoing corridors. Ash is important, but for the moment, he's as safe as I can make him. Ange will get him to her people and keep him hidden until he can regain his strength. Then he'll stop the Mara and bring down Refuge. Until he can make everyone safe, I'll be the one to fight back.

I ignore Cadence as she rages at me. Of course I don't want to leave Ash. Of course he would hate me doing this for him.

Of course I don't want to go back. It's not like I want Serovate to chase me down these endless corridors.

But this is what I choose: to put an end to this one source of hurting in the sea of misery that surrounds us.

HE'S ALMOST TOO delighted to chase me, abandoning the children—two cowering in the corner, not yet shackled, another unconscious on a table—without a second glance. The pounding of boots behind me makes my knees shake, but it's slower than my racing pulse, slower than my own racing steps. He's in no hurry to catch me.

"I wondered when you'd show that pretty head of yours, superior," Serovate says, practically skipping down the corridor behind me. He's enjoying this, drawing it out, getting some sort of sick pleasure out of the chase. He doesn't believe I could ever be a threat.

His mistake.

I put my head down and run faster.

"It won't do any good, you know," he calls after me, not even panting. "Did you think you could escape? You and your little friend? Did you think you could hide from us?"

I sift through the threads in the air, feeling for the ones that vibrate and snag at my fingers to signal a dream, an imminent death.

"We know what you are, princess," he croons. "They showed me what you are. Did you think we didn't know?"

I grin. It's good if he still thinks I'm a failure. He can keep on thinking I'm some scared, powerless little girl, right up until I spring my trap.

My fingers snag a thread that's thicker than the rest. A pulse runs down the line. I tighten my grip. It feels as if it's going to pull away at any moment. I'm too slow; it'll be over before I get there. Another pointless death.

My head spins. Darkness clusters at the edge of my vision. It's starting. It's calling me, drawing me in, but if I let go, if I fall now . . . I release the thread and reach for another, one that whispers of longing and hunger and shadows gathering.

"Clever, princess." He sounds closer now, too close. His voice bounces against the bleak walls, multiplied to a crazed chorus by the echoes. I pick up my pace, breath hissing between my teeth, muscles already burning. "Such a clever, scheming little thing. Hurry, hurry, princess. Maybe you'll outrun me. Maybe your friends will escape. Hurry, hurry."

"Faster," Cadence says. The thread tugs in my hand. "Faster. Get out of here. Go now. Lose him in the crowd. Get back to Ange."

I race on, outpacing Serovate. I dive around corner after corner, guided back to the press and furor of Freedom by the threads dragging me toward death. They grow brighter and stronger the closer I get to Freedom. I can feel them brushing against me, growing solid under my touch as I focus on one, then another.

The deaths are coming faster than before. One barely passes, the thread thickening, then evaporating before another starts the process. The Mara's hunger grows, and I allow them to claim their victims by not stepping into the dreams, not fighting back. I'm responsible now. I have to choose the right battle. These deaths are on my head, just like Serovate's will be when at last I feed him to the Mara.

My fingers trail across dozens of threads. I select a pale, insubstantial one. It feels right somehow, pliant in my hand with a whispered hint of danger. It will give me enough time to lure the monster behind me in.

"Almost there," Cadence says. "You're almost free. You can do it. Get out of here. Give it up. Don't use our power to kill. Don't do this, Cole. You don't have to do this."

She doesn't understand. That's fine. I'll protect her, too.

Serovate's singsong, mocking tones echo down the corridors, letting me know he's still in pursuit, "Hurry scurry, princess."

He's too far behind. Freedom is near. Will he be able to follow me through the crowd? His wickedness seems legendary, as if he embodies the lies of Refuge and all the endless evil hunger of the Mara, but he's only a man. Despite his threats and insinuations, I can't overestimate him. I have to lure him carefully.

I dart to the next corridor. There's an access point to Freedom's violet hall there. Muffled music presses through the fabric barrier. I won't hear Serovate until it's too late. I have to go now—but how to make sure he can follow me?

I consider the thread in my hand, stronger but not yet darkening. The death, or the potential for death, is distant still. I reach with the other hand for a murkier cord and hesitate. Then I throw off Ange's cloak and let it puddle on the ground behind me. Tall and unmasked, I should be easy to spot in the crowd.

I seize the heavier cord and taunt, "You're too late, sixer. You'll never catch me." I dive into the fray.

I press through the crush of dancers, struggling against their flow. Without the spotlight of Ravel's presence and Victoire's haughty elegance, I feel invisible, despite my height and vulnerable-feeling bare face. I hunch my shoulders, afraid of feeling Serovate's hand dragging me back too soon or Ravel bursting in and ruining everything.

It hurts, going against the surge of the dance, shoving through every opening, getting bruised and knocked aside. The fabric fluttering around me catches on the edges of other costumes in the churn. I jerk to a stop. The jewelled studs pasted along my skin tear away and scatter like heavy, shining tears. The chains dangle and swing, hooking on spinning limbs and snagging at every turn. They cut bloodless white lines into my skin when I tug away until a delicate link breaks and I'm free for another few steps.

I keep close hold of both threads through it all, focusing on their pull despite the distractions, letting them draw me forward.

It's hot and dark in the middle of the crowd. The heat moves in a low-lying cloud, carrying the heavy reek of sweat and too much perfume. The lights strobing overhead make it hard to see the best path; a shadowy opening too often turns into a sharp blow as I stumble on. I try to match the rhythm of the beat, to move through the crowd effortlessly as Victoire does, but her fluid grace is foreign to me. I can't help but be awkward and out of place, shoving forward with my arms raised and my hands clamped around both threads—until the darker one puffs apart in my hand and is gone.

Another one dead.

Thankfully, it's dark enough and the revels have gone on long enough none of the dancers seem to really pay me much mind. Hands reach out too often to touch, to grab, but there's enough of a press that I squirm away before their owners really manage to focus on the girl bumbling through the crowd.

"He can't be far behind," Cadence urges. "There's still time to escape. Hurry."

I peer through the masses of feathers and beads and lace, looking for stained white. If I can spot him coming, I might have a better chance of timing this right. But there's no sign of pursuit. There's nothing for it but to press onward, following the pull of the thread in my hands, batting away the darker, heavier ones that surround me. They thicken with the screams—anguish, a rising crescendo, cutting off raw and unfinished.

I break into a run, elbows tucked against my ribs, holding myself together. I let the thread pull me forward past one death after another toward a more distant attack. I have to hold on for the perfect moment. I have to be able to snatch up the nearest dreamer and hurl Serovate into his place just as he catches up to me.

It's dizzying, whirling toward the call of the dreams that shift every moment. The screams are closer, then further, louder, then softer, then gone, then louder again. I go from horrified and frightened to furious—furious at the waste, furious at the excess, furious at the pointlessness and the pain of it all. I just want it to stop, just want to make it stop, but I can't, not yet. All I can do is hold on and wait for the chance to end this one key threat amidst the multitude.

The crowd eddies around the latest attack. A patch of fog and shadows churns and grows. A figure at its centre flails and howls as blood flies. Then another dancer is caught up in the destruction. The cloud grows and darkens, cracking the floor and furrowing the ceiling. How much damage can Freedom take before all of Refuge is threatened?

There are shapes in the darkness; cutting shapes, tearing shapes, crushing shapes, the Mara at work. A flash of impressions, of sensations and feelings not my own ripple against the edges of my mind: longing, need, desire, hope, shattering, betrayal, rending, tearing pain.

But not my pain.

Her pain, a voice guttering out through a throat choked with blood.

His pain, fresh and sharp as the bone jutting bare.

Their pain, an avalanche of pain as the ravenous Mara rage through Freedom. I can't understand how there's anyone left, why the dancers don't flee. Is their faith in Ravel so great they refuse to believe the danger before their very eyes? Is whatever they're hiding from really worse than this carnage?

Although I'm cold and stiff with terror, I am also fiery with a rage more enormous and powerful than Refuge itself. The world strobes dark-bright-dark. Silver floods my vision, clearing my head and stoking that terrible fire within. This time, the sharp-edged light doesn't wash away the world. It brings it into focus, overlaying the dream like a phantom over the waking world.

DREAMSCAPE

NSTEAD OF BEING drawn in, I've pulled the dreamscape to me. I can end this. I will end this. I see it all now: the threads, the way they wrap and bind, muddying the scene with braided, entwined longings when really, each has a single source.

It's so simple. It's our longings—literally our dreams—that kill us. I can see it through the shadowy fog of the Mara. I see the insubstantial vision of a single dancer's dream, bound to him in threads of wanting that the beasts chase back and use to tear him apart.

I take the thread and pull, tugging it away from the Mara. The dancer wakes, shrugging off his dream and continuing almost without missing a beat.

The Mara go after another victim. This time, I twist the length of the thread to loop around them in a noose. When I draw it tight, the nightmare dissolves. I coil the thread and shove it at the dancer. She tries to take my hands. The thread touches her body and vanishes.

The next beast I turn to hulks spider-like over a snarl of threads spooling from a body collapsed on the ground. The first thread I pluck does nothing, nor the next. I dig my fingers into the knot and tear it apart. The fog, the waking manifestation of the Mara, thins.

"Get up." I pull the victim's arm, trying to raise him.

His mask has fallen. He stares at me, terror blanching his face. I hold my palm before his face to show him the shining threads. His dreams. He cringes.

"Take them." I grab his hand and press the mass into it. "Keep them close. Don't let them be taken again."

He curls away from me. Long gouges trail across his back. They weep blood over his once-shiny costume.

"Cole, there's no time," Cadence says. "Serovate will be here any second. You have to run. You have to get away before—"

The air explodes from my lungs as an arm catches me around my middle and hauls me back. My fingertips splay with the force of it, scattering silver sparks.

I twist. Ravel, his jaw set, is dragging me away. His eyes widen. They reflect twin hoops of silver light, washing out his own golden irises. I lash out, scratching and kicking, then let my weight drop to slip out from the circle of his arms. He stumbles back. I surge away.

Too late. There's a choked-off cry. I turn in time to see the last tendrils of sickly fog dissolve. The drops scattered by the splashing of my feet as I skid to a stop are the only sign of life left at the centre of the destruction. The dancer lies in pieces, no sign of the silver threads I'd pressed back into his hands.

"Victoire," Ravel calls. I'm not sure what his tone holds. Shock? Frustration? Horror?

Fear?

The still-warm liquid splashes to my knees with each step. My own blood mixes with it. I skid and slice through rubble—bone, concrete, steel, tile, glass.

They're dying. They're all dying, calling Mara down into them with every miserable beat of longing, and I have to let them. Why don't they run?

"Hurry," Cadence says, as if I've forgotten, as if I don't remember why I have to turn away, why I have to let the threads thicken and shatter into nothing in my hands. "Go to Ash."

"Victoire, get back here. How dare you—Victoire!" Ravel tries to seize me again.

His threads are bright with the strength of his longing. One leads right to me. I swat it away, and his grip loosens. As soon as I stop pushing, the thread snaps back in place.

"Victoire, flame," he pleads. "Come back with me. I'll make it better. I can give you what you want."

There's a disruption in the crowd behind him. A glimmer of white parting the dancers in a beeline toward us. I cast about, sifting through the threads around us. The Mara have moved off. I can feel them, still attacking, still feeding, but they're learning to avoid me.

I have to get their attention.

I tighten my hand around Ravel's threads. He stares at me, the gold in his eyes swirling. "Flame?"

"Stay away from me."

"Victoire, please. I just want to help. Trust me."

"You want to help? Do something about that."

He wheels and spots Serovate pushing through the dancers. He throws himself at the enforcer without a moment's hesitation. I blink, astonished, and take off in the opposite direction toward where I can feel the Mara's attacks.

Racing forward, I reach for the next thread, and the next, each crumbling away faster than the last. Ravel's voice rings out behind me, and Serovate's, but I'm gaining ground, whipping around one dancer after the next.

They whisper as I run: "Hurry. Your friends aren't far ahead. We'll slow him down. Hurry."

I feel the tug of a familiar thread and wrap my fingers around it as it thickens, still a clear silver, bright and strong.

This is the one. I can feel it. A part of me cries out at letting it cloud over with darkness, but I have no choice. Just one more dream—it's the only way to stop Serovate. The timing has to be just right . . .

I risk a glance back and stumble, bouncing off someone and tumbling to the floor.

"Get away!"

I meet Ange's desperate stare, her hands wrapped around the white-uniformed arm pinning her to the wall. Ash is slumped at their feet.

Cadence moans.

I'm afraid to look up. How could I have thought Ange could get Ash to safety on her own? Serovate's languidness had been an act. Of course he went on ahead to trap me instead. Of course. How could I have been so stupid?

The thread gives a tug in my fist, demanding my attention. Its surface clouds over. I follow its taut line up, up to—

I look, and then look again. It's not Serovate, though he wears the Refuge Force uniform.

Inspector Haynfyv blinks down at me, brows furrowed over the neat white mask covering his nose and mouth. His goggles are missing. "You! What do you want? Do you know these two?"

He looks back at Ange, then down at Ash, and swings again to stare at me, clearly debating whether it's worth letting go of the two he's captured to grab hold of another. Only a dozen steps to his left is the dark corner Ange said hides the escape route. They were so close.

"There's no time," Cadence moans. "What have you done? He's going to catch us all. Ash—"

"Shut up," I grit between my teeth. "I know. I'll handle it."

45

HAYNFYV

"WHAT DID YOU say?" Haynfyv leans closer. "You're that missing surveillance tech, aren't you? You're supposed to be dead." Ange kicks out harder, shakes her head behind his back. "Ravel. That devious little—I knew I should have insisted on inspecting the body."

That deep grey skin, eyes that might have been like his brother's if Noosh hadn't leeched them of warmth . . . I have to distract him. I have to give Ange a chance to get Ash away before Ravel and Serovate catch up to me.

I tug hard on the thread in my hand, the one that arrows straight into the inspector's chest. "Shame about your brother, Inspector."

His brows tent in confusion, but another thread nudges out the front of his uniform, slender and translucent.

"Haynfor." I watch his eyes widen and his shoulders snap straight.

Ange goes limp behind him, her gaze darting down to Ash and back up to me. I cut my eyes at her, willing her to understand. "Cass Hayne, right? You did realize that was who died the other day? No? That's terrible. Imagine not recognizing your own brother. Or didn't you even look at the victim? Careless work, inspector."

"You're lying."

That second thread thickens, darkens. I catch it as it drifts by. Haynfyv's eyes cloud over. His grip loosens.

Ange sets her feet and pulls away. He doesn't seem to notice. Ash stirs. His skin is too pale under the slow swirl of silver mist. I have to buy them more time.

"What an admirable commitment to duty, Inspector. Or was it on purpose?" I take a step backwards. Haynfyv steps toward me as though pulled. I tug on both threads at the same time, twist them together. I feel the Mara's attention snap toward him. "Maybe you resented him? Resented being abandoned? After all, a big brother's job is to protect, right?"

"Cole, stop," Cadence says.

"I didn't know," Haynfyv whispers. "You're lying."

"You didn't even spare him a glance." I can't look away from the twisted cords now, the sick tint from one leaching into the other as shadows swarm the inspector's heavy boots. "You didn't care enough to spare your dying brother a glance. You don't know how he longed to see you again, Kurt."

Haynfyv shakes his head, horrible lines etched around his eyes. "Don't."

I look past him and mouth *hurry* as the shadows creep up, up, and out from the inspector.

"Cole, don't do this," Cadence pleads.

Ange heaves Ash up, staggers under his weight, and sinks to her knees, panting. I don't know how she made it this far, but she's not strong enough to take him farther on her own.

I yank the twined threads that lead back to the inspector. The Mara coalesce out of shadows, fog thickening around his inert form. I let the threads slacken a bit and edge toward Ange. A strong tug almost pulls them out of my grasp. I haul back, keeping the fog from taking hold of Haynfyv too fast.

"We almost made it," Ange says. I pull Ash's arm over my shoulder. "Maybe this is for the best. It's not safe for you."

I let her talk, gritting my teeth and paying out the darkening threads of Haynfyv's dreams between my fingers. Ash moans. His eyelids flutter. He lurches. I stumble under his weight. Ange grunts.

Ash squints at Haynfyv in the midst of the Mara's fog. "I have to stop them. He's under attack. I have to."

His eyes roll up and he slumps once more, but now I'm the one who can't look away. Haynfyv is on his knees, the floor around him cratering under the force of the Mara. Long rents in his uniform weep blood. They're taking him slowly. It's as if they're taunting me with his death. They know I'm watching. They're waiting to see what I'll do.

It's not like I don't understand Cadence's objections or Ash's compulsion to fight back. I hate letting the Mara take even one more life. But to give Ash a chance to survive, to recover to fight again? To end the threat of Serovate once and for all?

I check the crowd for a second pale uniform. Haynfyv is lost in his dreams, and no one else seems to be paying us any mind.

I wait until we've pushed through the folds of velvet cloaking the corner exit. We're in another back corridor, this one dimmer and grubbier than I'm familiar with.

"I'm going back." I shift Ash's weight to prop him against the wall and step away.

Ange just looks at me, her dark eyes reflecting silver. I glance down at myself. Ash's light has rubbed off onto me. The mist swirls over my skin, my costume.

Ange takes my hand. I don't know how much she can see or how much she's realized. "Follow when you can." Her voice is low and rough, as if there's something caught in her throat. "I'll take care of him."

I swallow, turn and push back through the barrier into Freedom's black hall.

"I knew you wouldn't let Haynfyv die. Hurry." Cadence says.

I can hear her relief, but she doesn't understand. I shake my head. "I have to do this."

"But—"

"If I can keep the Mara from killing, you know I will. But I have to stop Serovate."

"You can't—"

"Cadence. This is my choice."

I dive into the polluted fog of the Mara. My vision doubles. I clutch the threads of Haynfyv's longing. They tangle in the dreamscape, his longing for a lost family snagging against his resolute sense of duty. They're crushing him, the beasts in the fog twisting his dreams and longings into something hopeless, whispering to him of failure and loss.

I have to slow things down. If I can hold off this man's death long enough, I think I can draw Serovate into the attack. I focus on separating the strands. They lighten in colour, becoming clearer. The fog around us thins. The Mara hiss their displeasure. I hold the threads a little closer, tugging to keep Haynfyv's dreams strong in his mind.

I can do this.

It's so easy now to catch sight of the threads even outside of a dream, to hold it off or let it in. So simple, once the threads are in my grasp. Why couldn't I have realized sooner? How many could I have saved?

"It's a miracle you can do this much," Cadence says. "It's not your fault. You couldn't have known."

"Did you?"

"What?"

"How long have you known?"

She doesn't answer for a long moment. "It's not your fault. It's not anyone's fault. We were never supposed to be like this."

I tense, ready to argue, but something catches the corner of my eye. Is that a white uniform, there at the edge of the crowd? A pale streak plunges through the ranks of rainbow-plumed dancers. Almost there. Almost . . .

But another bright spot closes in from the side, racing right up to the edge of the fog.

"Victoire, no!" Ravel throws himself toward me, seizing my arm and yanking me off balance even as the threads surrounding him snag and tangle against Haynfyv's.

"You have to get away from there, flame. I won't let them take you."

The fog whirls around us, howling. Ravel tugs my arm, but I can't hear, can't tell what he's shouting. His gaze turns inward. He slumps to his knees.

Outside the fog, a white-uniformed figure sneers and waves mockingly. Serovate stays just out of reach. Try as I might, I can't catch hold of his threads, can't draw him in to the attack.

But if I could take the Mara to him . . .

I take a careful step toward Serovate, feeling the threads pay out between my fingertips. He wags a finger and skirts the edge of the attack, fog coiling against his boots and oozing off as if they're oiled. He's headed for the corner behind me. I swivel to watch as he pushes through the opening and vanishes after Cass and Ange.

I can't fail them. I have to go after him.

But first, I have to untangle myself, and to do that, I have to stop this attack. I grit my teeth, dig my fingers into the knotted cords of Ravel and Haynfyv's mingled desires, and plunge into their dreams.

A boy with black hair and gold eyes watches a blond woman from behind a curtain. The mayor, Maryam Ajera. She stands over the broken body of another woman shrouded in silver mist. A girl screams in the arms of an enforcer. She goes limp, the mist vanishing from both in the same instant as the woman on the floor breathes her last.

I recognize the scene—the memory? It matches the one that cropped up in the midst of the street girl's dream earlier. I look closer. This girl has long, dark brown hair and a starburst pattern surrounding her eyes—a mask-like birthmark just like mine. Cadence might have resembled me, but there's no way we could've looked that much alike. Have Ravel's delusions gone so far as to see me in every female in his past . . . ? But there are more dreams, Haynfyv's and Ravel's overlapping and crowding each other out.

A brown-skinned child runs to the boys and men who troop wearily through a broken door, their eyes lighting as they see him. His brother lifts him up and whirls him through the air as he laughs.

Older now, the gold-eyed boy stands at a window, watching the still form of the girl under white sheets, tubes snaking around her, hooked up to a machine with blinking lights.

A young man admires the crisp white of his new uniform. He covers eyes that have lost their warmth with the goggles of an enforcer.

Ravel as an adult stands with Serovate, watching a worker who scurries into the elevator without a backwards glance. I recognize myself.

Haynfyv kneels at Mayor Ajera's feet to accept a shimmering length of gold fabric, the Mayor's Commission, from her hands.

Ravel raises his arms to accept the adoration of an endless crowd. He curves one arm around the waist of a glittering woman at his side. She wears gold, but her skin is silver.

This isn't working. I need to find a way to separate the two men before I can end this.

I haul my arms apart, stretching the twisted cords, and yank my hands out. The fog snatches at the ends as they whip free.

"Tell me," I say, but both men are lost in their dreams, unable to hear.

I reach for a loose thread, plucking it from the insubstantial grasp of the Mara. They hiss at me. I snatch away another. It's much harder to deal with two dreamers at once, but there's no way around it. I'll have to be strong enough. I grit my teeth and focus.

"Tell me," I say again.

I pull away two more threads, holding them still and straight between my fingers.

"No. Ash!" Cadence's cry distracts me.

I nearly lose my grip. Serovate leers at me, one hand around Ange's neck, the other fisted in Ash's hair. Ange kicks weakly. Ash is limp on the floor. Ange's struggles slow, stop. Serovate throws her down. She doesn't get up.

I howl, surging toward him, but the threads tangled around my hands jerk my attention back to the two men trapped in the dream. I flex my fingers, wanting to cast the threads aside, wanting to throw myself at the monster standing smugly with my friends crumpled at his feet.

"Cole," Cadence begs, for what I'm not sure, but it's enough to make me pause. I'm not strong enough to beat Serovate in a physical fight, but maybe now he thinks he's won, I can draw him in.

"Tell me what you want." I gather in another thread, another desire.

Ravel's threads, though more numerous and tangled, are brighter and stronger. He responds first, his lips moving. The fog hisses and roars around me. I can't hear his words. I see it, though, his desperate desire, reaching out, again, again, again, to the golden mayor of Refuge at the heart of dream after dream, but also to others, more and more. I see my own face in the mix, the way he pictures himself, reaching out and being tossed aside even in his dreams. I falter, seeing too much of myself in the way he chases their gaze, their affirmation, their acceptance.

I gather each thread and pull it tight, adding more, untangling, combing them straight, separating Haynfyv's dreams from Ravel's and sorting them into simple desire: love, acceptance, belonging, honour, trust, worth. The threads pull taut as the Mara snatch and grab at them. I stand firm, weaving the loose threads into strong, bright cords. The Mara turn on the men, but I swathe them in the new-made fabric of dreams, a shining barrier to hold death at bay.

"You did it—you saved them! Set them free, Cole."

I glance at Serovate, panting, planning the exact cast of the wrist it will take to snag him in a loop and drag him into the zone of attack, the precise tug it will take to coil Haynfyv's dreams in his hands and send him to safety, the way I'll dig my fingers into Serovate's threads to hold him captive while I free Ravel and turn back to finish this.

Then there are more threads, and more dreams, flailing, filling the space. The Mara go into a frenzy, filling the air with a fine mist of blood as I scramble to catch the loose ends without letting go of those I already hold.

It's Serovate's doing. He grins wildly, his mask dangling from one side of his hood. He shoves more dancers toward me. They stumble through the fog and into a nightmare of their own desires. I spin and grab, catching the threads, weaving them together into strong cords and shining fabric that I can control without the monsters tearing them away from me.

Sweat runs into my eyes. I gasp for air, choking on fog. I can't help fumbling some—voices are cut off, bodies collapse. My feet slip in the carnage, but I can't lose focus, can't stop fighting to catch the lives Serovate throws at me. I'm drowning in it, a sea of threads, an ocean of emotion and desires and unfulfilled dreams.

Serovate leans too close, exulting in the sight of my flailing, and shoves one more victim in. Ash, propped up on one arm, hooks a battered hand around the enforcer's shin. He grits his teeth as the enforcer stumbles and stomps on his hand, but it's enough to throw Serovate off balance, just close enough. I cast out my chain of dreams and drag him through the outer rim of fog.

46 SEROVATE

EROVATE STRUGGLES TO pull away. I tighten the rope, the chain I've formed of so many lives, and bind him there, surrounded by leering faces at the edge of the fog. I tie off one set of dreams after another and cast the dancers out of the circle.

The last to go are Ravel—aware and resisting as I push him out, shaking and yelling when he realizes I can't come with him—and Haynfyv, unconscious but still breathing. I have to shoulder him aside, fighting against the grasp of death that surrounds us, aware my sturdy ropes have unravelled to bare threads as I free one victim after the other.

Serovate stops resisting. He raises one hand to tap on the side of his mirrored goggles. It's just the two of us left amidst a whirl of sickly yellow, half-formed shapes churning in the fog. I'm sucked inside his dream.

We hate them, but they're long gone. We made sure of that. We hated everything about them, about that pathetic existence on the edge, about the way we were made nothing by them just because we were least and last, smallest of too many children in too weary a family. So when the fog whispered promises to us, we listened. We ended them. Bright, bright blood on our hands. We had to stand on a chair to finish it. They bought our way in.

The effort of tying off so many dreams and holding the Mara at bay from such a feast of dreamers has worn me down.

I can't pull away. Serovate's dream—his memory—draws me back under.

After, we scrubbed the blood from our hands and changed our clothes and followed the whispers in the fog to the white uniforms. We raised our arms and let them take us to the seat of power. We'd never be small and weak and hungry again.

The dream fades, nothing more than the whisper of a nightmare of a memory given flesh. I stare at Serovate. He wavers behind a sheet of hot tears. There has been no victim more destroyed by the Mara than this man. They promised a child everything, and he believed what they offered was worth the sacrifice. A child.

"Well done, princess," he says, smirking. "Looks like you caught me."

I reach for his threads. I'd planned to end his threat, to save everyone from him. But now . . . maybe I can weave something out of what's left of him. Something good. Something that will make it better, make him better.

My fingers are raw from the burn of so many wants and desires, so many people longing for so much, for so many reasons. The dreams aren't bad or good, in and of themselves. The way they cross and tangle and trip the dreamers, the way they call the Mara, that's the real problem. If I could untangle Serovate's threads and give them back to him made straight and whole . . .

I reach, but there's nothing there. Serovate shows no sign of a single dream or wish or longing or ambition.

Impossible.

He sweeps a mocking hand at the pale wisps of fog. The Mara are fading away. There's nothing here for them to feed on. Then he reaches up and pulls his mirrored goggles off.

His eyes are blank. Not dead, or blind, or fake. Blank. Mara-taken blank. Pearl-white orbs spin below the barely-there wisps of his eyebrows. Corpse eyes in a living body. They've already fed on everything he had and ever was, leaving behind some sort of monstrous shell. I can't save him. I can't end him.

He laughs. "Problem?" he mocks, running his hands through the fog. "Something wrong? You seem to be at a loss."

"That's not right," Cadence says. "That's not . . . He's a monster."

I take a step away from the grinning creature without dreams. No. He's alive. He's moving. There has to be a way.

"Embarrassed, princess? I would be. Then again, my plans never go like this." He gestures toward me.

The fog swirls and the shapes within it grow darker. Faces leer. Talons grasp. I run my hands through the air, but there's not a single thread. I have to find a way to bind him, to make sure the Mara take him and only him. But without the threads . . . As I watch, the silver light that had shone from my skin flickers and evaporates as if it had never been.

Serovate cocks his head and peers at me sideways, then flops his head to the other shoulder and shows his teeth. "Can't see your own either, can you? Don't feel bad; we rarely see our own failings until it's too late. Tell me, princess, what do you dream of?"

He's the one who's supposed to be trapped, not me. I can control this. I have to. I'll be the one to save Ash.

But there's nothing to work with. This man's dreams were all taken by the Mara long ago, and yet he lives. And . . . and . . . I hadn't noticed. It hadn't occurred to me to even look, but I have no threads of my own to manipulate. I never have.

"Cadence," I whisper. "The threads. The dreams. I don't . . . I can't . . . "

"No," she says. "Don't ask me."

"Cadence. Please. There has to be something. Another power. Some kind of trick you haven't told me about. Please."

"I—I can't help you."

People stare from outside the fog. People with wants and desires and dreams. People made up of countless threads. The endless music is muffled, distant sounding.

Ravel stands among them cradling his arm, relief written across his face. He raises a hand—not an expansive, showy gesture meant to impress the masses but a simple invitation.

I shake my head, grateful anyway. I've seen his longing, his hurt, his secret dreams. I can't hate him. But I don't want to go back to him, and I can't use him. I can't use any of them to attack. Cadence is right; I can't use their dreams to end a life. I won't endanger them like that.

The spot where Ange and Ash were once crumpled is empty now. I hope they escaped. I have to believe they made it out. I have to believe this fight means something.

Ravel's gaze flicks back and away. I turn. The fog pulls into a murky silhouette. It's as if it's being sucked into Serovate.

Then it explodes. Waves of darkness sweep me off my feet. I'm stopped by a pair of bloodstained white boots.

Serovate stands over me, grinning. Darkness weeps from his mouth. His voice holds the same slimy tone as ever. "Welcome to your nightmare, princess."

I scramble away from the prick of talons at my back and drag my hands through the air, desperate for a single thread to put between myself and this monster. There's nothing but fog and darkness with teeth.

The Mara surround us—no, that's not right at all. The Mara are in him. They always have been. He dreamed of power, and they gave it to him in the ultimate Exchange, gaining flesh. I never had a chance of defeating him. The Mara took him long ago. What's left is just a shell.

I try to stand and fall instead. The ground gives way beneath me. His hissing, cackling laughter surrounds me.

"What do you dream of, Traveller princess?" A chorus of voices hiss from nowhere and everywhere at once.

There's an opening in the fog. Blue lights trail off at the edge of Freedom. The escape route. It's so close. If I jump, I might reach it, might escape.

"Just run," Cadence pleads. "It's enough. You've done enough. More than enough. More than anyone could ever have expected. Just go to Ash, Cole. You don't have to be a hero.

You don't have to do anything except live. No one expects this of you. You don't have to impress me, or Ash, or anyone. Just live."

It's exactly what I want to hear. It's not my problem. Not my fight. No one expects it of me.

It's also a lie. If I go, there's no one to hold back death, no one to keep the Mara from taking every life here. I can't win. I can't beat this. My one skill, the one thing that I can do, that I only just learned to do, is useless now. All I can hope for is to stall as long as possible. I have to give Ash and Ange every chance to survive. I hope they're escaping even now.

It's almost a relief to realize there's no way out. This is the end, or nearly there, anyway. There's no one left to impress, to obey, to please. I'm never going to grow or change into anyone else. I'll never be a perfect, flawless drone, or dazzling like Victoire, or a powerful hero like Cadence and Ash. I'll die as I lived: a failure.

It's a strangely comforting thought. I don't have to be a hero. I just have to hang on a little longer. And maybe do this one other thing.

"I'm sorry for doubting you. Sorry for fighting you every step of the way. I know you just wanted to help, to make things better. It's going to be okay now. Go to Ash, Cadence. You don't have to stay for this part. Go be with him."

She doesn't respond, already gone. I shudder at the emptiness. But this is right. I can be alone. I should be, here at the end. I'm glad she won't have to stay and watch. I hope Ash can hear her, but even if he can't, I hope she'll find some joy in haunting him instead.

I stagger to my feet and take one last look at the light. Then I turn my back on it and face the Mara in Serovate's skin. Death snarls back at me. Darkness closes in.

47

DREAMS

I 'M SURROUNDED BY corpses.

Rows of cots stretch in every direction. Floor 6: the Corrections dorm. A pallid body lies on each, some slack and peaceful, others twisted and ravaged by anguish. I walk between the rows, watching the way the low light caresses their stillness, waiting for tingling fascination to wash up over me and draw me in. I'll be like them soon. I won't be one of the peaceful ones, either.

But not a single one of the dead calls to me. I've been too close to pain and darkness without end, my fingers tangled up in emotion: love, longing, hope, despair, loneliness, lust, pride, fear. I've felt the brush of death for myself. It's no longer alien, no longer fascinating.

I reach out to one of the bodies with trembling hands. The waiting darkness holds its breath—and hisses with disappointment as I pull the sheet up over its head.

"I do not dream of death," I whisper, kneeling and drawing my arms in close, bracing for the inevitable blow.

There's a sensation of falling, as if the floor drops out from under me.

Then I'm sitting, surrounded by light. I'm in Refuge, back in the superior's suite, dressed in a softly patterned uniform. There's a console in front of me. The display reads WELCOME, SUPERIOR.

When I reach out to press a button, gentle music streams into the air, soothing, like the light fragrance that surrounds me.

I stand to peer at the colourful wall hangings. I walk to the next room, look at the neatly made bed in it. There's rustling behind me. A woman dressed—barely—in gold. Maryam Ajera, mayor of the Towers of Refuge.

She smiles and pulls up a chair, learning forward as if we're friends. As if this weren't in violation of regulation. As if I've been accepted into the upper echelons of Refuge.

It's a heady feeling, to feel her touch on my arm, to be accepted by the very highest of authorities. But I draw back before she can part her full lips, before she can say a word. Perhaps once I dreamed of acceptance, but I never dreamed of this.

I shake my head. Maryam frowns. It doesn't matter. I don't need her. I don't need anyone's acceptance—I just need to hang on a little longer, to stall the pursuit and give my friends another moment of freedom. And even if I did . . .

"I do not dream of acceptance," I say. Cadence accepts me as I am. I accept my failure, my weakness. I am what I am.

Her face warps, dark lines threading through it, eating through the fabric of her skin and the room around me. I screw my eyes shut and wait for the rending talons.

But the blow does not fall. I open my eyes to Ange's smiling face and uncurl cautiously, waiting for the shift. It comes as I knew it would. Her smile falters and turns hard and cold. Her eyes cloud over. She lashes out. The Mara are losing patience with their own game, rushing the dream along toward death, but—

"I do not have to dream of friendship." I stare at the warped form of the first friend I ever made. The real Ange reached out to help me before she even knew me. She forgave me when my actions caused the death of her lover. She helped me save Ash, risking the position she'd fought for. And though Ash doesn't know me—will never, now, know me—I claim him and Cadence as friends too, because

I choose to help them, to sacrifice for them. I choose them as worthy. Someone always has to choose first.

I'm starting to see. Serovate has no threads and no dreams because the Mara ate them long ago. But I don't have the threads of dreams, either, and without that, it seems the Mara can menace, but they can't or won't finish me. They're searching for my dreams, my desires, my most desperate longings. But if I can hold out and keep them from finding something to grab onto, something to tear me apart with . . .

The creature that was Ange growls through bared fangs and lashes out. It throws me back with a blow that knocks the air out of my lungs. When the pressure eases, I'm staring at an unfamiliar scene.

A small girl with long dark hair holds the hands of a man and a woman who look very like her: broad high cheeks and wide mouths, deep-set eyes narrow with laughter. She looks at me and grins.

It's the girl from Ravel's dream. It's Cadence, but she looks just like me, with the same starburst spatters of dark stains around her eyes.

It's a strange blending, to see the Mara pull Ravel's memories and fantasies out to use against me. It gives me hope they really can't reach me. Maybe it's because I remember so little, only a few years' worth of hurt and longing, pain and determination.

I enjoy watching Cadence with her long-lost family for another moment before I tell them, laughing, "I do not dream of family."

If I ever had a family, I don't remember it now. I don't feel its loss.

The Mara exact their revenge for my dismissal, melting Cadence and her parents down inch by horrible inch. I look away. When I risk another glance, Ravel is there.

I tense. He was near enough to have been pulled back in for real. But this Ravel shows no signs of injury. He draws me close and tilts my head back, the swirl of his molten eyes too close, dizzying. His touch is fire, but I have no desire to burn.

Freedom offered every possible sensation, every want fulfilled—but I turned my back on it for Ash. No, I'd seen through it for myself long before I left to help him. The mission was just an excuse to accept what I already knew: desire without purpose is empty.

"I do not dream of desire," I breathe.

I close my eyes, too conscious of Ravel's touch. He doesn't pull away. What if the Mara don't care what I want or don't want? What if they're coming for me either way?

When I look again, the eyes focused on mine are not molten but starlight. Ash holds me close. I nearly relax into his touch, nearly let go. It's not desire, not really, or not entirely, but something else: raindrops, not flames. Longing.

I long for Ash, long to see myself reflected in his eyes, with no shadow of Cadence in sight. I hold my breath, just for a moment, and let myself see that reflection. I touch his face, promising myself it's just an illusion. It's not really him. It's not really a betrayal.

And then I step back. Ash belongs to Cadence. He always has. It was never me he wanted. And I will not try to steal from my friend, my sister, my ghost.

"I do not dream of longing."

There are other dreams, closely entwined. I will not give voice to them if I can help it.

Ash's face splits in a grin that drools darkness and eats away the light around me until I can't see. But I am untouched. I have no way to end the attack, no way to kill the Mara or divert their attention. I don't have blades like Ash, and there are no threads to use against it. But a tiny light of pride swells within me at the thought of how long I've held out already, how many minutes, how many inches toward safety I've bought my friends.

I can't hold out forever. But maybe, maybe I can hold out long enough.

48

TRUTH

"OH, VERY WELL done, princess." Serovate's voice is at the heart of an endless chorus. It hisses and echoes through the darkness. "Very well done, indeed. You're much cleverer than anyone gives you credit for, aren't you? But even you aren't as empty as you'd like to have us think."

There's a tugging, a brush all around me of movement: sharp things, hard things, bristles and fangs and damp and heat.

"Hopeless," Cadence says, startling me. I grit my teeth and brace for another onslaught. "I can't take it anymore. You still don't get it? Don't tell me you haven't had your suspicions."

This is the most convincing attempt yet. It sounds just like her, right down to the annoyance in her tone.

"I do not dream of—"

"Cole. Seriously? It's me. You really thought I'd leave because you told me to? Why'd you even think I could? When are you going to figure it out?"

"I do not dream—"

"Cole. Think. I know you've seen us. Me. You. Gah. There's no clear way to say this, and I shouldn't anyways. But come on. Why do you think Ravel remembers a kid with the same face as you? Hint: not 'cause he's obsessed with us. I mean, he is, but . . . Why don't you remember anything before a few years ago? Why don't you dream of family? Other supposedly 'brainwashed' workers do— you've seen them. Suzie. Liwan. You must have wondered why they remembered and you don't."

I hadn't, actually. It had never occurred to me. Why . . . but it's just another trick. The Mara are getting better at this. I can't let them get inside my head.

"I do not dream of . . . of . . ."

Cadence sighs. "Okay, look at it this way. What's your ID?"

"18-Cole-" I answer without thinking. If this is some new gambit of the Mara, it's working; she just seems so real. So familiar.

"What's an ID?"

"A compilation of work division code and production series identifier."

"But Refuge doesn't grow people. They can't. They take them. Ange told you, remember? Not a series ID, a family name. What was your name, Cole?"

"Don't."

"It's time. I'm pretty sure mom didn't mean for it to go on this long. She wouldn't want you to die over it. It's not like we were ever that good at listening to her anyways. She must have expected us to disobey eventually."

"Stop it."

"Who are you, Cole? Or better yet, who were you? Why can you walk in dreams? Why can you see the threads of desire? Why can you save the dreamers from their desperate longings? Why do you look like me?"

"I don't—"

"When are you going to remember, Cady?"

Cady. The one Ash came to save. The child who watched her parents slaughtered by Refuge. The dead girl who haunts me. Whose powers somehow passed to me. Who looks just like me in Ravel's dreams.

"You're lying. I d—do not dream of—"

"This one's real, Cady. Or Cole, if you prefer. Both are right, though I admit it gets a little confusing even for me. To be fair, I only started remembering a little while ago.

And really, it all came back, oh, maybe an hour ago? It's getting hard to keep track of time. Which reminds me. Ours is running out."

"I . . . I don't—"

"We broke, you know. Well, more like splintered. Mom made us forget—it's a dreamweaver thing. One day, you'll remember. Or relearn, I guess. And Refuge conditioning probably had something to do with how long it took us to start remembering. Well, that and all the gold. It's kind of amazing we survived at all, actually."

"You're dead."

I finally said it. I suck in a breath, expecting the world to crumble, but Cadence just keeps talking.

"Yeah, that's the thing. I'm really not. The result of all of it, mom's order, and the shock of seeing dad and her . . ." Her voice falters. "Um. The result of that, and probably Refuge's best effort at brainwashing too all coming together at once was, well, me. Our memories and, I don't know, consciousness, I guess? They separated. And it's more complicated than that, even. I'm not sure how complicated, except that I need you to accept it, Cole. I know you need me."

"I—"

"There's really not a lot of time. You have to accept us, accept it all. I'm going to give you your dreams back, okay? It's the only way to win. Just work with me."

I shake my head. I feel the brush of the Mara on all sides. The frenzy of their attack has slowed, as if they're listening in to Cadence with as much astonishment as I am. Or maybe this is all their doing. But as insane as it all sounds, I can't push it away, can't stop listening . . .

"We were never alone. Having you as an anchor helped me hold on. Though it would've helped a whole lot more if you hadn't insisted on being so boring all the time. We'll have to work on that. Anyway, I think I helped you resist too, helped you not get brainwashed, at least not all the way. But Refuge's conditioning is strong. You have to see through it, Cole. You have to see you were never a failure."

I couldn't get a word in if I tried.

"The way you couldn't sit still, couldn't fit in? It's because you really were different. We were different. We stayed awake in a way no one else could, because we had each other. And your so-called obsession with the dead? That's the echo of the dreamweaver powers. Our powers. It was never wrong, you just weren't able to understand it.

"And your drive, your determination to pass probation, to be accepted? The Mara never took anything you didn't let them take. They couldn't change you. You worked so hard to obey. We've always been driven, Cole. We were the best, the strongest. The dreamweavers are the strongest of the Travellers, that's why we were sent in first. This was always our place.

"You can fight back. We can fight back. We're strong, Cole. You just have to stop believing that all your strengths are wrong. Fight back. Stop waiting. Stop looking for someone else to save us. We're enough, right now, just as we are."

"This game grows dull," the Mara scoff. "What do you dream of, girl? What do you all dream of?"

The darkness fills with overlapping whispers:

Ambition.

Influence.

Power.

I stand, feeling my heart race toward its ending. There's no way out. No way I can outrun, outlast, outwit. I thought I could control my responses, find a way to persuade even myself that I don't want what they offer. But Cadence's crazy pleading is pushing me closer and closer to breaking. Sooner or later, the Mara will realize the truth.

I want all of it. Desperately. Greedily. Selfishly. Every dream and wish and desire, and none of them at the same time. It feels wrong to admit just how hungry I am. I thought I could stuff it down and away, just a little longer— but not forever. I can press my lips together and ball my hands into fists and set my shoulders, but sooner or later, I will crumble.

"Ah, power," the Mara say. "We might have known it would be power. It nearly always is, you know."

"I do not dream of power." My voice wavers at the thought of being strong enough to defeat them, at the thought of having a voice the Mara couldn't help but listen to. At the thought of saving everyone.

The Mara hear it.

"Lies," they hiss. Within the glee, there's a hint of relief—even, perhaps, weariness. What if their power isn't endless?

Fight back. Fight with me, Cole. Let me help you. Cadence's words echo from inside. Maybe they always had. Maybe I knew all along and tried to suppress it, or maybe it just feels inevitable now I've accepted it.

I feel warmth stir in my chest and bring my hands up to cover the light before the Mara notice.

"I did lie," I say. "You caught me. I've lied along. I'm full of wants. But you'll give me what I dream of? Anything?"

"Anything," the Mara lie.

I twist my fingers together as if uncertain, curling down and over them to protect myself.

"My deepest, truest wish," I say slowly, testing the words.

The Mara lean in. I hunch down tighter as if afraid. It's barely pretend.

"Yes?" the Mara whisper in many voices, caressing my skin with talons and tongues, tasting my fear.

"The thing I want most in all the world—"

"Tell us," they urge; eager, too eager.

"I dream of you, destroyed. I dream of you gone, defeated. I dream of being the one to end your threat and make everyone safe. I dream of a world without you."

"You lie." Serovate's voice rings clear at the heart of theirs. "Lying, clever girl thinks she can trick us."

"I wish for you to be gone," I say again. "And I'm granting my wish."

This time, I lash out with the cord I've braided, the shining cord of dreams and wishes and longings woven from the threads Cadence gave back to me, the threads I finally allowed myself to hold. A pure, brilliant silver light grows where the threads meet my chest and sweeps across my skin.

The Mara roar, swiping out at me with claw and fang and more beside, but their blows weaken. I radiate light against their darkness, binding the nightmare with the threads of my dreams.

"You can't, you can't," they wail.

As it turns out, I can. The darkness thins and lets in first the omnipresent beat of Freedom, then the wild skirling of melodies and the murmur of voices, and finally a kaleidoscope of coloured lights that scythe through the rapidly dissipating fog.

I slump to my knees in a pool of blood and shattered tiles. I'm too spent to be disgusted. Serovate's body isn't the only one that lies empty-eyed and spent in the aftermath, but it helps to know his threat, at least, is over now.

When I feel the first touch, I can't even summon the energy to jerk away.

"You stopped it," the stranger whispers, staring at me from behind a green mask.

"You won," the woman beside him says, slipping a hand under my elbow.

"Victoire." Another dancer crouches at my other shoulder, working with the first two to lift me.

A ring of faces spins and glitters above me, whispering and murmuring: *Victoire, Victoire.*

Then the light spins away. The last thing I hear is Cadence's voice, saying: *Well done.*

49

CADY

I WAKE SLOWLY, swimming up to consciousness to the sound of familiar voices: Cadence and Ash.

They're both alive, then. Or I'm dead—not an entirely unpleasant thought. The ceiling is unfamiliar, raw concrete with a single bulb.

Ange leans over me. "Welcome back. Took you long enough."

"Easy, Ange," Ash says from the next bed over, grinning. "She did well for her first big battle."

He looks good. Too good, considering how much blood he'd lost.

"How?" The word grates past my lips as if I've been gargling concrete. I cough and try again. "How long?"

"You've been out for three days," Cadence says from nowhere, as usual. "He's just faking. Typical—always trying to look tough. Don't let him fool you; he'll be recovering for ages yet."

"You needed your sleep," Ange says.

"Cadence said three days," I tell her.

Oops. Ange's brows draw together. Ash blinks.

"Who's Cadence?" A woman leans past Ash from another bed. There's a row of them, two more empty ones past her. She looks a lot like Ange. Her voice sounds vaguely familiar.

Ange takes in my gaping mouth and Ash's frown. "Let's give these two some time to talk, Amy."

There's a curtain—white, threadbare—just past the foot of the beds. The two women vanish through it. I'm alone with Ash. I pick at my blanket, fiddling with the threads.

"Seriously?" Cadence huffs. "Get it over with. You'll feel better."

Battling the Mara is nothing compared with facing him. I don't look up. "I'm sorry."

"Whatever for?" Ash sits up a little straighter, then flinches and sags back, looking as if he's trying not to gasp. "You did great, Cady. If anything, I ought to be the one apologizing. I was supposed to help, not make things worse for you."

"Don't you get it?" I finally meet his eyes. "I'm really not her. I mean, maybe I was once, but I'm not now. I meant to tell you sooner, but . . . Well anyways, you know now. You were . . . How were you talking to her?"

His eyes widen. "She said you'd be able to hear, but wow. Wow. You really are separate. Um, Cole, right? Okay, um. So, Cady—wow. Sorry."

"Wow." I try not to laugh. Ash is kind of awkward in real life. Or waking life. Or whatever.

"Yeah, wow." He laughs, winces. "Anyway, um, Cady tells me she's retained more of your training than you, so she can talk to me in the dreamscape, which is pretty easy from here. Ange's place isn't shielded like Refuge. And then she can talk to you because she's, well, you. So, you hear her no matter what, because of course you can access the dreamscape too, you just don't remember you can. So, um, wow. There's a lot to explain."

"Maybe start with where 'here' is?"

"Oh. You didn't know? Okay. Um. So it turns out Ange is the head of the Underground, and—"

I stare blankly. "The what?"

"The Underground. She's the leader of this secret organization that basically helps people get out of bad situations. And other stuff. It's complicated—I think they might have been left over from an early Traveller resistance when the borders closed. Anyway, she got me out after we got captured, apparently, which—I'm so sorry.

It wasn't supposed to go like that. My plans usually work out better. Just so you know."

I wave a hand magnanimously, as if it was all no trouble at all. "Turns out I can take care of myself." Then I remember just what went on and let my hand drop. "I should be the one apologizing. If I hadn't been so selfish, I never would have insisted on you coming in the first place."

"You've got to stop saying that," Cadence says.

Ash sort of jumps, which looks pretty strange from a sitting position. "Wow, it's weird to hear you—both of you—at once."

She ignores him. "It's okay to want things, Cole. It's okay to go after them, too. It's not like you knew Serovate was gonna shoot him. And we really do need to do something about Refuge. Besides, I'm not sure there's much you could do to surprise Ash at this point. He's known us since forever. Show her, Ash."

He reaches out a hand. Silver mist swirls up in a cloud. The moment his fingertips brush mine, everything changes.

WARM EYES AND wild hair brushing rounded cheeks. A brilliant smile in a sunburnt face. Not a man, a boy; beautiful and full of life, glowing with health, the whites of his eyes and teeth bright against the tan of skin as he laughs.

We played in a place that did not exist, he and I. It had never existed, except for us. It was a place of our own making, a fantasy come to life behind closed eyelids. Our own personal dreamscape.

We met there night after night to press back the edges and explore the cracks and crannies of our own imaginary wonderland. If I stopped and watched, I could work it out, see the things I'd brought pressing up against his magic. His was the sky, a shifting wonder of endless depth, crystal pale to deep blue-black. He brought the trees, huge and friendly, always moving, laughing in whispery little chuckles as we tickled them with toes and elbows, climbing and swinging through their branches.

He saw and felt so much. All the colour and light and form was his, the brightness that warmed my skin and painted the ground in a lace kaleidoscope when the trees rustled. The world he saw was beautiful.

But I heard more than he did. I heard the secrets the trees passed, the stories that made my blood boil and my hands curl into fists. And I smelled the darkness that seeped around their roots, the sharp sap when we scraped them, careless.

I was the one who brought the wild salt scent of the sea gusting through the trees. And then we ran and dived and played in the waves off the cliffs, splashing and laughing.

⁕

THE WAY HIS face is lit up makes it easy to look past how much it has lengthened and broadened, the way his skin has roughened over the years, the way the silver has settled like a shimmering cloud over him. It's easy to just bask in the joy of his presence.

But these are his memories, and Cadence's. My eyes prick with tears. I pull away.

His face falls. He shakes his head and tugs me back under.

I see through his eyes now. There's a wild, wiry girl with tangled hair and fierce eyes, eyes full of silver. The marks around her eyes stand in sharp relief, tracing lace-like patterns, a mask of silver etched on her skin. But when she smiles, the silver draws down and back and the marks darken, blurred to a familiar, smudged birthmark.

"Cady," he says, tugging a lock of hair. She grins back.

I surface, gasping.

"It's true," Cadence whispers. "I didn't remember either, at first. But between his memories and mine, I think we can give it all back to you. All you've lost."

Cadence pushes against the walls in my mind, slipping bits of dreams and memories and knowing into the hollowed shell that Refuge made of me after our mom—I don't know what to think of that. If what she's told me and what I've seen is true,

291

our mom is the one who took my memories from me. But it's too much all at once. I can't help curling against it, fighting the waves of memory that surge and ebb like the tide. A red wash of pain blanks out all thought for a moment, and then in the brief gasps between attacks, more pieces fall into place.

Dreams. Beautiful dreams. Safe dreams of a place where there is no danger, no hurting, no fear.

A time before Refuge.

Family: a mother, a father, a place at the edge of the water. Love. Warmth. Acceptance.

Terror. Fear. Loss. Blood. Hurt.

Nothing. A nightmare time of blankness and terror, unending, bland sameness.

And then something. Returning, a new start. Cole. And Cadence, there with me, though neither of us knew the other.

I hadn't fought it. For so long, just existing, forgetting him, forgetting myself, forgetting my family, holding Cadence at arm's length.

"Hang on," Ash whispers. The pitch is so deep now, so much more resonant than the high, bell-like voice of the Traveller boy I knew. But I know him just the same. It is marvellous and terrifying at once that in all those cloudy, distant dreams, I hadn't known him, hadn't reached out to him.

The past few days rush back in all at once, bringing a new and different pain. Cadence hadn't given up on me, on us. She wore down the armour and kept my eyes and ears open. She kept my mind switched on. There was Ravel, dangerous and different, a goad and a lure to break out. Victoire, a dream, a nightmare, a discovery of something more in myself and beyond myself, someone I didn't want to meet but couldn't ignore. Freedom, dangerous and deep, shifting the foundations of my world.

And Ash, haunting me, reaching out to me, drawing something out in me until I couldn't go back. I chose to reach for something more. I chose. I fought. I rebelled, though not in the way I'd expected. I escaped.

"Do you remember now?" Ash leans back, exhausted by the effort.

I stare at him, then at my hands. "I'm really not her. I'm not the girl you remember. I don't think I ever can be again."

His smile wavers but pulls through. "No, but you're you."

It's everything at once to me: acceptance and friendship and power and more besides.

"It's enough," Cadence says. "It has to be."

"What happens now?"

Ash answers first: "We heal. We regain our strength. We continue the mission."

"It was a victory, but only a temporary one." Cadence sounds fierce. "Refuge still stands. The barrier still holds, and within it, the Mara attack. Dreams are still dangerous here. The mission continues."

"Can we do it? Can we win?"

Ash doesn't answer right away, and Cadence is silent.

"Once, I would have said yes," he says. "Now, things have changed. You're different, Cady. Sorry. Cole. I'm not enough on my own. But maybe . . ."

" . . . if I were still her?"

His brows draw together. He won't say it, won't tell me I'm not enough as I am, but his silence makes me afraid. Without my past, without my memories, without years of skill and training, I'm a fragment of what I should be.

Failure. An echo of the Mara's voice—or maybe it's my own—hisses in my ear.

No. Not a failure, but . . . not quite finished. I am enough—for now. But I could be more. I want to be more.

I meet Ash's gaze. "Help us. Help us regain what we were. I want to win."

"We will win," Cadence says. She's both the child Ash remembers and the determined woman who pushed me to fight once more. Together with her and Ash, I can almost believe we have a chance.

But even if we don't, I choose to fight.

THE STORY CONTINUES in book two of the THREADS OF DREAMS trilogy, coming in **2019**.

Out now: LETTER FROM THE END OF THE WORLD, a short villain origin side story. Learn the truth behind Maryam, Ravel, and the monsters of Refuge.

Or sign up at kaie.space/newsletter for news, giveaways, and exclusive content including a free ebook of prequel novella UNDER and explore Cass, Ange, and Ravel's adventures in Freedom before Cole came onto the scene.

ACKNOWLEDGEMENTS

T O THOSE I promised I'd thank in a book one day: Not everyone gets great teachers; I had many. You helped me believe I could do this. Thanks for the dream and the tools and confidence to get there. Greg, you showed me real people could write. I still have the story you wrote about our 2nd grade class. Lenora, you not only saw the writer in me, you made me look at all the other people in the world I was inclined to avoid. Myopically introverted fourteen-year-old me needed that. Diane, thanks for not laughing in the face of a pretentious teen with delusions of grandeur.

To my parents, who raised a compulsive reader, an independent thinker and a relentlessly stubborn problem solver: You supported this insane dream more ways than I could have imagined. I'm still not sure why you thought I could do this, but thank you so much for asking what I wanted to do, waiting for me to figure it out, and sticking by me while I blundered my way toward publishing.

To Līssí, who was probably the first person I told stories to—and definitely the first to ask for more. And to Joshua, who pushes me for better answers. And to all the other family, friends and obliging strangers who graciously read and commented on drafts: I seriously can't believe the amount of time and effort you guys put in. Sandi, "Maggie", Kevin & Emily, Josh & Krystal, Becky . . . All-stars, you guys.

To Lisa Poisso, without whom I'd probably still be staring down an unreadable literary epic: You probably know exactly how I couldn't have done this without you. Thanks for putting a map in my hand . . . and pointing me back at it again and again until I learned to follow.

To Regina Wamba, who took the incoherent ramblings of a first-time author and turned them into this sheer gorgeousness: I bow in the face of your art.

To Catherine Milos, with thanks for a brilliant proofread and the much-appreciated encouragement: Any and all errors in this book can be wholly attributed to my lack of diligence and stubbornly "creative" use of language (a.k.a. wilful errors.)

To the West Highland Hotel where I found a much-needed Scottish escape while I figured out how the heck one goes about polishing up a manuscript, as well as to the Paperbacks & Prosecco book club and all the other businesses, groups, acquaintances and random strangers over the years who have graciously humoured my delusions of writerliness: Crazy though I may be, let it be known that I have now, in fact, published a book.

To the authors of my childhood: I lost count of the times I read and re-read Tolkien, Lewis, L'Engle . . . I still remember dashing around the playground hollering battle cries from Redwall. Thanks for truth in fiction, and beauty, and magic and heroism and some really sweet swords. To Canadian author O.R. Melling, who showed a dorky anglophile teen that great stories could take place at home and magic isn't the sole provenance of Britain. And to the Y.A. authors who have inspired me: Holly Black, Scott Westerfeld, Kendare Blake, Laini Taylor, Melissa Marr, and so many more. You're brilliant. Thanks for all the hard work you've put in to tell your stories.

To the one to whom I am always enough: I can't imagine life without you. I'm so grateful I've never had to.

And finally, to all the awkward, prickly kids out there who are afraid to try, who try too hard, who try and fail, who try and keep on trying: You're enough. You're not done yet. You never will be. But you're enough. Keep fighting on.

ABOUT THE AUTHOR

K.A. WIGGINS WRITES YA Fantasy with an edge for ages 14 and up. BLIND THE EYES is her debut novel and book one of a planned trilogy, THREADS OF DREAMS. Born in Vancouver, BC, she freelances as a business writer and marketing consultant in the Pacific Northwest.

Kaie has been creating urban legends about witches in the back wood and fairies in the snow melt since she was seven years old and writes prickly misfits challenging the borders of the mundane, inspired by current stars Brenna Yovanoff, Kendare Blake, and Laini Taylor, and fantasy legends J.R.R. Tolkien, C.S. Lewis, and Madeleine L'Engle.

Find her at kawiggins.com or @kaiespace on social media

11422454R00173

Made in the USA
Monee, IL
10 September 2019